The Wrong Box

Andrew C Ferguson

ThunderPoint Publishing Ltd.

First Published in Great Britain in 2017 by
ThunderPoint Publishing Limited
Summit House
4-5 Mitchell Street
Edinburgh
Scotland EH6 7BD

Cover image, Harvey Meadows
(www.meadowsfineart.co.uk)

ISBN: 978-1-910946-14-5 (Paperback)
ISBN: 978-1-910946-16-9 (eBook)

www.thunderpoint.scot

Dedication

For the other two musketeers, who know some of this…

Acknowledgements

This book couldn't have been written without the support, criticism and general good company of Writers' Bloc. Two of its members in particular should have a mention: Hannu Rajaniemi, for lots of patient help with plot and structure; and Gavin Inglis, for his constant enthusiasm, including the text at 11 o'clock one night that just read: JUICY FRUIT. LOL.

Thanks also to Michelle McDermott for typing the first draft of the manuscript, even the bits it didn't feel right committing to tape for her.

Undying gratitude to Seonaid and Huw at ThunderPoint, for believing in Simon, Karen and the supporting cast, and taking the whole project over the line with me.

Last but not least my family, without whom nothing I do could be possible.

Chapter 1
Jimmy Takes A Bath

By the time I wake up, the duvet's stuck to my leg and the sun's lancing me like a boil through the half-shut curtains. No wonder I'm not ready for the dead man in my bath.

'Fuck!' I say as I stumble in and see him. 'Fucking bastard!'

Not his real name, obviously. His actual name is – was – Jimmy Ahmed, and he was the M.D. of one of my firm's clients. I'd been detailed to show him Edinburgh on the expense account ('no lap-dancing bars on it, mind'), and to keep him out of any major mischief. Mission accomplished, or so I thought, till I get up with the hangover shark biting my head and there he is, naked in my bath, large as life. Only dead.

Well of course I check. I'm not totally without any human feeling for my fellow man. Try for a pulse on his wrist that feels like a fatty slab of cold marble. Nada. Somehow though – and there's a part of my brain, that bit that has the very sickest sense of humour, that says, *Typical* – his hand slips out of mine, bounces off the side of the bath, and lands full square on his cock and balls so it looks like he's died having a ham shank.

Nice work, my friend, says the same sick bit of brain. It's enjoying itself, I can tell. I'm glad some part of me is. I go to move his hand, wondering if that counts as altering a crime scene, when an ominous rumbling tells me that last night's bucket of Thai food has worked its way through my system, along with the bucket of red wine, and the bucket of beer. I sit down on the bog, just in time to open proceedings with a fart like the foghorn on the Titanic.

Then my arsehole descends its crop sprayer attachment and I'm stuck there, shitting a reduction of Tom Yum and Tennent's, while my dead client stares at me from the bath. Not the best of starts to a Saturday, I can tell you.

It's not like I make a habit of waking up with a body in my bath. I do try to make a habit of waking up with a warm, female one next to me in bed, preferably with a Buddha belly and ready for breakfast with her eggs unfertilised.

Yes, that's right, you heard it right. That's my little predilection. I don't often have the time to ponder if God exists, but if he does, there are two main things I'd thank him for. The crop top, and the modern Western diet. These two things produce a significant proportion of fit birds with a visible Buddha belly, and that's what gets the old one-eyed python snaking through the undergrowth for me.

Now, I know what some people will say. Here's another man objectifying women, and all that. But before the Germaine Greer horror mask goes on, I do really like women, and get on with them. It's other men I can't stand, quite honestly. Cunts and wankers to a man almost. Except my brother, Tom. And my Dad, before he ran off with his PA.

Anyhoo, that's a whole other barrelful of monkeys. I have plenty of time to think as I sit on the bog looking round at the appalling décor Bruce Reid has bequeathed to me in the flat exchange for my pad in London. If that sounds unfeeling, believe you me, there's only so many times you can catch a corpse's eye. Especially if he's got his hand on his cock. I stare at my dressing gown, hanging on the back of the door, and let my thoughts drift back to last night. Hadn't there been a woman – women?

Nope. I'm still not ready to piece it together yet. All I know is, I'm in exile in Scotland, and there's a dead Scouser businessman in my bath. With his toe up the tap.

At last I'm done. I wash my hands in the sink, cursing the tight Jock bastard Reid for only having night store heating in the flat. I badly need a shower, but since Reid hasn't put in a separate one, that would involve turfing poor Jimmy out of the bath, and I'm not feeling quite up to that yet.

Instead, I pull my dressing gown back round me and inspect Jimmy more carefully. His eyes, now I'm off the shitter, stare straight ahead of him. His mouth is open, as it so often was last night as he told staggering stories of unbelievable bollocks from pub to restaurant to pub to – where? No, still blotted out. Scent of booze despite the other smells in the bathroom, but then that could be coming from me, too.

Gently, I move his hand from his genitals. It slumps back, but at least it now looks as if he was just thinking of knocking out a crafty one instead of having died mid-bash of the bishop. At the far end, I look more closely at his left big toe, where it's lodged securely up Reid's stingy Jock one-microlitre-of-water-at-a-time bath tap. That strikes me as odd right away, but doesn't compute as any more than that right then.

I stumble backwards out of the bathroom, and take the shaft of sun from the skylight square between the eyes. A rucksack-full of wind bellows out my arse like a broadside at Trafalgar and I sink to my knees, overcome by the smell for a moment. Forget the stench of death: it's the living you have to watch out for.

After a minute or so, the smoke clears, and I go into the kitchen to collect my thoughts. What exactly are you meant to do when you find a dead body in your flat? Which authorities do you inform, exactly? Another fucking potentially useful thing they don't teach on the law course.

I eventually decide to phone the firm's staff partner, Tony Hand. There are two sound reasons for this. Firstly, I don't have the number of anyone else in charge at the firm; and second, even if I had, I'd rather climb in the bath with Jimmy Ahmed than phone either the Velociraptor or the Rottweiler with this news.

As it is, it's not going to be easy.

'Hi, Tony? Simon here. Simon English? Yeah. Ehhhhmmmm …look sorry to bother you and all that on a Saturday, yeah, it's just about Jimmy Ahmed…

'…well not so good actually, he's actually dead. In my bath, at the moment.'

The words seem to ring around the empty flat for quite some time and I have the leisure to admit to myself that, tight Jock bastard that he is, Reid has done all right with the kitchen – good spec units; proper quarry tiles on the floor, currently blasting cold up into my marrow via the soles of my feet. Neff appliances. Splashed out a bit there, old Brucie.

Still a radio silence from Tony Hand and only me and Jimmy Ahmed waiting this end. Then, eventually, he says, 'Dead?'

Then, 'Fuck, they – '

Then, 'How?'

'…err, dunno. I just woke up and went to the bog and there he was dead in the bath with his toe up the tap.'

'His?'

'Toe. Up the tap. Left toe, actually.'

'It's probably not important right now which one, Simon,' Tony says, a little tersely, I feel, in the circumstances. 'Okay, let me think. You'll need a lawyer.'

'I am a –' I start to say, and then I see his point.

'A criminal lawyer, Simon. Gordon Drummond's in-house with us now. I'll call him and get you sorted. He can contact the cops and arrange for them to turn up at the same time.'

'Meantime…'

'Meantime sit tight, Simon.' Tony's voice is calm now, soothing. 'We'll get you through this, ok?'

'OK.' I put the phone down and make a job of sitting tight, if by that Tony means going back on the bog three more times, dousing myself in Hermes to mask the Thai spices pumping out of my pores, getting dressed, drinking a full carton of orange juice, and then putting coffee on.

I do wonder briefly about what message the last bit might be sending out. I mean, you brew up coffee when you're selling a flat, but what about when you're receiving Lothian and Borders' finest?

'Ah, officer. So sorry to trouble you when you should be out catching happy slappers and giving them a stiff kicking down the cells. Dreadful business for a chap, finding a valued client cluttering up the bath in the morning. Care for a cup of Guatemalan to kick things off?'

Anyway, I make the coffee. While I'm waiting, I make a call that would be almost as tricky as waking up the Velociraptor, my London boss, on a Saturday morning: my mother.

'Simon? *Come siete, tesoro?*'

'How are you, Mum?' Forty years in this country and she still can't stop gabbling Italian. I've noticed she only does it when she's talking to me or Tom, though.

'What's happened?' She always expects that something's gone tits up when I phone her. Can't think why.

'Oh, nothing much.' I can fill in the details later. 'I was thinking of popping home, actually, just to see you guys. Maybe stay the night?'

'*Si, si, naturalmente* – that's great news. I'll need to change the sheets on the bed.'

4

She starts prattling on about domestic arrangements, and I go to the window, looking out at my new Lexus, where I've shoe-horned it into a resident's parking place in the street below. *Everything's small and tight in this place*, I'm thinking, when I realise my mother has stopped talking.

'Are you sure everything's all right, Simon?'

What can I say? She gets in a panic if I leave my toothbrush behind after a weekend there. The news that Jimmy Ahmed is, quite literally, tits up in my bath can wait for later. Or possibly never.

'Absolutely tip top, Mum.' I could hear voices in the background at her end, or one voice at least. 'How's Tom?'

There's a slight pause. 'He's not having one of his good days, Simon,' she said, lowering her voice. 'He's upstairs shouting at the plumber.'

'Really? That's great, Mum. Well, there's someone at the door, so I'll see you soon.' I ring off quickly, as a sudden realisation hit my hangover-ridden brain. The cops are coming to the house, and I have something rather stronger than coffee to stash away from their prying little piggy eyes.

***

There are two of them, of course. They always hunt in pairs: they've seen it on the telly. There's an older one, with cropped hair, a whisky-sour complexion, and bags under his eyes he could take his Farmfoods shopping home in. The younger one is dark-haired, whippet-thin, and in a suit so nasty you could probably get a cream for it.

'Mr English? DS Martin, and this is DS Futret. You have a body,' the first plod says, looking tired out already. I'm rehearsing a line about saying fuck all till my brief arrives, when the buzzer goes again. As I go to answer it, the two cops barge in, and head for the bathroom without so much as a by-your-leave.

'I'm from Gordon Drummond & Co.,' a metallic female voice says. I press the buzzer, and hear the door clunk open in the stairwell.

The two cops are standing in the bathroom doorway,

5

muttering to each other, and I'm trying to act casual whilst standing close enough to overhear them, when the flat door opens and a whiff of Chanel announces my lawyer's arrival.

The voice had warned me not to expect the old soak Drummond himself. I've seen him preening himself in front of a set of Session Cases on the news often enough to know he wouldn't pull himself out of bed on a Saturday morning, not even for a thousand of Tony Hand's favours.

I'm still not prepared for the sight that I turn to see. She's in her late twenties, I reckon, although she looks younger. Pert, upturned nose, brown eyes, masses of chestnut curls.

'I'm Sylvia McMonagle,' she says, putting out a china-white hand. I blurt out something while I take in the rest of her. The neat dark suit isn't this year's, but it's crisp enough. She's obviously dressed in a hurry, because she's left the top two buttons of her white (my favourite) blouse undone, as well as (first real bit of luck this morning) the bottom one.

Thereby showing a little fold of tummy above the skirt line that, with appropriate guidance, could develop nicely into a Buddha belly. I take to her right away.

As soon as she's shaken my hand, though, she goes straight past me to DS Martin, standing in the bathroom doorway.

'This him, then?' she says to him. Martin smiles in recognition.

'Well, Sylvia, it's the only one we've found so far.' He leans towards her casually, his grin getting ever more ugly. The younger one has disappeared into the bathroom, presumably getting a closer look at Jimmy. I've opened the window since my last contribution to the world of fishes: don't want them to think I've gassed the poor bastard to death.

'We'll have to treat it as a suspicious death, Sylvia,' Martin says. She hasn't moved away since he came in close, despite the fact the man stinks of fags. 'It's no normal for a man to die in a dry bath with his toe stuck up the tap. We'll get SOCOs in.'

I clear my throat. 'Ehhmm. I was wondering when I'd be able to use the bathroom again?' It's a stupid thing to say, I know, but I kind of feel left out of things here. Bit of a spare prick at the party. Martin deigns to look in my direction.

'Can't say sir. That'll be SOCO's call.'

I should just stay schtum, of course. My mouth won't flap shut now, though. 'Oh I see, yeah, Scene Of Crime. Of course. Only, would I be able to use the toilet before they…'

Martin's looking at me like I've suggested doing a dump on the deceased himself. He shakes his head. 'No.'

Now Sylvia, my lawyer who stands too close to cops, is looking at me. 'I suppose you'll want to interview my client, Jim? Can we arrange a time now that suits everyone?'

Martin blinks his baggy eyes slowly and glances over at his colleague, who has poked his rat-like head out of the bathroom doorway at that moment.

'How about now? Down at the station, since we're all up and aboot on a Saturday? I was hopin to get to Tynecastle later, as it happens.'

Sylvia smiles, and flutters her eyelashes at him. 'Yes, okay.' Shouldn't she ask me? 'Can you give me ten minutes with him, first?'

'Sure.' Him now, is it? Mister Fucking Third Person Suspect? The two cops tramp out, Martin giving me a look like he wishes he could just lock me up now and save the paperwork, the cunt.

As the door bangs shut behind them, I go into the kitchen to rescue the coffee, which is getting petulant.

'Want a cup?' I say over my shoulder to Sylvia.

'No thanks.' The way she says it makes it sound like even thinking about coffee at a time like this is another character defect. My head's pounding like a fucking construction site and anyway it's my flat, sort of, so I pour myself one and take it through to the living room where Sylvia has planted herself, legs crossed, and notepad at the ready.

After some preliminaries like name, age and so on, she asks me to describe the previous night. 'I'd had a bit to drink,' I say, doing my guilty schoolboy look. She peers at me intensely. 'Any charlie?'

'Since you ask, once we're clear of the cops I'd be glad to – ' her look makes clear she's not amused. 'Ehm, yeah, we did a line in Jimmy's hotel room before we got going. That was all for the night, though. Just good old fashioned booze from there on in.'

She says nothing to that, scribbling in her notepad, so I blunder on with the story of the evening, the Oyster Bar, the Thai restaurant, Indigo's even though it was rammed, then…then a club, that was it, Rum-Ti-Tum-Tums in the Cowgate. And then…

'…and then it all gets a bit blurred, I'm afraid.' I give her my best smile. 'But I'm fairly sure I left Jimmy at his hotel.' I was fairly sure, wasn't I? But weren't there women…?

I looked at Sylvia, who looks as if she'd been given a lemon to suck. 'I'm going to ask Jim Martin to give you a blood test, see what's still in your system,' she says, tapping her pen on her notepad.

'What? Why?' I'm starting to get really pissed off with her now, the way she's looking at me like I'm some kind of a criminal. I mean, I'm a fellow lawyer, after all.

'Just a sort of intuition,' she says, shifting in her seat, and re-crossing her legs. She puts her head to one side. 'Tell me. When you first woke up, did you feel anything out of the ordinary? Disoriented, maybe?'

I think back to the moments before I stumbled into the bathroom. 'Sort of, yeah. Yeah, when I first got my eyes open I didn't really know for a minute where I was. But then, I've only just been transferred from the London office, so I've just been in this flat for a few days. Why?'

Sylvia's smiling slightly now, in a way I find incredibly annoying. 'Just wondered. Call it woman's intuition.'

I open my mouth to question her again. I'm not at all keen to open up my bloodstream to the inquisitive snout of the Lothian and Borders Crime Lab.

Then I notice that, in shifting position, Sylvia's blouse has ridden up a bit to reveal her belly button. I look up, to see Sylvia's smile has gone, to be replaced by her what-the-fuck-is-this-I've-stepped-in look.

'Why are you looking at my stomach all the time?' she said. 'Is there something wrong?'

'No, not at all,' I murmur. 'Rare eye condition. Look, if you recommend I take a blood test, I'll take a blood test. You're the expert in this field.'

Little does she know it's the jewel in her navel that's convinced me. Terrible curse, male hormones. Especially the hangover horn. That's the worst of all.

Chapter 2
My Name Is Karen Clamp

I must finish up and get the bairn in from the green. I have to get some of this down though. There's somethin really, really no right about those lassies down the stairs from me.

My name, for the record, is Karen Clamp. Age: 40. Dress size: 20. Means of support: zero. I live in a third floor maisonette in Ivanhoe Court, on the Auchendrossan Estate. No exactly your Edinburgh tourist destination, by the way. Unless you're a fan of *Trainspottin.*

Oh aye. I read that filth. Makes us all out to be druggies and scumbags. Full of swear words. I heard that that Irvine Welsh used to work down the housin department in Leith, and blagged all their best stories. Don't see him down there much now though.

Well that's no me. Don't drink, don't take drugs, don't swear. You can ask anyone that kens me about that, even the people in the Cooncil. 'In many ways, Ms Clamp, you're the perfect example of community empowerment,' one of them says to me recently. In many ways. Sarky cow.

Anyway, that's another story. Those two lassies down the stairs from me are involved in somethin and they're in it up to their filthy wee necks. I heard them talkin this mornin on the baby monitor.

Aye, that's right. The baby monitor. I ken how that sounds, but hear me out. I have my reasons, believe you me.

The folk the Cooncil have had in that flat below me over the last few years would make *Trainspottin* look like *A Room With A View.* Convicted paedophile, at one point, before the locals nearly lynched the guy. Then a couple of chancers who ran it as a party flat. Raves every other night. Then, of course, a cannabis farm. That was actually ok, because they were keepin a low profile until they'd got the crop fully grown. The worst thing about it was the police raid, burstin our door down by mistake.

When the Cooncil gutted the flat downstairs, after they finally threw out the last set of druggies, I took the chance to nip down when the Cooncil workies were away havin their two hour lunch break, and install some handy wee devices. Never too early to ken what the neighbours are up to. Never too early to ken what the Cooncil are up to either, for that matter. I may be the size of a number eight to Muirhouse, but I'm no stupid.

See, I kent the lassies had been out on the randan on Friday night and came in late. Woke me up as usual with all the doors bangin and that. Luckily, the bairn would sleep through a thermonuclear strike on her toy cupboard.

Then, this mornin, just when I'm on my second coffee of the day, I hear them through the baby monitor talkin to each other, almost whisperin like, except the East European lassie can't keep her voice down ever and that other one, wee Debi Murray, it's never long before she starts pumpin up the volume too.

'So, what happen to him?' The East European one, Elena I think her name is, says.

'Never you mind, hen,' says Debi. 'The less we ken about what went on after we left that flat, the better.'

By now, I'm mildly interested, although I'm still thinkin it's some kind of low level drug deal. I've got bigger fish to fry than that, especially all that corruption that's goin on in the Cooncil that I'm just one step away from blowin the lid on. Then the other one says somethin that makes me sit up and pay attention.

'But it's on the radio, Debi,' she says. 'Top businessman found dead in Stockbridge lawyer's flat.'

That nearly sends me scamperin for the laptop, to check the news websites, but I'm no wantin to miss any of this. I'm wishin now I'd put in recordin devices that are compatible with Windows. That way I could be recordin all this. Course they didn't have them when I needed them. They're releasin bits of technology one bit at a time, just to make us buy more. Plain as anythin.

'It isn't our problem, Elena,' says Debi. 'We did what we were told to do. We weren't to ken he would react that way.'

Just then, the ice-cream van starts up below the deck access again. If I could get down the stairs fast enough, and if it weren't for my confidence issues, I'd stick that guy's head down his freezer with the Vanilla Flake. Either he's got one of these ham radios, or it's signals given off by his chimes, but whatever it is, it throws the baby monitor out of whack every time he comes round here with them on. Ice-cream van, eh? What a joke. Fags'll be the least of what he's sellin to the kids.

I take the chance to check on Candice again. She's eight, now, so you can't keep them wrapped up in cotton wool forever. She's a good wee lassie though, always plays down on the common bit drying green where I can see her. She gives me a wee wave and I wave back. It's the McLatchie lassie with her, from the looks of it. Low risk.

Anyway, by the time heid-the-baw in the van has gone off again, the lassies have been out to him for fags and come back to a different part of the flat where I can't pick up what they're sayin. It's only in the livin room, you see, that the listenin device still works. One out of three isn't a very good success rate but, given I ordered it off the internet and it's installed semi-legally in the flat downstairs, I don't suppose I can do much about the guarantee. Probably the batteries come to think of it.

So I go onto the internet and, sure enough, down a wee bit from the top stories, a wee piece sayin:

BUSINESSMAN FOUND DEAD IN CITY SOLICITOR'S FLAT.

A prominent Liverpool businessman has been found dead in a flat in the city in unusual circumstances. The flat's tenant, a solicitor with prominent city firm Benzini, Lambe and Lockhart, is said to be helping police with their enquiries. No charges have been brought and police investigations continue. It is understood, however, that the body was found naked in the bath.

They couldn't resist that last bit, could they, eh? All sex, sex, sex. It gets my mind racin though, for a different reason. How do those lassies ken about it? Solicitors and businessmen — sounds like it might be the Freemasonic thing again, although it could be somethin to do with the Coonci and their Black Ops Division. I just can't tell at this stage. No enough to go on.

See, I've been collectin all this evidence for years and it's startin to add up. See that Freedom of Information? That's been a Godsend for me. Places like the Cooncil have to send me the information I ask for or some posh bloke up in St. Andrews can get them the jail or anythin. No that they make it easy, of course. 'We'll only answer the question that you ask us, Ms. Clamp,' says one of them to me, last time I went through the complaints procedure. And kennin the right question, the one that nails them to the wall, is the thing.

Take that Caltongate Development the Cooncil was involved in, for example. You ken the one that was in the papers: big property deal involvin tearin down old buildins just off the Royal Mile and puttin up somethin that looks like it was made out of Lego instead. Sixty FOI requests and ten complaints to the Chief Executive later, I'm still no much the wiser for the whole process. Still, I'm no givin up. As one of the Cooncil lackeys says to me one time, 'Ms. Clamp, you're a determined individual, I have to give you that.' They all speak posh at the Cooncil like.

There's another property deal goin on at the minute, though, where the Cooncil's sellin some more land down the Cowgate. Now, if you're no from Edinburgh, you'll probably no have heard of the Cowgate. It's down the hill from the Royal Mile – kind of runs in parallel ken, underneath the Bridges and that. It's basically where all the workin class folk stayed, before they built them all hovels away in the outskirts of the toon, places like Auchendrossan. Now it's full of old tenement blocks, warehouses, dodgy pubs and clubs, places like that. Ripe for redevelopment though: right in the centre of town, like I say, close to that monumental white elephant the Parliament building, the Royal Mile, all that. What the Americans would call prime real estate.

Anyway, the Cooncil owns some of that and there was a report I saw when I was scannin the Cooncil papers online about it. 'Oho,' says I to the bairn. 'This is somethin that requires a Clamp Investigation.'

Rememberin this, I'm just about to do an email to the Cooncil about it when there's more movement downstairs. The lassies' pimp has arrived now, and there's a bit of chat goin on on the baby monitor. Another check on the bairn – the McLatchie lassie's away, but she's playin away happily enough, with the two wee laddies from 17A. The younger one's no the full shillin, but he's a nice wee soul. The other one needs watchin though. I'll call her in in a minute.

Meanwhile, I go back to the baby monitor and listen in.

Pimpy boy's somethin else like. He always wears the same manky white shell-suit, and cuts about like he's Don Corleone out of *The Godfather*. His actual name is Derek Boyes, and there's more to him than meets the eye, let's just say.

I go back through to the bedroom to catch what's goin on. The main PC's in the livin room, so the bairn can do her homework and play games on it. I couldn't have her listenin in on what goes on downstairs though, when she's here.

'Milk and two sugars, hen,' I hear Pimpy Boy sayin. It's loud and clear: he must be sat in the livin room while one of them goes to make a cup of tea for him. It's weird havin to reproduce what's goin on just from the conversation at times: a bit like listenin to River City on the radio. An x-rated version of River City at that.

'You're lookin no bad the day, Debi, considerin,' he says next. Must be Elena on tea duty. Debi says somethin else back I can't catch: it's like she's in the doorway of the livin room.

'Aye, wait till the other lassie gets back and we'll talk about it, likes,' he says. 'Oh aye, there you are.'

'What happen last night?' This is Elena, back with the tea.

'That's what I came to tell youse both,' says Pimpy Boy. 'Youse two ken nothin about it, right? No cunt kens you were there and no cunt needs to either. So just keep it zipped, right?'

'Aye, but we were there, Deek,' says Debi. 'And the boy died. I'm no wantin mixed up in some murder.'

He says, 'It was an accident, right? He wasn't meant to...'

'...number four, number four, can you go to 53 Whitecraigs Terrace. It's Rab, he's wantin a cab up the club. Where are you, number five?'

Aw shoot! That cab company up the road seems to use the same channel as the baby monitor, and just when things were gettin interestin, one of their cars has come past and knackered the signal from downstairs.

After a couple of minutes of hearin Kwik n Eezy Cabs' business, downstairs comes back on.

'And that's it, right?' Pimpy Boy is sayin. 'Anyway, Debi, come ower here.'

'What for?' she says, but you can hear the sly smile in her voice.

'I've got somethin here for you, a package,' he says, and she giggles.

'Woah!' he says. 'Look at it! S'like a bairn's arm holdin an apple!'

Pimpy Boy likes to sample the goods, like, and soon they're at it there and then, in the livin room. I have to turn the baby monitor off. Disgustin. And anyway, it's time I got the bairn in.

I go down to get her. On the way down, I nearly collide with a man comin the other way on the stair. Tall gadgie, button down shirt, chinos. Not your usual Auchendrossan Sunday attire. More Calvin Klein than JJB Sports. I used to work in Burton's years ago, and I ken a thing or two about clothes.

The gadgie's got a huge head, like a melon. Now then, I says to myself, you're a wee bit out of context here. Strangely enough though, I feel like I ken him or recognise him from somewhere. He even gives me a sort of half-smile, half girn, but that could just be the smell of the stairwell at work.

Down at the green, Candice has got her jeans dirty again. 'Mammy, Mammy,' she says, runnin over to me. 'Can we go up town soon?'

'Aye, soon, hen, soon,' I say, just as my mobile chirps in my handbag. It's Jessie, one of my old ones, wantin me to take up some curtains for her. I tell her I'll pick them up later as we start back up the stairs. Thing is though, I ken I won't wait till after dark to go over to her block to pick them up. Not with that Odd-Job character livin next but one to her. He's Pimpy Boy's muscle, and he gives me the willies.

Just on a hunch, I decide to go along the second floor access to the far away set of stairs. Sure enough, when I glance in, the well-dressed gadgie is in the flat with the two lassies and Pimpy Boy. He's no a happy bunny.

'What the f*ck were you thinkin of, Deek?' he says. It's strictly Prime of Miss Jean Brodie, his accent, but that's not stoppin him effin and blindin away. 'You should have f*cking called me right away, instead of leaving me to pick up the f*cking pieces. Just what – '

'Tony, Tony,' I hear Pimpy Boy say.

But by then I'm out of earshot again. Can't hang around

outside there, especially with Candice in tow. If things are about to get ugly, Odd-Job's just a phone call away.

Back in our flat, I hurry her along. 'Never mind changin your jeans hen, it's just a speck. Come on, we'll get the one on the half hour at the main road if we get a shift on.'

Sure enough, when we leave our block I look left and there's Odd-Job, prowlin across from Redgauntlet. He doesn't have the bowler hat, but there is somethin about him that minds you of that Bond villain. He's no Chinese of course, but he does have a kind of sallow skin, and he's thick set and always smilin. Like I say, somethin creepy about him.

***

The bairn likes us to go up the town on a Saturday, and if we walk to the main road, we can get a bus all the way to Morninside. Don't laugh. The bairn is really into those Maisie books at the moment, ken, the wee cat that lives in Morninside? I think they're a bit young for her, but she enjoys it, I think because of the Edinburgh thing, ken?

So most Saturdays we bus it up there, and spin a coffee and an ice cream out for an hour. How the other half lives. No money for taxis, no money for anythin much: how the government expects anyone to survive on sickness benefit at the level they have it at beats me. Don't drink, don't smoke: Farmfoods my only extravagance. Don't even get me started about that bedroom tax.

On the way to the bus, I pass a couple of wee neds smokin: they must be first year at secondary at the most, or would be if they were ever in school.

'Haw missus,' one of them pipes up, 'you ever considered usin your arse as a billboard? You'd make a packet off the advertisin, likes.'

The two of them are laughin away like a couple of underprivileged hyenas.

'Shut it youse two or I'll come and sit on your heids,' I shout at them, but they're already away down the road. That does nothin for my confidence issues of course. I briefly consider goin to see the GP again on Monday, but he's a total waste of space. Just wants to give me prescription drugs all the time. Well it's no happy pills I need.

We're just at the stop when the bus hoves into view round the so-called regeneration area housin at the top. The bairn wants to sit on the top deck, to look out, so I hoist myself up the stair while the driver puts the foot to the floor. It's more like bein on board a lifeboat in high seas than a Lothian Region bus: I'm nearly seasick by the time I get to the top.

'Look, Mammy, you can see the Castle from here!' The bairn's all excited cause we can get a seat at the front and get a panoramic view as we head into town. Uphill all the way from Auchendrossan, of course: through Stockbridge and then up through the New Town, the Unesco World Heritage site that the Cooncil's tryin to ruin, and up to Princes Street and beyond. Up, up and away: no wonder the bairn's excited to escape from Auchendrossan. Even she can see what a cowp it is.

I look down at the bairn: all blonde curls and wee cheeky face. She is another kettle of fish entirely. She's no got her father's red hair, thank goodness, and let's hope she hasn't inherited his other so called qualities.

'Can I have a chocolate egg when we get to the coffee place, Mammy?' the bairn says.

'A chocolate egg? But it's no even Easter, hen,– ' I say. To be honest I'm distracted, thinkin about the flat downstairs and the dead businessman. What are those two lassies into? Didn't sound like they're happy about it either. And who was the gadgie with the chinos and the melon sized head doin all the shoutin?

'Come on, now, Mammy,' Candice says, and takes my hand down the stair as the driver has one last go at breakin our necks with his cornerin ability. She likes to think she's the one lookin after me.

It's the same lassie in the coffee place, same one that serves us most weekends and looks at us like we're somethin the cat dragged in. Today though I've got too many things to think about to be bothered. Half of me is thinking about Edinburgh Cooncil and property deals. The other half, though, is thinking about Pimpy Boy, the two whores down the stair from me, and a man in pricey weekend clothes. Plus a dead businessman that they seem to ken all about.

Chapter 3
Ill Wind

Fuck knows what that stingy jock bastard Reid would have said about the mess the cops have made of his flat by the time I get back from the station. Sylvia drops me without a word in the street: then it's up the stairs, past a posse of gossiping neighbours, who only stop yapping long enough to turn and stare at me as if I've grown an extra head.

In the doorway, there's a uniformed cop, about twelve years old. When he sees me coming up, he shouts something into the flat and this woman in a white paper suit appears, with a face like a bulldog chewing a wasp. She's also the size of a small transit van, so I'm not about to argue with her.

'Can't come in here, sir. This is a crime scene,' she crows.

I look past her and, right enough, it's an episode of CSI Stockbridge, with her as Marj Helgenberger on a very tight budget: ghostly figures in white moving about, dusting things and putting that black and yellow tape they use across the bathroom door, like it's some sort of bizarre Christmas decoration. I presume they've already taken poor Jimmy off to the morgue, or at least taken his toe out of the tap.

'No, that's fine,' I say. 'It was only, I was wondering if I could maybe get a suit and a couple of shirts…'

'Absolutely can't let anythin out the flat 'til we've done our preliminary sweep,' she says, triumphantly. 'And I'll need your flat keys.'

She looks at me as if she's expecting an argument, but as I say in the seminars when I'm teaching negotiation skills, don't fight the battle if you can't win the war. Except if you just want to be arsey about it. Ancient Chinese proverb.

I march down the stairs past the neighbours, who go all quiet again, avoiding eye contact with me as I pass. I decide to ignore them: with any luck, I'll be out of this exchange and back at the London office within six months, so they can think I'm Dennis fucking Nielson for all I care.

Besides, as I get into the Lexus and gun the engine, I realise there are some reasons to be cheerful, despite everything:

> (a) my defence lawyer has a jewel in her navel;
> (b) I had the presence of mind to remember my moby, wallet and car keys, so I can make it back to Livingston and, fuck it, the pre-served London salary I'm on will certainly stretch to a couple of new suits;
> (c) Yvonne.

This last one is the real deal closer, and I text her before sliding the car down the cobbled street and nosing out into Saturday morning traffic. At the lights, my moby bleeps and I sneak a quick peek at it.

> GARY HOME BUT OFF TO
> FOOTBALL AT 2. SWING BY AFTER.
> LOL. YVONNE.

Excellent. The python stirs in his nest, my stomach rumbles, and I set about escaping Edinburgh Council's seemingly random system of roadworks. Then I point the Lexus down the M8 for Livingston, and put the foot down. Just enough time to get something to eat, and do a bit of suit shopping, before I see her. Then off to Mum's before Gary and his blue nose pals have swarmed out of Ibrox, and into the pub.

Yvonne was one of these things that just kind of happened to me. She almost literally fell into my lap at one of my Mum's parties: there she was getting pissed on the Sangria faster than anyone else and, before I knew it, I was getting the whole story of her life.

Next thing she was in tears about the whole fertility thing, and I had to take her home. Fortunately, Gary was away on the rigs, so a shoulder to cry on soon turned into damp patches of a more interesting kind. Thank fuck for the late flowering of the oil industry.

I think about her text as I turn off the M8, and can't help smiling. She's not just a dumb hairdresser by any means, Yvonne: owns three salons, two of which I did the leases for.

18

But she still hasn't worked out that LOL doesn't mean lots of love in text speak, it means laugh out loud. Or maybe she has and she just can't stop using it. Anything's possible with Yvonne.

A ham and cheese panini and two Ted Baker suits later, I nose the Lexus into Yvonne's cul-de-sac. As I walk up to the house, I realise that I'm actually nervous for once: usually my rumpy pumpy with her happens when the big monkey is safely tucked away 200 miles out into the North Sea off Aberdeen. My nervous system's connected to my arsehole on a morning after like this, of course, so there's a nasty breeze blowing just as I go up the driveway.

Hopefully that's the last of it though. I stand there, thinking, *If Gary comes to the door I can always have a go at being a Jehovah's Witness.*

When Yvonne opens the door, she's a vision in lycra. Some black and white two-piece aerobics thing that shows off her – regrettably flat – stomach.

'Well hello, you,' she says, with a grin. 'You'd better come in before the wind blows you over.'

As I follow her into the four bedroom mansion that her and Gary kick around in, I think to myself again how totally not my type she is: but then, show me the man who says he would kick a six foot blonde with a perfect all over tan out of bed, and I'll show you a lying bastard.

In the living room, the exercise DVD is yelping to itself and a variety of hand weights and other instruments of torture are scattered around the laminate floor.

'Would you like a drink of something?' she says, taking a swig from her mineral water bottle. She's still got that cheeky grin on her face, teasing me. 'I'm fine,' I say, stepping closer and getting my paws on that lycra-clad behind. 'Where are Rangers playing today?' The air is thick with Yvonne's scent: the python starts to stir itself again, stretching and yawning.

'Oh, they're at home,' she says. 'Gary usually goes for a pint with his mates after, so that's him away till at least six.'

'Excellent.' I feel my anxiety levels relax and the hangover horn start to kick in again: then I realise that my headache has gone too. Things are looking up, in every way.

Yvonne sashays out of my grasp. 'I need a shower,' she says, heading for the hall.

Normally I would protest that she's fine as she is, lightly glowing, but any slight movement on my part reminds me last night's Thai food still hasn't worked its way through my pores and I badly need a shower too. Besides, I'm not above a bit of soapy action.

As if reading my mind, she pauses at the bottom of the stairs. 'There's room for two in the power shower,' she says. Of course there is.

Twenty minutes later, we're towelling each other down and getting ready for the main feature when Yvonne asks, 'Any charlie?' I nearly tell her she's the second woman that day to ask me that, but instead go into my trouser pocket where the stash would usually be, then freeze.

'Err…no, sorry, not today, babe,' I say. Of course! Fuckfuckfuck. When I got back to the flat, SOCOs had moved in and I didn't get a chance to retrieve my coke from where I'd stashed it, under a loose floorboard in the bedroom. I picture Transit Van Marj rootling about on her hands and knees, shifting my bedside table.

Yvonne looks disappointed, but the lathering up has done her a power of good, and she can see the python's out to play, charlie or no charlie.

'You mean I've to put up with you sober?' she says, purring slightly and lying back on the bed.

'I'm sure you'll cope,' I say, letting the towel finally drop.

The train of thought has knocked me right back into the interview room with DS Martin and Sylvia, though, and a mental image of Martin's expensive complexion isn't one I want in my head right now. I nuzzle Yvonne and we roll about a bit on the bed, while I try to get the action replay of this morning's interview out of my mind's eye.

I can still see Sylvia, sitting next to me, saying in that high, whiny voice of hers: 'I know you know this, Jim, but, just for the record, my client is here voluntarily. He hasn't been charged with anything, and all he wants to do at this stage is to assist.'

Down below, the python regains interest at the thought of Sylvia and I wonder what kind of astronomical odds there would ever be on me getting her and Yvonne into a sandwich style situation.

'As you say, Sylvia, you ken I ken that,' Martin says, his dead eyes boring into me. 'All we all want today is to clear up how a client of your client's ended up dead in his bath with his toe stuck up the tap.'

(Python starts to lose interest again. I kiss Yvonne's neck and then start to move in a southerly direction. She gives an appreciative gasp.)

Martin's still in my head. 'What can ye remember?'

(Yvonne's bedroom smells of patchouli oil and some other feminine scent of some kind. The only fly in the ointment is Gary's framed, signed photo of John Greig on the opposite wall. And the memory of Martin's fag smell.)

What can I remember? Pub. Thai restaurant. Two more pubs and then us walking up Lothian Road, along by the West Port (I seem to remember having to drag Jimmy out of one of the joints in the Pubic Triangle) and then down to the Grassmarket, another pint in the Last Drop, and then along the Cowgate to the club. Rum-ti-tum-tum's...

'Oh fuck, that's fantastic!' Yvonne's voice brings me back to the here and now. God, if he does exist, gave us a tongue in our head for one main reason (well, two if you count talking) and Yvonne's been getting quite carried away while I've been thinking of DS Martin. I clamber up onto the bed, look at Yvonne, and stop thinking about DS Martin altogether. Soon we're at it at a gallop that would win us the Derby.

For me, sex, when it's good, is very, very good indeed. Come to think of it, when it's crap, it's better than a poke in the eye with a sharp stick, but hey. Anyway, things are going well and Yvonne's moaning like a porn star and things are building nicely when –

Choose one of the following options of what you would like to hear at the *moment critique*:

> (a) oh yes, oh yes baby you're the best ever;
> or,
> (b) oh fuck that's my husband's car in the drive.

Thought so. Me too. But unfortunately Yvonne comes out

with option (b).

I slam on the brakes, but it's not that easy when you're half way through, believe you me. There's no way the python wants to come out of there with the job half done, but eventually I manage to get into reverse and out it comes, still firing on all cylinders. Down below me, Yvonne has gone all wide eyed.

'Quick!' she says. 'Get in the wardrobe, Simon!'

I wonder briefly whether this has ever happened to her before, but downstairs I can hear the key rattling in the lock. Fuck! What is this guy, some sort of record holder for the driveway dash from car to front door? Yvonne, still naked, is shooing me into this huge walk-in wardrobe, which is absolutely stacked full of her stuff. I just have time to get into it, cracking my head on a shelf, before she grabs my clothes, stuffs them in with me, and shuts the door. My iPhone clatters off into the darkness.

Then I'm on the floor of the wardrobe, trying to get my arse down in the middle of a shoe collection that Imelda Marcos would be proud of.

'Oh, hi, babe!' I hear Yvonne say as she goes downstairs. I'm hoping she's had time to put on a dressing gown or something to hide the friendly fire. 'Did you forget something?'

'Aye.' Then he mumbles something I can't hear. What is it? What the fuck is it that he's forgotten? Blindly, in the darkness, I feel around at the clothes hanging in the space around me. The wardrobe has that same feminine scent of Yvonne that the whole house has, but what if the big monkey's forgotten something that he needs to come in here for?

I'm fairly sure the thing slapping against my face is one of Yvonne's blouses: it's too thin material to be a bloke's shirt. Then, as I reach further along the rack in the dark, my hands connect with what feels like the loops of a pair of men's trousers and a belt. The trousers slide easily off the hanger and clump to the floor at the far end.

'No, it's ok, I'll get it myself.' I hear heavy feet on the stairs and suddenly my racing brain switches from panic about what's in the wardrobe with me, to panic about what might not be. Did Yvonne throw in my shoes for example? Or is there going to be one guilty looking man's trainer waiting to greet Gary when he comes in here?

I can hear him scuffling about in one of the other rooms, as I grope around trying to reassure myself Yvonne got all my clothes in. In the meantime, my arse, which has only just managed to reach floor level through the layers of heels and sensible flatties, decides it's time it needs some sort of comment on the situation. I'm only just able to spread myself enough to make it mostly silent, but, boy, is it deadly.

Tramp, tramp, tramp. I can hear Gary in the next room muttering to himself and swearing, because he can't find whatever the fuck it is that he feels is so important he has to turn the car around and come back to get. I mean, how inconsiderate is that? People have no manners these days.

The sick part of my brain, the same part that said to me, *Nice work my friend*, when Jimmy's dead hand dropped out of mine and bounced onto his cock and balls, now finds some humour in this whole situation, despite the fact that my backside is pumping out methane fast enough to melt the polar ice caps all by itself. For some reason, I now have to stop myself from laughing.

'What was that?'

Fuck! Has he heard me? More tramping of heavy feet. No, the tone of his voice meant he was responding to something from Yvonne downstairs.

I have actually seen Gary once, in the distance, when I saw the two of them together at the shopping centre in Livingston. He's smaller than Yvonne, one of these stocky little Jocks that wears short-sleeved shirts too tight for his neck: a sandy-haired bulldog type with, the day that I saw him, a scowl on his face which is either because he's a grumpy little bastard or he didn't understand what Yvonne was telling him at the time. Come to think of it, given that he's a Rangers fan, it's probably the latter.

The point being, all things being equal, in a straight fight, if I was lagered up, I could probably take him. But then, I think, as I sit on the floor amongst Yvonne's shoe collection, butt naked and with the python trying to draw itself up into my body cavity, all things are not, in any sense, equal.

'Where the fuck is it?'

Suddenly, he's arrived in the bedroom. My mind is racing, trying to think of the best opening line to greet him if he opens his wardrobe door and finds me there:

'Ah, Gary, so glad you could make it.'

'Quick, let me out of here before she comes back: the crazy bitch has got me in here against my will.' I force my mind, like the rest of my body, to go very, very still.

A few feet away from me, the big monkey is silent. Then he says, 'Funny fucking smell in here.'

'Have you found it yet babe?' This is from Yvonne, who's keeping herself downstairs. Trying to play it cool, I suppose, so as not to arouse his suspicions. 'Naw,' he shouts back. Then, in a voice low enough that she won't hear, he adds, 'D'you think I'd still be standing here like a daft cunt if I had found it?'

'I'll phone it and then you'll be able to work out where it is,' I hear her say.

His moby, then.

Suddenly, a light goes on somewhere in the darkness beyond my right foot. Fuck! It's my moby she's dialled...I wait, like I've got my head on the fucking block and the executioner's swung his axe up, for the strains of Frank Sinatra to blare out of the wardrobe. If it weren't for one of Yvonne's blouses having wrapped itself round my face like a shroud I'd be seeing my entire fucking life flash in front of my eyes.

Then, instead, I hear a Deep Purple riff start up over on the other side of the room and she's realised her mistake, cut off the signal just in time, and phoned Gary's instead.

'Aye, that's it,' he grunts down to her. Not a word of thanks, the charmless cunt.

He starts to go out of the room and then stops. I hear the floorboard creak right next to the wardrobe door. Has he seen something? Then, in the same low voice, he mutters to himself, 'What's she been eatin now to make that smell? Just hope she's no ovulatin tonight so's I can get some peace to watch Match of the Day.'

Then he's away, the cunt, down the stairs, saying something out loud to Yvonne as he gets ready to go. Which, finally, he does.

I sit in the wardrobe too far into shock to move, until Yvonne comes up the stairs and opens the door for me. I realise I'm actually shaking.

Yvonne looks almost as white as me in her dressing gown. 'What's that – ?' she starts to say, but by then I'm halfway out the wardrobe door and heading for the en-suite. If Gary's got early onset Alzheimer's and has forgotten something else, I'm buggered, but it's worth it just to reach the toilet and let everything go.

By the time I've sorted myself and come out, Yvonne has nearly stopped laughing, and she's sitting on the bed with a gleam in her eye.

'Now, where were we?' she says, with that same cheeky grin. The python's near death experience in the wardrobe doesn't seem to have fazed it and, before I know it, we're at it again, this time mercifully without any interruption. Even DS Martin stays out of my head for the duration, although Sylvia's belly button makes a guest appearance near the end.

The sum total of which means, by the time I climb back in the Lexus at half past three, everyone's happy. Me, Yvonne and the python, certainly. It turns out later that by then Rangers are three nil up so presumably Gary's happy, too. I stick some sounds on the CD and head for Mum's.

***

Her house isn't anything near as grand as the new build palace Yvonne and Gary live in, of course. It's a three bedroom end-terrace in the best of the ex-development corporation estates, though, and I can park the Lexus there overnight and still have good odds on most of it being there in the morning.

Mum meets me at the door. 'Simon,' she says, but instead of the usual Italian style slobbering over me, she just steps back to let me and my new suits in.

Tom, meantime, is sitting on his stair-lift at the foot of the stairs. This usually makes me smile: it must be the only Stannah that's painted in military camouflage colours. However, the look on his face wipes the smile off mine and I remember what Mum had said on the phone: not one of his good days.

Tom looks me in the eye as Mum closes the door behind me.

'Cunt,' he says, and presses the button on the Stannah so that he then slowly disappears back upstairs.

Great welcome. You can always count on your family to bring you down, can't you?

CHAPTER 4
LIVING DEATH IN LIVINGSTON

There's an ominous silence, broken only by the whine of the Stannah, taking Tom upstairs. Then Mum bustles through to the kitchen without a further word, and I know something's up.

I hang my suits on the stairs, put my bag down and follow her through. There isn't far to go: the house is pretty small, with the kitchen off the hall and then leading through to the living-room in open plan, to make things easier for Tom to get about. Mum has put the kettle on, but she still isn't meeting my eye.

'I'll take a coffee if it's going,' I say, hopefully. She turns, and gives me a look as if I've told her I pulled the legs off insects for a hobby.

'Oh Simon, how could you do this? It's just not right, you know.'

Fuck. They say mothers always know, but how could she know about Jimmy Ahmed? I feel a prickle of fear run down my spine. And if she knows, who else does? Then she picks up her house brick of a mobile and hands it to me. 'Go on. Read it.'

I look at the thing. The screen is blurry behind the scratchy old plastic cover. I keep telling her to get a newer one.

SIMON ON WAY. LOL.

At last I understand. Thank fuck it's fuck all to do with Jimmy Ahmed.

Mum is still looking at me with those spaniel eyes of hers. 'Simon. You know she's married. She's trying to have her own family. She doesn't need any complications like being involved with a boy like you.'

I take a deep breath. I feel like laughing, I'm so relieved that this is about Yvonne, and not about the little matter of a dead bloke in my bath in Edinburgh.

I look at my Mum. She's still a good looking woman for her age; got that olive Italian skin and brown eyes that she's passed on to me. And, of course, Yvonne does wonders with her hair.

Perhaps, I'm thinking cynically, that's the issue. *She doesn't want to get another hairdresser.*

'Yvonne and I are just good friends,' I tell her. I'm not even convincing myself. 'I just popped round to see her about the lease of a new shop in Falkirk. She's a client, remember?'

Mum says nothing at first, turning and putting the kettle on. Then I hear the sound of voices upstairs. I see Mum's shoulders slump. Without turning round, she says, 'You'd better go up and see what you can do. Tom's got the plumber trapped up there. He says he won't let him leave until the taps in the bath get fixed.'

Great. I'm obviously not going to get a coffee until I broker a peace deal in what sounds like the Middle East crisis upstairs. I pick up my suits and the overnight bag, and take them up with me.

'What I'm saying to you, Mr. English, is that this is a low flow system. I…'

'You keep saying that. Then you launch into a long explanation about what a low flow system is like you're some kind of fucking plumbing brain of Britain. I don't care what a low flow system is. I just want the bath taps fixed, ok?'

Tom is blocking the entrance to the bathroom. Inside, looking like an overweight bunny trapped in the headlights, is Mum and Tom's plumber, Ballingall. He must have a first name, but all Tom ever calls him is Ballingall. The van, which has been abandoned across the driveway outside, just says AB Plumbing. Well, it also says 'All your plumbing needs, no matter how small' like plumbers' vans always do. But you get the gist.

Ballingall also looks like every Scottish plumber I've ever met: in other words, shaved head to hide the receding hairline, about three stones overweight, arse falling out of his trousers and a permanently puzzled expression. Or maybe that's just when he's dealing with the wheelchair kamikaze that is my brother, Tom, these days.

When I appear in the doorway, he looks up as if I'm the Seventh Cavalry coming over the hill.

'Oh, hello, Mr. English. I was just explaining to your brother that this is a low flow system and – '.

'Don't let the cunt explain to you what a low flow system is. You'll lose the will to live.' Tom says through clenched teeth.

'…so what I really need to do is get some extra parts and fit the right kind of tap. I've got something out in the van that would do for now.' The poor guy is sweating like a paedophile at a kids' party.

'Don't let the cunt out. He'll not come back.'

I ignore Tom. 'So, you're saying that you can get something fitted just now that will improve things and then you can come back later with something more permanent?' Establish the parameters of the deal on the table. Important in any negotiation. Of course, most commercial property transactions don't actually involve trapping the other party in your house until the deal is done. It's usually your office.

'That's right.' Ballingall is looking at me pleadingly now: he's probably told his wife he'd be home three hours ago. I've driven from Edinburgh, had lunch, bought suits, shagged Yvonne, hidden in a wardrobe and shagged Yvonne again while this luckless cunt has sweated over some bath taps. I look beyond him to the bath. It takes up most of the bathroom now, being one of these walk in jobs for Tom.

Actually, he uses the shower most of the time, so I'm not quite sure why he is getting so excited about things. I can see that the bath taps are in bits on the floor, along with a variety of tools, a roll of sticky tape and the obligatory empty mug of coffee. At least Mum has managed to smuggle that in to him, the poor bastard.

'Ok,' I say. 'Why don't you go and get some stuff from the van and fix us up something temporary then? And can you come back later on?'

Ballingall's already gathering up his tools. 'I don't think it can be today, but I can manage tomorrow for sure.'

'Tomorrow's fine,' I say, ignoring Tom, who sounds like a pressure cooker about to blow. I grab the handles of his chair and haul him backwards.

'Be back in a second,' Ballingall says, sloping out with his tools and edging down the stairs faster than a rat with diarrhoea down a drainpipe.

As the door shuts behind him, Tom turns to me and says, 'Nice work indeed. That's the last we'll see of him.' He wheels himself round and heads for his room. 'I had him cornered in there.'

'Oh, he'll be back,' I tell him. When I saw the plumber's van, I had anticipated this. 'My Lexus is blocking him in.'

Tom stops en route to his bedroom, turns and looks at me. 'You're not quite so fucking clueless as I thought,' he says, then continues on his way.

Negotiation. It's what I do.

***

Later, when Ballingall has left us with some sort of working system and taken himself and his builder's arse out of the bathroom, things seem to be thawing a bit. The shagging of Yvonne isn't mentioned again, and Mum even makes her proper Italian coffee for me. To be honest, I think she's grateful for the distraction I can provide when I'm at home. Tom can be pretty intense when he's in one of his moods.

'Right. That's us off to the pub Mum. Be back by eight.'

That's Tom. Once he's decided something, everybody else has to fall into line or there's trouble. At least, that's Tom nowadays.

Mum looks at me. 'There's some Pinot Grigio in the fridge, Simon,' she says hopefully.

Tom's already halfway through the door. 'We'll have it with the pasta,' he says. 'Bro will have been missing his Tennent's lager. They don't have it in the gay bars he goes to down south.'

I smile, and shrug at Mum. She doesn't look best pleased, but just says to me quietly, 'Don't let him forget to take his medication, Simon, ok?'

I nod. Tom's had a few seizures since the accident, so he's on Epilem. Not meant to be mixed with the gallons of lager he's about to pour down his throat, of course, but I suppose Swiss drug companies don't factor in Jock culture when they're doing their R&D.

Tom has wheeled out past my car and along the path, which means we're walking. Which means we're going to the nearest, nastiest pub, Legends. To get there, we have to leave the relative safety of Mum's estate, cross what was originally conceived of as a landscaped area but is now, in reality, a no-man's land for warring tribes of Jock neds, and go through a neighbourhood shopping centre with all the charm of Beirut on a bad night.

'Do you want me to push?'

'No thanks. I've had enough of your driving to last me a lifetime.' Tom can never resist twisting the knife about that, every time.

'Suit yourself.' I watch him spin along ahead of me, like something out of the Wheelchair Olympics' 100 metre dash. After last night, more fizzy Jock lager is the last thing I feel like. I decide to go along with it though, just to keep the peace.

Legends is surprisingly empty for a Saturday night. Perhaps half the regulars are in prison. Or still at the Rangers game with Gary. There's a step to get into the pub, but I notice that someone has put an insecure looking block of wood over it, as a makeshift ramp. I go ahead and open the door for Tom, who rolls up it, eyeing it suspiciously.

'Aye,' he says. 'If they think that's complying with DDA, they've got another fucking think coming.'

Here we go. Since the accident, Tom has been well into all the Disability Discrimination stuff. I kind of know what's coming next as he rolls up to the bar.

'Lager, cunt face,' he says to me. 'And we'll have a seat over there.'

'Tom…' He's indicating the part of the bar which is three steps down. There are plenty of other tables on the top level near the bar but, of course, that isn't his point. 'Oh, that's right,' he says, loud enough to get the barman's attention. 'I can't because it's not DDA compliant, is it?'

The barman's a big scary looking bastard with tattoos on his neck. He looks at me. 'What's he sayin?'

I must say, I hate that, when people don't talk to Tom directly.

'Errr…two lagers. Tom, the pool table's empty just now. Why don't I show you how to play that?'

He knows what's going on, but he looks at the barman, then me, and shrugs. 'Suppose so. You can bring the lagers over.' The barman gives me my lagers, takes my tenner, and gives me change without another word.

I take the beers over to a side table while Tom racks up the balls. The pool room, such as it is, is an alcove off the main bar with a couple of tables in the corner. The walls are decorated with the so-called legends of snooker that give the bar its name, pride of place being given to the Jocks of course, including Stephen Hendry, the ugliest man in snooker (now there's a closely contested title).

Speaking of ugly, one of the corner tables is occupied by a couple of neds drinking bottles of Bud. They could be brothers, but that could just be the inbreeding that's endemic amongst Jocks outwith the cosmopolitan centre of Edinburgh.

'Toss for break?' I say, keeping my voice low.

'Aye,' Tom says. That's another annoying habit he's picked up since he moved to Livingston. A bit of the accent. On the other hand, I'm proud to be English, although not so proud that I'll risk a kicking for it.

But the neds have already picked up on my voice. I don't hear exactly what he says, but one of them mutters something about 'tosser,' and the other one laughs.

I let it go, toss the coin, win and bend down to break. Tom, however, is already steaming towards the two of them.

'What did you say there?' he says.

The ned eyes him coolly. 'Didn't say nothin,' he says. Tom stares him down for a second, turns, sees that I've broken and not potted anything, and wheels up to the table.

The neds, meantime, have finished their drinks and stand up. I make the mistake of catching the eye of one of them as Tom lines up his shot. He sticks his finger in the Bud bottle, swings it gently from side to side then lets it drop back on the table. It rolls to the floor as they go out of the pool room, but doesn't break.

Tom, meantime, is hitting an ambitious shot, a cannon at a narrow angle to take down one of the stripes hanging over the bottom corner pocket. As the balls kiss together, he says, loudly, 'Cunts.'

The other ned, the one that hasn't spoken yet, turns on his way out of the alcove and strokes his earlobe, gently, to indicate he's heard. 'We'll be waitin,' is all he says. Then they leave the bar.

That's all it takes to get yourself in a fight in Scotland: have the wrong accent. Oh, and a stupid brother that won't let things go, I suppose. I had had it in mind to talk to him about the whole Jimmy Ahmed issue, but our night is now taking a different turn.

A couple of pints later and I finally persuade Tom it's time to go. Sure enough, Tweedle Dum and Tweedle Dee are waiting for us out on the path.

'Aw, here's the English boy with the crippled brother,' one of them says. The way they're moving, swaying slightly, make me think either they've gone home for a carryout, or else taken something stronger than Budweiser. The bigger of the two walks over to where we are on the pavement outside the pub. He reaches out and ruffles Tom's hair. I can feel something rising in me, a burst of adrenalin, ready for fight or flight. *Do something,* I tell myself but, for some reason, I'm frozen to the spot. 'Aw,' the ned's saying. 'Nothing to say the now – '.

He never finishes what he's saying. Tom may not be able to walk any more but he spends a lot of time down the gym. He reaches up and grabs the ned by the hair, pulling him down till his face is level with his own, and side on.

'I've plenty to say,' he says and then head butts the guy right on the cheek bone. I can hear the crack, and the ned springs back.

The other one has come up behind me so I spin round and, while he's distracted at the amount of blood coming out of his brother's face, boot him as hard in the balls as I can. He goes down, howling. Then I grab the handles of Tom's chair and run for it.

'Where the fuck do you think you're going?' Tom's shouting at me. 'We've only just got started on them!'

'I'll explain later,' I say, thinking, *This would please the Edinburgh cops no end, hearing that I've been done for assault the night after they found a body in my bath.*

There are roars of rage and pain behind us but no running feet. I used to run a bit at school, before I grew big enough at puberty to bully the little bastards back, so even pushing a wheelchair I reckon I could outpace them.

'Have you taken your Epilem yet?' I ask him as we reach the relative safety of our own estate.

'Took it with the first pint of Tennent's' he mumbles, unconvincingly. *That's great,* I think, *it would just crown a perfect day if he had a fit when I was in charge of him.*

We're half an hour late for dinner, so Mum's face is, predictably, a picture. We sit and eat our rubber pasta in silence, as Tom works the Pinot Grigio bottle like it's going out of fashion. At least Mum has had the sense to have two bottles in the fridge.

'How long are you likely to stay, Simon, just the weekend?'

'Er, yeah, or maybe a couple of days. Having a few problems with the new flat, actually.'

'Oh?' Mum's eyebrows go up. 'What kind of problems?' Parents always love to hear about your problems, don't they?

'Ah, just a few things needing done in the bathroom.' Which is, technically, true. 'Few plumbing problems.' Mum looks even more worried. There's just never a good time to tell your family you're a murder suspect and there's a corpse in your bath, is there? *I might tell Tom later*, I keep thinking.

'And you're not using Mr. Ballingall?'

I'm having to make up a lot of stuff on the spot. 'I phoned him but he said he was too busy. I've got a local guy in Edinburgh. He'll be fine. Name of Martin.'

That seems to satisfy them both, and I finish the rest of my pasta in silence. We're putting stuff in the dishwasher when my moby bleeps at me.

GARY GOT TOO PISHED AND IS STAYING OVER WITH A MATE IN GLASGOW. FANCY ROUND THREE? LOL.

Laugh out loud, indeed. I tell Mum it's an old pal I haven't seen in ages and get round to Yvonne's as soon as I can. Probably shouldn't have driven, but I'm not risking meeting up with Tweedle Dum and Tweedle Dee again. As I waltz through the roundabouts, I do wonder about Gary's excuse. It wouldn't be that he has some bit on the side near Ibrox, does he?

You never know. You can't trust what anyone says these days.

CHAPTER 5
AT HOME IN AUCHENDROSSAN

From: Karen Clamp
ubinclampit@hushmail.com
To: foi@edinburgh.gov.uk

What is the current status of the
Caltongate transaction?
Please can you tell me how much of the
land involved in the Caltongate land sale
is held on the Council's common good
account?
If the answer is none, has it been checked
to see whether it may be common good
land?
What land does the Council own in the
Cowgate? If possible, it would be useful
to have a pdf plan of the landownership
in this area.
Does the Council hold any information
on who owns the Castle Esplanade?
Does the Council hold any information
on whether it is permitted to take
photographs on the Castle Esplanade, and
if not, what legal right the authorities have
to stop the taking of photographs?
All under FOI. Sincerely Karen Clamp

Monday mornin and I'm just back from seeing the wean to the
school gate. I say school: it's more like a holdin tank for future
Saughton inmates. There's fencin all round it that would keep a
suicide bomber out. No barbed wire on the roof yet but give
them time. Should be twinned with one in Kabul.

The current teacher's all right though. I've only had to mark
her card twice: once when she said Candice's trousers were the
wrong shade for the uniform, and another time for some cheeky

comment she made to the class about obesity. Needless to say, I've seen more fat on a greasy chip than there is on her, but that doesn't give her the right to start preachin about fat people when it's hormonal for some of us. Did my nerves no good whatsoever, that.

Anyway, rather than go back to my own flat, I decide to go and see old Jessie on the opposite block about the sewin she needs done. Since it's the mornin, most of the crims and druggies round here will be flaked out for another few hours yet. On the way, I do a sweep of the drying greens for needles and broken glass. After my last complaint to the Chief Executive at the Cooncil, I managed to get them to promise extra patrols by the Community Wardens to try and pick these up. Mostly, though, I still see them dodgin around outside the Council offices, having a fag, so I just do it myself.

Not even a dog turd today though. I should be pleased but it's like in the old cowboy films when they're waiting for the Indians coming over the hill and they say, 'It's quiet. Too quiet.'

Jessie's flat is on the fifth floor. No lifts in these maisonette blocks, of course, and never mind the DDA; so by the time I get to the door, I'm like a whale that's swum the Atlantic. This block is called Waverley Court. My own block is Ivanhoe. When they built them they decided to call them after Walter Scott novels, like that would turn all the inmates into literary geniuses overnight.

'I'm glad you made it over,' says Jessie, showing me ben the house. Her flat is like a shrine to porcelain figurines, although the commemorative plates of Princess Di get pride of place, of course.

'Would you like a cup of tea while you rest up?' she says, bustling through to the kitchen before I get a chance to answer. She makes it sound like I've crossed the Sahara, rather than walk back from the school two streets away.

'Aye.' I hear her rattling about with the mugs and the kettle. She's probably only about 65, Jessie, but she's kind of been 65 ever since I knew her twenty years ago: she knew my mum and stayed in the old part of the estate, like we did then.

'How's the bairn?' she shouts through from the kitchen. From where I'm sitting, I can't see her, just her hands as she sticks the mugs on the bunker, pours the kettle, pokes the teabag and then slops it into the other mug. Even the mugs are porcelain, with pink flowers clambering all over them.

'She's fine.' I have to think about how to answer questions about Candice. Accentuate the positive, as they say. 'Her teacher says she's doing really well at some subjects, maths especially. She can't get difficult enough books for her, she's that good at it.' Art, too, surprisingly.

'I got that book I ordered out the library,' Jessie says, coming through. 'The new one about Diana.'

'Oh aye?' Jessie's convinced that Diana was done away with by the Establishment. I tend to agree but, to be honest, it's no the most interestin conspiracy theory as far as I'm concerned. I mean, there's much stranger goings on happenin here under our noses, especially what the Cooncil is up to.

Anyway, we chew the fat about Henri Paul and whether he was drunk or drugged, or both, and what Prince Philip was supposed to have said when he was openin a Tesco in Chingford one time and then I say to her, 'You said you had some sewin for me, Jessie?'

'Oh aye, I nearly forgot hen. It's just this skirt needs widened a wee bit – too many extra helpings of tatties at my daughter-in-law's, ken?' she laughs.

I take the skirt. I'm sure it's the same one I've let out for her before. If she doesn't cut down on the tatties, she'll be my size soon, and then she'll know all about confidence issues. Still, I think Jessie's more interested in a blether than the sewin.

I ask her if she noticed anything unusual happening in my block over the weekend.

'Me? Oh, I'm usually too busy to be looking out the window, as you know but...' She always says that but there's a chair that just happens to be by the window and it's amazin what she sees by never looking out of it. 'I did see Mr. Bump going across to your block – och, but you must've seen him yourself, you were going out with Candice at the same time, was that Saturday, you go up to Morningside? Candice likes to do that, doesn't she?'

'Mr. Bump? You mean Oddjob?'

She giggles a bit. 'Oddjob? His real name's Kevin, you ken. Kevin Taylor. But I've heard he likes to call himself Mr. Bump now. Anyway, he didn't stay long at your bit. I saw him standing in the doorway of the flat downstairs, then he came out again. There was that laddie Boyes there and another man I didn't recognise. The Boyes character and the other chap stayed a bit longer, then they left together. I saw the other one drive away in a big black car – an Audi or something.'

As I say, she sees a lot for someone that never looks out the window.

I nod, still thinking of the man with the head in chinos. 'I'll get these back to you by Wednesday, ok?'

Jessie says that's fine and shows me out. Down the stairs and across to my block again: nothin to do until I pick up Candice apart from a wee bit sewin and some outstandin FOI requests.

***

I've no always been the size of the number 18 to Pilton, ken. Never quite as thin as that skinny bitch that teaches Candice, mind. But then I had the bairn and my hormones got a turbo charger strapped to them. Not that I would swap having the bairn for anythin, of course. How she came about is hardly young love's sweet dream, but the result I wouldn't change for anythin.

Back in the door, I check the baby monitor. Nothin stirring downstairs. Ten years ago, I'd never have thought of bugging the downstairs flat. Then Derek Boyes moved in. Oh aye, it's a small world, Auchendrossan, right enough. He's no actually that much younger than me: in fact, I knew him when I was growing up in the old bit of the estate. He was a nasty wee ned then so I suppose he should get the credit for being consistent.

I put up with him downstairs for two years. He had what the Cooncil people call a chaotic lifestyle – in other words, drugs, drinks, parties till 5 o'clock in the mornin when I had my work the next day at that time. Rave music beltin out the windows so hard the furniture used to shake.

Then the Cooncil re-housed him just down the road and, after the paedophile, surprise, surprise, downstairs was let to part of his criminal empire. That meant I got the ravers, and then the cannabis farm. I went to the police but, well, the police, don't get me started on them. Half of them are in cahoots with Pimpy Boy's gang. I'm never sure if that's the same half that's in the Masons.

I'll say this for having a cannabis farm in the maisonette below, though: it's actually quite quiet. A lot of comings and goings, obviously, but it was just a boy and his lassie and they needed to keep a low profile. Eventually, the police busted them but, again, surprise, surprise, hardly any drugs were found in the flat the mornin they raided them.

When they were moved out, and the Council was doin the flat up, that's when I installed the baby monitors. That was a year past August. I suppose the batteries on the other two baby monitors have gone: that's probably why they don't work, come to think of it. But, surprise, surprise again, who should be moved in but a couple of lassies in the other part of Pimpy Boy's ever expanding empire.

There's a movement downstairs. 'I go and get the kettle on.' It's the Elena lassie. I do feel a tiny bit sorry for her: she came over in the back of a lorry from Romania, probably thinking she was going to pick tatties or somethin. No much of a life for her: no wonder she's on smack all the time.

Of course, I'm up at the Housing Department almost every week with my evidence. No the transcripts from the baby monitors, obviously: that would probably get me and Candice thrown out of our flat on our ear. But the anti-social people have told me to keep a diary, so I do. Sometimes the two of them have up to five men a night visiting. How you're supposed to bring up a bairn in a place like this is beyond me.

The flat below is quiet again: the lassie must have just made herself some tea and gone back to her pit. I fire up the computer and check for FOI responses. The Council never keep to their deadlines, but they never keep to anything anyway. What a mess this city is in. They tried that congestion charging idea but the turkeys wouldn't vote for Christmas so they gave up on that. They got their revenge with all the road works, though. And some laddie up in City Chambers never got a train set when he was a wean so they've put in trams at huge expense to the ratepayer.

38

***

A wee bit later and I hear the lassies movin about down the stair. After they've clattered about in the kitchen they go ben their livin room, and I pad through, to listen on the baby monitor.

'Deek say to me, I should have taken the pictures anyway, but how can I do that with the other man dead in the other room? And then by the time Deek and the rest of them come, this Simon had passed out. What were we meant to do?'

This is Elena. *So they were mixed up in the murder.* My mind's racin, thinkin, *How can I get the lot of them nailed for this? Who could I go to, and would it ever mean I got half-decent folk livin down the stair from me?*

'Look, hen. I've told you. Nothin to do with us now. If that firm want this guy Simon English fitted up with somethin, they can do it another way. We don't have to be the fall guys in all of Deek's wee schemes.'

'I know, Debi, I know. But when we –

'Number four, where are you now Bobby? Rab's needin a pick up from the club… aye, a couple of the regulars'll give him a hand out, just make sure you've got the rug on the back seat again…'

Blast it! It's the taxi firm again, usin the same channel as the listenin devices. It seems to go on forever, so I go through to the livin room to pick up my sewin, while I wait for the airwaves to clear.

I try to recall everythin they've said: *Simon English.* An unusual name, likes.

I've got my bits and bobs out and I'm doin the alterations to Jessie's skirt, lost in thinkin about what those two whores are into, when there's a hammerin on my front door. I ken right away it's a man: any woman would have the sense to ring the door bell. Through the frosted glass, though, I can see it's no just any wee gadgie.

'Mrs. Clamp?' Oddjob just about causes a solar eclipse single-handedly. He's even more massive close up than he is from a distance, which is how I like to see him normally.

'That's right,' I say to him, squinting up at the great bulk of the guy. His eyes are really heavy lidded, and he keeps them half closed all the time, which is why he reminds me of the Bond character. He looms over me. 'Deek Boyes said I should come and see you,' he says. I'm no easily scared, but I have to admit, looking up at him when he says that, I feel something running up and down my spine. There's a long pause and then he says, 'About gettin my alterations done.'

I notice for the first time he's got two or three pair of trousers on his arm.

'Oh, aye, right? You'd better come in then,' I say, leading him then to the living room. The door shakes in its frame, the way he shuts it, but that is probably just the way he always shuts the door. 'I'll need to measure you up, you see, to see what size to alter them to.'

His lips turn upwards in what I think is meant to be a smile: it makes his cheekbones go up and his eyes close altogether. He pats his stomach. 'Too much Chinese,' and for a horrible moment, I have a mental picture of him tearing the guy down the local takeaway limb from limb, like Hannibal Lecter.

'I ken the feelin,' I say, although, in reality, I can't stand Chinese food. Give me a curry every time. No that I can afford that more than once a month, especially since Candice doesn't like them yet. Too spicy for her.

I have to stand close to Oddjob as I pass the tapes round his waist. He smells of fag smoke and Old Spice: could be worse I suppose. I measure his outside leg but decide that I'll take a guess at the inside one: the main one's the waist measurement, obviously.

'A centimetre will do it,' I'm sayin, just as Debi Murray, in the next room, says, 'Where's the pain killin cream, Elena? That last one last night was rough as f*ck,' clear as day.

Oddjob looks up 'What was that? It sounded like…'

'Och, I must've left the radio on in the bedroom,' I say, and breenge through to get the baby monitor before the wee slapper downstairs says anything else. When I come back through though, he's still frownin.

'One of these kitchen sink dramas they do on Radio 4,' I say.

The corners of the mouth go up again and he nods. 'Oh aye, I see. Mostly listen to Forth FM myself.'

'I could just do the alterations just now if you've got half an hour to wait,' I hear myself saying. Why on earth did I say that? Most of me is desperate to get him out the door again just as soon as I can. On the other hand, the prospect of having to have him back here or, even worse, go across to his flat, is too much to bear. 'Would you like a cup of tea?' I say to him.

'I'm fine.'

So, Oddjob sits on my couch looking round the room at all my knick knacks and everything, while I do the fastest set of trouser alterations known to man. At the end, when he asks me how much it is, I blurt out a fiver, just because I'm no thinkin straight by then.

'I thought it was £3 per trouser, that's what Jessie said,' he says, frownin a bit again.

So. He's been up to see old Jessie. That gives me the creeps almost as much as if he'd said something about Candice. Have him and Pimpy Boy been keeping an eye on me? How much do they ken?

'Special introductory offer,' I say, trying to smile at him. He grins that weird grin of his again, pays me the fiver, takes the trousers and leaves. I'm sweatin like I've just run a marathon. I need a strong cup of tea, and a couple of chocolate digestives, just to get my heart rate down again.

When I was a kid, our mum took us to the zoo for a day out. Just the one time that I can remember. In fact, it's about the only thing I can ever remember her taking us to. Anyway, there was me, my sister Elaine, and our wee brother Brian.

I always remember Brian at the lion's cage. He was being a bit of a wee so and so, lobbin bits of stick and stuff at this lion through the bars. It was a Tuesday mornin, so there was hardly anyone else around and my Mum was distracted or she would've told him to no do it.

Anyway, this big old lion took it for a while, just twitchin its ears with its eyes shut, as if it were asleep. It was a huge thing, a bit scabby lookin, like it had had a few run ins with the chief lion, and no come up smellin of roses exactly. I suppose there's a peckin order, even amongst the lions.

Brian kept lobbin bits of stick through the bars: had to reach through them to get a good shot. He'd hit it on the napper, it'd just make a rumblin noise, twitch its ears a bit, ken? Clonk, twitch, twitch.

Then suddenly it opened its eyes, growled and charged at the bars, trying to get its paw through to grab wee Brian in. He just got his hand back through in time: they've got perspex on the cage now, of course, but that was back in the old days. Mum had to take him to the lassies' toilets afterwards to get him cleaned up.

That's what Oddjob reminds me of. A big scabby lion you don't want to annoy. Difference is, there aren't any bars on the windows in Auchendrossan.

CHAPTER 6
HARD DAY AT THE ORIFICE

'Rohypnol,' she says.

'Can you repeat that, please?' I think I have heard her right but, in the middle of the open plan office, I'm trying not to give the bastards any clue at all that it's Sylvia on the phone telling me what the plods have found in my blood.

'Rohypnol,' she says again. 'After effects include disorientation and memory loss. That's why I recommended you have a blood test. It's commonly used as a – '

'Date rape drug,' I say as quietly as I can, covering the space between receiver and mouth with my hand. Nobody around me looks up. 'Somebody must've slipped it in my drink.'

There's a pause at the end of the line. 'Well, that's one explanation certainly. It's also used for recreational purposes, particularly amongst the gay community. Couples take it to loosen up their inhibitions.'

This does ring a bell with me. My mate Chris and his girlfriend took it once after two bottles of Chilean Cab.Sauv. He told me when they woke up the next day, neither of them could remember what they'd done but the sheets were a mess and his knob hurt for three days afterwards. They only did it the once.

Don't like the mention of gay sex though. What's she implying?

'Look,' I say to her. 'It's a bit difficult chatting this through on the phone.' Heads are starting to pop up now, above the screens: they've all heard about Jimmy Ahmed, of course, so they've been very sympathetic to my face, but now their ears are flapping big style. 'Why don't we meet at lunchtime and have a chat about this?'

There's a pause before she says, reluctantly, 'Ok,' and names a place in Bread Street which is roughly half way between the offices. Although Sylvia's firm has been taken over by us, they still operate out of the same crappy little office in the Old Town, and are resisting getting shifted.

The main office is in one of the smaller new blocks off Lothian Road. The firm occupies floors 3, 4 and 10: when it was built, they had first dibs on the accommodation. Sandwiched in between, there's some accountants and one of the medium sized insurers.

After hanging up the phone, I go to make myself another coffee. Reasons to be cheerful: it's Thursday and I'm back at work and back in the flat at long last; and I'm getting a chance to have another gander at Sylvia's jewel in her navel.

On the other hand, work means Floor 3: the seventh circle of hell. If you're a client or a solicitor from another firm coming to cut a deal, you'll never see Floor 3, which is basically the business end where all the grunt work gets done. It consists of two big open plan areas on either side of the lifts and stairwell: one side mainly taken up with lawyers and the other mainly with support staff, other than the two offices our com. prop. partners have had made for themselves. That's the Rottweiler and Tony Hand, of course.

The top floor, on the other hand, has a reception area the size of a football pitch and a series of glass walled meeting rooms where all the meeting and greeting of clients goes on, as well as deal cutting. Very grand, with a view down to the New Town to stun the clients into thinking their money's being well spent.

When everyone's in, on this floor, it's more like the fucking black hole of Calcutta but, at least at the moment, most of my team are upstairs on one deal or another so there's a bit of space to sit and think as I drink my coffee.

So, somebody slipped me a Mickey Finn. Who, though? I suppose the prime candidate would be Jimmy Ahmed, since I fetched up in the flat with him but, then, why would he? The suggestion of gayness bothers me more than I would admit openly if I was being politically correct and all that, but I really don't think Jimmy was that way inclined. Besides, there were these two girls…

It's a brain equivalent of something being on the tip of your tongue. I can almost picture them now, one blonde, one brunette. I don't remember them at all before Rum-ti-tum-tum's, which suggests we met them there. I can almost picture meeting them: that buzz that you get when you're out and you meet up with someone and you think something's going to happen but, at the moment, their faces are blank. I sip my coffee, thinking.

An email pings up and I ignore it. Then a second one arrives, from the same source. It's the Rottweiler, wondering how I'm getting on with what he's given me and when I can hope to have things tied up. I email him back to say it will all be done this morning just to give myself something of a challenge, and then try to concentrate on my work again.

The Rottweiler has given me three rent review memorandums to sort out. For those of you who aren't lawyers, right, when you lease a shop or some other type of commercial property, built in to the lease is a regular pattern of rent reviews when the landlord can try to screw the rent up – generally every three or five years depending on the type of property. Got that? And once the review is sorted out, then there's a document of a couple of pages that has to be signed up, recording what the new rent is.

Sounds exciting, huh? Right. In. com. prop. terms, it's the equivalent of what they give the remedial kid in primary school when the rest of them are doing hard sums. Or, in McDonald's terms, it's having to sweep the shit out of the back shop because you're not trusted to flip burgers at the front.

And that's exactly the kind of shit they've given me to do since I moved to the Edinburgh office. Oh, and looking after Jimmy Ahmed, which was perhaps a tougher assignment than I'd imagined. While people I'm meant to be the boss of have been swanning about cutting some fairly juicy sounding deals, I've been sweating down on the third floor over bollocks like this.

Well, bollocks to that, I say to myself. Half an hour later and I've made a couple of calls, run off the standard styles of memorandums (there's not even anything interesting to argue over with the lawyers on the other side in these types of things) and have them sorted and ready for the final versions. Only another hour to go before lunch with Sylvia, so I set off for the tenth floor in search of something more interesting.

Gemma, the receptionist, is pretty slick and professional with me, a bit too skinny for my taste, but I wouldn't kick her out of bed all the same: fake tan, make-up and hair all beautifully done. She speaks like she's been to one of the posh Edinburgh schools, you know: that drawl. 'Bradley's got Edinburgh Council and their agents in Room Three,' she's saying, as I gaze out at the view across the New Town to avoid gazing down her blouse. 'Al is in Four to do with that shopping centre development at

Livingston.'

That decides it. I've had enough of Livingston for a while. I thank her, sneak a peek down her blouse anyway and head for Three.

Al and Bradley. Al an' Bradley. Al + Bradley, like some sort of shit law firm all of their own. Another fucking Edinburgh merchant school in joke. When I first got here, I thought they were just one person called Alan Bradley but it's just that they're so joined at the hip that people refer to them as a collective noun. Gemma seems to think the sun shines out of Bradley's arsehole in particular, so I take it she fagged for him or whatever they did at Stew-Mel or wherever.

They're both technically in my team and, therefore, technically, under my command but, as I say, I've been downstairs farting out rent review memorandums while they've been upstairs doing the good stuff. Well, thinks I, all that's about to change, buddies.

'You can't possibly expect my clients to accept that,' a smooth looking character is saying to Bradley as I walk in. 'Councils can't give guarantees in that way.'

'Why not?' I say, swooping behind the guy, taking a bit of the shortbread and helping myself to a coffee from the filter machine in the corner. As I say, all mod-cons on the tenth floor. The smooth guy twists round in his seat to look at me in a, who's this wanker then, type of way, so I deliberately move slightly in the other direction so that he has to twist round again.

Two basic strategies of competitive negotiation: ask the awkward question and get the other side to explain themselves, and ruffle the cunt's feathers by catching him off guard. Bradley looks up at me with those sleepy eyes of his. 'This is er, Simon English. He's the senior associate in our team.'

'Hi.' I come round and sit next to my boy. The smooth looking guy is looking none too pleased. Good. 'Sandy Crombie,' he says, reluctantly, as if it's some sort of state secret. The other guy, a bearded bloke in a suit that should've been retired ten years ago, mumbles something I don't catch but I'm assuming he's Mr. Edinburgh Council.

I smile pleasantly. 'I was asking why the Council can't give guarantees?'

Crombie looks exasperated. 'Have you heard of the *Credit*

Suisse cases? It would be *ultra vires.*'

I hate it when the cunts use Latin. They do it all the time up here and think their legal system's better than the English one because it's based on Roman law rather than Norman French. Well, fuck all of that. It's a second rate legal system for a second rate country and they should be glad they're joined onto a better, more successful neighbour, although, if I had it my way, I'd dig a big fucking trench at Hadrian's Wall and float the bastards off into the North Sea.

Actually, a bit further south than that. They can have the Geordies. We'll keep the Lake District for the water supply.

I chew the last bit of shortbread and then say, innocently, 'Don't you guys have power to advance well being up here?'

I appreciate this will all sound like absolute bollocks to you non-lawyers but, basically, what I've done there is had Mr. Smooth lay down four queens then trumped him with a royal flush.

There's a quick mumbled conversation between Smoothy and Mr. Edinburgh Beardy before they reluctantly admit that, yes, they do have that piece of legislation up in Jockland and, yes, that might be a way forward. All the time I'm wondering why Bradley hadn't spoken up while I finished my shortbread.

I borrow his copy of the draft missives to look at while the rest of them chunter on, trying to get a feel for the shape of the deal. Bradley looks at me sideways as if to say, *What the fuck? I was doing fine before you came in* but, from the look of the missives so far, I've got other ideas.

By the time it's time for me to go to lunch with Sylvia, I've managed to mess things around big style and got them much closer to something that works for us, rather than being in the Council's favour. It appears we're buying land from them down the Cowgate for some property developer clients of ours but in a crowded, shitty kind of place like Edinburgh's Old Town, things are never straightforward.

Feeling cheerier than when I took the lift up, I leave Bradley to pick up the pieces while I go to meet with Sylvia.

***

'There's been a development.' I love it when Sylvia looks serious. Unfortunately, from where we're sitting, across a table from each other at a little Italian restaurant she's chosen for our meeting, I can't see if she's left the bottom button of her blouse undone again.

Focus, Simon, focus. 'Which would be?'

'Jim Martin says that they've got the post-mortem results on your client back. He died of an adverse reaction to Rohypnol.'

'So we were both drugged?' I tried to think this through. Who would've done it, and why? I mean, I don't think I have any actual enemies up here.

I can see Sylvia has been thinking about it too but from a different direction. 'It's a very rare allergic reaction,' she says, as the waiter drifts up with two bowls of pasta for us. Must get a game of squash in, I think to myself, eyeing the carbohydrate overload that is my mother's native country's staple.

'So, what do the cops think?' I ask her. I notice DI Martin is Jim to her, by the way.

'They have a couple of theories,' she says, reaching for the Parmesan. Personally, I never put that stuff they have in restaurants on my pasta: no idea how long it's been sitting there, or who's been pawing it.

She sniffs. 'How well did you know Jimmy Ahmed?'

'Not well enough to know I could murder him by giving him Rohypnol,' I say. 'Besides, why would I then dose myself up?'

She twists her mouth into an unusual shape: I realise she's actually trying to stop a smirk. 'Well, that leads me to one of the theories.' She pauses.

'Which is?'

'It was a gay sex act gone wrong.'

I have to choose my words carefully. 'It wasn't a gay sex act gone wrong, Sylvia. Trust me on that one. I'm not that way inclined and, from my brief acquaintance with Jimmy, I would say he fairly definitely wasn't either.'

She looks at me over the steaming pasta and allows herself a smirk. 'Well, I did tell Jim that,' she says. 'I've been doing some research by myself with your colleagues in the London office, and I was certainly given the impression that you were what might be called a red blooded male.'

So she's been checking me out, I'm thinking to myself, when she spoils it all by saying, 'Of course, there was that unfortunate incident with the female trainee that triggered your transfer up here. I didn't tell Jim about that, for the moment.'

Fuck. Of course she would hear about that. Well that has been completely misinterpreted, let me tell you. When we were found in the boardroom, of course Rebecca Cropley was going to claim it was all my fault: only way she could keep her job, probably.

I finish a mouthful of pasta and then say to Sylvia, 'Anyway, as I told you, there were two girls. I'm pretty sure now they came back to the flat with us. They must've dosed us with Rohypnol.'

Sylvia wriggles her nose but I'm guessing it's my story and not the Parmesan. 'Oh yes, the two mystery girls who you can't remember very much about, who reversed gender roles for the night and decided to dose up guys with Rohypnol for their own perverted purposes. It's a difficult sell to Jim Martin, Simon.'

Another rule of negotiation: never show your anger unless it's going to help in the negotiation. 'I appreciate that. But that's what seems to have happened.'

She shrugs, as if it's all the same to her whether I go down for twenty years as the gay Rohypnol murderer or I get off Jock free. 'Do you remember anything else about them?'

What do I remember? I keep asking myself that. Little by little, tiny details seem to be bleeding in: one was blonde, one was brunette; one of them had a pair of black lacy gloves on; and one of them had...

I look up from my pasta. 'Sussies!' A boring looking couple of guys, bankers probably, look round at the sound of the word. Amazing what a reaction it produces, actually. In a lower voice, I go on, 'One of them had stockings and suspenders on. Which means, if I know that, we must've been fairly intimate to say the least. And back at the flat is the most likely place for that to have happened.'

Sylvia's got that look on her again, like I'm something nasty she's discovered underneath her sink. 'I suppose,' she says, in that whiny voice of hers I would find incredibly annoying if I didn't know she had an incipient Buddha Belly and a jewel in her navel. 'Have you heard of the toe in the tap murders? They happened a couple of years ago now, down in London?'

***

When I get back to my desk after lunch, it's fair to say I've got plenty to think about, so I don't respond to the Rottweiler's message that I've to go and see him straight away. For a while, I sit staring at the computer screen, ignoring the emails that come pinging in from time to time. Not that many, of course, when you're just the guy that sweeps the shit out of the back shop.

According to Sylvia then, to sum up, the cops have two theories about me: either I'm Mr. Gay Rohypnol who had a bizarre accident drugging up his new found boyfriend; or I'm the toe in the tap murderer, your friendly neighbourhood serial killer just up from London and looking to make some new pals.

The more I think about it, the more unconvincing both of these sound. I mean, if it was some kind of gay sex act gone wrong, how did Jimmy end up in the bath with his toe stuck up the tap? I don't even want to think about what kind of perverse act the cops have in mind that we were about to do when he went and pegged out on me.

On the other hand, moving up to Edinburgh and keeping the same signature method of sticking your victim's toe up the bath tap doesn't make a hell of a lot of sense either. Nor, for that matter, does killing the guy in your own flat and waking up in the next room.

At the same time, I guess I was starting to understand at that point how unconvincing my story sounded. I was out on the town with a guy and we met these two girls who came back to my flat, dosed us up with Rohypnol and calmly left, leaving no traces of their existence, when one of us went and died on them.

I'm just pondering this and starting to Google 'Toe in the tap murderer' when the phone rings. It's the Rottweiler's secretary, Linda, telling me he wants to see me. Now, if not sooner.

The big doggy's kennel is on the other side of the building from me, tucked away beside all the support staff. I've been in it once before, when I was getting shown around. Predictably, the Rottweiler wasn't there then, as he was away cooking up some massive deal down in London. Probably snatching it from under the London branch's noses, come to think of it. I thought at the time it was a very spare, spartan office for a senior partner: just a desk, a big chair and a meeting table where he tortures his victims. View not too bad, although not nearly as good as the one you get from the meeting rooms on the tenth floor.

Not that I suspect Bonzo takes much time to look out the window and enjoy the view: I kind of shudder to think what it is the Rottweiler gets his jollies from.

On that occasion, as I say, the office was empty. This time the Rottweiler's very much there and looking at me as I walk in with what appears to be barely suppressed fury. Mind you, when I've seen him going about the office before, that seems to be his standard expression. Although I've also seen one that could probably be characterised as thinly disguised contempt.

He starts on me as soon as I come in. 'I was speaking to Jim Maloney when I was down at Pret à Manger at lunchtime,' he says, in that dull, disinterested tone he uses for almost everything. 'He was saying how much he enjoyed dealing with you on that rent review memorandum I gave you.' He picks up a document I recognise as the final version I had biked round just before lunch. 'Especially when you gave his fucking client 90% off the increase.'

And then he throws the thing at me. I don't mean he just slaps it down on the desk a bit hard, he actually picks it up and throws it at me, as if he expects it to behave like a Ninja death star and take my head clean off.

I catch it and look at the figure. Right enough, instead of 300,000, the numbers are missing a zero. No matter that the words would over-ride the faulty figure or that I would've picked it up when I got it back to have signed by my clients; the thing's just so fucking careless.

Strange thing is though, even as I'm thinking that, I'm also thinking that I'm sure I hadn't made that mistake. I can be pretty quick and easy when it comes to shooting out final versions, but I do always double check them. However, it's not like I'm going to land Sandra, my secretary, in the shit with the Hound-Dog.

'I'll get it sorted,' I say, staring him down. There's a moment's silence. Then he says, 'Actually, that wasn't what I wanted to see you about. I understand you've been sticking your nose into the Edinburgh City Council deal.'

I shrug. I'm determined not to let the bastards smell any fear off me. 'I did swing by, yeah,' I say.

'Well, don't bother in future,' he growls and then stands up as if he's going to come across the desk for me.

Just then, there's a cough behind me.

'Actually, Simon came up with a really good suggestion to sort out one of the sticky points,' a voice says. I turn round and it's Bradley, my rugger bugger assistant, standing in the doorway. 'It'll involve restructuring the deal a bit, but I think it's probably better for the clients.'

The Rottweiler looks from me to him and back again. 'Did he now?' Back to the thinly disguised contempt expression. The guy should really play Hamlet, he's got such a huge range. 'Well, it doesn't need the two of you to close a pissy little deal like that. Sort it out between you who's going to take it forward, though I wouldn't have thought it would need someone of Mr English's alleged talents to do.'

There's an awkward silence. Then the Rottweiler says, 'Now get out of my sight, the pair of you.'

As we walk back through to our half of the open plan, Bradley says to me, 'His bark's worse than his bite, you know. Give him a couple of days and he'll come round to the idea.'

'Yeah,' I say. Then, 'Thanks.'

Bradley turns to look at me. 'No problem. Me and Al usually go for a couple of sherbets on a Thursday: one of the places down George Street. Fancy coming along?'

'Sure, why not?' I say, thinking, *Here comes the initiation rite by alcohol.*

But by the time I've got back to my desk, the dubious pleasure of going for a drink with Al + Bradley has taken second place to a shard of memory that's dropped into my head about the night out with Jimmy Ahmed.

The blonde was called Debi something – D-E-B-I. She was at pains to spell it to me, like it really mattered. She was a blonde wee Jockette. The other one, Elena, I think, I'm fairly sure, was Eastern European, darker skinned, brunette.

But it was Debi that had the Buddha Belly.

CHAPTER 7
ARSEY KATE

'Had the thing tied up by three in the morning, opened a couple of bottles of pop and then straight down to Rum-ti-tum-tum's. Got absolutely bladdered and didn't make it back into the office until noon. The Rottweiler called me in and I thought he was going to chew me out for being late, but it turned out all he was bothered about was I'd used the last case of champagne in the office.

'Fortunately, Tony came through and rescued me before the Rottweiler chewed my bollocks off. Of course, they do that all the time, the good cop, bad cop thing.'

The cops. I'm not really wanting to be reminded of DS Martin and his rodent-like sidekick, Futret, right now. They want me to provide them with alibis for three dates three years ago when I was in London, to prove I'm not the toe in the tap murderer. Which involves phoning Kate, my former girlfriend, who is the only person likely to remember what the fuck I was doing on any specific dates three years ago. That's if I can still get her to speak to me.

First though, I have to take one for the team and put up with a drink with the two goons, Al + Bradley.

The place they've taken me, Tiger Lily, isn't at all bad. It's one of these big suit magnets on the West End of George Street, where all the professionals unwind after a hard day of wage slavery up Lothian Road. Some perfectly acceptable totty in tonight, too: pity the gruesome twosome are blocking most of the view.

Al, or, to use his full moniker, Allan Till, is the slightly taller of the two. He's a ginger (which in Jock speak is pronounced to rhyme with minger). He's the one telling the slightly more interesting war stories about life in the ever thrusting world of com.prop, but then that's damning with faint praise, as Bradley's a very dull boy indeed.

We've already had the one about the guy – who they claim to know, of course – who got the police called at Gleneagles for what he was up to with his girlfriend ('Basically, it was your garden variety knobs out call, taken out of context,' according to Al). It was in *The Scotsman*, no less. Then the old favourites about various partners in the big Edinburgh firms and their anger management issues – the guy who allegedly plunged his pen through a trainee's chair when he found out she was en route to Glasgow with the wrong settlement cheque. Honestly, these guys wouldn't last a second down in London.

'Of course, this weekend it's all about Goldenacre, eh Brad?' Al looks sideways at Bradley, who is just appearing with three more pints clutched in his massive paws. Bradley Knight is one of these squat, swarthy rugger buggers that are ten a penny round these parts. Too many upper cuts in the front row to be pretty, but, according to Al while he's been away, he's irresistible to women.

'Look at him,' Al's saying. 'Brad the Impaler. Darling of Heriot's seconds: sole reason why half the women round here walk funny with a smile on their face.'

Brad looks suitably modest, scanning the bar for new victims. 'So, do you still play for Hutchie's?' I say to Al, stifling a yawn.

'Plays for a proper team now his citizenship papers have come through,' Bradley answers for him.

Of course. I must have died and left my body briefly with boredom when they told me that. Al, the ginger one, went to Hutcheson's Grammar, the Glasgow private school, but must now be playing rugby for Heriot's, one of the posh Edinburgh places, and Bradley's old school. This gives them plenty of opportunity for so-called amusing banter about Glasgow and Edinburgh.

If there's one thing Jocks from the east coast hate more than the English, it's Jocks from the west coast. And vice-versa, of course. There are more Weegies but the Edinburgh ones have had the sense to inter-breed more with other superior countries like us so there's a bit more hybrid vigour there. That's why Edinburgh is the financial centre and Glaswegians generally keep their suits for their court appearances.

'More a squash man myself,' I say, taking another scoop of over-priced Stella.

Al brightens a bit. 'Really? Give you a knock some time if you like. I'm in Edinburgh Squash Club.'

'Sounds like a plan,' I say, and after thumbing our iPhones for a couple of minutes, we've arranged our first play date. Bradley takes the opportunity to scan the bar again.

'Too many of Leonora's pals in here,' he says.

Al winks at me. Leonora is Bradley's girlfriend, and is also in charge of the other com.prop team back at the office. Not had the pleasure yet, but I can't help feeling a pang of sympathy for the girl, going out with the uglier of the two monkeys.

'We could go for a couple of laps after,' Al suggests to Bradley, and from the way he says it, I know he's not talking about jogging round a track somewhere.

'Why not?' I say and, before I know it, I'm drinking up and they're taking me to some dive of a place at the end of Princes Street.

'Bit early to go to Rum-ti-tum-tum's,' Bradley says. Just at that point, I remember that he was the one that had recommended the place to me, for my night out with Jimmy Ahmed.

The girls in the lap dancing bar aren't too bad but, by then, I'm starting to think about my little predicament with the cops. I have a couple of dances and then leave them to it, saying I have a couple of things to sort out. Need to know basis: if these guys thought by being pally they'd get all the juicy details about Jimmy Ahmed, they must be pretty disappointed by now. I've told them precisely the square root of fuck all.

Come to think of it, I think as I walk back down to my flat, Bradley was quite insistent about me taking Jimmy to that particular club. 'Rum-ti-tum-tum's is the only decent place you can take him at the moment,' he said. 'You absolutely must go there.'

In fact, he nearly overdid it and made me think I'd take Jimmy anywhere but where he suggested, but at the end of the day I couldn't think of anywhere else to go, so that's where we did end up. And the rest, as they say, is history. Or would be, if I could just remember it properly.

***

If Edinburgh's got one thing going for it, it's that it's quite small, so that there's none of the hassle there is in London getting about by tube and train. It's just a twenty minute walk from the West End down to stingy Jock bastard Reid's flat in Stockbridge.

To be honest, I'm not quite sure what to make of Al + Bradley tucking me under their wing the way they have. I thought once they took me out for a pint they would be pumping me for information about what happened to Jimmy Ahmed, what the cops have been saying and so on. Not a bit of it though – and it's not like they're subtle enough to have left it if they really wanted to know.

But then, nobody in the firm has asked me anything much about it: when I got back to work after the weekend, I had a chat with Tony Hand, the partner I phoned up originally, but, other than that, it's as if either they just don't want to know or, if I was being more paranoid, they know all about it already. Couple of sympathetic grunts, as I said, but nothing more. No cross-examination at the water cooler.

It's a coldish night but dry, with that biting Edinburgh breeze that chills the bollocks on even the warmest day. Speaking of which, the lap dancers may not have been of the highest quality, but they have kind of got the old python stirring in his nest, so I'm half tempted to go back up and rejoin the gruesome twosome at Rum-ti-tum-tum's. Gary's at home just now so, even if I hadn't had three pints, driving over to see Yvonne is not an option. And even if I had Sylvia's mobile number, she's definitely playing it cool.

I can imagine her saying in that whiny voice of hers: 'Let's keep it professional, Simon.' Knickers definitely in need of defrosting before it could be python time.

I'm thinking about all this as I get back in the outer door of the block (at least it's got an entry phone system, I think to myself) and go upstairs. It's a second floor flat and, I have to say, the stairwell's kept neat and tidy. Doesn't seem to be any noise coming from any of the neighbours, either: I might just have struck lucky and not have any students above or below me. Bloody students. Too busy getting off their tits on drink and drugs and playing their music at full volume to do any work. Not that I was any different, of course.

I have to admit, there's a bit of a creepy sensation letting myself back into the empty flat. It's not so much ghosts or anything, it's just the knowledge that somebody – and I guess it was those two girls, Debi and Elena – was in here that night with me and Jimmy, before Jimmy ended up tits up in the bath.

I'm needing to go and get rid of some of the three pints I had with Cheech and Chong and I stand there looking at the now empty bath. I'm guessing Jimmy flaked out here at some point, the girls panicked and I was too out of it to know what was going on. But why did they drag him into the bath? Come to think of it, how did they do that – Jimmy was a big lad and, when I think of the girls, I'm fairly sure they were both pretty small. And more to the point, why did they do that and run away, leaving no trace of themselves?

I finish up, flush and wash my hands then go through to the kitchen to grab something to eat, before I phone Kate. The cops say there was no trace of anyone else in the flat.

So, if they did slip us the Mickey Finns with the Rohypnol here, why were there no glasses? Did they wash them up and put them back in the cupboard in the kitchen, where I'm now standing? The cops said the flat was surprisingly clean of fingerprints and asked me if I'd just cleaned all the surfaces. That's a laugh, but then I'd only been in the flat for a week and maybe Reid had cleaned it all before he went south. It did seem pretty spick and span, I have to hand him that.

I make myself some toasted cheese, all these thoughts going through my head. None of it makes any sense. When I woke up that morning, I was super-glued to the sheets. DI Martin did say there were some unidentified blonde hairs, but didn't seem that interested. But does that mean the girl I remember as being called Debi was in here with me?

I finish my toasted cheese, and then make a phone call I've not been looking forward to.

'Hi, Kate?'

'Who is this?' She sounds suspicious and pissed off already. Not a great starting point.

'It's Simon.' I take the phone and wander through the hall to the living room as if walking about is going to make this any easier.

'Simon who?'

Oh, fucking fantastic. 'Simon English, you remember? We did live together for eighteen months.'

I hear her cover the phone but not so carefully that I can't hear her say, 'Old boyfriend. Don't worry, I'll get rid of him.' Then she takes her hand away from the mouthpiece and says, 'What is it you want, Simon? I'm kind of in the middle of something here.'

Is she indeed. 'Er, that's great for you. Listen, I was wondering if you still kept your old diaries? And, if so, if you would know what we were doing on 17th January, 15th March and 3rd June three years ago?'

Another muttered conversation which I can still hear. 'Don't know. He's asking about random dates.'

The thing is though, I can't hear anyone else's voice at the other end. There's a bit of a pause, just long enough for my brain to disengage itself from my tongue. There is a value to just keeping quiet in a negotiation and letting the other side do the running, although I don't suppose Kate is seeing this as a negotiation. Blame the three pints of Stella on an empty stomach. Blame the python taking more of his share of the blood supply.

Whatever, something makes me blurt out: 'There's no-one else there, is there Kate? I mean, you're just talking to yourself, aren't you?'

Not the cleverest thing to say. 'Yes there bloody is someone else here, Simon. It's my new boyfriend, Mark. A huge improvement on you I may say, in every department. And that includes the bedroom before you even think to ask. You always over-rated yourself there, let me tell you. Do you want to speak to him?'

The Stella's clearly playing havoc with my negotiating technique. 'Er, no, sorry. Look, Kate, I know it's a bit much me calling you out of the blue and everything, but it's important that, if you do have these diaries, you dig them out. I gave the cops your contact details, you see, because they wanted to know what I was doing on those dates.'

There's another pause, and then she says, 'The cops?'

'Yes,' I say. 'They want me to provide proof I wasn't out

murdering people and sticking their toes up the taps of baths. Crazy, isn't it?'

She starts to laugh, but it's a laugh like glass breaking, a nasty kind of laugh. I do wish now she hadn't caught me in bed with her best mate. That probably wasn't one of my smarter moves. It was the python made me do it. Although her best mate kind of had a hand in it too, to be fair.

'So, let me get this straight. You need me to give you an alibi for three dates while we were still going out, because the cops think you're some sort of serial killer?'

'Got it in one.' She always was quick on the uptake, especially when it came to seeing her mate clambering out of the – fortunately, ground floor – window of the flat we were sharing in Crystal Palace at the time, and legging it down the road. There's a smile in her voice this time, but it's worse than the laugh. 'And why, exactly, should I help you? Sarah and I have never made up, you know. She was my best friend right through school and university. And then you came along.'

So that's it. She's going to be arsey about it all because of a little misunderstanding that was, oh, nearly a year ago now. I ring off shortly after, after appealing to her common decency. Not that I really feel like she's got the milk of human kindness for me right at this moment. I still think I was right that there was no new boyfriend: but if there wasn't, that probably makes it even less likely she's going to help me.

The only compensation – and it's not much compensation right now, I have to admit – is that Sarah was ten times better in the sack than she was. Or at least was shaping up to be until Kate came home unexpectedly. My life seems to be turning into a series of interrupted shags.

***

The next day is Friday. Tony Hand calls me into his office first thing. Unlike the Rottweiler's, which is pretty immaculate, Tony's office is full of half chewed leases, files, and other unidentified bits and pieces. Dress Down Friday is a concept they had in London about ten years ago so, of course, Edinburgh's only just catching up. Tony's in an expensive looking blue shirt and brown chinos: I have to admit, though, he looks fairly fit for a guy in his late 40s. Tall, obviously stays in shape somehow, dark brown hair and a sunbed tan, although he's not too orange. Huge head.

'Just thought I'd have a quick chat and see how you're getting on, Simon,' he says, indicating a chair at the table. 'I hear you've been helping Bradley with the Edinburgh City Council deal.'

Has he indeed. Heard, I mean. Again, I get that paranoid feeling at the back of my neck that everybody knows everything about me in this office. It's good to be the centre of attention, of course, but not in this way.

'That's right,' I say and then say nothing else. As I mentioned already, silence is a very handy tool when you don't know where things are going.

'That's great, of course,' Tony says, eventually. 'Brad's in your team, so you've got to handle things the way you want to.'

Another silence. Eventually, I say, 'It's just that, to be honest, Wallace – ' I remember, just in time, to use the Rottweiler's first name instead of calling him Big Doggy – 'hasn't given me much to get my teeth into as yet. I was interested to see how Brad was getting on, so I swung by.'

'Sure.' Tony's nodding now, looking concerned. 'I guess Wallace and I felt that you had a lot on your plate with this business to do with Jimmy Ahmed, so we didn't want to overload you. Let me see if I can find something a bit more interesting for you to get involved in. To be honest, the City Council deal isn't really complex enough for someone of your calibre.'

I'm nodding, now. 'Of course,' I say, putting my own concerned face on. 'It's just that, with Brad one of the key guys in my team, I wanted to show him some support. I do take my management responsibilities seriously, Tony.' As if. My management style down in the London office consisted of dishing the mail out to my team in the morning and then letting the fuckers sink or swim. Unless I thought it would bounce back on me, of course.

On the way back to my desk, I see that Brad the Impaler is practically canoodling with some woman I haven't seen before. He sees me and looks round. At least he has the decency to look slightly guilty.

'Oh, er, Simon, this is Leonora Buchan.'

Ah. A light bulb goes on in my head, not to mention the python stirring sleepily down below. 'The famous Leonora Buchan,' I say sticking out a paw.

She smiles, vaguely. 'And you must be Bradley's new boss. Sorry we've not met up before: I've been locked away in an office in Glasgow for most of the last fortnight trying to tie a deal down.'

There's something about the way she talks about tying things down that makes me think of bondage and, specifically, of her lashing me to a bed post and standing over me with a leather whip. I don't know why that should be: however, as I may not have said already, the python has certain psychic powers.

Leonora's not really my type, as such. She's got bleached blonde hair, cut in a kind of page boy look, but her dark eyebrows suggest it's not a matching collar and cuffs kind of scenario. She's wearing a pale blue jacket and skirt combo that looks pricey, with just the top frill of a white blouse appearing from the top. Black tights.

Just as I'm noticing this, another memory from that night out with Jimmy Ahmed drops into my head. Specifically, the girl called Debi, straddling me wearing nothing but stockings and suspenders. I push the thought out of my head just now, hoping it'll come back later.

Leonora is arching one eyebrow. 'Are you okay? You were looking confused about something?'

I could say that I'm confused as to why such a good looking bird, and an associate to boot, should be wasting her time on a dumb fuck like Bradley, but I restrain myself. 'No, I'm fine. Brad, what are we doing today?'

Leonora makes her excuses and leaves: I watch her backside disappear over to the other side of the office while Brad, looking a bit sour, explains that the Edinburgh Council guys are thinking over their position and aren't likely to come back to us before Monday.

'That's fine,' I say to him and go back to my desk to scroll through my emails, such as they are.

Of course, I don't give a fuck whether Bradley's pissed off

with me for interrupting a conversation with his girlfriend. I just wanted to see how quickly a message can get back to the partners. I'm none too happy about being warned off doing the Edinburgh Council deal, when they've given me fuck all else to do. I don't buy the line Tony gave me about not wanting to overload me: they'd be the first two partners I've ever met who didn't want to work you into the ground, even if your entire family had been wiped out in the same car crash the night before.

The more they warn me off the Edinburgh deal, the more I fancy doing it. I guess I just don't like people telling me what to do.

There's not much in the way of emails. Sylvia has sent me one to say that DS Martin wants to meet us early next week, to discuss "developments". Other than that, some pleading email from a guy in the London office for help with something I was working on there (delete) and a couple more rent review memorandums from the Rottweiler, there's not much to get me through the day.

By five o'clock, I've had enough and head off out the door. Al says something about going for a pint but I pretend not to hear him properly: two nights running of anecdotes from these two dull boys is too much to bear. Besides, that paranoid part of my brain is telling me Al + Bradley have been detailed to be my minders.

Instead, on the way home, I phone Tom. 'Fancy coming into Edinburgh for a pint?' I say.

'And how exactly would I get there, cunt face?' he says. 'Wheel myself down the M8?'

'I'll be there in three-quarters of an hour and pick you up,' I say, and then ring off before he gets the chance to say anything else. I've had enough of arsey Kate without him starting on me.

It's a relatively easy job, even at this time on a Friday night, to dodge the worst of the traffic on the M8, pick Tom up from Mum's house at Livingston, give Mum some old chat and head back into town. I manage to get parked outside the flat and wheel Tom down into the village to get something to eat, before heading to Bert's. It's about the only pub in Stockbridge that Tom can get into easily, but even that doesn't remind me.

'I hope those are both for me,' he says, eyeing the two pints I bring back to the table suspiciously. 'If you're driving me back, that is.'

'Yeah, right,' I say, edging into the seat opposite him and sitting down. The place is absolutely rammed, of course, it being Friday night. 'I thought you could just stay over, actually.' Forgetting completely, of course.

'Yeah, why not? Sweet.' Tom says, looking genuinely pleased for once. He's desperate to get away from under Mum's skirts. Probably do her a power of good to get a break from him, too, I'm thinking, as I sink the Deuchar's like my throat's on fire.

'Fucking expensive though,' he says, as I hand him his change from his round.

'Yeah, in Livvy the lager's cheap, but the psychos are sheer class,' I say and we have a laugh about him wanting to take on the two neds all by himself last weekend.

After that, Tom's on good form for once, and I want to tell him about the cops, Sylvia, Jimmy Ahmed and everything, but decide it'll be better to do that back at the flat. It's only when, six pints later, I'm wheeling him up St. Stephen's Street and he says, 'I take it it's a ground floor flat you've got?' that I remember.

'Oh. Fuck. No.'

He turns in his wheelchair to look at me with a look that actually reminds me a bit of the Rottweiler: barely concealed disgust turning to non-suppressed fury.

'You stupid, stupid cunt,' he says. For once, I can't disagree with his analysis. 'How the fuck are you going to get me up the stairs? Please tell me it's the first floor?'

'Er ….. second actually,' I say. 'I'll just carry you. It won't be a problem.'

It is, of course. A major problem. Tom's only a little smaller than me and his years in the wheelchair haven't made him any lighter. Added to which, of course, by the time I get him up out of the chair into my best go at a fireman's lift, he's practically incandescent with rage.

'You absolute arsehole,' he's saying, shouting now, as I struggle with him on the first few steps. 'Are you trying to fucking kill me all over again?'

And so on, and so on, up four agonising flights of stone steps.

The trouble is, he's right: all that Deuchar's isn't exactly helping my balance and we're in severe danger of toppling back downstairs and breaking both our necks. Him keeping up the volley of abuse and punching me on the back doesn't exactly help, of course.

Back in the flat, I plant him on the couch, go down and fetch the wheelchair and get us both a drink. Tom, by this time, has started to see the funny side at long last. There are tears in his eyes, I think from laughing, 'You fucking stupid plank,' he comments, as I stick a bottle of beer in front of him. 'How you hold down some sort of job as a lawyer is completely beyond me.'

Just then, there's a hammering on the door and I go and answer it.

It's DS Martin and DS Futret. 'Mr. English?' Martin says. He and Futret are trying to look casual, but there's something in the way they're holding themselves that makes me realise they're on edge. Futret, in particular, looks coiled, like some kind of killer rodent ready to spring if I say the wrong thing.

'We've had reports of a disturbance. The neighbours thought you were murdering someone else.'

From through in the living room, Tom's voice says: 'What does he mean, someone else?'

CHAPTER 8
FLIGHT OF THE PYTHON

The following Thursday morning, DS Martin's dead eyes are boring into me. He has a look of disapproval on his face, but then I'm getting used to that from people.

'How is your brother now?'

'Still disabled but, other than that, fine,' I say, giving the bastard nothing. Tom was, understandably, a little put out initially that I hadn't told him I was being investigated for murder. 'He gets a little upset at times these days, particularly when he's had a few beers.'

'You said there were some more developments, Jim?' Sylvia says, sitting beside me in the interview room. Good girl, trying to get things back on track. This actually is, for once, all about me, after all.

Martin looks at me with that same sour look again. 'Aye. Your former girlfriend, Miss Stanton, has come forward with some information, Mr. English. She can provide two out of three alibis for you for the London murders when people were found with their toe up the tap. So we're closing that line of inquiry for now.'

The cunt looks genuinely disappointed. I suppose he was probably enjoying a quiet drink in some cop pub on Friday night when he got the call to come and stop me adding to my murder tally. 'She did give you some sort of character reference. She said she didn't think you were capable of being a serial killer. Just being a complete bastard.'

Beside me, Sylvia snorts. *Thanks, Kate.* I had been thinking of asking Sylvia out once we got clear of this today, but that's hardly going to help. I look at Martin. 'So, I'm not the toe in the tap serial killer. Where does that leave you?'

Martin casts a look at Futret. I can't quite read what the story is with these two. Futret says nothing and Martin very rarely asks him to. He just sits there like an undernourished whippet most of the time. I do get the impression that Martin would rather be doing it all himself, like some low budget Rebus, if you can imagine that.

'Well, Mr. English,' Martin says slowly, with a face like he's just found a fly in his whisky. 'I have to say we're at something of a dead end. Our other theory about this incident – that it was some kind of gay sex act gone wrong – starts to look less likely when we speak to your former colleagues in the London branch of your firm. Quite apart from your string of former girlfriends, there's the sexual harassment allegation with the trainee that got you shifted up here in the first place.'

I shift uncomfortably in my seat. I glance at Sylvia but she's looking straight ahead, not catching my eye. Not a good sign. Oh, great, I'm thinking. They'll have me on the sex offenders' register next. I'm surprised they haven't dredged up that time Mr. Blackley, the geography teacher, caught me having a Sherman in the toilets in fifth year as well.

'That was all a misunderstanding,' I say. 'Rebecca was put in a very difficult position.'

'Aye,' says Martin, slowly. 'Legs akimbo on top of the board room table probably would be.' Futret at least has the decency to switch his smirk off when I catch his eye.

Martin goes on. 'So, that leaves us with your rather incredible story that two girls met you in Rum-ti-tum-tum's, went back to your flat with you and Mr. Ahmed, and then dosed you both up with Rohypnol for reasons of their own. Can you tell me again what you remember of them?'

What can I remember? I look round at them, huddled as we are in Interview Room 3 in Fettes, where we've spent so many happy hours together: it's almost a family scene now. DS Martin is expressionless: only the Nicorette packet on the table in front of him and his working jaws suggest that he's actually a simmering, nicotine-starved volcano waiting to erupt.

Futret, on the other hand, seems to be constantly on the move, even when he's sitting still: eyes darting all over the place, scribbling furiously in a notebook the minute I say – or even do – anything. He seems to have an endless supply of badly fitting cheap suits – or at least two: a grey one and a blue one. His hair is slicked back today, making his head look even more rat like.

Beside me, Sylvia has opted for a long skirt with a split up the side, thigh length boots and, most importantly, a creamy blouse that allows me a furtive glance now and then at an exposed fold of tummy. She re-crosses her legs, sending a whiff of her perfume under my nose: the python stirs, stretching sleepily along my right leg. *Not now,* I tell it. As I say, almost a family scene by now. And like a family, they inspire a range of mixed emotions.

'One of them was blonde, one of them was brunette.'

Martin's expression changes ever so slightly. 'Well, that certainly narrows it down, Mr. English,' he says. 'Thank goodness there are so many gingers in this city or it really would be a needle in a haystack job.'

'Er, yeah, I suppose I see what you mean. Okay.' I sit and think for a moment. I still don't know to this day why I didn't tell them the names at this point. Probably something to do with the little matter of a missing bag of Bolivian marching powder. 'The blonde one was quite skinny, but she had a bit of a Buddha belly on her, if you know what I mean by that. She had a tattoo of some sort on her ankle. And an ankle bracelet, come to think of it.'

I must've spent quite a bit of time down at the foot end. Random images of various bits of her swim into my mind.

Martin chews a little bit faster. 'And the brunette?'

'She was skinny as well,' I say, 'A little taller maybe and a fuller figure. Quite big … er … well made, I mean. She was wearing black if I remember rightly, black low cut blouse and leggings I think.'

Futret, to my surprise, speaks up for once. 'It sounds like you saw a bit more of the blonde than you did the brunette.' He has a surprisingly low voice. Martin glances sideways at him but, as usual, he's expressionless.

'Yes, I think that's right. I went into the bedroom with the blonde and I presume Jimmy stayed in the living-room with the brunette.'

Martin's chewing jaws have an almost hypnotic effect on me. I'm beginning to wonder if the whole set-up of the room, the dull paintwork and the yellow light, are all part of a cunning plan to get crims to confess. Maybe it's not really the product of dull municipal minds and budget cuts. Maybe highly trained psychologists have made it all look like this and Martin's chewing gum is really a psychological tool. I need a coffee. 'Was there sexual activity?' Martin asks, making it sound like some kind of unfortunate disease.

Ah, here comes the sticky bit. 'Yes. I had sexual activity with the blonde girl.' I nearly say that I *committed* sexual activity with her, he makes it sound all so fucking guilt ridden and Presbyterian. 'Did you find any DNA evidence?'

Martin allows himself the briefest of smiles. 'Well, Mr. English, we found enough of your DNA to start a whole civilisation of commercial property lawyers, certainly. We did find a couple of blonde hairs which clearly weren't yours, but there was no match in our files for them. Did you use a condom? We didn't find one.'

I glance sideways at Sylvia, but she's as expressionless as Martin, staring straight ahead. No idea how she's taking all this.

'No, I didn't, but then if I remember correctly, the type of sex we had didn't involve penetration.' Then, to lighten the mood, I add, 'Think of a number between 68 and 70 and you're right there with us.' Nobody laughs.

The interview finishes soon after, with Martin admitting, grudgingly, that I'm no longer a prime suspect, but that they're still treating poor Jimmy's demise as a suspicious death. 'Folk suffering an adverse reaction to Rohypnol don't usually get themselves in the bath and stick their toe up the tap,' he tells me, as he shows Sylvia and me out.

At the door of the main reception, he says, 'Try and remember what you can, Mr. English. You've given us very little to go on so far. But if there are two lassies out there dosing up random men with Rohypnol, then I'd like to have a word with them.'

Fettes police station is a greasy mark in the middle of a very smart district of Edinburgh. Outside, the birds are singing and the sun has come out as Sylvia and I walk the half mile to where I managed to get the Lexus parked. Sylvia's not saying much as we head back into town. 'You could drop me at the top of the Meadows, instead of the office,' she says, as we rumble through Stockbridge. 'I'm working from home today.'

'Okay,' I say, and wait. Then, when she doesn't say anything else, I say, 'Anywhere specific near the Meadows?'

'I'll direct you,' she says. Then, after a pause, 'I'm still trying to think what these girls were doing. I mean, there was no evidence they robbed you and Jimmy. You say nothing was taken from the flat. The only other sensible motive I can think of for them to drug complete strangers and then have sex with them is blackmail. I mean, it's not as if you and Jimmy were going to play hard to get, were you?'

I pull up at the next set of lights, trying to remember how I get across a city that is so totally dug up for tram works. 'Oh, I don't know,' I say, trying to sound offended. 'Blackmail? I suppose Jimmy might've been involved in some dodgy business dealings and somebody was trying to get to him. The girl called, er, the blonde girl, was a Jock – I mean, Scottish.'

She looks at me and I wonder if she's picked up on the fact that I nearly used Debi's name. But, no.

'Is that what you call us, Jocks?'

'Just my little pet name for my Celtic brothers and sisters,' I say. Pet, as in most of them need to be kept on a tight leash, if not actually muzzled. 'Why, does it offend you?'

She actually laughs, and I realise it's the first time I've heard her do that. It's quite musical, actually, much more so than her usual whiny speaking voice. 'No, not at all.' The lights change and I pull away, hanging a left along Queen Street. 'Tell me something, Simon. You mentioned that the blonde girl had a Buddha belly. Is that why you keep staring at my stomach? Do you think I need to lose weight?'

I glance over at her. 'No. Not at all.' *Quite the contrary.* 'It's the jewel in the navel thing. It's just something I've always liked.'

'Oh, this? I actually forget I've got it in, some days.' And she flips her blouse up a bit to expose her perfect little Buddha belly with the green emerald nestled in the middle.

Thank goodness we're stuck at another set of lights. The python gets so excited, he nearly reaches across and grabs the gear stick.

'That's the one,' I say, trying to sound cool, but my voice comes out a little strangled. There's a pause and the lights change again. 'So. Now that I'm no longer prime suspect for the toe in the tap murders, I was thinking. How would you fancy meeting up after work tonight and maybe grab a coffee or something?'

Coffee. Everybody goes for a coffee these days, even up here in the frozen, alcohol sodden north. If I had any spare money washing around, I'd buy my own fucking plantation in South America. Just down the hill from the coca farm, obviously.

There's a long pause, then she says, 'I don't think so, thanks. I'm meeting my boyfriend.'

Ah. A boyfriend. That does complicate things. Funny she didn't mention it before, though.

***

When I get back to the office, I've just logged into my computer when Al pops his head above the screen like an overfed meerkat.

'Think Tony was looking to have a chat with you when you got in, Simon,' he says.

I nod, and decide to scroll through my emails first: there's eight in succession from Tony Hand, all with attachments, and all with different headings. He seems to be bombarding me with work, and the tiny paranoid part of my brain says, *Is that just because you sat in on the last meeting about the Edinburgh City Council deal, old pal?* Not quite sure why my paranoid voice calls me old pal, but it might have a bit of a point.

I get up and stroll through to Tony Hand's office, next door to Big Doggy's. He's sitting there chatting to Leonora Buchan, who's looking fetching today in a powder blue trouser suit.

I'm still not sure what it is I find attractive about Leonora: no Buddha belly on offer, and she dresses quite mannishly, like some female lawyers do, with her bleached blonde hair cut short, and the minimum of make-up. Still, there's some sort of twinkle of mischief in her eyes that makes the python say to me, *I would.*

Tony Hand has a very unusually shaped head. You know when you go back and look at old school photos and one of the kids has this massive head like a melon? You never noticed it at the time, but looking back at the photo, years later, this kid's got a head so big it's got its own solar system in orbit round it? Well, that kid would be Tony Hand: massive thatch of brown hair, which makes him stand out even though he always dresses well. Suit, today, if I'm not mistaken, by Aquascutum.

'How did things go?' he says. He's the only cunt in the whole office who has shown any interest in whether I get banged up for murder or not, I have to give him that. Mind you, he is supposed to be staff partner.

'Some progress,' I say. 'At least I'm no longer prime suspect, and they're starting to take my version of events seriously.'

'Great,' he says, nodding that huge head of his. 'Well, life goes on, and if the two of you hurry, you can just catch the next one to Glasgow Queen Street in time for the meeting. I hear you're looking for something more to keep you out of mischief, so Leonora and I thought you might be able to take this one from her.' He pushes a file across the desk at me. I glance at Leonora and she's smiling, encouragingly. 'We're the landlord and we've got Chooseus4shoes in seven of our premises. They're wanting to re-profile the rent.'

'Sounds good,' I say, thinking, *I'd still rather be doing the Edinburgh Council deal. But I can wait.*

***

We catch the train by the skin of our teeth, and I spend most of the journey trying to come up to speed with the existing leases, while Leonora seems to be doing her best to distract me. She prattles on about the deals, other deals, the weather, her dad's football team (he coaches some junior lot, apparently), the restaurant she was at last night with her girlfriends, yada yada.

It's only when we get up to get off at Queen Street that she says, 'So how's that deadbeat boyfriend of mine getting on working for you? Is he doing okay?'

'Fine,' I say, avoiding the obvious question. Which is, what is an attractive, intelligent bird like you who's clearly going places in the firm doing with a plug ugly rugger bugger with no brains or personality like Brad? Is it because he is Brad the Impaler? I've had a couple of games of squash with him, as well as Al, and seen him in the showers afterwards and, boy, the python wasn't quite so pleased with itself when he saw the monster that Brad's got. Doesn't so much as shake it dry as slap it about the jaws, that kind of thing.

Anyway, I have to put these unpleasant images of Bradley's anatomy out of my head, as we walk to the Glasgow lawyer's offices where the meeting is. I don't know Glasgow at all, but

Leonora, who has the tiniest tint of Weegie beneath the standard issue Edinburgh professional class quacking noise, leads me to it.

We've got the lawyer and the surveyor for the other side there, as well as our own surveyor, who's got there separately. The deal's not that unusual, in these recession hit times: retailers are going to the wall every week and even the big guys like Chooseus4shoes are struggling. They're locked into our leases and the existing rents pretty securely but, at the same time, big retail tenants like this have a lot of muscle. And, boy, does the Glasgow lawyer acting for them want us to know about it.

The cunt is big, probably about six foot four. Probably a rutting stag in Hutchie's back row about fifteen years ago. Since then, late nights in the office and takeaways have sent him out to chub a bit, so he's one of these big, baggy guys with the waist band straining on his suit trousers. He is, Leonora has told me, something of a legend in his own lunchtime: kind of a Rottweiler in waiting. I noticed when we did the standard round of introductions and getting to know you banter, he just grunted. Never a good sign.

'Look,' he says, looking studiously bored, 'We've already wasted a lot of time on trying to do this deal, Leonora, and now you're bringing someone new in. Frankly, our clients don't have time to piss around any more: they're going through some serious debt restructuring and if the banks don't hear from us by five o'clock today that most of the rentals across the UK have been reworked substantially, you'll be dealing with their administrators and getting crumbs off the table.

'This deal is way the smallest of the twenty-five our clients are trying to close, so let's not waste any more time. It's not like your clients are going to get any other commercial tenants in this climate.'

There are three main schools to negotiation: competitive, which is what this guy is doing, which involves trying to screw your opponent into the ground; co-operative, which kind of speaks for itself; and the Harvard method. Nobody quite knows what the Harvard method is, I suspect not even the guys at Harvard, but it basically involves using a blend of the two other styles to get your objective. In other words, knowing when to be a cunt and when to be a good guy.

Now is the time to be a cunt, so I cut in ahead of Leonora.

'I've been doing some brambling on the way over about your client, Mike,' I say. Which is true: once I'd scanned the leases, I got on my Blackberry and had a look at the latest company results. 'What's surprising is that people are still buying loads of shoes. What's even more surprising is they're still buying the crap shoes that your clients sell by the shed load, so the last quarter's results – which were coincidentally just in and announced today – show they're doing well. If the vultures are circling, they're not swooping down yet.'

I pause, just to see the expression on the guy's face. He looks bored but surprised at the same time. Time to switch from competitive to a blend, for the benefit of the surveyors. 'So let's not have any more false deadlines or stories about how unimportant this is to your clients. If it was that unimportant, you wouldn't be here, it'd be the trainee. If we work together on this – ' here comes the co-operative bit – 'I think we can pull together a deal that leaves everybody happy, looking at the numbers.' Here comes the competitive bit. 'But if we're just going to have grandstanding from you guys,' I check my watch with a flourish, 'there's a train back to Edinburgh in ten minutes from Queen Street.'

We don't get the train back till three hours later, when the deal's done so nicely you could put a pink ribbon round it.

'I don't think I've ever seen that prick brought down to size quite so quickly and easily,' Leonora says, smiling. We're sitting opposite each other in the carriage: it's pretty busy, so we're crushed in amongst the commuters escaping from Glasgow. She crosses her legs and her foot brushes my ankle. Was it deliberate? Her eyes are twinkling.

I shrug, hearing the drinks trolley rattling through the far end of the carriage. 'Fancy an over-priced warm Chardonnay to celebrate?' I ask her.

She wrinkles her nose, still smiling. 'Tempting, but no. I've still got stuff to do when we get back to the office. Maybe some other time.'

Definitely maybe. A thought occurs to me: if size really is important to her, Brad has probably told her he's seen me in the shower and that the python's the size of a grass snake. Other than whipping the big fella out here and now on the 5.30 to Waverley, there's not much I can do about that. As Al himself said, nobs out call has to be in context.

Still, I remember something else. 'Well, if Tony's got you all tied up, I guess ....' I say.

She smiles, rising to the bait. 'Oh, it wouldn't be Tony I'd have tie me up,' she says.

Definite chemistry there. The python is almost never wrong.

***

When we get back to the office, I last exactly half an hour then head home: there's only so much brilliance you can manage in one day.

Back at the flat, after I've had my Waitrose Sad Bastard Single Meal for One, I'm kind of at a loose end. If I were in London, there'd be mates I could phone up and go out for the night with, even if it would take half the night to cross town to do it. Here in Edinburgh, of course, I'm Billy No Mates, apart from Al + Bradley and, frankly, there's only so much rugger bugger talk that you can take.

Still, I've got itchy feet and the python, after his moments of excitement with both Sylvia and Leonora in the same day, is clearly looking for action.

Which is what drives me, at about eleven o'clock, to head out up through the New Town, up Lothian Road through the drunks, down through West Port (tempted but only briefly by the rough looking lap dancing bars in the Pubic Triangle there) and down into the Cowgate to Rum-ti-tum-tum's.

Which is where I see Al + Bradley chatting away to Debi and Elena like they're old pals, and everything changes.

CHAPTER 9
THE SCENT OF THE SCHEME

I'm walkin home with Candice from the school when I see Oddjob headin our way from Redgauntlet. He gives us a big cheery wave.

'Hello, Mrs. Clamp,' he says. He always calls me Mrs, and I never find a reason to correct him. 'I was just coming to see you.'

My heart sinks, but then I see he's got a jacket slung across his huge paw.

'Oh, aye? You'd better come up, then,' I say to him.

In the stairwell, there's a couple of teenagers I've never seen before, smokin, a bottle of Buckfast on the step between them. Sometimes it's like the whole of the scum of Auchendrossan think they can come and park themselves anywhere they like in our block: never know what you're goin to see when you go round a corner.

'Hey missus,' one of them starts up and then he sees Oddjob come round the corner behind me and he shuts up fast. I suppose there are some advantages in havin the local hard man as a sewin customer. Luckily, Candice skips on up the stairs ahead so she doesn't see what happens next.

Oddjob smiles down at the two teenagers. Scrawny wee things they are, but they've had a few tokes of the Bucky so one of them looks up at him towering over them and says, 'You have a problem big man?'

Oddjob smiles, and picks the ned up by the front of his shirt. I mean, bodily lifts him off the steps. Two quick strides and he's got the laddie up against the glass of the stairwell wall, his legs swingin in mid air.

'Aaaaaayabasa!' the boy says.

'I haven't got a problem,' Oddjob says. 'Next time I see you and your pal hangin around here botherin respectable folk like Mrs Clamp, though, you'll go out through this wall head first. Then you'll have a medical problem.'

Then he drops the boy, and says, quietly, 'Oh, and clear up that broken bottle before you go.'

75

Then, before either of them can say, 'What broken bottle?' he's booted the Bucky to the bottom of the stairs, where it smashes, spreading red wine up the stairwell wall like a bloodstain. I've never seen two teenagers move so fast in all my puff.

When we get in the flat, Candice is all giggly like she is with strangers, hidin behind me as Oddjob goes ben the livin room and sits down. Then she surprises me by goin over and askin him, 'Would you like a cup of tea?'

In the kitchen, I quiz her. 'Oh, I just ken him from when I go over to Aunty Jessie's after school,' she says.

My flesh creeps at the thought of him being anywhere near my lassie, but I make him the tea and give him a chocolate biscuit.

'Braw, thanks,' he says, as I put the mug down, but he's lookin at it kind of strange. The biscuit is next to the mug on the plate, so there's a bit of the chocolate melted on the biscuit. He looks at it as if it might bite him.

'What was it you were wantin done?'

He looks up at me, distracted from the biscuit for a minute. 'Oh, just if you could make the arms a bit longer, like,' he says. 'I've got long arms, you see.' He dangles one of his arms like an Orang-utan, just in case I hadn't noticed. Then it's back to staring at the biscuit and the chocolate mark on the mug.

I have a look at the coat. It's no exactly high quality tailorin, and the only way I can lengthen the arms is to cut it away from the linin, take what little spare there is, and make a new edge to it. It'll be messy, and I'll need to re-attach the linin, but it will give him an extra couple of centimetres on the arm. I explain this to him, but he still seems more interested in the chocolate mark on the mug.

'That's fine, thanks,' he says, picking the biscuit up by the digestive bit, as if it was a crab that would nip him. Candice, meantime, goes round to sit down next to him, until she sees the look from me, and sits on the other chair, puttin the telly on first.

'This will take a wee while,' I tell him. 'Can I bring it round to you tomorrow maybe?'

He's eatin the biscuit in delicate wee bites, like it might bite him. He looks up. 'Aye, okay,' he says, finishes the biscuit, takes a big slurp of tea and stands up. 'Do you mind if I wash my hands before I go?'

I show him ben the kitchen and watch him wash his hands twice to get rid of a wee speck of chocolate on his fingers and suddenly I twig what's goin on. He's got that OCD.

'Thanks,' he says, seein me watchin. 'I just like clean hands, ken?' *Oh, I ken, son.* 'No problem,' I tell him. Everyone in Auchendrossan's got a special need. Why shouldn't Deek's heavy have one as well?

***

Single index of multiple deprivation. That's the thing Auchendrossan is at the top of the league on. They used to call us an area of multiple deprivation, that used to be the jargon. Although I did see one smart alec official at the Cooncil refer to it as area of multiple satellite dish installation instead, in an email I got under FOI. Aye, well, he should come down here and try stayin for a bit, and see how much he laughs then.

Anyway, Auchendrossan apparently ticks all the boxes in terms of this index for poverty, anti-social behaviour, poor housin, the list goes on. Low business start ups. That one made me laugh. Take Pimpy Boy, Deek, for example. He's runnin a big business these days, although, apparently, drugs doesn't make him as much money these days as human traffickin. These two down the stair had better make the most of havin a three bedroom maisonette all to themselves: before they know it, Pimpy Boy will have seven Eastern European migrant workers to a bed down there.

I'm thinkin about all this as I lie awake at two in the mornin, listenin to the two of them with their latest customers. I'm a light sleeper, so I get no choice in the matter. No need for the baby monitor either, to hear all the shriekin that goes on.

When the two punters leave (no from round here from the sound of them; a taxi arrives for them and I hear one of them, Bradley I think Debi says his name is at one point, tell the driver to go up to Bruntsfield) I put the baby monitor on low. It's when the lassies are finished their shift for the night that I often get the most information out of them.

They're back to talkin about this guy who died with his toe up the tap.

'But why did they do that?' Debi's sayin. 'The toe up the tap, I mean.'

I can hear stuff clatterin about on the table in the livin room: gettin their fix ready, no doubt. They'll soon be flaked out for another night. 'How do I know?' Elena says. 'Maybe he thinks that's another way to have something on this boy.'

'Who kens what Deek does and for why,' Debi's sayin, her voice gettin slurred. Then, sharper for a moment, she says, 'Did you hear somethin? Almost like an echo?'

I put the baby monitor off quick and lie in the dark, thinkin. Things go all quiet downstairs: the two wee whores are obviously smacked out of their heads again.

I don't quite know why I feel I have to do somethin. It hasn't taken much effort on Google to find out about Simon English. It's quite an unusual name, after all. He's a lawyer, in one of the big firms. The older references had him down in London, but I found out the firm has a branch in Edinburgh. I suppose one thing I find interestin is that the company that, accordin to the papers, are in talks with the Cooncil to buy that land off them down in the Cowgate, has them as their legal advisers.

The company, strangely enough, is called Ivanhoe Enterprises. As in the name of the block of maisonettes I'm sittin in at this very minute.

All of this is goin round my head as I lie there in the dark, thinkin and thinkin. After a while, I get up and go through to check on the bairn: still sleepin, safe and sound. She's got her wee Maisie cuddly toy tucked under her chin.

When I go back to my own bed, I can actually hear, very faintly, one of the lassies downstairs snorin.

Walls have ears in Auchendrossan, right enough. I must remember to turn the baby monitor down when it's as quiet as this.

***

The next day is Saturday. The bairn's girnin a bit at breakfast: says she didn't sleep well.

'I kept dreamin about bein tied up in a garage, somewhere, Mammy,' she says. 'Some bad men had done it and they were lookin for you as well. The concrete was really cold and sore on my bum.'

Why is she havin my worst nightmare? 'Ach, nonsense, Candice,' I tell her. 'Come on, it's Saturday. Let's go up to Morninside and get a coffee. You can have an ice-cream at that posh place, since Oddjob's paid me for his alterations.'

'His name's Kevin, he told me,' Candice says, quietly.

Somethin turns over in the pit of my stomach. 'When were you talkin to him, likes?'

'Ach, just when I was out playin down on the green one day and he was passin,' Candice says, cool as you like. 'Don't make a big thing of it, Mammy. It's no like he was tryin to take me away and hide me in a garage or anythin.'

For once, she takes a bit of persuadin to go up to Morninside, but I have plans of my own. I need a cover story to get to speak to this Simon English guy. I've had a look at the firm's website: it deals in things like commercial property, somethin called just 'corporate': tax, agricultural law and so on. I don't even know what half of these things are. I think briefly of posin as a farmer, but I think he would probably see through that right away. The wee spiel about him on the website – which still has him down in London – says he does commercial property.

On the bus, I'm scannin the shops. No sewin alteration shops in Morninside. Perhaps there should be, though, I think to myself.

'Come on now Mammy, it's our stop,' Candice says, but when we get off the bus I surprise her by goin back the way we've come a wee bit and then off down a side street.

'This is no the right way, Mammy.'

I take her hand. 'We'll go for ice-cream in a minute. Your Mammy just wants to see a house.'

Jessie and the rest of them would kill themselves laughin if they heard me say this, but if I had loads of money, likesay a proper sewin business, and I didn't have my confidence issues and I'd married somebody decent instead of havin a one night stand with an utter eejit, and if I wasn't the size of a killer whale, this is where I'd live. There's a wee bit of Morninside which has streets all called biblical names, like Canaan Lane, Nile Grove and so on. There's a wee street called Jordan Lane. If it was in

Auchendrossan, I'd think it'd been named after the guy who was Hearts manager for a while, but it's no.

We stand in front of the house and I note down the number.

'Are we goin to move here, Mammy?' Candice asks me.

'Let's go and get that ice-cream, Candice,' I say. It's all I can say.

***

It's the next Friday at two o'clock, and I'm on the bus up from Auchendrossan into the city centre. I've arranged for Jessie to pick up Candice, just in case I'm no back in time. Of course, I meant to do this in the morning.

I'm absolutely bricking it. I've taken two Diazepam I had in the back of the cupboard from when the GP prescribed them for my anxiety attacks, when I was havin words with Candice's last teacher. Couldn't eat more than a plate of beans on toast for lunch to wash them down with, so my belly's rumblin like a cement mixer. I sit on the top deck at the front like Candice would, but I'm no even takin in the view.

When I get to the offices, I'm headin for the lift when the wee janny gadgie stops me. 'Excuse me, Missus. Do you ken where you're goin?'

'Aye,' I say and keep headin for the lifts. My heart sinks as I hear his chair scrapin behind me. Then he's right next to me, the wee tin pot Hitler, just as the lift door opens. 'It's just I have to get you to sign in, likes,' he says.

'Oh. Aye. Right.' Breathe a sigh of relief just as my stomach gives another gurgle and the gas from the beans starts to make its first escape. The wee janny wrinkles his nose so I go back to the desk quickly, to escape the smell. It occurs to me as I sign in that I should probably have used an assumed name, but then I've got my false address sorted out so it should be ok. Then it's back to the lifts and up to the top floor.

In the lift, I check my hair and everythin is no too bad. I was kind of amazed I could still get into this dress, but as long as I don't make any sudden movements, it should be fine. I washed my hair this morning, but you ken what it's like. Can't do a thing with it. The lippy I borrowed from Jessie is the wrong colour.

She thinks I'm goin on a date, likes. 'Just you take your time comin back, hen,' she told me. 'Me and Candice will be fine. We can get somethin from the chippy if things go well for you, likes,' and she gave me this big wink, like I was meetin Tom Cruise up Lothian Road. All I told her was that I had an appointment. Jessie's a nice old soul, even if she is a bit batty about Princess Diana, but she's still got a hotline to my Mum and I certainly don't want her stickin her boozy snout into what's goin on.

The lift doors ping open and there's a view over the New Town that gives me vertigo. Then it's through the double doors and across about a mile of carpet, to get to the reception desk, where a lassie who looks like she's spent a small African country's budget on her make-up is sittin behind a screen.

'Can I help you?' She doesn't even look up, or no properly.

'Does Simon English work here?'

This time, she does look up, although she manages to make it lookin down her nose at the same time. 'Yes, we do have a Mr. English working here. Do you have business with him?'

'In a manner of speakin. I want a word.'

She goes back to her screen, tapping away. There's a pause, so I say, 'I'm a new client of his, likes.'

'Okaay,' she says, as if that's the most unlikely thing she's ever heard in her life. 'I'll just see if Mr. English is available. In the meantime, we have a new client details form. Do you think I could ask you to fill that in?'

'Well, I can write, hen,' I tell her. And her eyes widen.

'I never said you couldn't,' she says, and just for a minute, her accent goes from being posh Edinburgh to Auchendrossan Edinburgh. *Aha,* thinks I. *You're a long way from home, lady, but you've still got the scent of the scheme about you.*

Just at that moment, the baked beans start to make their scent obvious again, so I scribble the form down quickly and hand it back to her. 'Thanks. Would you like to take a seat?' She's back to pure Morninside now, of course. After I've sat down, she makes me sweat for about five minutes before she picks up the phone. 'Simon? I've got a Mrs – ' she looks at the form as if my handwritin was difficult to read or something – 'Mrs. Clump here to see you. She says she's a new client.'

There's a pause, then she turns her head away from me and

says in a voice I can still hear, 'Shall I tell her to come back then?'

'I need to see him urgently,' I say, gettin up from the comfy seat.

'She says it's urgent…okay.' She puts the phone down and turns to me. 'Mr. English will be right up.'

'Right up,' in fancy lawyer speak, obviously means ten minutes, by which time more of the deadly baked bean gas has escaped and the snooty receptionist's wrinkled her nose about a dozen times.

He appears, carrying a pile of papers. 'Mrs. Clump?'

'It's Clamp. Karen Clamp.' I say, shootin the snooty lassie that came from a scheme long ago a look.

'Oh, er, right.' He's tall and dressed in a fancy suit: jet black hair and olive skin. He's got one of those posh English accents, of course.

'Shall we go into a meeting room to discuss your details? Gemma, is Three available?'

She nods her head, havin gone back to her screen. Probably just lookin for make-up bargains in Superdrug Online.

'Have you had far to come to get here?' the boy says, as we go into this huge glass walled meetin room. Big shiny wood table, expensive lookin chairs and a kettle with coffee and biscuits on hand. Outside, there's the same view of the New Town to give me my vertigo again. Have I come far? You have no idea.

'No, no far at all. Just got the bus down from Morninside,' I say, stickin to my cover story.

He looks at me kind of strangely and laughs. 'The bus? Gosh, you're brave.'

'It's a sustainable solution, like,' I say. You pick up a lot of Coonreil jargon with all the FOI requests.

The boy Simon looks unimpressed, and produces a laptop from under the pile of papers he's been carryin. 'I just need to take a few details, as you're a new client,' he says and fires up the laptop.

Great. Here we go again. It's as bad as the benefits office. 'Karen Clamp. 17 Jordan Lane, Morninside, Edinburgh.' My stomach gives a gurgle, like it can't believe I'm pretending to come from there rather than Auchendrossan. Neither can the rest of me, to be totally honest. No for the first time, I wonder what I think

I'm doin here.

He takes a few more details, then looks up. 'And how can I help you, Karen?'

I should just have told him there and then, of course, but what with the Diazepam and the coffee he's now produced for me and the wee bit of shortbread givin me a sugar rush, I just kind of get carried away.

'I run sewin alterations, that's my business. I have three shops, so far, all in Morninside, and I'm lookin to take over the lease of a fourth. I've heard you're the best lawyer there is for leases and so forth, so I thought I'd come and see you.'

He's still tappin away at his keyboard. Can these people never actually look at you? 'I see. And how is the sewing alteration business doing? I must admit, it's not one of the usual sectors I deal with.'

'Have you heard of a city called Wenzhou?' I say. No idea why this popped into my head. 'I didn't till I read it in the paper last week. Apparently, it's one of the most successful places in China, since they allowed them to make money under the communists, likes. They do it by makin all the wee bits and bobs that the rest of the world needs but nobody gets around to makin.'

'Really?' Tap, tap at the laptop.

'Aye, yes, that's right, they do. For example, all the fixins for bras are made in that one place.' That's true, likes. Don't know why I'm tellin him this, of course.

I seem to have got his attention, though. 'Really? That is interesting. Pity they couldn't make them easier to undo, eh?' He looks at me as if he still doesn't know what I'm on about, though. 'So, are you looking to set up in competition to them? Is that part of your business model?'

'No, no. It's just an example, likes. With Stitchin Time – that's the name of my shop – we're tryin to provide somethin that no-one else does.'

'I see, I see.' He is still lookin at me slightly strange. 'Do you have a web presence?'

This kind of throws me. 'Oh, aye. My cousin's set somethin up for me, but I can't remember the website, likes.' He's back at his keyboard, tappin away furiously. 'Of course, if you know any marketin consultants, I do need to develop that side of things.

We are startin to get internet orders in, likes.'

He stops typin. 'Just a little question on your business model. You've got three shops in Morningside already and you're looking to take on the lease of a fourth. Do you not think it might be better to expand into other areas of the city?'

I ken I'm diggin a hole and gettin deeper and deeper, but I just can't stop myself by this point. I grab another piece of shortbread and say, 'It's total market saturation, likes. Lots of posh people in Morninside have old clothes they want repaired...' but he's lookin at me now with that same look the snooty receptionist had.

'Look, Mrs. Clamp. I've been doin some Googling whilst we were talking. I can find about three zillion hits for Stich in Time, which must be about the most unimaginative sewing alterations shop name ever. None of them relate to any premises in Morningside. I don't know what this is all about, but I think I'm going to have to ask you to leave.'

I feel somethin buildin up in me: all that effort for nothin. Why on earth did I bother tryin to help this guy?

'That's fine, then. You can fend for yourself. It was stupid of me to come here.' I stand up and I'm just about to go out the door when I see who's goin past.

It's the guy with the huge melon shaped head that I last saw comin up the steps of the Ivanhoe block in Auchendrossan, wearing Chinos. He glances at me, then Simon English, then moves on. He disappears into one of the other glass walled meetin rooms with some other gadgies.

The Simon English boy has seen me lookin at him. 'What do you mean, fend for yourself?' he says.

'Like I say, forget it. But I wouldn't trust anyone in here, likes.'

And with that, I'm out the door, turnin my head away from the other glass walled meetin room where the melon head guy is sittin. And then it's out through the doors and down the stairs, leavin a trail of baked bean explosions behind me.

I hear Simon English shout after me at the top of the stairs, but just keep goin.

Stupid, stupid, stupid, I'm thinkin to myself.

CHAPTER 10
RUM-TI-TUM-TUM'S

I told you the python was psychic. We'll come onto the mad woman in a minute, but, first, let's go back a step, as I always say when negotiations are starting to go tits up. Let's go back to Rum-ti-tum-tum's, where, if you remember, the python had led me the night before.

There were the four of them. Al + Bradley, and the two girls who had been with me and Jimmy Ahmed, Debi and Elena. All sat round a table as nice as pie. They were in one of the back rooms of the club, a little alcove away from the dance floor, where you could just about hear yourself think, or hear other people speak, for that matter. I was working up to steaming in and telling the guys they were about to be dosed up with Rohypnol and taken off somewhere to have something nasty done to them, when some sort of instinct took over, and I ducked behind the nearest wall.

And that's when I heard Elena say, 'I tell you last Tuesday, Brad, I'm not that kind of girl.'

And that's when they all laughed like drains, and everything changed.

If they had met each other more than once, then either Al + Bradley liked being dosed up with Rohypnol, or the guys had a different relationship with these two than Jimmy and I had had, in our brief encounter. I listened for a bit but couldn't make out much more: lots of laughing and carrying on and the Debi girl screeching like a train with its brakes on, but I'd heard enough by then anyway. Outside the club, I shook my head in the fresh air, as if that would bring me back to some kind of reality I could understand, then hailed a taxi for Stockbridge.

Back at the flat, I paced up and down until about two, thinking things over. When I went to bed, I must've lain awake for the whole night apart from the two fucking precious minutes of sleep I had just before the alarm went off. Then it was back to the office, ready or not.

Now I know what you're thinking. Why did the stupid cunt

not just phone the cops, when he had the two girls there in the club? Fair question, I suppose, apart from that little bag of Bolivian marching powder I mentioned a short while ago, the one that I had stashed below the floorboards, which had disappeared after the SOCOs had investigated Jimmy Ahmed's death, but which DS Martin had said absolutely nothing about so far.

It shows how sad my life in Edinburgh was that I hadn't felt any need to have a coke and a smile until that night I carried Tom up into the flat and we were talking after DS Martin had left. Now, if I'd been down in London, my mate Ben or I would have been making a call to our good friend Scuzz, for supplies once or twice a week, Scuzz being our favoured purveyor of the fine white stuff.

Up in Edinburgh, though, I have zero mates to share a toot with, apart from Yvonne, of course. And I'd forgotten it the time that I'd gone to see her. So, it was only when Tom was at the flat and we fancied something stronger than single malt that I remembered to check under the floorboards. Where there was a big bag of cocaine shaped hole in the air where there should have been a big bag of cocaine.

All of this is still going through my head as I reach the office and discover that Bradley has called in sick. A moment of concern hits me, that perhaps I've got it wrong and that, in fact, he's another victim of the Rohypnol assassins, when I look over and see Al's carrot top above the screens in the open plan.

'You guys on the lemonades last night?' I say, just one guy to another.

Al's face is a picture of innocence. 'Not me,' he says, even though the cunt's bloodshot eyes are telling a different story. 'When I last heard, Brad was off out for dinner with Leonora. Maybe he's got food poisoning.'

Then his eyes widen. 'Ah, I think Brad was due to meet with the Edinburgh Council guys today on that Cowgate deal. Do you want me to cover for him?'

'No, that's fine, Al, leave it to me.' The Edinburgh City Council deal, which the Rottweiler had warned me off of, and Tony Hand had given me a pile of work to keep me away from. 'I'll handle it for today, don't worry.'

After that, I have an interesting morning working over a deal with the guys on the other side. They haven't made much progress since I'd last stuck my oar in but, with a bit of co-operation, we manage to move things forward well by the end of the morning. It's basically a development deal: our mysterious client, Ivanhoe Enterprises Limited, is taking some crappy buildings and gash land in the Cowgate off the Council's hands, but they want their sticky little fingers on a share of the yield our guys are going to get from the redevelopment into a massive hotel, leisure, retail and resi complex. It's even managed to take my mind off whatever the hell else is going on with Al, Bradley, the two girls and the cops.

By lunch time, though, I'm sitting at my desk chewing on a chicken tikka wrap made of blotting paper, thinking things over again.

Why haven't the cops done me for possession? The fact they haven't, just makes me all the more suspicious. It has to be one of the cops that's removed the bag of coke from under the floorboards. Isn't it worth a mention? Or is it something Martin's keeping in reserve for when he runs out of options? Whatever it is, it doesn't smell right; it doesn't make me trust the cops enough to go to them with what I have on the two girls either.

Then, when I've just about finished my blotting paper, Gemma, the permatan piece on reception upstairs, phones me to say there's a woman asking for me by name. Her name, she says, is Karen Clump.

I see through her right away, of course. It just takes a little time to browse the net to find enough holes in her story to get rid of her. Then the weird thing with Tony Hand happens.

The woman's getting up anyway. She's saying something about, 'Well, you'll just have to fend for yourself.' That in itself would be a weird thing to say. But then she turns, and sees Tony Hand walking past, and her jaw drops about a foot. It's like she's seen a fucking ghost or something.

'But I wouldn't trust anyone in here, likes,' she says and bolts out the door, pausing only to look up right in the direction Tony Hand's huge melon head has gone. Then she's off, like a twenty stone rabbit that's seen a fox.

I sit there for a moment, after the Clamp woman leaves. I'm thinking about Tony Hand, thinking about what he said that first morning when I phoned him from the flat with Jimmy Ahmed in my bath.

He said 'Fuck, they – ' and then stopped. Then he said something else which made sense, but it was that 'fuck, they – ' that had me thinking now. Who were 'they'? How did Tony Hand know them? Did everyone in Edinburgh know the Rohypnol girls apart from me? 'Fuck, they.' What did it mean?

I go out to where Gemma's filing her nails, not even pretending to look busy. 'I wanted to double check that new client's address. Can you show me what she gave you?'

She pushes the client info sheet across the desk at me and goes back to her nails. It's the same address that the Clamp woman gave me.

Gemma looks mildly interested. 'Problems? She seemed a bit odd, your client. Do you know her personally? She asked for you by name, you know.' She wrinkles her nose. 'Bit of a, you know, personal wind issue, to be honest.'

'Never met her before in my life,' I say. At least she's saved me one more question, but I've reached the stage where I feel I can't trust anyone. 'Could you do something else for me?'

She smiles suddenly, and there's a glint in her eye when she says, 'Almost anything.'

Why is it that you get the sniff of it when you're least able to take it up? Still, noted for future reference. 'Er, yes. Mrs. Clamp has left some papers behind. Could you call me a taxi, please, Gemma? I'll need to get them back to her.'

She frowns. That's not the answer she's expecting. 'Don't you want me just to order a courier?'

'No, that's fine, thanks. It's a nice day, I'll take them myself.'

She orders the taxi, a little huffily, and I give her some chat before the taxi arrives.

You would think getting a taxi would be straightforward enough but, in Scotland, everything has to be complicated.

I'm walking out the door when a voice behind me says, 'Excuse me, sir. Is that your taxi?' I turn and there's Bobby, the security guy behind the desk, one of the most officious little buggers you'll ever come across. 'Yes?' I'm not in the mood for him, but then again, I never am. 'And your name?'

'Simon English.' I turn and go through the doors and get into the taxi, ignoring him shouting after me about my identification. What a tool.

Up at Jordan Lane, there are no surprises. The address the mad fat woman had given me is an extremely nice looking Victorian villa.

The woman who answers the door is one of these high born Edinburgh types who looks down their nose at the rest of the world, like Edinburgh's the centre of the universe instead of a chilly little regional town. Athens of the north, indeed. More like Bristol, with Buckfast.

'Yes?' I would have thought the cut of my suit might have defrosted her a bit, but she's still staring down her long nose at me.

'Er, hi. I'm looking for a Mrs. Clamp?'

'Clamp? What a curious name. Of course no-one lives here called Clamp. Whatever gave you that idea?'

'I'm sorry,' I said, smiling through gritted teeth. 'Well, perhaps you can help. I represent a company that sells a new wonder brand of laxative. Are you in need of any?'

That gets the door slammed in my face, all right. I trot back down the steps and decide to walk back to the office.

Don't get me wrong, okay? Edinburgh has its good bits and Morningside is probably one of them. It runs into Bruntsfield, where a lot of lawyers live now: slightly less pricey than Morningside, but still at the top of the hill where they can look down on the rest of Edinburgh.

It's a nice spring day for a walk, but I'm not really taking much of that in as I head back down to Tollcross and Lothian Road. All I can think about was how shitty my life has become since coming back up north. And there was only one person I can speak to about it.

I phone Tom on the mobile.

'Can't talk now,' he hisses. 'Ballingall's back, trying to screw extra money out of us for new bath taps. Termination with extreme prejudice.' He rings off.

Back at the office, past the tin pot Hitler on the desk downstairs, and up to the office. I don't have any meetings scheduled for the afternoon, but there's plenty to do.

I can't concentrate, though. Partly it's just trying to get my mind off the obvious. Partly also, though, it's this incredibly fucking paranoid feeling I keep getting now, that everyone in the office is watching me. It's like something crawling up the back of your neck.

About five o'clock, I can't stand it any longer. I finish up what I was doing and leave, even though most of the office is still there. Not good practice to be seen to be one of the first to go, of course, even on a Friday. However, at least now I have a plan.

Bradley's presumably too hung over to go out a second night running, and I doubt that Al will be going down to Rum-ti-tum-tum's by himself. Not the way they're joined at the hip.

Which leaves the way clear for me.

***

It's somehow crawled round to nine o'clock. I've had a couple of Waitrose baguettes to eat, although, to be honest, I'm not all that hungry. I've also demolished most of a bottle of Chilean Cav Sauv while watching some rubbish on the telly.

In retrospect, I should've stayed later at the office, of course. The club doesn't even open till half nine and doesn't really get going till a couple of hours after that.

I keep using delaying tactics on myself: I've even fixed a couple of the light bulbs in the kitchen, but it's quarter past nine now, and I'm good to go. I neck the rest of the wine and grab the flat keys. One last check in the bathroom mirror: I can't help glancing over at the bath, picturing Jimmy Ahmed laid out there. *Well, maybe I'm going to get to the bottom of it at last*, I think to myself.

Just as I open the front door, the phone rings.

'What's up, cunt?'

It's Tom. 'So you got Ballingall sorted out?'

'Yeah. Pretty much had to hold his head down the bog to make sure he got it right, but we got it over the line in the end. So what were you phoning about?'

Tom already knows most of the story, so I explain about my trip to Rum-ti-tum-tum's the previous night, what I saw, what I heard and so forth. I leave out the bit about the mad woman for now.

'And you're planning to do what, exactly? Go down and find these girls again by yourself?'

'That's pretty much it.'

'And then what? Tie them both up using a boy scout knot and stand outside waiting for the cops like Lord Peter fucking Wimsey?'

I realised I haven't exactly completely thought this through. 'Something like that.'

There's a sigh on the other end of the line. 'Oh, for fuck's sake. Mum must've dropped you on your head a couple of times when you were a baby for this. Why don't you just phone the cops, give them a description and leave them to it?'

Right now, that does sound like an attractive option. I could go and pick up a carry out, open a second bottle and watch Sky Sports. So I've no idea really why I say, 'Yeah, great idea bro. And then the cops go to the wrong club, pick up the wrong women and I spend the rest of the night looking at I.D. parades of schemies. Look, I'd better go, okay? I'll let you know how I get on.'

I put the phone down and head out the door. My moby bleeps but I put it on silent: time to sort things out by myself, in my own way.

Time to negotiate with them.

CHAPTER 11
IVAN'S HO'S

As clubs in Edinburgh go, Rum-ti-tum-tum's isn't too bad a joint: it's rave stuff, mainly, but they mix it up a bit so it's bearable. All the same, I'm wishing I'd had some pills with me once all the lights and the dance floor get going.

My life right now seems to be full of guys on the door with too much power. The bouncer isn't going to let me in initially, I suppose because I'm a bloke on my own. But then, on an impulse, I tell him I'm meeting mates inside: Al + Bradley.

He perks up. 'Oh, you're pals with those guys? I haven't actually seen them in tonight, likes, but in you go anyway.'

The club is on three floors in the Cowgate: the ground floor level is mainly the bar and chill out area, with lots of little rooms, then it's upstairs to the main dance floor. Upstairs beyond that is always roped off with a sign saying, "VIP Lounge".

I decide to switch to bottles of Corona. Little tip if you think somebody's going to slip a Mickey Finn in your drink: any bar worth its salt serves Corona with a squeeze of lime on top, making it extremely difficult for said Mickey to be slipped. At least, that's my theory.

It takes a couple of hours for me to find them, or for them to turn up. I'm prowling round the dance floor for the tenth time when I see them, giving it plenty to some coked up R&B number I'd never heard before.

Most guys would probably fancy Elena more. She's quite dark skinned and more conventionally pretty, with one of those long East European noses. She's got her hair scraped back into a ponytail with some sort of glitter stuff through it and she's wearing some sort of corset thing with lots of laces and stuff on top and a pair of black trousers down below. Pretty toned in the middle: not much Buddha belly there, although she does have a ring in her navel which flashes as she bops about.

Debi, on the other hand, has had longer exposure to pies and bridies, so there's a very satisfactory bit of Buddha belly and muffin top between her electric blue cut-offs and lime green crop top. Her bottle blonde hair is scraped back too and she's got one of these little freckled faces that a lot of Jocks have: quite pretty in its own way, I suppose, if it wasn't usually scrunched up into a bored expression. In fact, the two of them look totally disinterested, despite the music and the lights.

As I'm watching, a couple of guys come up and try to dance with them, giving it plenty of that dodging about type of dancing that the young ones go for these days. The girls just turn away, and the blokes get the message after a couple of minutes. I lie in wait for them until the song ends and they're heading for the bar.

'Can I get you girls a drink?' I come up behind them laying a hand on their bare shoulders. Debi turns round, ready to give me the brush-off, until she sees me.

I do my best to look puzzled. 'Sorry, I know this sounds like a line, but haven't I seen you girls somewhere before?'

I can hear Debi's brain grinding, trying to take this in. *So he doesn't remember us,* she's thinking. At least I hope to fuck that's what she's thinking. I turn to Elena, who looks a bit like a rabbit caught in the headlights. 'It wasn't in here though, was it, it was that other club?'

'Oh, yeah. That's right. It was Po Na Na's, wasn't it?' This is Debi, obviously thinking on her feet. 'Do you always chat up two girls at once? You were on your own last time, weren't you?'

We've reached the bar, which is about three deep, but I manage to nudge my way in. 'More fun with three,' I say, and then to the barman, 'A bottle of your best champagne, my good man.'

That makes their greedy little eyes light up. They're obviously not used to guys buying bubbly for them.

Elena nudges Debi. 'We should be going, really,' she says, glancing at me and at the barman fetching down a bottle of shampoo that's probably sat there cooking for three years. Can't see many Jocks being prepared to splash their cash on champagne, even in Edinburgh.

'Just a quick one,' Debi says, looking at me and the size of my wallet as I take it out to pay for the champagne.

We go and sit down in one of the quieter alcovey bits and I pour them out a glass each.

'Where's yours?' Elena says. Debi looks suspicious. 'You trying to get us pissed and no have any yourself?'

93

'Course not,' I say and take a swig from the bottle. *Let's make it that little bit harder for them to dose me up this time.*

Funnily enough, we're in the same alcove that I saw them with Al + Bradley the night before. The place is pretty rammed with it being a Friday night, so that there's only room for us if the three of us sit side by side. They make room for me in the middle: excellent.

'So tell us about you,' Elena says. When she smiles, it makes a huge difference to her face. She really is very fit indeed and sitting squashed between her and Debi, the python is starting to take a stroll through the trouser department in a big way.

'Oh, nothing much to tell. I used to work in London, but I've been posted here for a while,' I say, distracted by the fact that Debi, on the other side of me, is busy texting away. I can't stand it when people do that to you, actually. Plus it worries the hell out of me who she might be texting.

'Come on, let's dance,' she says, suddenly, necking her champagne. She grabs my hand and drags me up and Elena comes with her.

The dance floor is stuffed full of pilled up Jocks giving it plenty, but Debi's not shy about barging past them. Soon we're right in the middle floor and Debi's pressed up against me, wriggling like a salmon in her crop top and leather trousers against me. Then Elena joins in from behind and the python's in hog heaven. Crushed up against me, I can smell Debi's scent: somewhat surprisingly for a schemie, it's one of the more expensive perfumes. In fact, it's the same perfume, Chanel, I think, that Kate used to wear. Except Kate never gave me a vertical lap dance like this. Especially not with a pal.

'I think I might even fancy you,' Debi shouts in my ear and suddenly we're snogging, right there on the dance floor. Then she spins me round and I snog Elena, while Debi's hands slide into my pockets. Then, when the music changes, Debi slips round in front of me and she and Elena start giving it major bump and grind. By the time they lead me off the dance floor, it's almost a relief, the python's so over-extended.

Back at the table, we finish the champagne. Then I see Debi check her mobile. 'Why don't we go somewhere quieter?' she says, exchanging a look with Elena across me.

'Do you want me to come too?' Elena says, and I look, and there's that twinkle in her eyes.

'Of course,' I say. 'Like I said, it's always more fun with three.'

Now, I know what you're thinking. What the fuck is Simon doing? I mean, these two girls had been involved in Jimmy Ahmed's death, right? Plus they dosed me with drugs, and not in a good way.

Well, that's all very well for you to say, especially if you're a woman. You weren't there, with a bottle of wine, four lagers, and a good few slugs of champagne inside you. You hadn't had Elena in her corset and Debi with her leather trousers and her Buddha belly giving you major friction. At times like that, the python kind of takes over any brain cells still working.

Out in the Cowgate, there's a taxi hovering, and the three of us jump in. 'Ivanhoe Court, Auchendrossan,' she shouts at the driver and we're away, the street lights sliding past at a speed that reminds me how much I've had to drink.

Still, there's the two girls to snuggle up to. 'Have you ever had two lassies at once, likes?' Debi says, giggling. She's got her hand in my trouser pocket again, teasing the python big time.

'Only the once,' I say. Actually, that's true. What I don't tell them is that it was when I was a student and I was so out of it on booze and pills that I crashed out and left the two of them to it. When I woke up in the morning, I had the mother of all hangovers and they had decided to move in together. They still are together, come to think of it. Which is nice.

Thinking about all this makes me sober up just a bit, although Debi's isn't helping and now Elena's joined in, nibbling at my ear. The taxi driver keeps glancing in the mirror to see the action, which is hardly comforting given the speed he's reaching, hurtling down through the New Town like a maniac.

People talk about being conflicted about things. Well, that night, I knew what it was to be conflicted. Part of me is waking up to what I'd got myself into. For those of you who don't know Edinburgh, Auchendrossan is, in Monopoly board terms, the stuff just after you pass Go. In fact, Muirhouse and Pilton are Mayfair and Park Lane compared to Auchendrossan. But, at the same time, there are more than reasonable prospects that I might get the shag of my life. What a piece of work is man.

The taxi eventually pulls up outside what I take, at first, to be a derelict block of flats. Then, as we get out, I see that there were one or two lights on in the windows that haven't been boarded up. The girls lead me up the first flight of stairs: it's one of these maisonette jobs, with an access way leading along the front of the flats on the various levels.

Debi, giggling, pulls her keys from somewhere and lets us in. The living room looks like a bomb's hit it: pizza boxes scattered about the floor, a red leather sofa that's seen better days, and a couple of opened cans of super lager on a wooden table. Paper thin carpet with some very dodgy looking stains on it.

Debi's watching me. 'Have you ever had a penguin before? I think I'm going to give you a penguin for starters,' she says, and then she's on her knees in front of me and undoing my trousers and hauling down my boxer shorts. Before the python can spring into action, Debi leaps up and takes two paces back.

'Come on then,' she says and I get it, as I waddle forward like a penguin. The two of them start laughing. Then Elena, who's disappeared off into the kitchen, re-appears with a bottle of what looks suspiciously like Buckfast and two glasses. The two of them are laughing like drains by now. 'See you in the bedroom, big boy,' Debi says and the two of them disappear off, past the kitchen and through a door.

At least I have the sense to pull my boxers up and keep them on. Of course, I leave my shoes and trousers in the living room, don't I? Idiot.

Through in the bedroom, they've got the Buckfast poured out into the two glasses. I pick up one of them and drain half of it, just about throwing up in the process. That stuff is disgusting: I've no idea how people manage to drink it. When I put it down, Debi is eyeing me suspiciously.

'I thought you just drank out the bottle, likes,' she says.

'I was trying to be classy,' I say, refilling the glass from the bottle. Game on.

Then the two of them are on me like a couple of wildcats, tearing my clothes off, tearing each other's clothes off, and pulling me down on the bed. The python, who's been a bit quiet since we got into the flat, begins to take over my brain again.

I don't know if you've ever taken part in a threesome, but

although it may sound like a great idea, actually, there are some logistical difficulties. For a start, even double beds are designed for two people, not three. And there's – how can I put this? – only one place you can put your python, from the several on offer. Maybe it's something to do with men and multi-tasking.

Apart from that, though, even as Debi and Elena are clambering all over me, I'm beginning to sober up to what I've got myself into. Or what the python has got me into, more accurately. From the look on their faces, it's obvious they'd done the penguin thing on me to give them time to dose up the Buckfast bottle with Rohypnol, or something else. Which means, despite all appearances to the contrary, they were still up to no good.

Which is probably why, after about a minute of licking, fondling and digging elbows in each other, Debi says to me, 'Do you want us to put on a show?'

'Excellent idea.' I kneel on the edge of the bed, putting on the emergency condom I always carry in my wallet (I'm certainly not going any nearer to them without it) while they do a lesbian act.

'Hey, you guys are professionals,' I nearly say, but fortunately manage to stop myself. I finally have to admit to myself that that is exactly what they are: they have every move down pat, just kissing or licking each other in the right places to get me going and then moving on into a new position. How stupid exactly can I be? What did I think they were, Benny Hill-style nymphomaniacs?

After a minute or two, they've worked through their repertoire and lie, snuggled together, looking at me.

Then Debi says, 'I've got her warmed up for you, Simon. Why don't you two have fun while I go and get us something else to play with?'

'Sounds good to me.' Elena says, and then she's all over me, while Debi takes her Buddha belly out the door, shutting it carefully behind her.

I start at Elena's neck and head southwards: you know those films when the agent's special training takes over? Well, in situations like that, the python's training takes over. I reach the business end and am pleased to find Elena isn't faking it, at least not entirely. Just as we're about to get to grips properly, though, she slips out from under me, slippery as a salmon.

'I forget something, I have to tell Debi,' she says, sliding off the bed and heading out of the bedroom. When the door closes behind her, I stand up and go across to the window. The python's drooping like a flag at half mast, with no-one to salute him. Fortunately, this allows some blood supply to get back into my brain and I'm just thinking about how to get out of this, when the thing I least expected to happen happens.

As I stand looking out the window, a piece of cardboard dangling from a string drops down from above. Something's written on it, but I can't see what it says at first for the reflection from the light inside. Then, by shifting position a bit, I can read it:

GET OUT NOW.
YOU ARE IN DANGER.

Then, just as suddenly as it's appeared, the piece of cardboard drops out of sight.

I don't need any fucking second invitation, though. I look around quickly for my clothes. Of course, my trousers are still in the living room, where I can hear Debi and Elena speaking in low voices. Shoes are there as well.

Fuck. In fact, fuck, wank, fanny bastard. I throw on what clothes I can find and then start on the window. It's one of those big aluminium jobs they have in flats of this vintage: the catch is a nasty little piece of work which seems to have welded itself to the surrounding metal. After a bit of fiddling, it comes undone, but the window still won't slide open.

Fuck. Of course, you can only get half your finger tips onto the narrow edge, and I pull at this for all I'm worth. Fuck. It won't budge.

Fuck. It won't budge.

Fuck. It won't budge.

Fuck. It won't – it does, at last, slide back with an awful screeching sound. I push it as wide as it will go, clambering up onto the ledge, just about slicing my bollocks on the metal edge in the process. Outside, street lights in the distance; darkness close up.

I'm pretty sure we only came up one flight of stairs. I glance down at the blackness below, as I manoeuvre myself to dangle from the window frame. It's some sort of landscaped area, if I can land just beyond the concrete end of the foundation. Pushing myself out a bit, I let go –

And just about twist my ankle 180 degrees as I land, falling backwards onto my arse.

I look up. Debi and Elena haven't appeared back in the bedroom yet, but one floor above, I see a face at the open window, gesturing madly. She seems to be pointing down at me, and then I realise – it's the cardboard sign which dropped out of sight. It's lying stuck in the bushes.

My mysterious benefactor is pointing it out. Obviously, she doesn't want it to be found. I raise my hand and nod and pick the sign up to take it with me. Then, as I back away from the building a bit, I see that it's the mad schemie woman, Karen Clamp, who's dropped the sign down to warn me.

A tiny piece of the insane jigsaw that is my life at the moment slots into place. So that's why she came to see me: she lives above Debi and Elena. I raise my hand to her, then turn and stumble off in my stocking soles, aware of the wet mud sticking my boxers to my arse and the light spring shower of rain which is starting to fall.

The block of maisonettes I've just jumped out of is separated by a raised grass area from similar blocks, looming out of the darkness like ships in the icy waters of the Atlantic. I can see what looks like a main road ahead and start walking: there are street lights there and possibly even the hope of civilisation. To my absolute amazement, I can see a bus, toiling its way up a hill along the main road. I break into a run, waving frantically at it, and I realise there actually is a bus stop I can reach in time.

Past the next block of maisonettes. I hear a bottle smash in the stairwell, so not all the natives are tucked up safely in bed. The ground rises again and I stumble up the grassy slope, trying to keep my stocking soles clear of dog shit and broken glass while still keeping up as good a pace as I can. I arrive at the bus stop, panting, just in time.

It's a night service, heading into town. Result. I step aboard and the driver stares at me.

'Where you going, son?'

'Anywhere you are.' I fumble for my wallet. Which is when I remember my wallet was in my trousers. And neither of them are actually there. 'Look, I don't have any money on me at the moment, but I really need to get this bus, okay? I'll pay you double when I get back to the flat.'

The guy just looks at me. 'It doesn't work that way.' He stares at me until, eventually, I step back off the bus. Not one of my finest negotiations. The doors hiss shut and the bus takes off.

And that's when I turn round and see the shape emerging from the slope in front of the last block of maisonettes.

In the darkness, I can't see the guy's features. However, I can see how big he is: he looks as broad as he is large. He could just be a guy heading for the bus stop, but I somehow don't think so because, when I set off in the same direction as the bus, and look back, I see him alter the direction he's walking, just slightly, to keep heading for me. The thing that gives me a really nasty feeling in the pit of my stomach, not to mention making the python shrink in on himself even further, is that he doesn't even seem in any hurry: just walking steadily towards me, big strides, no tearing hurry to reach me and do whatever he's going to do to me.

I set off, walking quickly, up the road. The estate has kind of petered out and there's a wooded area where I can picture myself being found, dismembered, months from now.

Pad, pad, pad. The guy's like some kind of tiger the way he moves, a tiger stalking its prey. I'm just considering whether it's worth breaking into a run when a taxi comes rattling round the corner ahead of me, going in the opposite direction from where the bus has gone. I cross the road and stand in front of the cunt, thinking at least if he runs me over, it'll be faster than the alternative.

The guy leans out his window. 'Are you wanting a taxi, mate? You just had to raise your hand, ken?'

'Am I glad to see you,' I start saying, but the guy's looking behind me, to where the figure following me has broken into a trot now.

The taxi driver's expression changes.

'Is that guy with you?'

I look round. You can just start to make out my follower's

features: a huge, round head, almost Chinese looking. He's staring right at the taxi driver. 'No, it's fine. We don't have to wait for him.' I have my hand on the door of the taxi. If he pulls away as soon as I get in, we can be away before there's any need to run the big guy over.

'In that case, pal, I'm not for hire.' And with that, the taxi driver revs his engine and accelerates away, just about taking my arm with him until I can let go of the door handle.

The big guy's fifty yards away now. When he sees he's scared off the taxi, he breaks into a smile and slows down to walking speed again. Somehow, though, in the process of changing pace, he slips on the wet grass, and falls face down, just stopping himself in time with his hands. I stand, frozen to the spot, as he gets up again, brushing himself down, over and over.

Something like a low growl escapes him: he wipes his hands on his trousers, then dusts them together. Maybe he's landed in dogshit. It occurs to me suddenly I needn't be hanging around to find out.

I turn and leg it along the road, feeling the tarmac starting to shred my feet through my stocking soles. Behind me, I can hear his footsteps on the tarmac as he breaks into a trot again. It sounds like he's got metal toe-capped boots on. That would make sense, I guess.

Ahead of me, the wooded area seems to stretch on into the distance as I go round the corner. Where the fuck am I? Wherever it is, it's a pretty deserted place at three in the morning with some huge fucking Chinese assassin on your tail.

I'm not even aware of the car engine until I look round and, just passing the guy behind me (twenty yards now, and closing), I see the headlights of a car. It screeches to a stop beside me and a face looks out from the open window, a face that's got a whisky sour complexion; a face that I could kiss right now for sheer fucking joy.

'Get in,' DS Martin says.

My last image of the guy following me is him standing in the middle of the road, dusting his hands together over and over, in the headlights of another night bus coming up the hill behind him.

I have no doubt at all it'll be the bus that'll get out of his way, not the other way round.

CHAPTER 12
ANXIOUS IN AUCHENDROSSAN

None of this is any good for my nerves. Just takin the bairn to school broke me out into a sweat, and now I'm back, I need a Tunnock's caramel wafer with my coffee just to get my pulse rate down.

I have no earthly idea why I decided to do anything on Friday night. Any man that was stupid enough to pick up the same two women and agree to come down to Auchendrossan with them almost deserves whatever Oddjob was goin to do to him. I mean, he must have agreed to come down with them: certainly, he legged it out of the window like he was still in possession of some brains at least.

I was woken up by the three of them arrivin. No great change there, of course. Every other night these two wee whores are bringin men back, and it's never a quiet affair. I got up and looked out the window and there was the same overgrown public schoolboy that had practically thrown me out of his office the day before. I couldn't believe it at first: I mean, how? Never mind.

I went back to bed and switched the baby monitor on, as low as I could. It was quite cold with the heatin off, so I pulled the covers up and put the baby monitor as close as I could to the bed itself without taking it out the wall. I remember how I used to have a torch when I was a wean to read books under the covers. Now here I am pullin them up to listen in on a couple of prostitutes. Some things don't improve with age.

The three of them started off in the livin room, getting drinks. I heard that Debi tell him that she was goin to give him a penguin. And then the two of them screeched with laughter and went away ben the main bedroom. I've heard them do that trick to a man before: he takes his trousers down, thinkin it's something kinky, and then they leave him to it, and he has to waddle like a penguin. Most men fall for it. Say no more.

The main bedroom, the one they use most of the time, is just below mine but the receiver I put in has gone on the blink long ago.

Anyway, there didn't seem to be anything to hear for ten or fifteen minutes. Still though, I lay in the dark wide awake. What on earth were they doin to him? The last time they'd been with him, the other guy had wound up dead in the bath with his toe stuck up the tap. I was frozen to the bed, sweatin buckets. What could I do? The cops? No way. Talk about Sleepless in Seattle. This was Anxious in Auchendrossan.

Then I heard the bedroom door shut downstairs, and someone come back ben the livin room.

It was wee Debi Murray. As luck would have it, she must've been right near the receiver, because I could hear her talking on her mobile even though she was keeping her voice down. She's on the phone to Pimpy Boy.

'Aye, we've still got him here, Deek. When are you coming to deal with him?'

Then a pause, then she hisses: 'I don't give a f*ck if you're in Glasgow! Have you no got anyone you can send round to get rid of him? He must be on to us, Deek...Aye, aye, get Mr. Bump round if you like. Just make sure he does whatever he does to him a long way away from here.'

Just at that, I hear the bedroom door close quietly again. It's Elena. As soon as I hear her say, 'What's going on? Is Deek sending someone round? He won't drink any of the wine, and he's getting hornier and hornier,' I realise here's my chance.

I couldn't lie upstairs and listen to someone gettin murdered. I couldn't phone the cops either, not without givin myself away. There's the bairn to think of, no just me. I get up, and find my legs are shakin. Still, I have a plan of sorts, cooked up as I lay there listenin.

I go through to the bairn's room where she's sleepin sound as ever. She's been doin some art project which involves drawin a clown's face on a piece of cardboard. I know where some string was in the kitchen, and scissors. My hands are tremblin, too, as I put the sign together. I can only hope that the lassies have left the curtains open: they usually do, right enough.

Back ben the bedroom, I open my window and lower the sign down. It would've been just my luck if the wind had caught it and Simon English ended up lookin out the window at a clown's face made of buttons but, luckily, there's no wind and the sign holds firm.

I have no idea whether he would even see it, of course. He might've been lyin on the bed fast asleep for all I ken. Then, of course, does the string no unravel itself and the piece of cardboard drop out of sight. I haul in the string but, just at that moment, hear the window open.

No a moment too soon, either. From the baby monitor, I can hear the lassies discussin whether they should go back through to keep the big numpty from gettin suspicious. Then his head appears out the window, quickly followed by the rest of him. He swings one leg over the ledge, then the other, dangles there for a minute, and then drops down.

He's about to leg it, and I realise that he's not thought of takin the sign with him. If Oddjob or the lassies find it, I'm done for.

Just at that moment, he looks up. I signal to him and he eventually gets the message, picks up the cardboard sign and trots off in the direction of the main road.

Just at that moment, back in the flat, I can hear the lassies say that's the door. They let Oddjob in, then the two of them scuttle back through to the livin room. Tramp, tramp, tramp go Oddjob's feet along the hall to the bedroom. I don't need the baby monitor to hear that. The door opens, and there's a pause of about ten seconds, then he comes back ben the livin room and tells the lassies, 'There's no-one there. The window's open. He must've legged it.'

As quietly as I can, I shut my window, tiptoe over to the bedroom light, and shut it off. Then back to the window, standin a wee bit back from it, so I can see what happens.

When I look out, I can see the English boy strugglin up the slope next to the Rob Roy block. He's makin heavy weather of it, but then the eejit doesn't have any trousers or shoes on. Then, out from underneath our own block, Oddjob appears.

Pad, pad, pad. Oddjob doesn't seem to be in any hurry to catch him. In fact, he stops and turns to look back at our block and, for a moment, I think he's seen me. I'm fairly sure no, though, cos I've stayed back from the window. He smiles in that creepy way of his and then pads on, just keeping pace with Simon English, or maybe just catchin him up a bit.

It's no long before they disappear out of sight. It would be safe for me to phone the cops now, of course, but then what do I tell them? There's a guy that looks like a James Bond villain about to do somethin bad to a big lummox that you'll recognise by the fact that he's got no trousers on. Couldn't even give them an exact location now, even if they got past thinkin I'm some sort of a fruitcake. Besides, I have my own reasons for no trustin the cops.

I go back to my bed but I can't sleep. After about twenty minutes, I hear Oddjob chappin on the lassies' door downstairs. They let him in, and I can just hear Debi say, 'What happened?' and Oddjob say 'Need to wash my hands,' when the sound from the baby monitor goes all fuzzy and then stops altogether.

The battery must've gone. Can't rely on anythin to last any time these days.

I go through to the kitchen and get a glass, moving as quietly as I can, and then go into the livin room with it. I've just got into position when the bairn comes up behind me. 'Mammy, why are you lyin on the livin room carpet with your ear on a glass?'

Of course, I hadn't heard her. You wouldn't think someone my size could jump five feet in the air from a prone position, but I swear I managed it.

'Shush now, Candice,' I say. 'What are you doin up? You need to get back to your bed.' But, of course, she won't settle then, and I end up lettin her sleep in beside me, all the time me tryin to hear what's goin on downstairs above her snorin. I hear the door go no long after, which is presumably Oddjob headin off. Then I lay awake the rest of the night, thinking, how long was he away? Has he left the English boy lyin in a pool of blood somewhere? Is that why he needed to wash his hands?

Then, just as I'm about to fall asleep, twenty minutes before the alarm goes off to wake me up again, I remember. Oddjob has OCD. Even if he'd got a speck of dust on his hands, he'd have to wash them.

***

A cup of tea and an extra biscuit and my palpitations are more back to normal. Like I say, I don't know why I'm worryin what happened to English. It could be that I'm worried they'll

105

somehow trace it all back to me and make it my fault somehow. That would be a wrong pattern of thinkin, accordin to that psychologist the GP sent me to once about my issues. Apparently, I do lots of thinkin in wrong patterns, kind of like those knittin patterns your mum or your Gran used to get except you've knitted it all skew whiff.

That did wonders for me, bein told I couldn't even think straight. I never went back after that first time.

Actually, I think it's probably the fact that English is gettin a hard time from the same bunch of criminals that have made my life a misery for years, so there's some sort of fellow feelin, even if he is a big obnoxious prat. Doesn't matter to me that he actually is English, at least from his accent. A prat's a numpty in anyone's language.

I log onto my emails, still thinkin about the listenin device, and how I might fix it. I suppose I could try doin it from this end: takin the carpet up I mean, and seein if I could get in under the floorboards. No literally in, obviously. I could imagine myself splashin down on the two skinny wee lassies because the joists wouldn't take my weight, like that wrestler my granny used to watch on a Saturday afternoon, Giant Haystacks. Except without the beard.

No, but I could see if I could work another listenin device in through the joists to just above their ceilin, somethin like that.

I've got the email programme set up to automatically generate a reminder when the Cooncil hasn't responded to my FOI requests within twenty days. There's a couple, now, mainly about the Caltongate development. I bang off a couple of reminders, just to keep them on their toes, and then scroll through all the junk that's come in to my inbox.

My hands freeze over the keyboard. There's an email from Benzini, Lambe and Lockhart. Are they on to me? Or is this Simon English tryin to get in contact?

My heart starts flutterin again. It's weird, but it's almost like when you've met a guy, and you're hopin he'll phone you. No that any of the deadbeats I've ever gone out with were worth the price of a reverse charge call, of course. And that includes Candice's dad, rat that he is.

'WELCOME TO BLL'S FREE COMMERCIAL

PROPERTY NEWSLETTER,' the email says. I start to laugh. Simon English might have given me the bum's rush, but now I'm on the firm's email list as a valued client. I scroll through the list and help myself to another biscuit to celebrate.

Actually, there's quite a bit to interest me in the email. There's a link to the latest news article on the Caltongate deal (I'd already read that of course). But there's also another wee piece of interest:

> '**Council close to closing Cowgate deal**. A report to Edinburgh Council's Finance and Resources Committee confirms that negotiations are ongoing to sell out Edinburgh Council's interest in a prime piece of city centre land off the Cowgate. The public part of the report was short on detail, but the Council's landholding is known to include the block which includes popular nightspot Rum-ti-tum-tum's, as well as several Fringe venues and undeveloped land with an extant permission for mixed retail and commercial use. A spokesman for Ivanhoe Enterprises later confirmed that negotiations were still ongoing. "It's with the lawyers now," the spokesman said. "We anticipate being able to close the deal by our deadline date of 1st May."

Ivanhoe Enterprises. Surely, it couldn't be? Of course, there are a million reasons why they might call their company Ivanhoe in Edinburgh. I'm no completely thick, you see. I do know it was a Walter Scott novel. In fact, it was one of the slightly less borin ones if I remember.

Definitely worthy of a Clamp investigation.

I log onto the Companies House website and I'm just about to start diggin, when the phone goes and it's Jessie.

'Do you do curtains, hen?' she says. 'It's only, you ken these ones in the front room that go all the way down, I was thinkin I would get more heat out of the radiator if I got them taken up to about half way, ken? It's terrible gettin old when you find you have to keep the house warmer and warmer..'

And so on and so on. She's really just phonin for an excuse for a natter, but by the time I get her off the phone, havin promised to come round and have a look at her curtains, it's time to pick up the bairn.

***

She fair skips out the gate, and my heart gives a wee jump when I see her, the same way it always does when I haven't seen her for a while. I ken it's only the length of the school day. I must be gettin soft in my old age.

She smiles at me, a wee arch kind of smile. 'I ken what you were doin last night, Mammy,' she says.

'Oh you do, do you?' What's comin here, I'm thinkin.

'Aye, because I asked Cameron at break time, and he said puttin a glass to the floor lets you hear what the folk downstairs are sayin. That's what you were doin, wasn't it Mammy? Listenin to what those two wee whores were up to?'

'Don't use bad words, Candice,' I say, buyin myself time. 'What's Cameron's second name again?'

'It's Cameron Wishart,' she says. 'You ken him, Mammy. He lives in Rob Roy. I can see him wavin at me through the window sometimes.'

'Is that right?' I never thought to sweep the bairn's classmates for criminal connections. If he kens I've been listenin in on the lassies downstairs, who else does now?

'You shouldn't tell other people our business, Candice. Anyway, I wasn't listenin in on downstairs. I was checkin the thickness of the carpet. That's how you do it, with a glass.'

She doesn't seem that bothered either way, and goes skippin off, happy as Larry.

Just when we get to our block, my heart sinks. Oddjob is comin out of our stairwell. When he sees me, he heads over. Pad, pad, pad, just like some big cat.

'Well, hello there, Mrs. Clamp,' he says, blithe as you like. 'Listen, I'm glad I bumped into you. I was wantin to apologise in case you were disturbed last Friday. The lassies downstairs from you had an unwelcome guest, and I had to go over and deal with him. I hope it didn't wake you up.' I give Candice a look, just hopin against hope she keeps her mouth shut. 'Never heard a thing, Mr. Taylor,' I tell him.

He beams at me. 'That's great. There's few enough decent people in this estate without youse bein driven away. I know those lassies downstairs aren't exactly angels so, if they ever give you any hassle, just let me know. By the way, if it's all right, I'd like to drop off some more trousers later on.'

Candice is still sayin nothin, thank goodness. 'Aye, that would be fine. I'm away then, see you later.'

He doesn't come round till two days later. That night though, I dream about the lion that scared my wee brother, Brian, at Edinburgh Zoo that time. In the dream, it's prowlin about the flat, and I can't get through to see if Candice's door is shut or not.

CHAPTER 13
BREAKFAST AT TIFFANY'S

'What the fuck did you think you were doing, going down after these lassies yourself? I think I must've under-rated you before, Mr. English, because it takes a very special kind of arsehole that puts himself deep in Auchendrossan in the middle of the night with no trousers or shoes.'

I have to admit, Martin has a point, but I'm still too busy watching the receding shape of the guy who came after me. There's a part of me that thinks he's going to come after us all the same, outrunning Martin's Astra, even though we've got the pedal to the metal and the blues and twos on, hammering on through a red light like a bat out of hell.

I decide this is going to be a competitive type negotiation. 'Maybe I thought the cops were going to be fuck all use, to be honest, Detective Sergeant. And do you mind me asking how you knew to come down and look for me in whatever that shithole was called?'

We've reached the relative civilisation of Davidson's Mains by now, and Martin takes the foot off the gas a bit as he gives me a sidelong glance. 'How do you think? Your brother, Tom, phoned me and told me you were going down to the club with this crazy scheme of finding them yourself. After your live sex show with them on the dance floor, it didn't take Hercule fucking Poirot to get a hold of one of my regulars, who told me you had left with working girls he half knew from Auchendrossan. That was all I had to go on, mind. I was just circling the estate, and I was just about to give up when I saw you flashing your boxer shorts at Kevin Taylor.'

Kevin Taylor. What a dull name for that big scary bastard. He'd reminded me most of Oddjob, that Bond villain from one of the early films, you know, the one where he's got a bowler hat with razor blades in it? 'So you know him?'

At the lights that turn us onto Queensferry Road, Martin stops at the red this time and turns to look at me.

'Oh yes. Taylor is well known to us. And from the description

I extracted out of Smithy, one of the girls is Debi Murray. Didn't recognise the other girl from the description but she's probably a more recent recruit.'

'You know them as well?' Martin's switched the lights and siren off now; in comparison to the speed we left Auchendrossan, he's positively dawdling along at fifty. At the Blackhall junction, the lights go green and we take a left towards Stockbridge. Looks like he's taking me home.

'Let's just say I know the network they're a part of,' Martin says. 'The question is, what do they have against either you or Jimmy Ahmed?'

I say nothing for a bit, trying to think this through. I guess so far my theories about why these two girls might have wanted to drug me and poor Jimmy up had been a bit fuzzy. I'd been less concerned about the why, and more about finding out who. I mean, there were a few people about that thought I was a cunt, but not anybody who I thought would go the length of hiring a couple of gangsters' molls to dose me up with Rohypnol and then do whatever.

Besides, there was the question of the *whatever*. They must have pretty much had me at their mercy. I suppose I'd always thought that Jimmy had been the intended target but that when he took the allergic reaction to the drug, they panicked and left him, albeit in the bath with his toe up the tap.

'None of this makes sense to me,' I say aloud, and Martin nods.

'You're no the only one, son,' he says. We're pulling into my street. Nowhere to park as usual, so Martin reverses back and shoves the cop car up on double yellows on the corner.

'I'll come in with you, and you can get as much stuff as you can carry down to your car the now,' he says. 'Then you can stick it in your car. You're probably still over the limit, so I want you just to take your car somewhere close by and park it: you can pick it up later. I'll follow you, and then we can go somewhere for a while until you're sober enough to drive.'

I've never felt more sober in my life. I feel a chill go down my spine. 'You mean, it's not safe for me to stay in the flat any more?'

Martin's already getting out of the car. 'It's maybe no even safe for us to go and get your stuff just now,' he says. 'After all, they know where you live. Depends how quickly they can get their guys mobilised. I don't think Taylor drives.'

As I get out, he looks over at me. 'By the way, what's that you're carrying?'

I look down. I'm still carrying the cardboard sign Karen Clamp dangled outside the window to tip me off. It's got wet by now, and I've scrunched it up so tight it's like a papier mache sausage.

'Oh this?' I say. 'Nothing – I just used it to get over the window frame of the flat, and avoid slicing my bollocks off.'

Martin seems satisfied with this, and I get the chance to dump it in a bin outside the flat, stuffing it well in with the polystyrene curry boxes.

Up the stairs, all is quiet, apart from my bowels. 'Did you leave it on the Yale?' Martin says.

I realise he's one step ahead of me, again. My keys will be in my trouser pocket, back at Debi and Elena's. I nod to him.

'That's good. It means I don't have to kick the door down.' He brings out a piece of wire and has the lock picked in about thirty seconds. Scary when you think even the cops can do that.

I've got an old holdall and I start throwing clothes into it, suddenly realising what a bloody mess I'm in. My flat keys and my wallet with all my cards in them have been left behind me in my trousers. Fortunately, I took my iPhone through to the bedroom with me – I think I had some vague idea I might be taking photographs. I sling on a pair of trousers and shoes and dig out what cash I have at my bedside. Until the banks open, that's all I've got in the world.

Then I stick a few more clothes into the holdall and say to Martin, 'Let's go.' Just at the last moment, I remember I have a spare set of flat keys as well as spare car keys and go and fetch them.

'Sure there's nothing else you want to take? We can get a joiner out first thing, but the guy those three work for will have had someone in to have a good look round by then.'

I stop for a minute, realising how little there is in Bruce Reid's flat that's really of any value to me. At least, that's worth risking these gangsters turning up before we leave. 'No,' I tell him. 'They're welcome to the porno mags.'

There's just the tiniest hint of a smile on Martin's booze-cured features when we leave, shutting the door and double locking it.

A futile gesture, I know, but we might as well make the bastards work.

***

I park the car in India Street, near the junction with Jamaica Street. On a single yellow, but even Edinburgh's traffic wardens don't crawl out from under their stones at four in the morning. I get back into Martin's car and he shoots off up the cobbles, along up Heriot Row, to Queen Street and then back down Broughton Street, then Leith Walk.

'We're not going to Fettes, then?' I say.

He gives me a sidelong look which I can't read. 'No. I thought we might need an unofficial chat. I'm open to suggestions, but the only all night café I know is down by the docks.'

And so it is. It must open early for the dockers or something: them and the working girls. There's a couple of them at the nearest table when we walk in, looking like they would castrate a man right now just for asking if they wanted a cup of tea. Must have been a hard night. Most of the punters are probably cunts, come to think of it.

The sound of the fry ups getting made is deafening: the atmosphere is steamy, a kind of greasy steam which takes in the bacon fat as well as the constantly boiling urn of water.

The café's called Tiffany's. I sit down at a table away from the other punters while Martin goes to get us teas, and scan the menu. On the bottom of the back page, it says, "PROP: Tiffany McSween". I look up, and decide the woman serving Martin is probably the right vintage: in other words, her parents had the bright idea after seeing the film. They probably conceived her half way through, come to think of it, with Dad thinking of Holly Golightly at the *moment critique.*

Sadly, any resemblance to Audrey Hepburn, alive or dead, is hard to see. If Darwin was wrong and somebody wanted to show we were evolved from bulldogs instead of apes, Tiffany is your actual missing link.

I watch the other punters clock Martin as he walks back with the mugs of tea. He's in plain clothes, but it just doesn't matter. There's something about him that has COP written all over him.

Apart from the two working girls at the table nearest the door, most of the other punters are guys that work on the docks. Big, solid looking bastards, some of them obviously Eastern European, others not.

Martin sits down and pushes one of the teas over to me. 'Fancy something to eat? Fry up? A good cure for a hangover.'

'You know, I might just do that,' I say, although, in reality, I don't feel that hung over. I feel slightly spaced, and incredibly awake for the time of the morning that it is, like all my senses are in overdrive. Very aware of everything that's going on around us.

'So,' I say. 'What happens now? Are you going to pull the two girls in for questioning?'

Martin sips his tea, staring at me. 'We could do that. But there's maybe bigger fish to fry here.'

'You mean the Oddjob guy?' The corners of Martin's mouth twitch ever so slightly again. 'You mean Taylor? Aye, well. Every monkey's got an organ grinder.'

I nod, sagely. I had Martin pegged as having a poster of the guy that plays Rebus on his bedroom wall, but actually, when you get to know him, it's more like early Clint Eastwood. Half expect him to say, *You gotta ask yourself that question*, or, *Do you feel lucky, punk?* Although apparently Dirty Harry never actually says that.

One of a group of guys down nearer the counter looks round at us, briefly, then goes back to his conversation with the others.

'And you know who the organ grinder is?'

'Oh aye,' Martin says. 'Derek Boyes is well known to us. He's no much to look at but he's managed to work his way up in the organisation. Quite a player now, our Deek is.'

'What organisation?' What the fuck is he talking about, organisation?

Martin sips his black tea with four sugars, looking at me over the rim of the mug all the time like I'm some kid who needs to be told there's no Santa Claus.

'Here's the thing, Mr. English. Commercial property is no the only big business going on in Edinburgh. It used to be mainly drugs this lot were into, but human trafficking is much more profitable for them. Smuggle ten Romanians in and you've got what you might call a captive workforce, either to work in one of your saunas if they're good looking enough, or sell onto one of the gang masters for any number of shit jobs that the locals can't be arsed getting out of their beds to do. These guys are big time now, Mr. English, at least in Edinburgh terms. They have connections everywhere.'

Just at that moment, the docker who's looked round at us twice now gets up from the table, avoids looking at us, and goes outside, taking a mobile phone out of his pocket. I decide it's time to offer something up in this negotiation.

'Do these connections everywhere include the police, then?'

Martin suddenly sits very still, his eyes narrowing slightly. There's a long pause, but I'm used to holding out in a silence. Eventually, he says, 'Maybe. What makes you say that?'

The guy who was on the mobile outside has come back in now. Something prompts Martin to look round at him: again, the guy avoids eye contact.

'Do you know him?'

'Probably,' Martin says and looks at me. 'Have you finished your tea?' I nod and we get up to go, feeling several pairs of eyes watch us leave.

When I was at university, there was a friend of a friend had a paranoid episode. Everyone said it was because he smoked too much blow, but then we all did. He was convinced that an ex-girlfriend was following him around. His mate told me they were on a bus once, and the guy just got up and got off at a stop somewhere completely random and started running. When my mate caught up with him, he was in a shop getting the shopkeeper to phone the cops. He had been convinced he had seen the ex-girlfriend sitting two rows back in the same bus. My mate hadn't, of course, but there was no convincing him.

Anyway, I'm starting to know how the poor bastard felt as we climb into Martin's car and set off in the cold light of dawn.

As we reach Junction Street and stop at the lights, Martin says, 'You haven't answered my question.'

I take a deep breath. 'Say, hypothetically, a previous occupant of my flat had left a bag of a certain substance – just a small bag, mind, for personal use only – under the floorboards.' Might as well blame Bruce Reid for it for now. 'And say, after your scene of crime people did the sweep, that bag of coke had disappeared. You would know all about it, right?'

The lights change and Martin guns the accelerator. 'Of course.'

'Do you?'

'No.' There's another long silence as we head up Leith Walk. Around us, Edinburgh is starting to wake up in a leisurely, kind of Saturday morning way: we overtake an early morning bus; then two taxis at Elm Row, dawdling along. At the top of Leith Walk, still saying nothing, Martin hangs a right onto Queen Street to take us into the New Town. Eventually, he says, 'Do you ken your Greek mythology, Mr English?'

'Not really.' What's coming here?

'Well, you might have heard of the Hydra, the many headed monster. Every time you cut one of its heads off, another one grows back. That's what organised crime is always compared to. Personally, I prefer to think of it as a squid – ken, the tentacles?'

As he's saying this, he's glanced once, then twice in the rear view mirror. 'I guess I see what you mean. And where do you think this one has got its tentacles?'

Another glance in the rear view. The cunt is making me nervous again. I look behind but all I can see is a taxi, one set of lights back.

'You could well be right that this organisation has an insider in Fettes HQ. I've been thinking that for some time now, to be completely honest with you. But I also think you should be thinking about somewhere closer to home.' This throws me completely. 'What, you mean Bruce Reid? Is that why he had to disappear down south?'

Martin hangs a right again, down Howe Street.

'Well, what do you think?' he says.

I think of Tony Hand, saying 'Fuck, they – ' when he heard about Jimmy Ahmed. Al + Bradley cosying up to the two girls as if they'd first met them at fucking Mary Erskine's.

And I say exactly nothing.

Martin pulls in just above Jamaica Street, the connecting street that will take me along to my car. The taxi that was behind us rattles past and then pulls in, about fifty yards further down. It sits there, its engine running.

Martin turns to look at me. 'Look. I can understand exactly

how you're feeling right now. I've just confirmed to you what you were beginning to find out for yourself: that the entire Edinburgh branch of the legal firm you work for is in cahoots with a gang of organised criminals and that had something to do with why you got dosed up with Rohypnol and a guy ended up dead in your bath.'

I nod, slightly.

'Okay,' he says. 'You've no particular reason to trust me, Mr. English. If I tell you I had nothing to do with your bag of drugs going missing, and that I'm as keen as you are to bring these bastards to book, I understand how you can't take that at face value.' He fumbles in his jacket pocket and brings out a slightly battered business card and a pen, which he uses to write a number on the card. As he hands it over to me, we both glance down at the taxi, which is still idling fifty yards further down the street.

'On that basis, I don't want you telling me where you're going to stay for now. I'll have to report the fact that I picked you up in Auchendrossan but I'll say that you legged it without telling me where you'd be. When you're ready to talk to me, that's my home number. Call me on that.'

I nod again. 'Okay.'

'Now, get out of the car, get to your own, and disappear for the rest of the weekend. I'll deal with our friend the taxi driver.'

The minute I'm out the door of the car, Martin takes off in a squeal of tyres on the cobbles, heading for the taxi. Just before I disappear down the lane, I look again and he's dumped his car right across the front of the taxi then sprinted round and wrenched its door open before the guy can reverse back towards me. That's enough for me. I break into a run that would make Usain fucking Bolt get a bit of a shift on and reach India Street in a new personal best. Me and the Lexus get the fuck out of Edinburgh, destination Livingston.

First stop, Yvonne's, since Gary is still away on the rigs.

I do text Tom first to tell him I'm okay, though. I'm not a complete and utter cunt.

CHAPTER 14
EVERYBODY WANTS TO RULE THE WORLD

Monday morning. By the time Mum has stopped faffing about with my breakfast and the train in has been delayed, I'm running a bit behind schedule when I get into the office. Funnily enough, I do notice that the tinpot Hitler guy isn't on the reception desk this morning as I go past: nobody there at all, in fact. I'm just wondering what we pay these cunts for when I'm met at the lifts by Sandra, the Rottweiler's secretary.

Sandra is the yin to Big Doggy's yang: she's about six foot tall but wears high heeled boots that make her about six five, blonde, and even her curves have curves. I suppose intimidating can be attractive in the right woman.

She gives a strange sort of smile when she sees me emerging from the lift. 'Wallace would like a quick chat with you, Simon,' she says and turns on her heel. I follow her through to the other half of the open plan, trying not to watch the serene movement of her arse too obviously. Particularly as it feels like every pair of eyes in the secretarial unit is on me. Or maybe that's just my paranoia kicking in again.

Sandra shows me in, but I'm surprised to find the Rottweiler has company already. Now I see why the reception desk downstairs was empty: Mussolini on a budget is sitting in one of the Rottweiler's chairs, arms crossed, legs stretched out, beady little eyes glittering as they watch me plant myself down in the other one. Just to complete the look, I notice for the first time he actually has a little toothbrush moustache.

Then I turn and look at the Rottweiler and see he's got the barely concealed fury face, rather than the mild disgust one, this morning.

'This is Bobby,' the Rottweiler says. 'He tells me you didn't follow correct procedure for getting a cab the other day.'

I look from him to my new friend Bobby, who's got a triumphant look in his eye. I'm still waiting for the punchline from Gnasher, preferably when he comes across the desk and tears Bobby bodily limb from limb for disturbing him. There's a nasty suspicion growing in my mind, however, that that's not going to happen.

'Oh,' I say.

'Yes,' says Bobby. 'You maybe weren't aware, Mr. English, but it's very important that we know when one of the tenant's staff has called a cab, and which firm they've used. As you're a lawyer, I'll expect you know that we can't just use any cab and we have to follow the proper procurement procedures. There's also the health and safety angle to consider.'

'Indeed,' I hear the Rottweiler saying.

Bobby's nodding.

'I just got Gemma to call a cab,' I said. 'Is there a problem with that?'

'All cabs have to be ordered through myself or one of the other building facilities personnel, Mr. English,' Bobby tells me.

I look at the Rottweiler. His face is contorted with rage as he pushes some grubby A5 forms across the desk at me. 'Bobby very helpfully brought these up for you,' the Rottweiler says. 'They're the form you have to fill in when you want to call a cab. Just make sure you do it in future, Simon.' I look back from him to Bobby, mainly because it's uncomfortable to look the Rottweiler in the eye at the moment. 'Sure,' I say. 'I didn't know.'

Bobby's not finished though. 'One other thing, Mr. English. I think your firm will have issued you with an ID badge. Can you make sure, please, that you wear it at all times? It took quite a bit of detective work for me to find out who you were so that I could speak to Mr. Brodie here and make him aware of the incident.'

I remember vaguely now that they did drag me into a spare corner of the office when I started here, take my picture and then issue me with some horrible little piece of plastic which I was meant to wear round my neck. Like that was going to happen. Well, it looks like it is going to have to happen.

'Oh yes, of course,' I say, thinking, not that I'd ever seen the Rottweiler wear his. Probably chewed it into pieces years ago.

As if he's reading my mind, Bobby says, 'Of course, Mr. Brodie doesn't need one. He's well known to us now,' and looks over at the Rottweiler as if the two of them used to bunk down together at Loretto. I sneak a look at the Rottweiler. If a volcano on the point of erupting could manage a wan smile, it would look like him right now.

'Well, thanks for bringing this to our attention, Bobby,' he manages to croak. Bobby nods and gets up to go. 'No problem,' he says. 'I'm sure it won't happen again.'

'Could you just see that you shut the door behind you on your way out, please, Bobby?' The Rottweiler's voice has a strange, strangled quality to it now. Bobby nods, pulls the door shut behind him and leaves me to my fate.

There's a long pause during which the Rottweiler doesn't say anything at all. I'm not even sure if he's capable of speech. Eventually, I say, as breezily as I can manage, 'Janitors, eh? The people who rule the world.'

Eventually, the Rottweiler hisses at me, 'Have you any idea how much time I've had wasted this morning by that man because of your stupidity? Yes, they do rule the world. They're impossible to replace and cost us a ridiculous amount of money through landlord's service charges. Don't ever, ever, make me do that again.'

He looks like he's about to launch into something bigger, a real big budget number, but then he just looks down at the pile of papers in front of him and says, 'Now get out. I'm busy and you're late for your prayer meeting.'

Ah, yes, the prayer meeting. Apparently, in the olden days, Benzini, Lambe and Lockhart really did have a prayer meeting: the senior partners then were a couple of god botherers who insisted the staff come in and join in a quick chorus of Kum Ba Yah or something. Nowadays, of course, it's all business.

I make a sharp exit and go up in the lifts, to the top floor. I'm almost distracted enough by thinking about how to get revenge on Bobby, to stop me thinking about what Martin's said to me.

Of course, he was just confirming what I'd started to suspect myself. There is something very odd about this firm and I think it's connected to what happened to Jimmy Ahmed. But how? And who? All of them?

I'm actually just about on time for morning prayers. I pour myself a coffee and take a seat halfway down the table, next to my team, Al + Bradley.

As the associate replacing Bruce Reid, I'm now head of one of the two teams that works mainly to Tony Hand. The other team is headed up by Leonora. She's there, across the table from me, chatting to Danielle, her senior assistant. Tony Hand's at the head of the table, stuffing coffee and shortbread into his huge melon shaped head.

'Who are we missing? Ah yes, Rhona,' he says, above the general buzz of conversation. Just at that moment, the door opens and Rhona bursts in, looking flustered.

Al leans over to me and says in a low voice, 'We call her the Boomtown Rat. Doesn't like Mondays.'

I nod, thinking all the time, so who here is in on what happened to me and poor Jimmy?

Now they're all here, and after my conversation with Martin, I can't help looking round at them all as if we're in some sort of play by Agatha Christie and wondering who's involved. I mean, Martin was right. There's something about the firm that just isn't right, the more I think of it. How they can be connected with the two schemies, Oddjob and the other character, the kingpin gang boss guy that Martin mentioned, is beyond me at the moment. Although I have my theories.

I take a sip of the coffee. Pretty rancid stuff they serve up in here: typical Jocks, too mean to buy the good stuff. So, I'm thinking: runners and riders. There's Tony Hand, who said, 'Fuck, they –' when I told him what happened to Jimmy Ahmed. He's got to be involved. The Rottweiler's not coming to morning prayers today: some major part of the universe needs its property deal restructured. I add him to the list of probable suspects on the basis that he's a complete and utter bastard and I can't see Tony Hand getting anything past him that he doesn't know about.

Below partner level in commercial property though, things get a bit more hazy. It occurs to me that the guy I exchanged jobs – and flats – with, Bruce Reid, can't be left out. Why did they choose him to go down to London? Did he not fit into their plans, or what?

Then there's my two goons, Al + Bradley. It certainly feels to me like they've been detailed to keep an eye on me: all these chummy games of squash, pints and trips to the lap dancing bar. Given that I'm their boss, don't have an old school tie or a first fifteen rugby shirt for that matter, I wouldn't normally be a prime candidate as New Best Pal. These cunts usually hang together in herds of their own kind.

Then, looking across the table, there's the lovely ladies. Rhona, the Boomtown Rat, just arrived, looking especially lovely as she's flustered: masses of dark brown hair, red designer glasses and white blouse that's struggling to hold the rest of her in. Then Danielle, all straight brown hair and sensible shoes, looking like butter wouldn't melt in her mouth. Not to mention Leonora, my fellow associate, who catches my eye and winks at me. Is she involved in some way with these gangsters?

It all seems unlikely yet, at the same time, I can't help feeling that I'm the only one in the room that isn't part of whatever's going on here.

A comment the Velociraptor, my boss down at the London headquarters made, just before I got posted up here, comes back to me. 'I don't know how these Jocks do it, Simon. Their fee income in the commercial property department is incredible, given its size. I wish we could sting our clients for those kind of rates.'

Money laundering? Maybe.

Tony Hand speaks. 'Okay, now we're all here, let's do a quick round of the table. Rhona?'

This is what has replaced praying, if they ever did really pray in the old days. A quick update so the partners – when Old Rottie's not out being a Big Swinging Dick somewhere, he sits brooding in a corner and eating shortbread – can hear how their wage slaves are getting on in making them richer. We have the same thing down in London but at least the Velociraptor has the decency not to call it morning prayers. I guess that's some kind of Jock Presbyterian joke about God and Mammon.

'Still just finishing off the leisure trust transfer for both the Councils. Then I've got the rent restructure for the Milton Place retail park coming on stream,' she says, hesitantly. Rhona's the most junior of the assistants and she's still being given the baby stuff to play with. The retail park deal is relatively complex but we act for the landlord and can call the shots. The leisure trust transfers for the two Councils are like most things when you act for a local authority: bit of a dripping roast, really, and you can take almost as long as you like.

I try not to drift off into a fantasy about the buttons on Rhona's blouse coming firing out in all directions as Danielle starts speaking.

'I got the last of the Redgauntlet portfolio rent reviews tied off on Friday,' she says, rolling her eyes. This is obviously a big thing for her. 'The Rob Roy transaction's going okay, and we should be able to close it by 15th April.'

'You will,' Tony says, quietly. 'Leonora?'

Leonora looks across at me again as she answers. 'Well, thanks to Simon taking all that extra stuff on for me, I'm able to concentrate on the Talisman transaction full-time now. There's a bit of deal restructuring needed to maximise the yield but...' To be honest, I lose the thread of what she's going on about. The buttons on Rhona's blouse, Danielle's cool as a cucumber discussion of her property transactions and Leonora's look across the table at me have all contributed to waking the python up. Three different feminine perfumes are wafting round the room and he just can't keep his head down. I barely notice that Leonora has stopped speaking, and it's Al's turn.

'Like Rhona, I've got the rent reviews up-to-date, Tony,' he says. 'There's a couple of Redgauntlet transactions as you know: the main one, the shopping centre in Hamilton, I'm just waiting for client's instructions on a rent free period and then we can do the turnover to the funders.'

'I'll get them for you,' Tony says. 'Brad?'

Bradley looks up with a frown on his broad features, thick lips pursed as if he's trying to remember what he's doing here. 'The City Council deal's still causing me some problems, to be honest, Tony,' he says. 'They're being difficult buggers about the guarantees still – '

'I can help with that,' I say quickly before Tony can come in. 'In fact, there might be one or two things we can do to give them comfort.' 'Give them comfort' is a great term in commercial property. It means pulling the wool over your opponent's eyes and stopping them lying awake at night worrying about stuff they really should worry about.

Tony looks at me, a little suspiciously, I feel.

'Well, Brad's in your team, of course,' he says. 'What about your own transactions?'

What about them indeed? As they've gone round the table, I've noted that most of the others have two or three big transactions on the go. That's normal for com.prop.laywers. You're talking about deals that involve documents of hundreds of pages sometimes, all of which have to be gone over with a fine tooth comb. There might be lots of other fiddly little things to be doing as well but, in the main, you have a case load of two or three.

They've given me five and all of them biggies.

'I'm managing them okay,' I say, 'Although I think Leonora's still to hand one more over to me. I'll be looking to spread some of the joy around the team a bit.'

Leonora smiles at me again, catching my eye in a way that I find intriguing. So does the python. Tony looks dubious and says, 'Okay, but bear in mind Brad's been working on the Ivanhoe deal with the Council from the start so he should lead it, really.' He shoots a look at Brad, who's still looking like the whole thing's far too clever for him. One too many against the head in the scrum, methinks.

'I'm sure we can work something out,' I say, as smoothly as I can. Getting my hands on the City Council deal they so obviously don't want me involved in is going to be a long negotiation.

Funny how most of our clients have the names of Walter Scott novels, I'm thinking as the morning prayer meeting comes to an end. None of mine, mind you, or Rhona's.

Not that I've read any of them, but I saw a TV adaptation of Ivanhoe once. It was rubbish.

***

Sylvia's waiting for me when I get back to my desk. It may be my imagination, but I don't think I've ever seen her in that suit before: she's taken the jacket off and hung it over the back of my chair while she sits on my desk. She's wearing pixie boots today and there is something pixie-ish about her: if pixies had masses of curly chestnut hair and a snub nose, I mean.

I also can't help but noticing the bottom button of the blouse is undone today, revealing the jewel in the navel and the beginnings of a Buddha belly developing nicely.

She catches me looking and smiles. 'Hi. I was just up to collect some files and thought I'd see how you were doing. I thought maybe we should grab a coffee some time and just close off the last bits and pieces of your file, now the police have seen sense.'

This is the first of me hearing that the cops have, officially, ruled me out of any wrongdoing with poor old Jimmy but I'm very aware of Al + Bradley coming up close behind me. 'Sure,' I say, as casually as possible, making sure I'm looking her in the eye and not the tummy. Don't want the python drawing extra blood away from my brain right at this moment. 'Thursday after work, say six?' Don't want to seem too keen.

We agree on a Caffè Nero instead of Starbucks, she smiles and says hello to the boys and then is gone, leaving me with the two monkeys grinning like hyenas.

'Woah, nice work Skip,' says Al, making growling noises. Brad the Impaler is still watching Sylvia's arse as she heads off down the open plan.

'Definitely doable,' he says, in that Merchiston Castle accent.

'Okay, boys, steady yourselves,' I tell them. 'She's got a boyfriend, apart from anything else.'

Bradley turns to me, eyebrow raised. 'From what we hear, that's not a major obstacle for a man of your abilities,' he says.

It's the first time either of them have said that they've heard anything about me at all. Interesting. I smile back at him and Al.

'It's true, I have many skills, and one of them is delegating. I'd like to talk to you both about workload.'

Here begins another negotiation. I plan to give these two clowns as much of the shit work that Tony has given me as he'll let me. And young Bradley definitely needs tucked under my wing on the Edinburgh deal.

Mind you, one of my other skills is being able to close a deal faster than anyone else in the firm. Half the transactions I mentioned at the prayer meeting are just about completed already, thanks to a fuck load of work last week. Not that I felt Tony needed to know that yet.

Just at that moment, Leonora walks past, giving me another wink over the top of Bradley's head.

Typical. You wait all week for a shag and then see two of them approaching at once.

***

'Oh, great shot, Si.'

The cunt is patronising me now, I know it. But I finally manage to scrape one of his impossible serves off the wall, mostly with the frame of the racquet, and jammily sclaff it into the far corner as a drop shot. First point in three games.

My serve, though, at long last. I hit one of my better ones, but Al just stretches out a long, ginger haired arm and pats it back without any trouble. It's not a great return, though, and I slam away a winner which even he can't reach. Then I realise he's letting me win the point. Fine by me.

Thirty years ago, lawyers like us would have knocked off at the back of three on a Friday and gone for eighteen holes at Braidhills, followed by six pints in the clubhouse and a slightly woozy drive home to the wife. Now, instead, you get to stay in the office every night till seven, followed by an hour of running ragged around a little glass box, a quick shower and then off to a lap-dancing bar. Come to think of it, I suppose some things have improved.

I serve in the backhand court. Al hits one down the side wall, but it's not quite far enough for it to drop annoyingly into the corner and die on me, so I just get to it and flick a half decent shot high to his backhand. He hits another gettable return and I slam it away again. He's definitely letting me win a few points and I'm definitely going to let him do it.

As I pick up the ball to serve again, I make the mistake of glancing at Bradley, who's sitting on the bench outside the court, legs akimbo. I do wish he wouldn't do that: the prospect of seeing his Donkey Kong peeking out of the leg of his shorts is not a pleasant one.

'Two love?' I ask the ginger one.

'Two one, actually,' he says. Just testing, cunt. My next serve is a screamer, that hugs the side wall and then drops like a stone into the bottom corner. Al still manages to play it though, and his return seems to hit about five surfaces before hitting the front wall and dribbling to a stop before I can get to it. When Al serves next, it's much easier than his usual, and the rally goes on for about ten minutes before finally I mistime a drop shot into the bottom plate and he takes the point.

And so on, for the rest of the game: Al just patting the ball up to keep the rally going, with the occasional killer shot just to keep himself in front. By the time he's finished with me, I'm like a slab of basted pork at gas mark six and I have to let Bradley go next against him just so that I can get my breath back.

Once I have though, and it's my turn again, Bradley's just as totally my squash bitch as I am Al's. He may be dynamite in the Heriot's front row and have a cock like a tree trunk, but Bradley's not exactly a gazelle when it comes to moving about the little glass box. I grind him into the dust for the first couple of games and then, for my own purposes, have to let him win.

'Good work, Si,' he grunts at me as we come off the court and head for the showers. 'Pity you misread my quadruple bluff at the end there.' If rugby's a game for hooligans played by gentlemen and football's the other way round, squash is a game for arseholes played by cunts.

I don't know when these bastards decided they could call me Si, by the way. I suppose it could have been English Bastard; probably will be, if we get any matier.

Still, keep your friends close and play squash with your enemies, as the old mafia saying goes.

CHAPTER 15
HOT DATE

I'm on my knees with the carpet up in the bedroom when Oddjob breenges in the door of the flat.

'Hello, Mrs. Clamp, are you there?' Then he spies me down the hall, just as I'm trying to get to my feet. That's no that easy for me these days. I've seen tankers in the Forth turn faster.

'Are youse having trouble with your carpet?' He's standin there in the doorway, smilin as always. His eyes almost disappear when he smiles, I notice. No a good look for anyone.

'It's – ' I'm usually better than this at thinkin on my feet, but him standin there, pair of trousers on his arm, half schemie enforcer, half great ape, is makin my brain freeze up.

'Is it a squeaky floorboard? These floorboards are rubbish, by the way, but what do you expect of Council flats, eh?' he says, taking a step forward into the bedroom. Quite at home, now, so he is.

'Ehm, aye, that's right,' I say, lookin down at the floorboard I've got half up. Thank goodness the listenin device is still in its padded envelope on the bed.

He puts the trousers down on the bed beside it, and kneels down beside me. 'Oh aye, I can see your problem. Couple of loose screws there.' Is he tryin to be funny?

Then he takes the screwdriver from me and screws the floorboard I've taken ten minutes to nearly get up back down, tight, his big paw givin the screwdriver about ten extra turns past where I'll be able to loosen it again. Then he stands up, still grinnin from ear to ear.

'There you go, Mrs. Clamp.'

I open my mouth to say something, but he raises a hand. 'No problem at all. Don't mention it. All part of the service.'

What is the big muppet on about? Does he think he's my handyman now as well as trouser alteration customer and potential Best Pal? My initial panic at him marchin in and findin out what I was up to is gone now.

'Aye, thanks. Are these the trousers you need altered?' I say, pickin them up off the bed. I start off out of the bedroom but he's lookin at the padded envelope on the bed, readin the label.

'Personal Devices R Us? Is that somethin electrical you're needin installed in here?'

This time, my brain is workin overtime. I do my best to look coy. 'Er, well, it's no a device you install as such, actually. It's a bit embarrassin. For personal use, ken?'

It takes a few second for the penny to drop; the frown on his big moon face takes a second more to unravel into a grin, although he does have the decency to blush.

'Ah, I see. Sorry. Didn't mean to pry. They say these things are really advanced, these days.' And with that, he clatters off down the hall to the livin room. I breathe a sigh of relief and follow him with the trousers.

He stops at the living room doorway. 'Any chance you'd be able to do them...'

I check my watch. 'Sorry, Kevin. It's nearly time for me to pick up the bairn from school.' That is true, although I'm early for her the now. I hang the trousers over the back of the couch, and go to get my coat on; although it's the start of April, it's still cold enough.

He nods, as if pickin up kids from school is all part of his daily routine too. 'Aye, aye, of course.' Then he brightens up again. 'Actually, I was heading up that way myself, to the shop. I'll walk you up the road if you like? First though, do you mind if I wash my hands?'

Do I have a choice? I lock up after us and we head up Auchendrossan Drive, just one woman and her psycho out on a stroll.

Mind, it does have some advantages. The two wee neds who gave me grief about my size slide past on the other side of the street, see Oddjob, and just keep on goin. Nary a word. Oddjob, meantime, wants to tell me all about his job.

'Deek calls me his security consultant, but, to be honest, the job is more complicated than that, like,' he says. 'Some of Deek's tenants need a bit of persuasion that what they're doing is no acceptable, right enough, but it's also about helping them with the authorities. Sometimes I feel more like a Social Worker with some of them. I've even picked up a few words of Polish.'

'Oh aye? Well, here's the gate.' It's about ten minutes before the bell, so I'm just goin to have to stand there like a lemon. Oddjob gets the hint, and heads on up to the shop. There's a couple of other mums pitch up after a minute or two, both of them drawin on their fags like it's their last request afore a shootin. One of them I half ken, Imelda. She's got the pit bull puppy with her the day. She nods at me and talks to the other lassie.

Sure enough, the bell still hasn't gone by the time Oddjob comes back from the shop, a bag of whatever it is he lives on in his paw.

'I meant to apologise, by the way,' he says. 'I mean, I didn't mean to interrupt you when I came in. It was just the door was open and it certainly goes no further about your, ehm, your personal device. It must be hard being a decent single woman in a place like this. So many nutters around Auchendrossan.' He grins again. 'I should know, I get to evict most of them.'

'Aye, that's right. Anyway, Kevin, I'm off up town after I pick up Candice, so I'll get the trousers to you tomorrow probably.' After waitin impatiently for nine minutes, I'm now prayin the bell won't go until I've got rid of him. Don't want him anywhere near the bairn.

'Oh, that right? Hot date, is it?' He frowns. 'I could look after Candice for you if you like?'

'No, that's fine. Jessie's lined up to do it.'

He's noddin. 'Oh, aye, right enough. Well, I'll see you later then.' He's only about a hundred yards down the road when the bell goes, but, fortunately by then, he's spotted someone he needs to enforce, a wee skinny gadgie, who dodges off down the path between Rob Roy and Redgauntlet as soon as he sees him. Oddjob just picks up his pace a little, pad, pad, pad, as if he's in no great hurry to catch him. No doubt he kens where the gadgie lives.

By the time Candice appears, I'm sweatin like a sealion on a summer's day, despite the cold air.

'Are you no done up for your hot date yet, mammy?' she says. She takes my hand and we start off back towards the flats. 'Jessie says she's got a ribbon you can wear in your hair if you like.'

Jessie and her ribbons. Why is it everyone thinks I'm goin up town to meet someone on a hot date?

Well, I suppose it's as good a cover story as anythin else. Particularly now Oddjob thinks I order vibrators by mail order.

What was it my gran used to say? What a tangled web we weave.

***

Of course, Jessie's no better. By the time I've got away from her and her suggestions on how to improve my hair and what shade of lippy I should have on, there's barely time to have a shower back at my flat. I do though. I don't want Simon English thinkin I can't manage personal hygiene, whatever else he thinks of me.

He's arranged that we meet in a pub called the Old Bell which is away over on the south side. It means changing buses at Princes Street but I don't suppose that would have occurred to the likes of him. Probably has a personal assistant to drive him everywhere.

Funnily enough, it does feel a bit like a date as the number 31 hauls up Nicholson Street. I've got butterflies in my stomach, except I suspect that's more about whether I'm bein followed than whether me and the big galoot are goin to hit it off.

Mind you, I do find myself wonderin whether the fascinator Jessie gave me makes me look stupid or not. Just as the stop comes up, I decide it does, take it off and stuff it in my handbag.

At least he has the decency to be there before me. He's standin at the bar, pint of lager in hand, wearin old jeans and a kind of salmon coloured shirt that suggests a touch of colour blindness to me. No a hair out of place, of course. He's tall, good lookin in an Italian film star kind of way, kind of like a young Robert de Niro. No my type at all, of course, my type bein generally feckless wee bauchles with someone else's teeth and bald patches.

'Hi Karen,' he says, casual like, as if we've known each other for years. 'Glad you could make it up. Drink?'

You couldn't make him up, I'm thinkin to myself as I say, 'Orange juice, please.' I don't really want an orange juice, because it'll play havoc with me later on, but it's all I can think of.

'Do you fancy a bite to eat?' he says. 'They've got a restaurant upstairs, which might be quieter than here.'

'Aye, that would be fine,' I say, takin the hint. The pub is certainly busy, one of these town centre places that's done up to look like it's old fashioned, all cosy with subdued lightin and all that. I have to admit, it's a million miles away from the places down in Leith my brother insists on draggin us to whenever he surfaces from Saughton.

'Did you find the place okay?' he says, as we go upstairs.

'Oh, aye. I've been here once or twice before, actually.' Don't want him thinkin that I've never crossed the Mason Dixon line at the top of Leith Walk and ventured into the posh bit of town. Actually, I think I maybe have been here before, with Candice's dad, once. He may have been a low down rat, but he did know some braw places to eat and drink.

Of course, that was when I was still drinkin, hence Candice.

We sit at a table in the corner, away from anyone else. Mind you, it's early evenin on a Tuesday night, so it's no too packed. The waitress bustles up and we give our orders.

'I have to thank you for what you did the other night,' he says. 'You probably saved my life.'

'Well, I'd a feelin Oddjob wasn't comin to you for commercial property advice,' I say, and he bursts out laughin. Is he laughin at me?

'I don't know why I'm here,' I mutter, just as the starters appear. I'm havin melon (more havoc with my digestive system later on, but I didn't fancy anythin else) and he's havin somethin fancy with prawns.

'I'm sorry, I'm not laughing at you, Karen,' he says, puttin on a concerned face. 'Is that his name, Oddjob? It describes him perfectly.'

'His real name's Kevin Taylor, although he likes to be called Mr. Bump. Oddjob's kind of my pet name for him,' I tell him, and explain how he comes to me for his alterations.

He's stuffin his face full of prawns, but I can see him noddin when I talk about sewin. 'So, A Stitch In Time is your long-term ambition, then?'

Oh, you can laugh, English boy. 'Ambition? I don't recognise that word. That must be somethin they just teach as a specialist subject at the private schools the likes of you go to.' The melon tastes sour. 'I've got to go. My babysitter's on a tight schedule.'

He takes a minute to answer, shovellin some more prawns in. Then he surprises me by sayin, 'Actually, I went to Livingston High myself. What I'm more interested in, to be honest, is what these overgrown public schoolboys in the firm I work for are up to. And I think you're the only person I can trust to help me, if you're prepared to.'

I was afraid he was goin to say that. I shouldn't have come. All the same, I reach down into my bag and pull out the printouts I did this afternoon.

'Well, for what it's worth, Exhibit A,' I say, handin him the info I've downloaded from Companies House. 'It's a fair bit for you to look through over your prawns but that's the corporate structure showin the links and directorships and so on between Rob Roy Limited, Redgauntlet Developments, Ivanhoe Enterprises and all the rest of them. It took me about an hour to track back through them to find the holding company, although I should have guessed it would have somethin to do with Walter Scott as well.'

He's leafin through the print outs when I hand him Exhibit B.

'Google maps isn't that easy to print out the right bit of, but here's an overview of Auchendrossan Estate. You'll see what the maisonette blocks are called. The one you legged it out of the other night is Ivanhoe; Rob Roy is the next one down; Redgauntlet the one after that.'

When he looks up, his mouth is still open, which is a pity given he's no finished his prawns yet.

'Benefits of a comprehensive school education,' I tell him. Then I walk out on him.

'Karen. Wait,' he says, but once I'm up I'm up.

***

I nearly fucking missed it. Typical of her to do it in some mental way. Quite smart, too, though, in fairness:

> BECAUSE YOU DESERVE IT! Is your
> lack of a degree holding you back from
> career advancement? Are you having

difficulty finding employment in your
field of interest because you don't have
the paper to back it up – even though you
are qualified? If you are looking for a fast
and effective solution, we can help! Call
us right now for your customized
diploma: Inside U.S.A.: 1-718-989-5740
Outside U.S.A.:[09981 805876]. Just leave
your NAME & TEL. PHONE # (with
country-code) on the voicemail and one
of our staff members will get back to you
promptly! A stitch in time saves nine!

It was only when I was about to delete it as yet another piece of spam email that I saw the last line. Then I looked at the "Outside USA" number again. Comes from all these years of scanning hundred page leases, waiting for something unusual to pop out. Most of these junk things don't have a normal mobile number with no international dialling code as the contact.

Sure enough, I texted the number and Karen Clamp was back to me in minutes. On as secure a line as mobile phone signals can ever be, as she said. Mind you, I'm not far behind her in the paranoia stakes right now. Just because you're paranoid doesn't mean they aren't out to get you, as the saying goes.

I'm still thinking about this on Thursday night, when I have my hot date with Sylvia. Talk about torn between two lovers. Or, in my case, one huge mound of schemie cunning with a chip on her shoulder, and the girl with the jewel in her navel. No contest, of course, in the bedroom stakes, but the Clamp woman is actually the only person I can trust right now. Well, her and Tom, I suppose.

By some random quirk of fate, by the time I've got the coffees up, Sylvia has managed to bag one of the sofas in the front window, rather than the hard little upright chairs. She crosses her legs as I pitch up with the goldfish bowls of latte: she's still in her work clothes, but I count two buttons undone at the top of the blouse, and one at the bottom. She smiles at me: an unusual event in itself.

'Jim Martin tells me he's been talking to you,' she says, taking a sip of her coffee.

Has he now. 'Oh?' I say, watching Edinburgh's Lothian Road hurtle past. It's only six o'clock, so it's still kind of mid-rush. My bag is stuffed full of papers to do with one of my transactions to take home, although I'd gladly take other offers if Sylvia is thinking of making any.

'Yes,' she says, one eyebrow arching. 'He shouldn't really do that, you know, talk to you direct, I mean. He says he just bumped into you one day.'

'Yes, that's right, actually,' I say, sounding as casual as possible. 'We went for a quick coffee, funnily enough, although it's not the same with two guys.'

She manages a second smile. 'No, I suppose my researches did suggest that wouldn't be the same for you,' she says.

She sits back, uncrosses her legs and smooths down her skirt. Down to business, in body language. 'So. I take it he told you that they're not treating it as a suspicious death anymore?'

'He did.'

'There'll be one or two final things to clear up, I suppose, which means we should probably meet again to tidy up any loose ends.' Back to sipping her coffee, looking at me over the rim of the coffee cup.

'Okay, sounds good. Why don't we do it over a spot of dinner?'

Sylvia looks surprised, then starts to laugh. 'What, the three of us? I'm not sure if Jim would go for that. He prefers his interviews to be a bit more formal than a chat over the starters.'

'Not really the threesome I had in mind,' I say out loud, although I was really meaning just to think it.

Then something odd happens. I can see her face descend into sub-zero temperatures but then, just as I'm waiting to get my head snapped clean off, the thaw sets in. She smiles for a third time, and there's a bit of a glint in her eye. 'Oh, so you had someone else lined up as well? I do have a boyfriend, you know.'

I give her what's meant to be my best, slightly guilty, smile. 'Oh, I think you'd be quite enough fun all by yourself. How about tomorrow night?'

She's still smiling: three's a charm. She finishes her coffee (fuck knows how she can do that so quickly: mine is still at molten lava temperature) and stands up to go; in the process, her blouse riding up to reveal the jewel.

She pulls her blouse down, wagging a finger at me. Caught again. 'You know, you are a persistent offender,' she says, picking up her bag. 'I'll take a rain check on dinner, Simon, at least for now.'

'At least for now?' She's already on her way out past me, but she lets her hand ruffle my hair as she goes.

'Let's call it a definite maybe,' she says softly, in my ear. Then she's off.

I sit and finish my latte, thinking. Or at least thinking as much as the limited blood supply to my brain will allow, what with the python misinterpreting all the mixed signals and getting ahead of himself. Eventually, I have to take a development agreement out of my bag and start reading it, just to calm him down a bit.

Then it's off back to Livingston on the train, via a chance encounter.

CHAPTER 16
A COKE AND A SMILE

The chance encounter is Jerry Mitchell, a guy I used to knock around with a few years ago. He's a surveyor, or something, with Standard Life, but our relationship was more founded on the large quantities of quality Bolivian marching powder he seemed to be able to get a hold of whenever I was up from London.

'Hey, Simon,' he says. 'Didn't know you were in town. How's the Big Smoke?'

Even though he's got a big grin on his face, he looks a bit kind of jittery, looking round at all the other suits marching down towards the station. It wouldn't take a genius to know he's carrying.

'Jerry, how's it going? Got time for a pint?'

He looks even more shifty. 'I can do better than that,' he says, tapping the side of his nose. He keeps edging towards me in a slightly weird way, and I realise that he's trying to nudge me out of the stream of commuters, off towards a side street. 'I've come into what you might call a bit of an over provision situation,' he says. 'Are you in?'

Of course I'm fucking in. I mean, this is quality stuff this guy peddles, although doing it in an empty shop doorway, twenty yards from the cream of Edinburgh's suburban professional classes, feels slightly dodgy. Even if half of them probably snort the same stuff in their spare time.

I pay Jerry in cash, we exchange our latest iPhone numbers, and I go on my way rejoicing.

Of course, since my little trip to Debi and Elena's maisonette, I've had to make do with cash. A loan from Mum to start with, and then a big wad of bank notes as soon as I could get to the bank on Monday morning after the prayer meeting. Fortunately, the first of my replacement cards arrived yesterday at Mum's address, my Mastercard.

Another reason to be cheerful. In fact, I'm feeling so uplifted by the thought of things getting back on track (and the two little bags of the white stuff now creating a slight bulge in my coat pocket) that I even buy a copy of the Evening News on the way to the train.

For those of you lucky enough not to be Jocks of the Edinburgh persuasion, the Evening News is the paper that put the och in parochial. Headline the day after the Titanic went down was 'Morningside man drowns,' that sort of thing.

However, this particular Thursday, I have to admit the advertising hoarding does a good job: ASH CLOUD GROUNDS SCOTS FLIGHTS. Commuters are milling round the newspaper guy like flies round the proverbial, buying copies. He's never had it so good.

I've been too busy all day working, sorting out my finances, and trying to sort out my sex life, to pay any attention to what's going on in the rest of the world. The headline intrigues me. Who or what is Ash Cloud? Some Red Indian Chief with special powers? A rock band, perhaps, behaving so badly on their private jet that the entire Jock air space had to be cleared for them?

In fact, the story turns out to be almost as bonkers as either of these. Some volcano in Iceland has gone off, and sent a whole load of stuff into the atmosphere that, initially, has only grounded flights to and from Scotland. Of course, at this point in the proceedings, I've no intention of flying anywhere, so the thought of hundreds of ginger basted turkeys stranded in Torremolinos only helps to lift my mood even higher. And that's just on coffee.

***

When I get off the train at the other end, I get the same prickly feeling at the back of my neck I've had all week. What if the cops are following me? What if the crims are following me, more importantly? They know where I work, after all. I'm lingering in the Lexus, waiting for the car park to clear, when my moby goes off. It's Karen Clamp.

'Will you stop phonin me? You've got what you want from me, now. This is no a secure line.'

'Nice to hear from you too, Karen,' I say and I really mean it. Three times I've left a message, which is twice more than anyone else would get.

'Aye, well, but –', she gets ready to launch off again, into some tirade about me being too posh to help, when I decide it's time to get competitive.

'Listen, Karen. This is a two way street here. You help me and I help you to get out of that fucking war zone you call home.'

'There's no need to swear.'

I take a deep breath. 'Sorry. No, there isn't.' Come to think of it, I've not heard her swear once yet. 'It's in both our interests to get to the bottom of this. You may think I'm a bit of a prat right now, Karen, but I'm your best chance of sorting things out with these people.'

I wait. There's silence at the other end, then a sigh.

'Melon Head was here again the day. He met Pimpy Boy at the flat. It was quiet, so I could hear them talkin, but I couldn't hear what they said.'

'Pimpy Boy?' Melon Head is her pet name for Tony Hand. Funny how she seems to be able to get descriptions of people dead on.

'Oh aye, you wouldn't ken him. I mean Derek Boyes, the guy I was tellin you about. Mister Supposed Gangland Kingpin. Anyway, the two of them had a chat, sampled the merchandise and then left. This was around one o'clock the day.'

No wonder Tony looked a bit flustered when I saw him after lunch.

'Which one did he – oh, never mind. Thanks for letting me know. Listen, you look after yourself, okay? Don't take any risks.' I'm scanning the car park as I speak but all I can see is stressed out wage slaves getting in their cars and roaring off home. No-one with cop eyes or the look of a Bond villain. Not even a white Persian cat to be seen.

'Aye, aye,' she says. 'I'm workin on gettin new listenin devices put in, but it's difficult with Oddjob always sniffin round here with his trousers – what's that, hen?'

In the background, I can hear a kid's voice, saying, 'What's for tea, Mammy?'

'Right, I'd better go,' she says and rings off. The car park is nearly empty. I drive back to Mum's house, thinking. From time to time I check the rear view mirror, but don't see anyone following me.

Back at the house, mum is cooking spaghetti carbonara and Tom has done his bit by pulling the cork on a bottle of red wine.

'Ah, Simon!' mum says, rushing up and giving me an Italian momma style squeeze. I've barely time to get my coat off.

'Just be a moment, Mum,' I say, heading upstairs.

'Hey, cunt!' Tom says, cheerily. 'Why are you taking your coat upstairs as well?'

Because I've got two bags of cocaine in the pockets that I want to stash, obviously, Tom. Out loud, I say, 'Just get a glass organised for me, will you bro?' I disappear upstairs as Mum tells him off for swearing again.

Upstairs in my room, I stash the coke under the bed, think better of it and hide it in the top of the wardrobe. Mum has a nasty habit of coming in and hoovering when I'm not here. Finally, I settle on the back of the sock drawer. I change out of my suit into my old Levis, and the same salmon coloured shirt I had on when I met Karen Clamp at the Old Bell; it's my favourite.

Just before I go down, I text Yvonne. *You in?* As I go downstairs, the moby bleeps back. *Expect so. LOL,* she says. Excellent. LOL, in fact.

Mum's served up already by the time I get down. Tom, meantime, is working the bottle of Chilean Cab. Sauv. hard, so I've got some catching up to do.

Mum has her only bottle of that thin Italian white stuff she always goes for. You could drink a case of it and still be on your feet, as the song goes.

'How was work today, Simon?'

'It was okay,' I say. 'How about yours?' Mum works part-time at a travel agents. How they keep going through the recession I have no idea.

'Ballingall was here again today,' Tom says, before Mum gets a chance to answer.

Ballingall, the poor bastard. This house must have worse plumbing than a ninety year old with Delhi belly. Still, shouting at him gives Tom a focus in life.

'And?'

'Fine,' Tom says. 'He did what he had to do and left. He was asking after you, actually.'

Tom must be having one of his better days. Mum smiles at me and says, 'Mr. Ballingall is always asking after you, Simon. I think he was hoping for some free legal advice.'

Great, just what I need: a plumber for a client. Still, I feel the poor bastard is owed something for putting up with Tom's not so good days. 'I'll give him a ring later on,' I say, lying through my teeth. I'm planning a busy night ahead, none of which involves sorting out legal tangles for stray tradesmen.

The spaghetti tastes like rubber: Mum must be the only Italian mother who can't cook to save her life. The carbonara sauce comes out of a jar, probably knocked up in a factory unit outside Hartlepool. Luckily, the garlic bread is Tesco's own, and all she has to do is stick it on a tray in the oven.

I manage to grab a second glass of wine, just before Tom empties the rest down his gullet, and starts work on a second bottle. Mum shoots me a warning look. 'Just make sure your brother doesn't drink too much,' she says. 'You know it's not good with his medication.'

Oh yeah, I forgot. I'm Tom's personal assistant whenever I'm in the house. When mum is clearing the plates away, I say quietly to Tom, 'Go easy on the vino, bro, I've got something more interesting for you later on.'

Tom pauses, mid-guzzle, and nods, once. When he takes his face out of the wine glass, he says, 'You mean…?'

'A coke and a smile,' I say, just as Mum comes back through.

'Darling, we don't have any coke in the house,' she says.

That's what you think, Mama. I smile, and nod.

***

By the time the dishes are done and Mum has got fed up enough of us to go to bed with her book, we've finished two more bottles of red, and Tom's switched to the whisky. It's all I can do to prise the stuff off him. As he nips off on the Stannah on an errand of his own, Mum takes me aside.

'Try to keep him off the whisky, Simon,' she says. 'You know how he likes to argue when he's on it.'

Too right. Too much of the Highland crazy water, and bro

gets pretty belligerent. It's the last thing I want tonight, particularly as he always dredges up the accident at some point as his trump card. As far as I'm concerned, the quicker I can give him a quick toot of charlie and get off to Yvonne's, the better.

So when Mum toddles off to bed, I nip up straight away, and bring down one of the bags. When I get back, Tom is busy at the DVD.

'Bit of retro stuff for you,' he says.

Antiquated would be more like it: Tom's taste in porn seems to run to Ron Jeremy Seventies era cheese. Still, if it makes him happy. I'm not actually sure what effect it can have on him now: he's always on at me to get porn mags and movies, but I'm just not sure what the accident did to him in that department. I mean, he's paralysed below the waist, but I'm not sure what that means for the old whanger. Not the kind of thing you can easily ask, even with your brother.

Anyway, things are going reasonably well. Ron is earning his corn with a couple of blondes and I've wrestled the Lagavulin out of Tom's mitts, then started cutting a couple of lines on the coffee table.

Here's another thing, though, that they don't think of in terms of access for the disabled. It's actually quite hard, if you don't have the use of your legs, to be able to snort cocaine off a low surface. In Tom's case, it involves getting him upright off the couch (difficult enough normally, without the addition of all the booze), levering him onto his knees and propping him up while he gets his elbows on the coffee table. I'm not sure who's grunting the most, me, him or Ron Jeremy. Then Tom gets a fit of the giggles, just about blowing the line of Colombia's finest export into Mum's shag pile.

I suppose, by that time, we were making quite a bit of noise. And the house isn't that big.

And I suppose there wasn't ever really a good time for Mum to come back into the living room, looking for her reading glasses. But the point at which Tom is in mid snort, and one of the blondes is saying, 'Get my Mom's vibrator, and shove it up my ass so I can come real good,' would possibly be about the worst.

All hell breaks loose.

'*Santo cielo!* Simon! What have you done?'

Oh great. It's all about me, suddenly. She marches forward, grabbing the rolled up twenty out of Tom's hand and glares at me. 'This is all your fault. Is it not enough that you nearly kill your brother with your drunk driving, that you have to kill him with drugs?' Before I can say anything, she rounds on Tom. 'And turn that filth off, Tom. I know you must have only got it to please Simon, but I will not have that on my television.'

She points dramatically at the screen, which, actually, shows old Ron in one of those awkward moments between active shagging when he and the actresses have to pretend that they can, er, act for the purposes of some wooden plot device, before they can get back down to it. He's even wearing a suit.

Tom, meantime, says nothing, just grabbing the remote and putting the telly off. He's not usually lost for words, but it looks like I'm going to have to negotiate us out of this one.

'Mum, this is not how it looks,' I say. 'I'd read this article in a science journal about cocaine being beneficial...'

Even I don't feel convinced by that. Mum stands up to her full five foot six and points to the door with a flourish.

'Get out, Simon. I don't want you in my house. And take this – this – *merda* with you.'

I look from her to Tom, who's still doing the dumb animal act, snatch up the bag of what's left of the coke and say, 'Fine. There's plenty other places I can kip down until I can get back into my flat.' Then it's as quick as I can grab up a few things from upstairs, and then off out into the night.

Actually, I'm thinking as I go, there's only one other place springs to mind.

***

She's rubbing her eyes and yawning even as she's answering the door.

'I'd given up on you,' she says and there's a tone in her voice that suggests she's not exactly bubbling with joy to see me. 'Did you leave the car round the corner?'

'Of course I did.' Probably shouldn't have driven, but at least I got here. Yvonne, meantime, is permanently paranoid about some neighbour spying on us through the net curtains. Which is ironic, really, because in a Spam Valley estate like this, they've all got vertical blinds.

Anyway, I pull what I expect will be my trump card as Yvonne goes ahead of me into the living room. She's wearing this white silky dressing-gown, the effect of which is only slightly spoiled by the fact I can see she's wearing some very sensible pants underneath.

'Question for you. What makes a Mexican mariachi band do the quick step in double time?' I hold up the bag of charlie as she turns round.

There's a pause, as her eyes take in the bag of coke. Then she says, 'No thanks, Simon. I'm really just not in the mood, I'm afraid.'

Not in the mood? This from the woman who has been badgering me for weeks to get a hold of the fucking stuff, which I have, now, at no small personal risk to myself, and managed to save from the marauding nostrils of my brother? Well, there's fucking gratitude, I'm thinking.

'Oh. Okay.' I sit down next to her, still with my coat on, and stick the coke on the table. Yvonne glances at it, as if it wasn't just the best thing since sliced bread, and says, 'Of course, go ahead yourself if you want.'

'Maybe later,' I say, taking the front of her dressing-gown and pulling her gently towards me, my other hand undoing the tie at her middle. We have a bit of a nuzzle, but then she breaks away and there's a strange smile on her face, one that I don't like the look of. Kind of a pale imitation. In fact, Yvonne just looks pale full stop: not the usual tanned tigress I've come to know and lust after.

'I'm afraid you've come at the wrong time of the month, Si.'

Si? Why has everybody suddenly decided that I'm a fucking abbreviated version? For a brief paranoid moment, I imagine that she's in cahoots with the two goons at the office, but it passes, thankfully.

I look down to see, where the dressing-gown has fallen open, that her pants are definitely of the time of the month variety. I mean, Yvonne is a woman who takes her underwear seriously. She has some well nice thongs in her collection, keeps the lady garden well tended, the full nine yards. But these ones look like they've been boiled for a month and then pounded dry on a rock.

'That's okay,' I say, trying a smile. 'We could just go to bed and chat.' Of course, that's the last thing I want, really, but this is a negotiation, after all. I'm keeping the suggestion of mouth to python resuscitation till later. Meantime, he's gone back into his lair, confused by the boiled pants.

She's still looking at me in that strange way. 'Yes, okay, we could do that for a while,' she says, and leads me upstairs.

Yvonne's house is quite something, if you like that kind of thing. Laminate floor all the way up, through the staircase, which is actually quite a nice feature in this particular model. Every surface gleaming, too: she gets a marvellous little Romanian woman in to do it, apparently.

In the bedroom, she gets under the duvet, taking her dressing-gown off, but not the boiled pants. As she watches me get my kit off, I can't read her expression: she's in a funny mood, for sure. Saying no to a coke is just so not Yvonne's style.

I clamber in beside her and the python begins to stir himself, boiled pants or no boiled pants. The strange smile is back on Yvonne's face.

'You don't give up easily, do you?'

'Sorry. It's my hormones. Terrible lust. Just can't help it.'

She sighs, raising herself on one elbow. 'Well, I suppose I could lend a hand.'

The python certainly thinks so. Right now he'd settle for anything. She grabs a hold of him and starts tugging away, although, to be honest, it's a bit more like she's trying to get the top off a bottle. I move closer and start kissing her neck, partly to try and make it seem a bit more romantic for her, but partly just to slow things down a bit, when she breaks off.

'I'm sorry, Simon. I think I'm going to be sick,' she says and gets out of bed, making a run for the en suite. I lie on my back listening to the sound of her retching, while the python's still seeing stars. Eventually, I decide I'd better go and do something, so I pick up her dressing-gown and go through to the en suite.

She's kneeling in front of the toilet. 'Thanks. I'll be through in a minute,' she mutters, taking the dressing-gown from me. Her eyes are shining like she's been crying, presumably with the effort of honking up whatever it was she had for supper.

Eventually, she comes back through, dressing-gown on, still looking whiter than I've ever seen her. I give her a bit of a cuddle but she pushes me away.

'You should go,' she says. 'I'm not exactly great company.'

'No, no. I can stay and look after you.' Plus it means I've got a bed for the night, of course, but I haven't actually got around to telling her that yet.

She's shaking her head. 'No, Simon. It's way too risky. The neighbours might see you. Besides, Gary's due home, tomorrow morning. We might sleep in.'

'The thing is – ' I start to say, but she interrupts. 'To be honest, I think we should cool it for a while. It's all getting way too risky.'

I'm aware that there's something going on behind all of this but, to be honest, I'm too fucking tired to try and work it all out. All I know is I'm not getting to stay the night, and she's close to dumping me altogether. I start collecting up my clothes without saying another word, hoping my silence speaks volumes. She disappears into the bathroom to honk up some more and the last I hear of her as I shut the front door on the Yale behind me is her retching up again.

Fuck. In fact, fuck, wank, fanny, bastard. I suppose I'm actually technically homeless. I have a flat in London I have handed over to a Jock for his flat in Edinburgh which I can't get into for fear of being rubbed out by a gang of criminals; and I've managed to get myself thrown out of my Mum's and Yvonne's all in one night. Just as well I've got that little piece of plastic to pay for stuff with.

I pat my pocket to be sure: my Mastercard's there, nestling beside one of the bags of coke. It's pretty fucking cold out here: it may be the middle of April, but nobody's told Livingston's weather system yet. Walking down the street, I see a light go on in one of Yvonne's neighbours across the street. Maybe she was right about them. Who gives a fuck? I feel like going over to piss on their immaculately striped lawn.

I get into the Lexus and fire up the ignition, feeling pretty knackered. All the good effect of the booze I had at Mum's has gone, but I bet, technically, I'm over the limit still.

As I drive off towards the nearest Premier Inn, this thought sets off Captain Paranoia in my head. What if Mum has sent the cops to look for me? A second drink driving conviction, plus being done for possession of nose candy, wouldn't look so good right now. Probably get defrocked by the Law Society, or whatever they fucking do when they find out you've been up to more high jinks than the President can manage at his age.

It's two in the morning, and Livingston is dead to the world. Of course, that just makes it all the more likely that there'll be some bored plods in a car somewhere, looking for someone to noise up. Even the kebab shops will be closed by now, so there's not that distraction for them.

Sure enough, there's a squad car sitting in a side street as I drive up the main drag towards the motorway. I try to drive as calmly and normally as possible: I've heard that they often pick you up for driving too slowly, so I step on the gas a bit. In my rear view mirror, I can just see their headlights snapping on and they start sliding out of the side street. Shit.

There's nothing I can do, really, except keep driving in as straight a line as I can manage. The cop car gains on me, quickly, then suddenly they've got their blues and twos on and they've shot past me. Do they want me to stop? Should I make a run for it? Then I realise it's not me they're after: they go shooting up to the next roundabout, go right round it and head off back down the dual-carriageway in the opposite direction from me. They must've just got a call at the same time I was going past. Fuck.

I get to the Premier Inn, dump the Lexus in an empty space, and turn off the ignition. As I sit there, trying to get my heart rate below two hundred, my moby bleeps. It's a text from Tom: SORRY.

I think about going to Mum's house, to beg forgiveness, but the thought of driving there puts me off. If Tom's feeling guilty, maybe he can work on her.

That sets me off thinking about the accident and my first drink driving conviction. I was twenty-one, Tom was twenty. I didn't even want to have that third pint, but Tom was egging me on, asking what sort of gay lord I was, so I drank it anyway.

Apparently, if you're going to hit something, don't make it a tree, because the cunts just don't budge. The guy I swerved to avoid had apparently had three times as much as I had, but none of that matters. It was the passenger side that connected: I didn't even have a scratch on me.

So I'm feeling fairly fucking low by the time I get out of the Lexus and go into the Premier Inn reception. Behind the desk there's about the only thing that could raise my spirits: one of the nicest looking Asian women I've ever seen in my life.

'Can I help you?' she asks with a smile. 'Hi,' I say, suddenly tongue tied, for once. She is actually stunningly good looking. 'I do hope so. I'm looking for a room for the night.'

'Is it just for yourself?' She's rattling away on the keyboard, her eyes off me now.

'Well, unless you've any better ideas,' I say, hopefully.

She doesn't take her eyes from the screen. 'Single occupancy is the same price as double,' she says.

'But less than half the fun,' I say, trying again.

Her eyes flick back over me and I'm thinking, she's either going to say:

> (a) I can see you're going to be trouble;
> (b) I can see I'm going to have to show
> you to your room myself; or
> (c) do you intend to pay by credit card.

(a) or (b) would be acceptable, of course. Especially (b).

'Do you intend to pay by credit card?'

Fuck. I hand over the magic little piece of plastic and she takes it without another word. I don't say anything more. Even I have to stop trying some time.

Half an hour later, I'm just about getting to sleep, when there's a knock on my door. I get up, the python's hopes springing eternal, and haul on some boxer shorts.

At the door, there's a guy with a shaven head, some sort of corporate blazer thing on and a Bluetooth. She's sent the security guard to tell me that I've parked the Lexus in a disabled space, and I'll have to move it.

Cunts.

CHAPTER 17
WHAT THE DOCTOR ORDERED

Fucking beds in these places are never any use for sleeping on. They're either like a slab of concrete, or the opposite, all soft in the middle like a couple of sumo wrestlers have been shagging for three nights solid on it. About half five in the morning, I give up, get my stuff together and check out. The Oriental girl has disappeared off somewhere and it's some surly big heifer who looks Livingston born and bred. In fact, she looks vaguely familiar: I might even have gone to school with her.

Thank fuck I got a half decent education down south before mum moved us up to Livingston after the break up, or I'd never have got to Uni at all. Most of the kids in Livvy were more interested in sniffing marker pens than keeping the noise down and letting the rest of us get on with any work. Fortunately, by then, I'd filled out sufficiently so any bullying that went on tended to be organised by my good self.

I just have time to take the Lexus down to the station car park and leave it there, with a backward glance of regret. I'm not much of a petrol head, but I have driven Porsches, and Jags, before. I even had a shot of a Maserati once. Let me tell you, the Lexus beats the lot of them. I stare out of the early morning train window at it in the rain, wondering when I'll see it again. Don't know when or if I'll be back to Livingston, so it feels a bit like saying goodbye to a friend.

But if I've got to live in Travel Lodges and Premier Inns for now, it might as well be one in the city centre, and not some hellish corner of West Lothian off the M8.

Definitely in need of something to pick me up, so I nip to the toilet and have a quick snort of sherbet for breakfast. Of course, the ancient Jock rolling stock doesn't exactly provide a level playing field for a toot of charlie, and there's always the worry that you've pressed the wrong button on the big sliding door so that half the wall will open up and show you in mid-inhale to all your fellow passengers.

I manage to hoover most of it up though, and by the time I

get back to my seat, I'm feeling a whole lot more fucking positive about things. Because despite being under constant threat of physical violence from the biggest criminal gang in Edinburgh, having split up with my girlfriend (although I realise, as I think it, that's the first time I've thought of Yvonne in that way) and been thrown out of my mother's house for getting my brother off his tits on drugs, there are reasons to be cheerful:

> (a) two bags of coke, virtually untouched, apart from the aforementioned breakfast refresher;
> (b) a text I got from Sylvia at some point last night which I'm only now catching, talking about meeting up again;
> (c) a scheduled meeting with Leonora this afternoon, which again takes us to another office and, therefore, Brad-free territory; and
> (d) my Mastercard. Okay, so everyone's got to have Mastercards, but when the rest of your cards are still being sent to an address where you're not welcome, the one piece of plastic that unlocks access to all manner of goods and services suddenly feels like your best pal in the whole world. I make a mental note that I should really check the credit limit on it at some point, but then with my London salary still piling into the bank account faster than I can spend it, I reckon that I can put that worry on the back burner.

So by the time the Scotrail boneshaker has hauled its sorry arse into Haymarket, things don't seem so bad. All the same, I'm feeling like getting out of Toytown for a while. As Dr. Johnston said, the finest prospect a Scotsman has is the fucking Easyjet flight to Stanstead. Or something like that. Anyway, the point is, he had the Jocks down to a tee, two hundred years ago or whatever, and he didn't even have to put up with the entire fucking country being run by a Tartan Mafia.

On the way to the office, I text Ben, my best mate in London:

Out of bed you lazy cunt and get the spare room organised. Coming down tonight for long weekend. Will bring charlie for flat warming.

Ben's just split up with his girlfriend, so he's moved to a loft apartment in Southwark.

Just as I get to the office, the moby bleeps and Ben's right back at me:

You woke me up from a dream of shagging your mother. Give me a call when you get into town.

My mother, indeed. That's not an image I wanted in my head, certainly. Another image I didn't want in my head was the face of Bobby, the security guard/janitor/trainee world dictator on the front desk. He's stuffing something pastry-based into his face: it occurs to me that he's always here, morning, noon and night, a strange little Gollum-like creature with his precious belt of keys and his Bluetooth.

'Morning, Bobby,' I say, preparing to swing past.

His piggy little eyes light up. 'Morning Mr. English,' he shoots back. 'Can I see your ID please?'

The cunt thinks he's got me but, in fact, I had, luckily enough, had my ID badge in the briefcase I'd snatched up whilst being thrown out of Mum's house last night. I slide it out of a pocket, flash it at him and head for the lifts without a backwards glance.

'Thank you,' he says and I can hear the disappointed tinge to his little voice. As I step into the lifts, he says, 'You should really be wearing the badge at all times, of course, Mr. English,' but it's all a bit pathetic, and too late, and I know I've got the cunt. I also know he'll be plotting his revenge.

Up on our floor there's nobody else in yet, so I take the opportunity to nip to the gents for a little more breakfast. The transaction file serves as a good enough table and the Mastercard actually does not too bad a job of chopping out a line.

Afterwards, on an impulse, I close the bag of coke I've been using, take it to the sinks, and wipe it thoroughly, holding it by one corner. Then I hold it using another tissue, wipe the corner where my finger and thumb were, and stick it back into my pocket.

Back out in the open plan, I check around quickly, just making sure nobody else has come in in the meantime. Then I go to Al's pod and, using the tissue again, stuff the half used bag of coke under the shitty little standard issue set of filing drawers that are for Al's exclusive use. Just a little insurance policy, I think to myself.

I'm back at my own pod and I've just logged onto the Easyjet site to check out evening flights when Leonora appears. Once again, I have that moment when I look at her, and wonder why it is I find her attractive: she's just so not my type. I mean, she's always turned out well, crisp white blouse buttoned up to the neck, but her blonde hair comes out of a bottle. Plus she's no figure to speak of, certainly not in terms of Buddha belly. Pencil skirt, which, I must admit, is attractive on the right woman and a set of high heels which might even be Louboutin.

Then she gives me that look, her eyes twinkling, and the python remembers why he's so interested in her. There's definitely some seriously kinky stuff she's into. The psychic python is never wrong.

'Something for the weekend?' she says, smiling.

'I've got plenty in stock – oh, er, I see what you mean,' I say seeing that she's indicating the website.

'Haven't you heard about the ash cloud?'

Fuck. I'd forgotten all about that. Just at that moment, a news feed comes up on the site advising that all UK flights are grounded.

'Looks like the train, then,' I say, turning briefly to log onto the Trainline.com. 'Are we still on for the Panjandrum meeting this afternoon?'

'Sure.' She's walking away now, towards her part of the open plan. She stops and looks back, that glint in her eye again. 'And that drink you promised me last time, if you've time.'

'I'll make time,' I say. The python, meantime, seems to be swelling with pride. *I told you so*, it seems to be saying. *Hideously kinky.*

By half past ten, I've got through a shit load of work. Given that I only managed to grab one suit and a couple of shirts in the madness at Mum's, I decide to go down and reward myself with some new outfits on the Mastercard. Half an hour later, I've closed the deal on a new Paul Costelloe navy number, two shirts, a collection of ties and a new overnight bag, when the moby goes and it's the office. Bradley is looking for me, urgently.

Of course, I knew that Brad was trying to move the deal forward today and had planned to swing by just to lend an avuncular hand; looks like he's saved me the bother of making up an excuse. I get back to the office in five minutes (flashing my ID at Bobby: he doesn't even look up, the cunt).

I drop my new threads in my pod and take the lift to the top floor. Brad is hovering by the lifts, looking as worried as a thick prop forward in a suit can look.

'I'm sorry to bother you, Simon,' he says. 'They said you were in a meeting.' Good girl, Sandra. Most of the secretaries here are picked for their ability rather than looks, but Sandra's got both. And obviously discretion as well. I remember hearing once of a Dundee lawyer's secretary who told a caller that the guy was out being sick in the street. I mean, how fucking disloyal can you get?

'What's the problem?'

Brad's forehead creases up a little more, and I almost feel sorry for him. I mean, these rugger buggers generally sail through school on a combination of good fortune and having it crammed into their thick heads, scrape their way through University whilst drinking the local breweries dry, and then get thrown out into the real world, where they actually have to think creatively. I mean, the ability to drink yards of ale, and being a legendary shagger, may both be admirable qualities, but they don't necessarily suit you for a complex commercial property deal involving sale, lease back, and option arrangements, all with an institutional investor at the back of you trying to slip you a length.

'The City Council don't think they can do the deal by the 30th April.'

'What do you mean, the 30th? I thought you had to close this by the 23rd, this Friday.'

Brad's eyebrows go up. 'No, sorry, that's the deadline they've been given so far but the absolute long stop is the 30th. And from what they're saying, they can't do it in that time either. They say they need to go back and get Committee approval. Something about *vires*.'

Brad says *vires* so that it sounds like *virus*. I'm not absolutely sure he knows much about the concept of local authorities and their legal powers to do stuff, which is all that *vires* means. Fucking Jocks and their stupid Latin tags.

'Leave it to me,' I say and sweep back through reception towards the meeting room, leaving Bradley to catch up.

It's the same two guys as before: Mr. Smooth, the City Council's external lawyer, and the bearded guy, who's presumably just along for the ride. Beardy looks seriously nervous: Mr. Smooth is trying to look smooth, but I can smell the fear when I come in the room. Either that or the drains have blocked.

'I hear you think we have a problem,' I say trying to make it sound as unlikely as a fucking volcano in Iceland exploding and grounding all the UK flights so that I have to take the train to London tonight.

It's Beardy, the City Council guy, who speaks up. The suit he's got on today was probably quite smart five years ago, before the dry cleaners at Asda put it through the mangle a few times. 'The deal has moved so far from what we reported to committee that we're going to have to take it back,' he says. 'This is what we reported before.' He shoves a committee report across the table at me.

I don't look at it right away. 'Here's where I think we are,' I say, slowly. 'We have to close the deal this Friday. It's not a question of drifting into another week.'

False deadlines. A handy tool to keep the other side's nose to the grindstone, although it doesn't do to overplay it. Complex deals always drift and you're left looking like a bit of a tool if you cry wolf too much about the earlier deadline. Beardy looks unimpressed so far, so I go on. 'Our clients are keen to close this, but they have other fingers in other pies.' *Like drugs, prostitution and human trafficking mainly, but I'm not about to tell you that right now, Beardy Boy.* 'If they walk away, then you have to go back to committee and tell them the deal is stuffed and I don't think you want to do that, particularly in the current climate.'

I let that sink in for a minute. Mr. Smooth tries to cut across, but I beat him to the punch. 'I had a look at the City Council's Finance Committee papers recently, and it's fair to say a deal like this will help prop up the budget, at least for now. Nice big cash injection to keep some schools open. You also need to factor in that there's not an awful lot of other players in the market at the moment, if you do put this back on. It's very tough to get commercial finance for a deal this size at the moment.'

Actually, all of that is true, apart from the bit about me looking at the finance reports. It doesn't take Einstein to work out the Council's budget is bust. As far as finance is concerned, it's probably only our client's unusual business model – i.e. being a bunch of money laundering gangster bastards – that makes the deal possible.

I let Mr. Smooth in at last.

'Well, we are where we are,' he says. 'What do you propose?'

I'm leafing through the report, deliberately looking bored. 'Well, there's always emergency powers in the Scheme of Delegation,' I tell him. 'You guys could go to the Chief Executive and get this one signed off. But even apart from that, the report gives you pretty wide authority to close the deal. Our clients have got enough comfort to move forward, so I think you guys should as well.'

I look across at Bradley, who's giving me a strange look. After a minute, I'm able to classify it: adulation. I swear, if I were wearing a robe, he'd fucking kiss the hem of it.

'That's absolutely right,' he says. 'Thanks, Simon. Now, guys, can we move forward?'

On the way down, I nip into the gents for another refresher. Just as I'm getting back to my desk, the moby bleeps: message from Tom.

Call me when you get a chance.

I delete it.

The meeting in the afternoon is another handover meeting with Leonora: in other words, her getting shot of any stuff that's not something to do with the Walter Scott companies and the gangsters. Our client is a gangster of a different kind: an administrator of a bust retailer, who's trying to suck the life out of a chain of shop leases. He's assigning them to a management buy-out, so it's a three way negotiation with the landlord, who doesn't care about anything except getting his rent paid, our guy, who's basically acting for the bust company's creditors, and the management buy-out, which is headed up by a couple of guys with more dreams than sense as far as I can see.

The truth is, though, what with having to take the train instead of the evening shuttle, I'm in a bit of a hurry. Before we go in, I take Leonora and the client aside and suggest a new deal which equalises the valuation a bit so there's a bit less money for our guy, but it hurries the whole thing up. Slightly to my surprise, our client takes it: maybe he's got plans for the weekend too.

A meeting that should have stretched into the night takes an hour and a half. Of course, having made a concession, the other two scent blood and try to get more out of us so I have to throw a planned tantrum to get things back on track at one point, but it all sorts itself out amicably enough and I've even time to take Leonora for a quick glass of Cristal at Whigham's to celebrate.

As I watch Leonora's arse going ahead of me into the pub, I realise that that's one of the reasons I like doing commercial property. No, not her arse: I mean, the fact that one of the skills is to take all your genuine emotion out of what you do. You never show the other side your true feelings. They try to rile you up, you don't ever show that you're annoyed. They offer something you're happy with, you hide that too. There's all that bonhomie stuff at the start of every meeting, asking how the guy's wife and kids are getting on, when actually you couldn't give a flying fuck.

And there's the planned tantrum, when you pretend something is so completely unreasonable you've lost the plot. Of course, it's difficult to know, with the Old Masters like the

Rottweiler, whether the tantrum is planned or unplanned most of the time.

We sit at one of the tables down in the lowest bit of the bar, which I find too dark, but which Leonora obviously prefers. Maybe gives her comfort that none of Brad's pals will see us.

'I must say, I'm impressed,' she says. 'Now I can see what Brad's been talking about.'

We've managed to lose the client on the way to the bar, so there's the full bottle of shampoo between us. I'm sipping mine slowly, but Leonora's already necked her first glass and is helping herself to a second.

'To be honest, I'm more impressed that you're impressed, than Bradley,' I say. Have to be careful what I say here.

Leonora smiles, tucking into the second glass of Cristal. 'I'm not sure whether I should take that as a compliment, or whether you just mean Bradley is thick,' she says, laughing. 'In any case, cheers.'

We clink glasses, and I sip a bit more. Women generally talk to you about their boyfriends for two reasons. One is to tell you that they've got a boyfriend, and therefore they're off the market. The other is to tell you they've got a boyfriend, but they're looking to trade up.

'Well, you should take it as a compliment,' I say, taking another sip. 'But I guess it's no secret that Brad is not the brightest bulb in the chandelier. I'm sure he has many other qualities.'

Leonora wrinkles her nose. She actually looks quite pretty when she does that. Still, I remind myself, she's not Sylvia. To my surprise, I feel a twinge of guilt about what I'm doing in here with Leonora, and the way it would totally blow any chances I have with Sylvia if she caught the two of us.

A crazy way to think. To compensate, I brush my leg deliberately up against Leonora's stockinged calf under the table.

She smiles. 'Actually, he's only got one quality I can think of. And even that's over-rated.'

I finish my first glass. Leonora pours me a second and tops up her own.

'Really? You'll be saying next that size isn't important.'

Under the table, she hasn't taken her leg away. Then, suddenly, she does. I think I've blown it in some way and then it's back, minus the shoe, and her black clad foot is snaking up to rest at the top of my thigh.

'Size isn't everything,' she says. Her foot strokes the python, just once, then slides back down my leg again. 'Although I've heard very good reports in that direction.'

I check my watch. 'I need to get that train,' I say, taking another slurp of the Cristal. I stand up. 'Let's continue this conversation some other time.' I look down, checking that the python isn't making too obvious a tent pole. Honestly, women have no idea the problems we have. Our hormones, I mean.

'We will,' Leonora says, and I leave her to finish her drink. Keep them guessing, that's the secret.

I head off for Haymarket, mingling with the other suits clogging up the West End, thinking about all the reasons to be cheerful. And that's where the weekend starts to go seriously arse about face.

My first mistake is to decide not to take the extra time to get to Waverley. For those of you who don't know Edinburgh, Waverley's the main station, whereas Haymarket is a nasty little place with no facilities and, usually, a single window open at rush hour.

The train's already in by the time I fight my way to the front of the queue. The girl on the desk is young and Asian, quite good looking, but with the cold eyes of a croupier in a Leith casino.

'Do you have a print out of your booking?'

'Sure,' I say, going into my Drizabone coat pocket and nearly pulling out the bag of cocaine. *Fuck*. 'Er, no, sorry, I must have left it at the office.'

Come on, come on. I can feel the people in the queue behind me willing me to drop dead on the spot so they can trample me into the ground and get their own tickets. The girl behind the glass looks unimpressed.

'Your name?' I can hardly hear her: it's that ridiculous round bit in the window you have to speak through. It's always at the wrong height, so you can either speak through it and not see the other person, or see them and talk to the bullet proof glass bit instead.

Which is why I say, 'Did you say, 'your name'?'

The girl looks disgusted with me. 'Yes, your name?'

Body language is everything in a negotiation, especially if it's not going well. Which is why I straighten up, smile at her, and say through the non-speaky-throughy bit, 'Simon English.'

I've never had such an extreme reaction to saying my name. A look of surprise, then one of rage, crosses her face as she says, 'I am speaking English.' At least, I think that's what she says.

'Sorry?'

'I said, I am speaking – '

'No, no. That's my name. Simon English.' Through the speaky-throughy bit this time.

'Your name is Simon English.'

'Yes.'

'I thought you said – '

'No. I said my name. Simon English.'

A mixture of sniggers and tuts behind me as she hammers away at the keyboard and, eventually, prints out the ticket I need. She doesn't even look at me as she sends it through.

I clear the barrier just in time to see the London train pull away from the platform. Arse. I go straight into the nearest pub and use a cocaine-stained twenty to buy some good old fashioned beer.

And so begins a lost weekend.

I won't go into detail, because none of it is pretty. Beer, coke and various eating and watering holes feature largely on Friday and Saturday. I steer clear of Rum-ti-tum-tum's for obvious reasons, and any time I see dodgy types I think might be part of Karen's pal's criminal empire watching me, I move on. A couple of times I think I might be being followed, but that might just be the coke.

Another feature of cocaine is, it adds extra points to your attractiveness to fellow coke heads. Which is how I find myself, somewhat slightly dazed, wandering up some street in Clermiston on the Sunday morning, making a sharp exit from some girl's flat before she wakes up, when the iPhone rings.

I squint at it with my one fully open eye. It's a London number.
'Hello?'

'Simon. Just thought I'd give you a call and check on your progress in the Edinburgh office.'

I nearly drop the phone. Fuck! It's the Velociraptor, my

London boss.

'Oh hi.' In my current state, I can't even remember his real name. 'Yes, things are fine here.'

Fine. The last refuge of the stiff upper lip. Wife and kids slaughtered by a maniac who set fire to your house and cut off your tadger as a trophy? Someone asks how you are, you'd say, 'Oh, fine, not bad, considering.'

'Really?' the Scaly One says. 'I heard you were up on a murder charge. Still, might be all in a day's work for you, I suppose.'

It's hard to say what the Velociraptor thinks of me, really. He's the senior partner now, and he certainly gives the impression he's seen it all. Even the little business of Rebecca and me shagging on the boardroom table only caused one eyebrow to go up a centimetre.

'Hope the cleaner gave the table an extra wipe at least,' was about all he said, before banishing me to the frozen North.

I look around me. Street after street of post-war bungalows. In the middle distance, I see a bus pass a road end and decide to head that way. The wind begins to pick up.

'Just a minor misunderstanding,' I say to the Velociraptor.

'Thought as much,' he says. 'Well, we've just taken over the criminal firm there, so there should be no problem with getting you representation. How about the office generally? I spoke to Wallace Brodie when he was down here on Friday and he seemed happy enough.'

Another paranoid flash of panic. What if the whole London firm is – ? But no, surely – I try to stop thinking too hard and concentrate instead on crossing the next side road.

Then the Velociraptor says something odd. 'Simon, you know I said about the com prop department's fee income? Well, it's still bothering me. Are they up to something...' he searches for the right word while I stumble on, in search of the main road – 'non-legal?'

And there it is. There's my chance to say to the Velociraptor, boss of all bosses, big enough and scary enough even to treat the Rottweiler as his lapdog that, yes, the Edinburgh branch is up to something non-legal, so non-legal you can't even trust the cops because they might be in it too, and that the dead guy in my bath with his toe up the tap might only be the tip of the iceberg. So get me out of here now.

And, given that he's phoning me at nine o'clock on a Sunday morning, he might be prepared to listen.

So I have no idea at all why I just say, 'I think there might be something. Give me another week or so to put some pieces together, will you?'

Stupid pride, I suppose. There's a pause at the other end of the line as the Velociraptor considers what I've said. Then he says, 'Okay. But tell me as soon as you've got something.'

Back in town, I remember I actually checked out of the Holiday Inn Express after a liquid lunch yesterday, just to put extra pressure on myself to get fixed on Saturday night. It's too early to check back in though, so I go into Harvey Nick's, have lunch, and spend the rest of the day wandering about Edinburgh's prime retail areas. It's getting dark by the time I've parked myself in a Costa, having yet another espresso when Tom phones.

'Where the fuck have you been, cunt?'

'Tom, so good to hear from you,' I say, and then the phone goes dead. I think at first that I've lost the signal, as happens so often in central Edinburgh, but when I look at my iPhone, I see the entire screen has gone black. Bugger. The battery is dead, and the charger is at Mum's.

I take out my netbook and plug in the dongle, surfing to see where I can get the cheapest deal for a replacement battery charger. That leads me on to surfing for other stuff and I see a couple of half decent shirts at John Lewis that I decide to just order and have delivered to the office. When I get to the final screen, though, it doesn't work. Bugger.

It's only when I head down to the Holiday Inn Express on Picardy Place, that the truth sinks in.

'I'm afraid your credit card hasn't been accepted, sir,' the woman on the desk says. 'It's saying your credit limit has been exceeded.'

Fuck. I have exactly £1.20 in my pocket. Not enough for a train ticket to Livingston, even if I did want to go back there. iPhone dead, so there's nobody I can call, and I don't actually know where Al, Bradley or any of the rest of them stay.

I trail back along Princes Street, with my overnight bag and my Hugo Boss suit over my shoulder. Half way along, I stop and sit down on one of the wooden benches. The inscription reads: 'Dedicated to the memory of George and Georgina Wilson.'

I measure it out by eye and reckon I can just about stretch out on it: the new suit in its plastic cover could go on top of me, and the overnight bag gets stowed underneath.

The least old George and Georgina could have done is sprung for an extra couple of fucking cushions.

CHAPTER 18
AN INTERESTING PROPOSITION

From: Jorg Muller
<Jorg.Muller @edinburgh.gov.uk>
To: ubinclampit@hushmail.com
Cc: Jennifer Watson
<Jennifer.Watson@edinburgh.gov.uk>,
Richard Herries
<Richard.Herries@edinburgh.gov.uk>,
Lorraine Bluedown
<Lorraine.Bluedown@edinburgh.gov.
uk>
Date: Tue, 18th April, 09:37:22

Dear Ms Clamp
Thank you for your further enquiry
regarding the Caltongate and Cowgate
land ownerships. I have noted below my
comments on these requests:-

1. Canongate – 35% of any receipt is
credited to the Common Good Fund.
This reflects that the garage premises
occupy approximately 35% of the total
site area to be sold to Mountgrange/new
purchaser.

2. Cowgate – As explained below, the
Council's land ownership is already in the
public domain and the Council is not
therefore required under the FOI
legislation to provide the information in
the format requested.

I trust that this information is of
assistance.

If you are not happy with this, or want to complain about the way in which we have handled your application, please write to the Director of Corporate Services, Level 2/7, Waverley Court, 4 East Market Street, Edinburgh EH8 8BG.

If, after you have received a reply from the Director of Corporate Services, you remain dissatisfied, you may ask the Scottish Information Commissioner to conduct a review. You can contact him at Scottish Information Commissioner, Kinburn Castle, Doubledykes Road, St. Andrews, Fife, KY16 8DS. Phone 01334 464610 – Fax. 01334 464611 – email: enquiries@itspublicknowledge.info

Yours sincerely

Jorg Muller
Property Development Manager
City of Edinburgh Council
Waverley Court
4 East Market Street
Edinburgh
EH8 8BG

The Cooncil are in this up to their filthy fat cat necks. This property deal, the one in the Cowgate. It's just the latest in a long line of SELLIN THE PEOPLE OF EDINBURGH DOWN THE RIVER TO LINE THEIR OWN POCKETS WITH.

I still can't quite believe that Pimpy Boy is some sort of kingpin in this whole operation. To look at him, you wouldn't think he could be kingpin of a fish and chip van, but I've obviously misjudged him. The Companies House website doesn't lie, and there he is, director of all these Walter Scott companies. All that dirty money from things like what those two wee whores downstairs get up to, laundered through into property interests: swanky offices, shoppin centres in Lanarkshire, the lot.

And now they're buyin up half the Cowgate off the Cooncil who are obviously hand in glove with them, with some complicated deal that means everybody makes a huge pile of money out of some scabby old flats and a dodgy night club called Rum-ti-tum-tum's. Simon English has explained the deal to me, although I must admit he lost me at one point. And then his iPhone lost its signal.

iPhones. Oh aye. I'm on to them as well. The latest way of monitorin our every wakin thought. Who do you think is behind it all? These so called apps on them? That's right, Big Brother government. And its special needs wee brother, the Cooncil.

Anyway, it's Saturday, so me and Candice have our usual wee trip up into town. There's a braw place called Peckham's up in Morninside. It's a bit of a pech up the hill to get to it from where the bus lets us off, but me and Candice love wanderin round the deli bit, just drinkin in all the smells of coffee and spices and all that sort of stuff. Then we go to a much cheaper café down the road and I get a coffee and she gets her ice cream. I say cheaper, but everythin's relative in Morninside. Still, I'm a wee bit more flush than usual, what with all these alterations I'm doin to Oddjob's trousers. I suppose it has some advantages.

So, we're sittin in the café when Candice says, 'Who's Simon English, Mammy? Is he your boyfriend?'

Oh, she's sharp, that one. She might be a bit different in the way she thinks things out, but she's no stupid. Fey, would be the word my mother would use. If she were ever sober enough to speak these days, that is.

'Simon who?'

Candice looks at me with those big blue eyes of hers. 'I saw you had emails from him the other day, when you were on the laptop,' she says and spoons up more ice cream.

'He's no my boyfriend, Candice,' I say. 'He's just a friend of mine. But you've no to tell anyone about him, because it would get us both in lots of trouble.' It sounds weird, describing him as a friend. He's no exactly anythin, except a sort of an ally in this particular Clamp investigation.

It occurs to me that he's actually the only person I can trust to speak to about all of this: I wouldn't trust the police as far as I could throw them, the Cooncil are completely corrupt and apart from old Jessie, who's half away with the fairies and is only really interested in what happened to Princess Diana anyway, there's no-one else I can rely on in the estate. Most of them are workin for Derek Boyes in one way or another.

Candice finishes her ice-cream. She's got a vanilla flavoured moustache from it, so I'm reachin for a paper hankie to give her when she says, 'Can you no talk about him because he's married? Is that why it's all a secret? Auntie Jessie thinks you've got a man up in town somewhere, but I've no told her about this Simon English man.'

Auntie Jessie indeed. I have a moment's inspiration. 'No, Candice, he's no married. The reason it's all a big secret is that we're plannin to set up in business together, you know, the sewin I take in from other folk? He's gonna help me start my own business doin it somewhere up here – ' I wave a hand round the café in a general sort of way – 'But he's in business with other people, who would be very angry with him if they found out.'

God forgive me for lyin to the lassie but it's for her own good. Her eyes widen a wee bit more.

'What, here in this café?'

I laugh. 'No, Candice. No here exactly. Morninside.'

'Oh.' She's lost interest by now and has her sketchpad opened up again. 'Look, Mammy. I've drawn a monkey on a rocket.'

***

We've no long got back to the flat when someone chaps the door. I can tell by the way the glass in it shakes it's Oddjob but, when I open it, I get my first surprise of the day. He's no on his own.

'Oh, hello, Mrs. Clamp,' he says. 'Mr. Boyes was wantin a word.'

Pimpy Boy pops his head out from round the back of Oddjob's huge tank like body. He nods at me. 'Alright Karen?'

I nod back. 'Deek.'

He looks up and down the deck access. 'Would it be alright if we came in? We have what we might call an interestin proposition for you.'

With Oddjob standin there, I'm hardly goin to refuse. I stand back and let them in, and the two of them disappear up the hall to the living-room, Oddjob paddin like some big cat, Pimpy Boy with that swagger of his, all hips and shoulders back, like he's cock of Leith Walk.

Candice pops her head out of her room. 'Hello Kevin,' she says, shy like.

'How's it goin Candice?' And I can see him smilin at her.

'Candice,' I say, 'Why don't you pop over to Auntie Jessie's, and see if she's got any spare biscuits for these gentlemen? I'm sure they'll need somethin with their cup of tea.' I try to make it as normal soundin as possible, although I have to admit, the thought of what sort of proposition these two might have for me is makin my flesh crawl. The quicker Candice is out of the way, the better.

'Aye, sure, Mammy,' she says, and then she's out the door and slammin it behind her while the two goons have gone through to the living-room.

Oddjob wants tea; Pimpy Boy says he just drinks water these days.

'Nothin too stimulatin, eh, Karen?' he says, with a weird sort of smile.

I make the tea and get the water and bring it through, tryin no to let the cups rattle as I carry the tray. Oddjob is sat in the armchair. Pimpy Boy is sprawled across half the settee, but since that's the only other seat, I've got to sit down beside him. Close up, he smells of cheap aftershave and somethin else, a sort of vanilla smell. It must be somethin to do with drugs. A sweetish kind of smell, if you ken what I mean.

'So what's this proposition?'

'Karen,' Pimpy Boy says, suddenly sittin up straight. 'How would you like to own this place? I mean, I know at the moment you rent it from the Cooncil. How would it be though to own this outright, no strings attached, and a mortgage you could pay off any time you wanted?'

He's totally floored me. I don't know what I was expectin him to come up with, but it certainly wasn't this. I thought they must have found out somethin about my Clamp investigations, maybe through my FOI requests to the Coonuil, but no this. I pause a minute and then say, 'And how exactly would that happen? In case you haven't noticed, Deek, I haven't a job. I'm on the sick. Doctor says I'll probably never work again. It's hormonal.'

Pimpy Boy is noddin, then he jerks his head at Oddjob, who's sittin in the armchair, smilin like some Chinese assassin.

'Kevin tells me that you do a bit of sewin on the side,' he says. 'Very enterprisin. What I'm thinkin though, is there's quite a lot of my employees could do with somebody like that. Someone that can do alterations, maybe run wee outfits up for them and such. You could have a steady income keepin you and the lassie comfortable instead of scrapin by on benefits.'

Stupid, stupid, stupid. I should've seen it comin. Now he's got proof that I'm on the high diddle diddle with my benefits, he's got somethin on me. What is it he's after though?

'What sort of outfits?'

Deek puts his hands together in a steeple, you know that kids game, here's the church and here's the steeple. 'Well, you may not know this, Karen, but I do have a fairly wide portfolio of business interests, likes. Some of these are quite specialised. For example, there's a kissogram company I run, and the lassies are always needin new outfits for nurses, police women, that sort of thing. You can get them off the internet, but usually they don't fit properly and the punters are very choosy these days.'

'Oh aye.' Deek takes a sip of his water. Oddjob drinks his tea. Just the three of us havin a normal kind of business meetin.

'And then there's the dancers.'

'The dancers?'

'Aye. Some of them have to change their costumes quite a bit and that plays havoc with the stitchin.

'Then there's the East European workers, of course. They tend to like to hang on to their own clothes, but a few months of livin off curry and chips usually mean they need alterations in their work trousers, as well.'

I know what's comin next, but I play the daft lassie all the same. 'That's all very well and interestin. All the same, I can't really see the Bank of Scotland goin for a business plan based on sewin costumes for kissograms and lapdancers.'

Oddjob's smile gets even bigger. 'That's the beauty of what Mr. Boyes has in mind for you, Mrs. Clamp,' he says, holdin the cup of tea in his great paw like it's out of a dolls set. 'One of his other companies can do the mortgage for you.'

Deek's noddin. 'I'd probably be lookin for you to diversify a bit, as well,' he says. 'A lot of my workers in things like the fish processin industry have a fairly regular need for clean clothes. You could take over the laundry downstairs, if I got a couple of my Polish boys to plumb in some extra machines.'

I think about the communal launderette down the stairs. 'I don't much fancy clamberin over the junkies who use it to shoot up at the moment,' I say. Everybody has their own washin machine now, so nobody actually uses the launderette, apart from the junkies and the alkies.

Oddjob leans forward in the armchair. 'That's where I come in, Mrs. Clamp. Mr Boyes has asked me to clean this block up a bit. He's got this drug rehab programme goin, through this regeneration company with the Cooncil, so they can be persuaded to go and get their methadone there and leave this place alone.' He smiles. 'I can be very persuasive at times.'

The Cooncil. Yet another instance of the Cooncil bein hand in glove with these types.

Meantime, Deek's noddin along to what Oddjob is sayin. 'It was Kevin's idea that we should take this block in hand. He said respectable folk like you could use a break. Which is why I've done a bit of consolidation of the tenancy portfolio and put Debi and Elena, the two lassies downstairs from you, somewhere else.'

'You've moved them out?' That would explain why the listenin devices weren't pickin anythin up. 'So who's goin in instead?'

Pimpy Boy takes a gulp of his water. I can hear the bairn comin back through the front door. Pimpy Boy says, 'Like I say, I've got quite a big interest in the docks and the fish processin industry these days. They're East European lads: very quiet. You won't hear a cheep out of them. Same in the flat above you, actually.'

I think of the old couple in the flat above. So they've been re-profiled as well. Just at that moment, the bairn comes ben the living-room with the biscuits from Jessie's.

'I got wrapped ones, Mr. Bump,' she says to Oddjob. 'I ken

you don't like gettin your hands all sticky.'

Oddjob couldn't look happier than if he'd won the lottery.

***

After Oddjob and Pimpy Boy leave, I get Candice busy on her homework, and fire up the computer. Simon English has set me up with an account for the Registers of Scotland site, so there's no problem about checking out ownerships in the block. And every title deed tells a story.

Margaret Thatcher would be proud. Every punter, apart from me, in this whole block of scabby maisonettes, has bought their own home under the tenant's rights from the Cooncil. And every one of them has taken out a mortgage to the Marmion Lending Company. A quick flick over to the Companies House website, and no prizes for guessin that, through a holdin company, the directors of Marmion are the usual three: Pimpy Boy, Wallace Brodie and Anthony Hand.

And, goin back to the Registers of Scotland, every one of the owners has sold their flat on to Ivanhoe Enterprises.

I'm the only Cooncil tenant left in the block. Amazingly, even Debi Murray supposedly had the wherewithal to buy her Cooncil flat, three months ago. For a minute, I almost feel sorry for her: hooked on drugs and nae brains, droppin her drawers for every punter just to keep up with the mortgage payments and the bill for the smack. Then havin to sell it on to Ivanhoe Enterprises and become a tenant again, because she couldn't stop. No doubt gettin Elena in was the last gasp attempt to help pay the bills.

And now they've been moved out. They've probably been stuck into some tiny wee flat above a sauna or somethin now. Goodness knows where the Finnies, the old couple above me, have been shifted to. Don't think Mrs Finnie would be up to a shift at the sauna. No now, anyway. No with her hip replacement.

Suddenly, the whole place feels eerie for a minute. Candice is ben her bedroom doin her homework. And then there's me. And apart from that, Ivanhoe is completely empty. For once, I'm glad of havin Oddjob no too far away. I can imagine him persuadin the junkies in the launderette quite effectively.

I'm not taken in for a minute about the sewin business, of course. I'm the fly in their Ivanhoe ointment. Pimpy Boy knows he can't sell my body, so he'd have me workin flat out as his wage slave washin workin clothes stinkin of fish, day and night, just to keep a roof over my head. And when I can't keep up the payments on the mortgage, I get converted into a tenant and shunted on somewhere else and he fills this flat with another lorry load of Romanians.

I go ben the lassie's bedroom and tell her to stay put; that I'm just goin out for some fresh air. I lock the door behind me and stand on the deck access for a minute: there's a cold wind blowin along it, despite it bein April.

I go upstairs first, to check on the Finnies' flat. No curtains and, when I look in, the place has been stripped bare. There's a better view from this level of the block: you can see right over Rob Roy towards the centre of town. If you lean out from the corner of the deck access, you can even see the Castle Rock.

When I get back down to my own level, I hear voices. It's Pimpy Boy and Oddjob, just leavin our block. They must have been surveyin Pimpy Boy's property portfolio. He swaggers away with Oddjob back towards Oddjob's flat, laird of all he surveys.

I walk carefully down the stairs to the next level. They've left the door to the flat downstairs open.

I ken it's mental to go in, but I can't help it. I'm like a moth to a flame. Even with the reign of terror Oddjob runs around here, they wouldn't have left the door open unless they were comin back. I just want to get the old listenin devices back if I can, before some enterprisin Polish tradesman finds them and reports back to Pimpy Boy.

There's no a stick of furniture in the place, so it's a stretch to reach the one in the living-room light fittin.

The second one I put in was under the sink in the kitchen. Come to think of it, I was never goin to hear much from there, other than the sound of runnin water. It was almost a relief when the battery on that one went. Made me want to go to the toilet all the time. It's a bit of a struggle to get that one off; the kitchen is absolutely stinkin. Three week old spare ribs in the sink.

Oddjob and Pimpy Boy have probably just gone for somethin

they needed at Oddjob's flat, so I'm hurryin as much as I can. I go ben the main bedroom, where the third listenin device was. I'm distracted for a moment by the sight of a stiletto mark on the ceilin and waste precious seconds wonderin how that got there. Then my moby goes: it's Candice, phonin from the landline.

'Mammy, where are you?'

'I'll just be a minute, Candice.'

Her wee voice sounds far away. 'I don't like it in the flat on my own,' she says.

'I ken, Candice. But your pal Kevin is keepin all the bad people away.'

There's a pause at the other end of the line. 'No all the dead people, though,' she says. This is her latest thing: ghosts.

'Aye, but it's the livin ones you have to watch out for. I'll be up in a minute.' I ring off and head for the walk-in wardrobe which is where the third bug is.

And which is where I am when I hear the door of the flat swing open.

CHAPTER 19
MYSTIC KNOB

It must have been the weekend's worth of booze and charlie affecting my brain, but it took me ten minutes to figure out there was somewhere more comfortable for me to sleep than a bench on Princes Street. One of the benefits of working in commercial property: no one turns a hair at you turning up for work at eight o'clock on a Sunday night.

I actually get a reasonably comfortable sleep on the leather sofa they have for clients in the reception area on the top floor. The only downside is a cleaning woman appearing at 6.00 a.m. with a Hoover that appears to have a Boeing 747 engine fitted, judging by the noise.

'Sorry, son. Did I wake you up?' The cleaner is a tiny, wizened, grey haired Jock. She looks as if the Hoover might run away with her. She peers at me through beer bottle glasses, which have the effect of making her eyes look unnaturally huge in her head. 'Have you been sleeping here, likes?'

I sit up, having a stretch. 'Yes. I was working late last night and it wasn't really worth me going home.' Actually, I did do a couple of hours downstairs before I crawled up here.

'Aye, they work you boys hard in here. I used to start at 6.30, son, but they said I was distracting the folk who were in already.'

'Yeah, they get their money's worth out of all of us, don't they?' and give her my best smile; she smiles back before beetling off down the runway with her Hoover.

I take my overnight bag into the bogs, hoping that the cleaner's been in here already. My armpits smell like a Turkish wrestler's jock strap, and my mouth's like a badger has decided to set up home in it. I wash myself as best I can with the tiny sink available and liquid soap: then a quick scoosh of Ted Baker deodorant and a brush of the old teeth and I'm good to go. I have a rummage through the overnight bag: the shirt I put on Friday night has probably seen least action, and though it's a bit crumpled, underneath the new Hugo Boss, it'll do until I can get down to Frasers.

Dressed, I check through the pockets of all my trousers just in case there's some extra moolah to be had. My personal fortune rises to £2.78. I raid the conference room of shortbread supplies and then go downstairs to start work.

In Com.prop., it's all very well to be a whiz at negotiating in meetings. You have to be able to back that up, though, with draft documents that push things as far as possible in favour of your clients. Leases, missives and so on used to look like medieval manuscripts, with all the annotations in the margins, but with tracked changes in Word now, you end up with a multi-coloured word puzzle on screen.

By 7.15, I have everything up to date. Leonora is first into our floor, although I've heard people moving about on the floor below since half six. She looks pretty damned good, even making allowances for the python's hangover horn. Crisp, smart grey suit. Red blouse with it, which somehow works. Still no Buddha Belly though. Not even a flash of midriff, but still the python is stirring.

Her expression changes to one of concern when she sees me. 'Simon. You look terrible. Do you think you're coming down with something?'

Something prompts me to tell her the truth. 'No, just a big weekend. Did you manage to finish the champagne in Wigham's?'

She laughs. 'Not all by myself. Actually, a girlfriend of mine came in five minutes after you left, so she helped me.'

I raise my eyebrows. 'Well, if I'd known you were bringing a friend…'

There's that twinkle in her eye again. 'Oh, you boys and your threesomes. Thank goodness Brad doesn't have your imagination. You really are a bad boy, aren't you?'

I smile and stand up, taking a step closer to her in the empty open plan, hoping the deodorant has done its work. 'Why don't you punish me, then?'

Leonora has a quick look around the office herself. Then she looks back at me. She lowers her voice, even though there's no-one there to hear.

'Go into your pod, bend over the desk and drop your trousers.'

Not the start to the day I had been anticipating, but the python is catching on quickly. I get as close in to my desk as I can:

fortunately, the pod is facing towards the main entrance doors to the open plan, so the baffle boards hide everything but my head. I fumble with my belt and then the trousers are down. I hear the sound of a zip behind me, then Leonora says: 'Shirt up, boxers down.' It takes a few seconds to untangle the python from my pants and then I'm standing over my desk, bending over, arse ready to receive whatever Leonora has in mind.

THWACK.

There's this searing pain across my backside and then, almost simultaneously, I see the lift doors beyond the entrance open and someone come out.

'Fuck,' says Leonora, and then she's gone, leaving me to crouch down under the desk and rearrange myself. By the time Danielle has appeared through the entrance door, I've got everything back in place and I'm on my knees in my pod so she doesn't even see me as she sweeps past, saying hi to Leonora.

My arse is pulsing, gently. I email Leonora, who, of course, is sitting like butter wouldn't melt in her mouth across the open plan.

WTF was that?

She emails right back:

A Lochgelly tawse. I'm an old-fashioned girl.

Means fuck all to me, of course, but a quick Google search reveals that this is a leather belt that Jock teachers used to hit their kids with until it was banned in the early eighties. She must have bought it on Ebay or something.

The python's psychic powers were dead on. Leonora is hideously kinky.

She emails back.

Enjoyable?

Strangely, yes, I reply, although, to be honest, I've never been that sure about all that S&M stuff. It certainly got rid of a few cobwebs first thing on a Monday morning though, and I decide to leave the charlie till later.

***

My arse is still tingling when I go up with the rest of them to the top floor to have morning prayers with Tony Hand and the

Rottweiler. S&M really isn't my thing, but there is something fairly stirring about the whole encounter all the same. *As long as she isn't into nipple clamps and all that stuff. We'll see*, I think to myself.

Tony plants himself down at the far end of the table while we get coffees. My stomach's rumbling like crazy and I couldn't face another piece of shortbread; but I have the coffee anyway for the sake of it. The Rottweiler prowls around behind the rest of us, stuffing his face and grunting from time to time. It reminds me a bit of that scene in the Untouchables where Al Capone walks round the table of his lieutenants with a baseball bat, except Big Doggy's got a half eaten stick of shortbread instead of a bat.

'Okay,' Tony says. 'Quick round of the table, just to see how we're getting on with the key transactions. Simon?'

If he thinks he's going to catch me off guard, he'll have to do better than that. 'Closed out the Panjamdrum deal on Friday with Leonora,' I say, looking across at her. *Also thought you should know she hit me across the arse with a leather strap this morning, in some strange Jock ritual, Tony. Not sure what the firm's dignity at work policies are, but I'll let it slide for now since I kind of enjoyed it. Oh, and Brad, the sun doesn't rise and set on your todger, apparently.*

I don't actually say that, of course, but Leonora smiles at Tony and says, 'Yes, Simon's been a great help. How he fitted me in with the rest of his workload, I don't know.'

Tony looks slightly confused. He obviously thought the Panjamdrum deal would keep me out of mischief, but he's in a hurry, so he doesn't ask about the other stuff. 'Fine. Bradley?'

Brad looks like he's concentrating hard on his coffee. 'One or two nips and tucks to the Edinburgh deal, but it's going pretty much on schedule. I've got the old quadruple bluff going on the guarantees.'

What is it about him and his quadruple bluff? He's not clever enough to work out a single bluff, never mind a quadruple one. The Rottweiler, who's passing behind his chair at that moment, obviously agrees.

'Don't try to be clever, Bradley. Just get it done.'

Tony Hand glances at the Rottweiler. There's something non-verbal passing between them. Then Tony says, 'Al?'

And so it goes, round the table. Everybody focuses on the deals involving Walter Scott companies, and everybody assures the partners that they'll be closed this week. I start to lose interest but, just at the end, when Tony quizzes Rhona about her transactions, my ears prick up. 'Sorry, who? Ron Ox?'

The Boomtown Rat looks a little less flustered than usual this morning, although she's still bursting out of her blouse, I can't help noticing. She smiles at me and the python begins to stir down below.

'That's the Wrong Box company, Simon,' she says. Turning to Tony, she says, 'Still waiting for the Scottish Government's lawyers to come back to me. I'm hoping to have the S.I. access agreement tied up so they can go in on Friday the 30th as you suggested.'

Big Doggy's on the prowl again. 'Hoping isn't good enough, Rhona. Wrong Box need into the building to do their S.I. that Friday. It's the optimum day for them to do it. Just get the other side off their lazy arses and get it signed up, okay?'

'Okay, no problem.' Rhona looks plenty flustered now. I must say, that makes her look all the more attractive, but for once I'm not just thinking the obvious thing.

'What building are they going into?'

Rhona looks across at me. 'New St. Andrews House. It's pretty hush hush Simon, so I understand.'

I bet it is. It was the name of the company that made me pay attention first of all – who calls their company Wrong Box, after all, or even Ron Ox – but the fact the Rottweiler is taking such a keen interest makes me all the more interested, too. S.I. stands for site investigation, but it's time for a Clamp Investigation, as my schemie pal would say.

The meeting breaks up soon after, but just as I'm about to go out with the rest, Tony says, 'Simon. Could you wait behind for a second, please?' The rest of them go out and I'm left with Tony Hand and the Rottweiler.

'We just wanted a quick word about how you're settling in, your workload and maybe a couple of other things.'

This is Tony playing the good cop. Here comes bad cop.

'What interests us, specifically, is that you've been given a package of work to do, but you seem to prefer interfering with a deal that Bradley's handling. You've been told more than once to stay out of the City of Edinburgh deal and let Bradley get on with it. Is there some reason you can't do that, or do you simply not understand straightforward instructions from us?'

The Rottweiler's tone of voice rises slightly by the end and he looks as if he's trying to control a murderous rage, and would really rather beat me to death on the board room table with a stick of shortbread than waste further breath on me. But then that's Big Doggy for you.

Before I can reply, Tony comes in. 'We have told you on more than one occasion, Simon. Do you have a problem with taking instructions?'

I've been kind of expecting this. They've not even let me sit down before starting on me, so I take a moment to pull a chair back, get myself comfortable and eyeball the two of them. 'No problem at all. You should know, though, that Bradley's struggling. Everyone else seems to be too busy to help. I'm his boss, or at least I thought that was the structure in place around here. Why wouldn't I want to help him?'

I lean back, settling into the chair as if this is just a cosy chat. 'Or is there something about this transaction you don't want me to know about?' It's balls on the table time. The Rottweiler has long ago switched from his barely concealed disgust look to completely unsuppressed fury. Tony – old Melon Head, as Karen would call him – has his lips set in a thin line. There's a long silence.

Eventually, Tony Hand breaks it. 'I hear you've got some accommodation problems,' he says.

I have to admit, that throws me a bit. Who's grassed me up? Bobby, Leonora? The cleaner?

'What do you mean?' Tony smiles slightly, seeing he's got a weak spot. 'There's not much happens in here that gets past me, Simon. For example, you spent last night in here, didn't you?'

Now it's my turn to bluster. 'Of course I did. I had work to do. I decided to try and sort some things out before Monday morning and, before I knew it, it wasn't worth going home. And that's because you guys have totally overloaded me with work, compared to the others.'

Tony's still smiling. The Rottweiler never really manages to twist his features into anything like that, but if he had a white Persian cat, he would be stroking it by now. 'And where is home these days?' he says.

Key thing in negotiation: telling a lie is usually not worth it, because you lose so much face if you get found out. I have no choice though. 'Bruce Reid's flat, of course. We did an exchange, remember?'

Tony has made a church with his hands. 'Okay, Simon. Time to stop pussyfooting around here. Wallace and I can't be there all the time to stop you helping out Bradley. We could discipline you, but you could make a stink that we're too busy to deal with. Although I wouldn't recommend testing us on that.

'But we'd really rather Brad does this one by himself, or gets help from Al, who knows the clients. How about if we gave you a hand with these accommodation issues?'

I'm having to think on my feet here. I wasn't expecting this, I have to say. The only thing I can think of at the moment, though, is Bruce Reid's flat. It seems like the loveliest flat in the world, now.

'In what way?' I'm playing for time now.

'These…redecoration problems you've been having at the flat. The firm is well connected with all sorts of trades people. We could make a couple of calls. You could be back in by tonight.'

And there it is. The first offer is down on the table.

'You're saying if I stay out of the Council deal, you'll call off the dogs?'

The Rottweiler's expression has switched back to barely concealed disgust. He thinks I'm going to roll over, the bastard.

'Something like that,' he says.

I stand up, 'I'll give it some thought,' I say, and get ready to leave. Tony's expression flickers, but he still has the church steeple thing going on.

'Don't think too long, Simon,' he says. 'Maybe you could let me know by close of play what you think.'

'I've got a meeting starting in five,' I say and leave the cunts sitting there.

Never, ever, accept the first offer. That's the first rule of negotiation.

First stop is the bank, where the woman is a bit arsey about it at first, but eventually arranges to transfer enough money to my credit card to de-max it, as well as giving me some basic spending money. She peers at me through steel rimmed glasses.

'What I don't understand, Mr. English, is why you didn't use one of your other cards.'

'Because they were at my mother's house in Livingston, and I had no way of getting there,' I say, which is true, at least.

Next stop is Dixons on Princes Street, to get a charger for the iPhone. Then House of Fraser for some clean clothes to go under the Hugo Boss.

Back in the office, there's the usual creepy feeling of my every move being tracked. At least I now know for sure that it's not just paranoia. Knowing what I know through Karen's research, I can see why they wouldn't want me poking around in the Edinburgh City Council deal. But it seems like a little more than that. Something has them so rattled that they are prepared to tell Pimpy Boy and his pals to lay off me. That could mean a couple of things, but the thing that is really starting to nag away at the back of my head is the date of 30th April. That's next Friday. Everyone's been told that's the absolute deadline for any of these Walter Scott deals.

Friday, 30th April is also the date that the Wrong Box company wants access to New St. Andrews House. And they've got Rhona, who's not involved in any of the Walter Scott stuff, doing the business.

A quick Google of *Wrong Box* turns up that it was some film in the Sixties about a couple of old guys trying to do each other out of some money. What are those cunts up to?

By lunch time, the iPhone is recharged, and I walk down to Pret a Manger with it glued to my ear. There are messages from Tom, DS Martin, Sylvia, Karen Clamp and, finally, my Mum.

It's a reasonable sort of day, so I take my paving slab sized tuna sarnie into Princes Street Gardens while I phone Martin. He answers on the third ring.

'I'm glad you phoned,' he says. His voice sounds a bit rougher than usual.

'I didn't think you'd be at home, to be honest,' I tell him, looking around me just to check there are no schemie gangsters blotting out the sun in the vicinity.

'Aye, well. They've taken me off the case and given me gardening leave. Which is fuck all use to me given it's no a garden flat.'

I arrange to meet him at his flat in Marchmont at nine o'clock. After I ring off, I call the official cop number I've been given for Martin and ask for him.

The girl sounds hesitant. 'Erm…DS Martin isn't available, I'm afraid. You'd probably be better speaking to DS Futret for now. Do you want me to put you through?'

I tell her that it's fine and ring off. So far, Martin checks out.

The schemie savant is next. 'Oh, it's you,' she says. 'I was beginning to wonder if you were part of the foundations of a new office building somewhere by now.'

'Not yet, Karen,' I say. 'Listen. Could you do a bit of research for me. There's a company called the Wrong Box Company. That's capital W – R – O – '

'Oh aye. Like the Stevenson novel? I think that was one of the ones he did with the stepson, Lloyd someone.'

The woman never ceases to amaze me with all the irrelevant stuff she carries round in her head. It's a wonder she can function at all. I arrange to meet her at eight at the Old Bell. A quick catch up and then I can get over to Marchmont and see Martin.

Lunch hour is nearly finished, so I decide to leave Tom and Mum for now. Instead, I give Sylvia a bell.

'The wanderer returns,' she says, a smile in her voice.

'Yeah. Sorry I've not been in touch. A few communication problems.'

'You're a man. It's par for the course.' She is in a playful mood. I just keep thinking of that Buddha Belly of hers.

'Can you stomach a quick drink after work? I've a feeling I'm going to need one.'

'Sure.' There's a note of concern in her voice now, something I'm not used to. 'You were telling me you were getting a hard time at the office, Simon. What's going on with that lot, do you think? My boss looks distinctly nervous every time he talks about us moving up there.'

An inquisitive little thing, so she is. 'It's fine.' I tell her. 'Say five thirty?'

'Okay. But I need to get to my step class at half past six, so it will need to be a quick one, Simon.' She giggles, realising what she's said. Is this the same Sylvia?

'I'll try to slow you up as much as possible,' I say and ring off.

The rest of the day goes past in a blur of phone calls, emails, planned tantrums and unplanned ones, deals being stitched together, partly unstitched and then stitched back together again.

At five, I retreat to the bogs to prepare to beautify myself for my encounter with Sylvia. I still feel like some old dosser, washing myself in the bogs, but at least House of Fraser has got decent deodorant and I change into clean everything, binning the rest. The last thing I need is dirty laundry holding me up.

When I leave the office, I get a text from Tom: *Wtf cunt?*

I phone him.

'Where the fuck have you been, you twat?'

I decide to play hardball. 'I've been busy on a number of projects, Tom. What exactly do you want?'

There's a silence at the other end. I think at first it's a negotiator's silence, trying to get me to crack first, but then I realise it's just hard for him to say it. Eventually, he says, 'Did you get my text?'

'What, the one that said WTF Cunt?'

Tom sighs. 'No, you fanny. The other one.'

'The one saying sorry?' He was never good at eating humble pie. 'Are you?'

'Yeah.' Another silence. 'I mean, you took one for the team, there. You didn't exactly have to force the coke up my fucking nostrils, did you?'

I smile. *True.* 'But it was my coke in the first place.'

Tom grunts. 'And my porn. She threw the video in the fucking bin, you know. I tried to persuade Ballingall to retrieve it for me, but he was having none of it.'

'Can't say I blame him,' I say, thinking of the plumber's arse sticking out of the wheelie bin as my Mum appears round the corner of the house. 'Anyway, get me on the road to forgiveness, and we'll see what we can do about something more sophisticated than 'get my Mom's vibrator and stick it up my ass so I can come real good."

Tom laughs. 'Deal. Listen. I do know you cover for me quite a bit these days. In fact, that thing with the accident. If I hadn't...'

'Ah, losing the fucking signal this end, Tom,' I say. Catch up with you later.' I ring off.

You know, it's weird. I know what he's going to say about the accident. That he was the one egging me on to have a drink in the first place, then arsing about in the car and making me lose control.

I just don't want to have him say it.

CHAPTER 20
HOME AND AWAY

I just manage to get the wardrobe door shut in time and then I'm trapped there, hearin Oddjob and Pimpy Boy as they fiddle about with somethin in the kitchen. There's a bit of bangin (oh great, they've got a blunt instrument they can use on me, when they find me) and then I hear Pimpy Boy say, 'That's it the now,' and the bangin stops.

All this time, I've been thinkin of excuses as to why I might be hidin in the wardrobe of the flat. No great inspiration though. It suddenly occurs to me that I've still got the listenin devices in my hand. I'm wearin a dress from Evans, although it looks like it could've been from Blacks Campin and Leisure. Despite that, there's no pockets in it so the only way to hide them is to stuff them in my pants.

I just manage to do this when I hear the two goons come out of the kitchen and stand in the hall, talkin. Because the bedroom door's open, I can hear what they're sayin a bit more clearly.

'That's it then,' Pimpy Boy says. 'Painters are comin in the morn, and then we can get Billy's next consignment in.'

'Aye, that's it then,' says Oddjob, and I hear them movin off down the hall. They've done whatever they needed to do in the kitchen and now they're goin out again. I'm goin to get away with it.

Then my mobile goes again. It's Candice, wantin to know where I am. I've had the sense to put it to silent, of course, but it still makes that wee vibratin noise that they do when they're on silent. In the quiet of the flat, it sounds deafenin. I stuff it down my pants with the listenin devices but that only seems to make it louder.

'What was that?' says Oddjob.

'Didn't hear anythin,' Pimpy Boy says, and I can hear that his voice is gettin more muffled. Must be just about up by the front door. Then it gets a bit louder. 'Let's just have one last look round and see how many we can get in here.' More footsteps, and they must've gone into the livin room, cos I can't hear what they're sayin at all again.

This would be my chance to jump out the window the way Simon English did when he was escapin from here. But then, he isn't eighteen stone and in danger of gettin stuck. That's even if I can get the window open, of course. The fitments on these flats are just rubbish. Typical Cooncil workmanship.

So I decide to stay put.

To give myself somethin to do, I text Candice back: *Be back in just a minute. Hold tight. Don't phone.*

They're just checkin how much space they have to cram the Romanians in. They don't need to check the wardrobes. They won't check the wardrobes. There's really no reason for them to check the wardrobes. They have a look in the other bedroom first, then the bathroom, and finally I can hear them approachin the main bedroom. Pimpy Boy's footsteps sound like a wee boy's beside the tramp, tramp, tramp of Oddjob's great paws.

'Four or five in here?' Pimpy Boy's sayin.

No reason at all for them to look in the wardrobe.

'Have a look in the wardrobe, Kevin, and see what you think. Do we need another cupboard for their clothes?'

The wardrobe door at the other end slides open. Oddjob's face appears. He looks at me, blinks and then his face disappears and the door shuts. There's a pause.

Finally, he says, 'No a lot of room in there, Boss. I would say stick another cupboard in here or you could put it in the hall, look. There would be room in the hall and folk could still get past.'

He's leadin Pimpy Boy out ben the hall. I suddenly find I can breathe again as they head up the hall and out the door, still goin on about furniture like some sort of married couple. I give them five minutes, then come out of the wardrobe, creep up the hall, and look out the spy hole of the front door. No sign of them. I open the door, very quietly, by a crack. No sound of voices.

I slide the door open and, very carefully, have a look around. Coast seems to be clear, so, keepin my head as low as possible so that it's below the level of the deck access wall, I go along to the stairs and back up towards my flat. As I turn the corner of the stairs though, my heart sinks. There's a pair of huge feet visible. I turn the corner and there's Oddjob, sitting at the top of the stairs, waitin for me.

He's frownin. 'I got rid of Deek,' he says. 'He's got some errands to run up at Ikea anyway.'

I come up the stairs, but he doesn't budge. He looks like one of those big trolls in one of Candice's books, you know, the one where the billy goats are tryin to get across the bridge and it won't budge.

'I suppose you're wonderin what I was doin hidin in the wardrobe downstairs,' I say to him.

'Aye.' He's still frownin. No a good sign. I've had time to think of this excuse, but it still sounds pretty lame.

'Night after night, I lay awake, listenin to those lassies downstairs. I just had to see what kind of state the place was in after all their shenanigans. I was thinkin, maybe it would be easier for me and Candice in the flat downstairs if it was empty. Closer to the laundrette, ken?'

Oddjob doesn't look completely convinced, but he's no frownin quite as much. 'Oh, right, I suppose I can see why you might want to do that.' Suddenly, his big moon face brightens up. 'Did you see the stiletto mark on the ceilin?'

I laugh. 'Aye, I wonder how they managed that?'

Just at that moment, Candice calls me again.

Oddjob frowns for a second, then his eyebrows go up again. 'Mrs. Clamp, I was goin to ask you what's vibratin in your pants but, really, it's no' my business.' He's smilin now. 'And don't worry, your secret's safe with me. As long as the next pair of trousers is on the house.'

'Definitely,' I say, and he lumbers to his feet to let me past.

'I could ask Deek, though, about the flat downstairs, if you like,' he says.

'No, that's okay. The one I've got is fine.'

'Well, if you change your mind…' I sidle past him on the way to the flat, home free. 'Aye, I'll let you know, Kevin.'

I've got my key in the door when he says, 'Don't forget about Deek's offer to you, though. He'll be keen to ken what your answer is.'

As if I could forget.

***

Candice is a bit weepy by the time I get in, but she soon gets calmed down, and I get in front of the telly watching some nonsense. Once she's settled, I go into the kitchen, dispose of the listenin devices and try to phone Simon English. Just the answerin machine. I tell him to give me a call and then go back ben the livin room.

'What do you want for your tea, Candice?'

She looks up at me. She's much more herself again, which is to say a bright wee lassie who doesn't fit into any of the school's pigeon holes. Some of the other mums at school tried to get me to have her diagnosed as autistic, just so that I would get extra benefit.

'Beans on toast, Mammy,' she says.

It's always beans on toast with her. It gives me terrible wind.

***

The next day is Monday. Candice is off the school, so she wants to go and play with her cousins in Pilton. My sister lives there with her man, who works for the Electric. Just as we're walkin to the bus stop to get back to Auchendrossan, my mobile goes and it's Simon English.

'Oh, it's you,' I tell him just as the number 42 pulls in. 'I was beginning to wonder if you were part of the foundations of a new office building somewhere by now.' I give Candice the ticket to show to the driver. He just grunts at her and we head down the bus, tryin in vain to get to a seat before he takes off like a bat out of hell. Lothian buses must train their drivers at Brands Hatch.

'No, not yet, Karen,' Simon English says. He sounds rough, but also quite up, you know, like he's had too much coffee or somethin. 'Listen, could you do some research for me? There's a company called Wrong Box. That's W – R – O'

'Oh aye. Like the Stevenson novel? I think that was one of the ones he did with the stepson. Lloyd someone.'

He cuts across me. 'Was it a film?'

187

This is turnin into some sort of game of charades. 'Aye, probably. Why?'

Suddenly Candice says 'Look, Mammy! A fox!'

Sure enough, there's a fox runnin across one of the patches of grass at the side of the road. Two wee radges are chasin it with a stick. Life in the suburbs.

Simon English says, 'Whatever. Listen, could you get some details about it for me, please? Also, what's happening to New St. Andrew's House?'

This throws me completely. New St. Andrew's House is a horrible old grey block where the Scottish Office used to rule Scotland on behalf of its English masters. That was before we got our own numpties at Holryood, of course.

The fox has disappeared from view, but there's a wooded area that the bus is goin through now, so there's half a chance it'll escape into there before the Pilton fox hunters get to it. I look round the bus again. I've already done a sweep for suspicious characters. Given it's the Pilton bus to Auchendrossan, there's plenty of them.

'Listen, Simon, I'd better go. There is somethin I want to talk to you about, though. Things are happenin down this end too.'

I want to talk to him about Oddjob and Pimpy Boy's offer, what I can do to stall them. Also, what lawyer I could use to hold them up with. They've recommended a firm of lawyers that have a branch in the shoppin centre in Auchendrossan, so they're obviously bent.

It sounds like he's crossin the road again. 'Yes, okay. How about eight o'clock at the Old Bell?'

'That's fine. I'll see you there.' I ring off and Candice is lookin at me. 'Was that your business partner, Mammy?' She manages to say "business partner" so that it sounds like it's in quotation marks, the cheeky wee scamp.

'That's right, hen. Looks like you're goin to be spendin some time at Auntie Jessie's again.'

Candice just smiles and says nothin.

Just then, the bus starts to pull into Auchendrossan. When we get off at the stop, one of the first people we see is Oddjob. My heart sinks, and for a moment, I think he's actually been waitin there for me deliberately, but then that really would be mental to think that way. I suppose his job as local enforcer does involve a bit of shoe leather after all.

'Oh, hello, Mrs. Clamp,' he says. He's got that big grin on his face as he usually has. 'Hello there Candice, as well.' He gives her a wee wave.

Candice goes all shy and tries to hide behind me.

'Oh, err, hello, Kevin. How's it goin?' I can't think of what to say to him, but I know what's comin.

'Oh, just doin my collections. Have you thought about Derek's offer, yet?'

I push Candice ahead in front of me. 'Oh aye. I've been givin it some thought, like. But I want to talk it over with my Mum first. She's out of the country at the minute, but she gets back soon.' It's the best I can come up with off the top of my head. Actually, my Mum was last heard of in some hostel for alkies down in Leith and would struggle to give me the time of day, far less any half decent advice on buyin a property. However, Oddjob doesn't necessarily know that, and it's kind of a need to know basis.

His grin gets a wee bit smaller. 'Oh, aye, I see. Well, if you could get back to us just as soon as...'

'Don't worry, I will. It's a good offer, like.' Candice has taken the hint and is stridin off ahead of me.

'I'd better catch up with the lassie. See you later, Kevin.'

***

I get on the Companies House register and, right enough, there's a company called The Wrong Box Company. First surprise, though, is that there's no set of holding companies as Directors, like there is with all the Walter Scott companies. Just one company, stand alone, with three Directors. No Pimpy Boy, though. Just Simon's two bosses: the melon headed one, Tony Hand, and the other one he calls the Rottweiler, Wallace Brodie. And a guy called Kinnaird with an address in Merseyside. Interestin.

I'm thinkin about all this as I call Candice in from playin on the green. Why have the two lawyers decided to set up a company without Pimpy Boy? Does he know about it? What are they doin pokin around at New St. Andrew's House?

Candice is full of questions herself, but not the same ones. She comes skippin in, not a care in the world, a big smile on that wee face.

'What's for tea tonight Mammy? Can I play outside again after? Are we going to buy the flat with Kevin's help?'

'It's fish fingers the night, Candice, and, aye, you can play downstairs as long as you stay where I can see you.'

She laughs, tuggin at my elbow. 'You didn't answer my third one, Mammy. It would be great if we owned the flat. Sky McLatchie's Mum bought hers, and now they've got new windows and doors. You can do that if you own your own place, Mammy.'

'Aye, maybe, Candice. I'll need to do my sums though. Remember I have to go out again tonight, so I've arranged for your Aunty Jessie to look after you. Okay?'

She looks a bit dubious. I'm thinkin, *To get up to the Old Bell by eight, I'll need to leave at seven to be sure; if I can get Jessie to come over to our flat this time...*

Candice is lookin at me in that sly way. 'Of course, Mammy. Sky McLatchie says her Mammy's out every night except Tuesday nights. She must be really busy.'

Kennin Maggie McLatchie, I can well imagine.

***

Jessie's no to keen to come over and babysit at our flat. I can't say I blame her: but I explain to her that Oddjob has been doin some clearin up. I even have his mobile number now, so she can phone him if anyone's givin her hassle. No that they'd get much in the way of money out of her. Any time we go to the café together, they practically have to surgically remove the price of a cup of tea.

It's a Monday night, so the bus out of Auchendrossan is fairly quiet. No that it's ever exactly stowed out. That's why the Cooncil built these estates so far out in the first place: to put the scum off comin into the city centre and spoilin the view for the tourists.

The bus rattles about through every sink estate it can think of, then heads up through the new town, wheezes its way up the Mound (the Cooncil have actually stopped the tram works for now, because they've mucked up the contract) and then I get to change buses on George IV bridge. By the time the 41 comes along and takes me down through Newington to the Old Bell, my stomach's growlin like a bear with a sore head.

I could get used to the Old Bell, if it weren't for its prices. I'm nursin a diet coke when the phone goes and it's Simon.

'Hi,' he says. There's a pause and he's breathin heavily like he's walkin along the street again. 'Listen, er, Karen, I'm not far away, but I've got company.'

'What? Your girlfriend?' He's no actually mentioned a girlfriend as such. I've just kind of assumed that somebody like him would have one. Some skinny bitch probably.

'Not exactly. I'm being followed.' The diet coke stays suspended in mid air half way to my lips.

'What did you say?'

'There's someone following me. I'm out on Causewayside at the moment, but they're staying back a block or two so they can't hear me. I'm just coming up to the Old Bell, so I'll keep walking and throw them off the scent. You'd better stay put for a bit, though, and I'll text you to let you know when the coast is clear.'

I feel my mouth go dry as he hangs up. First thing I do is go upstairs, to the restaurant. There are other pubs that Simon will go past, of course, but if for any reason whoever's followin him decides to check out the Old Bell, it's better if I'm not sittin in the bar.

'Table for two?' The waitress seems to recognise me.

'Er, aye, that's right.'

The minutes tick by. A couple comes into the restaurant and the waitress speaks to them as if she knows them. When she comes back over, I order the cheapest starter there is.

No-one else comes in the restaurant. The starter arrives: it's a thing with avocado. I don't much like avocado, but I eat it anyway: I am starvin after all. Just as the waitress is takin it away, my moby bleeps. Simon, to say it's all clear.

'I'll have the bill, please,' I tell her.

She puts her head to one side, sympathetic like. 'No-one joinin you then? That's men for you, eh?'

Why is it everybody thinks everythin is about sex? I shrug my shoulders and say, 'Just the bill.' She gives me a funny look and then beetles off.

Another wave of panic hits me when I come out of the pub. Maybe I've left it too late. Maybe whoever's followin Simon has retraced his steps already. Then, just as I get to the bus stop on the other side of the road, I see him.

His name is Futret. Kenny Futret. He grew up in Auchendrossan, and ran with the same team that Pimpy Boy and Oddjob do. Haven't seen him for a couple of years, right enough, but I'd recognise those weasel features anywhere. He's slouchin along, lookin this way and that. When he reaches the Old Bell, he stops a minute, obviously decidin whether to go in or not. I turn quickly away and start off up the road towards the next bus stop.

I don't think he's seen me.

CHAPTER 21
FLYING FUTRET

By half past seven that evening, I have a couple of reasons to be cheerful:

> a) Brad's clocked in and there's a meeting tomorrow on the Edinburgh deal I can clear space in my diary for, just to up the ante with Tony and Big Doggy;
> b) I've clocked in with Tom and he's going to smooth things over with Mum on my behalf; and, most importantly,
> c) the further coffee with Sylvia has gone well. I even got a peck on the cheek, and a promise that she would review the boyfriend situation.

Nothing more than that, though. I tried an experimental paw over the Buddha Belly, but she pushed it away. In fairness, Caffè Nero isn't exactly renowned for its romantic lighting.

So, anyway, by the time I'm heading up towards Newington, the Old Bell and Karen Clamp, I'm feeling distinctly chipper. The python's practically whistling.

Then I notice DS Futret on the other side of Lothian Road from me, waiting at the lights to cross.

That could be a coincidence, of course, but when I reach Tollcross and look back again, there he is, a couple of blocks back, looking in the window of the Bank of Scotland HQ as if financial products and services are the most interesting thing in the world to him right now. He's in plain clothes, if you can call anything by Matalan "clothes", but I'd still recognise him a mile away: that narrow, rodenty face, with the hair slicked back with what looks like the contents of that morning's chip pan.

The next bit of my walk doesn't provide him with much cover. I'm going across the Meadows which, if you don't know Edinburgh, is this big patch of park on the south side near the

University, with tree lined avenues and all that sort of crap. Kind of like Hyde Park, but not as big, and not as good.

Darkness is starting to fall but, when I look back again, he's still following me. Bugger.

Of course, it occurs to me that I could just turn around and confront him, but something stops me doing that. I just have this feeling he's not on official police business. Otherwise, why wouldn't he have caught up with me by now and felt my collar, officially? But, as it is, I'm leading him straight to my only contact who's willing and able to help me find out what the fuck is going on here, and I'm just not going to let him do that. It really is me and Karen Clamp against the world, strange as that may seem.

At the end of the Meadows I look back again. He's still there lurking about in the trees. I cross into Newington but instead of crossing Causewayside to the side of the street the Old Bell is on, I stay on the right hand side, picking up speed now, and phone Karen Clamp.

'You're late,' she says.

'Listen, er, Karen. I'm not far away, but I've got company,' I say.

I can hear her sigh at the other end. 'What? Your girlfriend?' I smile to myself. Just at that moment, I'm passing the Old Bell doorway on the other side of the street. I try to keep walking normally, not glancing towards it. 'Not exactly. I'm being followed. I'm out on Causewayside at the moment, but they're staying back a block or two so they can't hear me. I'm just coming up to the Old Bell, so I'll keep walking and throw them off the scent. You'd better stay put for a bit, though, and I'll text you to let you know when the coast is clear.'

I hang up, imagining her sitting there with her diet coke, like she's been stood up. Then I pick up the pace a bit, just to make Futret work that little bit harder. My mother's gift to me might be my Italian good looks, but my father gave me my long legs. I'm going to make the little cunt scamper. Besides, I have something approaching a plan.

One of the many annoying things about Edinburgh is the street names keep changing on you. I mean, the street I'm now marching down with Futret in hot pursuit is called Causewayside for most of the way, but it's probably called something else at the point I'm at. Which fucks about with the map app on my iPhone big style.

Fortunately, I recognise this area. Although I didn't go to university here, I have pals that did, so bits and pieces of the place are familiar from coming to visit mates and having a few beers.

One pal, Gav, did science at King's Buildings, and I realise that I'm now fast approaching this. It's a sprawl of science buildings, the kind of sprawl that you can maybe lose somebody in, then come out the other side. It's not much of a plan, but it's the only one I've got. I've got to do something to draw the little cunt as far away as possible from the Old Bell and Karen Clamp.

The light's starting to go now, but I don't dare look back anyway. It's probably fairly obvious to him that I've made him by now, but he's not to know that I've gone past where I'm meant to go. The minutes tick by and I cross a load of side roads: Lussielaw Road; Rankin Road; Rankin Drive. King's Buildings heaves into view and then plan B presents itself.

I'm aware that there are a lot of buses in Edinburgh, of course. You can't step out onto the road without one of them trying to run you over: I'm sure they speed up when they see a guy in a suit. It's just that I've never taken one. However, if my little encounter with the bus down in Auchendrossan has taught me anything, it's that they take exact fare, and the exact fare is £1.10.

As it happens, when I see the bus emerging onto West Street, I feel in my pocket and find £1.10.

As it happens, there's a bus stop just a bit further up with some random guy standing there with a bright blue parka on sticking his arm out to stop the bus.

As it happens, if I just pick up my pace slightly, I can make the bus just in time, pay my fare, and the bus can lurch off just before Futret realises what the fuck I'm doing and chases to catch it up.

As the bus hauls away, I see him, standing on the street, trying to look like he wasn't really trying to catch the bus now. He catches my eye and I use my middle finger to scratch my nose, up and down, the finger straight up. You don't have to be a genius lip reader to work out what he's saying back, as he disappears in the bus's wake.

The bus wheezes along and, before I know it, I'm back in another bit of territory I recognise: Morningside. I duck back in through the side streets, quite close to Jordan Lane funnily enough, where Karen Clamp wanted me to believe she stayed, and then out of Morningside proper and into Marchmont. It's a slightly scruffier area than Morningside, full of students. When I was staying with my mate, Gav, I actually got off with a girl who stayed up here so, again, I have a vague idea of where I am. I use the iPhone though to track down Martin: he has a flat in Spottiswoode Street.

I scan quickly up and down the street before I ring the buzzer, but there's no-one to be seen. No rodent faced coppers, no Bond villains, not even a taxi driver with his engine idling. In the stairwell, there's two bikes chained to the banister in such a way that it looks like they're mating, and dubstep coming from one of the ground floor flats. On the first floor, the scruffier of the two doors has a faded piece of card saying "James Martin". The door is ajar, so I push it open and go in.

'I'm in the living room,' says a voice. The flat is surprisingly well done out. Laminate flooring, not unlike Yvonne's; simple white walls and framed art posters all over the place.

In the living room, Martin is sat in an armchair that looks out the bay window. It's part of a suite of black leather. There's a flat screen TV mounted above the mantelpiece on one wall. On the opposite wall, there's a sleek Ikea book case with a biggish, well lit aquarium on top of it. Fish of various colours and shapes nip about inside it.

'Now I know you're one of the baddies,' I say. 'This is where you feed the fish while explaining the plot to me, just before you kill me.'

'Fucking cunt!' someone shouts, just beside my left ear. I jump about five feet in the air and Martin laughs. He gets up.

'Of course, you haven't met Cameron yet,' he says.

I turn round, expecting to see another person. Instead, there's a birdcage on a stand with a big grey parrot type thing giving me the eye.

'Cunt,' it says. 'Fucking cunt.'

'Just ignore him,' says Martin, coming up. 'Drink? You look

like you could use one.'

I notice now, on the coffee table, there's a bottle of Talisker with the neck taken out of it.

'Drop of whisky wouldn't go amiss right now, certainly,' I tell him. I'm not that keen on the crazy Jock water but if you're going to drink it, Talisker is about one of the best.

'Do you want water with it?' I see he's got a little jug next to his glass, so he's obviously not one of these hard line Jocks that think it's some form of heresy.

'Same again of it,' I say.

'Fucking cunt!' squawks Cameron. He's obviously old school, so far as water with whisky is concerned.

I sit down on the sofa and Martin sits at the other end of it, refreshing his own glass.

'Slàinte,' says Martin, raising his glass.

'Chin chin.'

'Cunt,' Cameron says, but it's more of a low grumble. He's stopped giving me the eye and has started to preen himself, as if he's lost interest in the whole whisky with or without water thing.

'So they've pulled you off the case?'

Martin nods. He's wearing a white t-shirt with no logos or brand names on it, and a pair of faded jeans. It's hard, actually, to place how old he is: his hair's a sandy brown colour and it's not receded much. Although his face looks like he tanks into the Talisker on a regular basis, physically he looks like a hard little bastard. Not a lot of fat on him, and fairly muscly to boot.

'When you've worked for the same place as long as I have, there's always some old file they can dig up and find to pin on you,' he says. 'Quite why they chose to do that now is the interesting question.'

I swill the whisky around in my glass and smell it. Actually, for me, the smell of malt whisky is better than the taste: I take a sip and it burns a track down my throat. I have to stop from coughing. 'I think I know why. But let's come to that in a minute. What do you reckon to your partner, Futret?'

Martin's eyes darken. 'Kenny? Wouldn't trust him as far as I could throw him. Why do you think I came and picked you up in Auchendrossan on my own that time?' I tell him about the other part of the evening, leaving out the fact that I was going to meet Karen Clamp. 'So you think he's working for the criminals?'

Martin takes a drink of his whisky. 'Of course. But why would he follow you round half of Edinburgh and make it obvious that he was doing that? He must have been trying to put the frighteners on you.'

I hadn't quite thought of it that way. 'I suppose if he'd been trying to hide it, he could have – '

Just at that moment, my moby bleeps and it's a message from Karen. *Got away ok. Don't think Futret saw me.*

So she knows Futret. Does anybody not know everybody else in this fucking village of Edinburgh?

'Who was that?' Martin says.

'Just a pal. Nothing relevant,' I say, trying to keep my voice as level as possible. They say cops can tell when you're lying better than almost anyone. I'm just not prepared to let Martin know about Karen Clamp yet. To change the subject I say, 'So you're saying Futret was there to put the frighteners on me? I guess that would tie in with my meeting with my two bosses earlier in the day. They wanted me to keep my nose out of one of the bent transactions, in return for getting safely back into my flat.'

Martin's watching me carefully. Cameron the parrot, meantime, has stopped chewing at his feathers and is gnawing at the bars of his cage, as if he can't wait to get out there and get wired into some of the whisky himself.

'Did they? That's interesting. Maybe you should take them up on their offer.' I nod, take another blast at the whisky. 'I think I need to do something, soon. Today's the nineteenth, right?'

Martin nods again. A man of few words. Leaves most of them to Cameron.

'Well, we have until the thirtieth, next Friday, to nail these bastards and find out why they killed Jimmy Ahmed,' I say. 'I think on that date they're planning to complete a whole load of transactions that will launder enough money for the lot of them. I also think, from the amount of chat that's been going on about the ash cloud from the lawyers at the firm, that they're planning to fly somewhere, presumably as soon as the money hits the firm's accounts.'

Actually, I've just worked this out, but I don't tell him that, obviously. But there has been a lot of mutterings about the ash cloud, and how it might affect the flights, and I distinctly heard Al say to Leonora on the other side of the open plan, something about needing to have a "Plan B".

Then Martin surprises me. 'I don't think Jimmy Ahmed had anything to do with any of this. I think he was just in the wrong place at the wrong time. I think you were the target for that night, Simon. I think you were dosed up with Rohypnol so that the girls could take pictures of you with them and blackmail you if necessary.

'That makes sense.' Actually, that makes absolute fucking sense. 'And then Jimmy developed an allergic reaction and they had to improvise. They stuck him naked in the bath and somebody – presumably the Oddjob guy – came to help them clear the whole thing up. But why did they stick his toe up the tap?'

Martin shrugs. 'That's probably not important right now. What we do need to decide is, how do we nail these bastards from here?'

'That is a good question. You've been hauled off the case and put in suspension, and they're watching me like a hawk. Is there anyone else in the whole Lothian and Borders police that you can trust?'

Martin looks amused. 'Oh aye. There's just a few bad apples and Kenny Futret is one of them. But before I can go to someone else with all of this, I need some sort of proof. And I guess that's where you come in.'

Cameron stops gnawing the bar of his cage, looks up, and starts giving me the eye again.

'Fucking cunt,' he says.

Wise words, indeed.

***

Three quarters of an hour later and we have a plan of sorts. I leave Martin to his whisky and step out into the Marchmont night. I wander down to Melville Drive, the main drag that separates Marchmont from the Meadows. Just as I cross the road, a taxi rattles up and I stick my hand out. I've had enough walking for one night. Besides, it's starting to rain.

'Holiday Inn Express, Picardy Place,' I tell the driver.

***

'Yeah, it was too late to get the train back to Livingston,' I tell Tom. I'm on the phone to him, stretched out on the bed. 'Still, Holiday Inn Express isn't so bad. Plus the porno's a bit more up-to-date than yours.'

'Ungrateful cunt. I did that for you,' he says but there's a smile in his voice as he says it.

Just at that moment, there's a knock on the door. 'Hang on,' I say to Tom and go to the spy hole.

It's Futret. Fuck. I open the door a crack. He's just a skinny wee guy after all, although it does occur to me that, by then, I've taken my trousers and tie off and I'm padding around the room in my boxers and shirt.

'Just want to talk,' the rodent faced one says.

I decide to take a chance and let him in. He takes a seat in the only chair in the room they provide. I sit on the edge of the bed.

'Well?' I feel tired all of a sudden. Let the little bastard make his play and then go: I've had enough for one day.

He smiles, a nasty, unnatural expression in his case. 'Nice work with the bus, by the way. I didn't know you rich lawyers took buses. Took me by surprise.'

'That was the idea.'

He reaches into the inside pocket of his George at Asda suit, trying to look as if he's just remembered something. 'Oh, I nearly forgot. I meant to give you this when I caught up with you.'

How did he know I was here? I hadn't told Martin or, indeed, anybody else where I was staying. Tom, obviously, is beyond suspicion. Then I realise. The taxi. Because I was a lazy bastard and didn't walk. Of course the crims will have contacts in the taxis: I should have remembered that from earlier.

He produces a little bag of white powder and dangles it in front of him. That's when I notice he's wearing gloves. 'You left this behind in the flat, Mr. English.'

'Or you planted it there.' That's not true, of course. He takes

200

the bait, though.

'Or I planted it there. It really doesn't matter. What does matter, Mr. English, is that it's got your fingerprints all over it.'

'What do you want?'

Futret's smile grows ever more nasty. 'It's not a matter of what I want, Mr. English. To be frank with you, you're becoming something of a nuisance so far as my employers are concerned. Who also happen to be your employers. They made you an offer today which it was foolish of you to refuse. '

'Who says I've refused it?'

Futret stops dangling the bag of coke in front of me and puts it in his lap. He looks puzzled. 'What do you mean? The deal was that you would get back in your flat tonight and, in return, you would stay out of any of the deals that the partners wanted you to keep your nose out of. It was that simple. So what are you doing still staying in a Holiday Inn Express?'

It's my turn to smile now. 'Maybe I like the corporate décor. Or maybe I want to improve the deal a bit.'

I go over to the bed and pick up my iPhone, which still has Tom's face showing on the screen. 'Did you get all that?'

I turn up the loudspeaker just in time for Tom to say, 'Every fucking word.'

I look at Futret, who looks like he's seen a ghost. 'Needless to say, Tom's been recording what was said as well, Detective Sergeant Futret.' I tell him. 'So why don't you fuck off out my room and go and tell Tony Hand that I'll be in tomorrow morning and I'll be looking to improve the offer.'

Futret stands up. 'Fine,' he says. Then he shimmies up to me, stands on both my stocking soled feet at the same time, and grabs my low-hanging fruit through my boxers.

His mouth is close to my ear. 'Just be aware, Mr English,' he hisses. 'You're playing with the bad boys now.'

Then he punches me, hard, in the solar plexus, shoves me backwards over the bed, and slides out the door.

I put the iPhone back to my ear. 'Were you really recording?'

'Actually, I was. Need to work out how to convert the file now, but it can't be rocket science,' Tom says. 'You okay?'

'Oh yes,' I tell him. 'Game on. Fucking game on.'

CHAPTER 22
GETTING TO KNOW YOU

A little later, I phone Mum on her land line, just to touch base with her.

'Oh, Simon,' she says. Her voice is all wobbly and she's fazing in and out of Italian. Never a good sign. '*Mio tesoro*. Tom has explained everything to me, all your problems. The drug thing, it is a problem. But together we can be strong, Simon.'

Oh, great. Thanks, Tom. Still, at least it means I can swing by tomorrow, pick up my remaining bank cards and start living somewhere near normally. Depending on how my little meeting with Tony Hand and the Rottweiler goes, of course.

Actually, one thing I did lie to Tom about was the quality of the porno in these types of hotel chains. Plus, of course, my bollocks are still a bit tender from Futret's loving squeeze. I turn in around midnight, although I kind of know it's going to be an uncomfortable night.

I mean, if Futret knows where I am, then that means the crims know as well. And Tony Hand. And the Rottweiler. It wouldn't take much for them to send a couple of folk into the Holiday Inn Express – no-one on reception is going to stop them, after all – break the door down and do me. Not a comfortable thought, although I've just about convinced myself that they won't want to do that. They're getting too close to their deadline to want the complication: they'll wait and see what I do in the morning.

About three a.m. I get up and put all the furniture in the room against the door. That helps, a bit. At least they would have to make a hell of a noise breaking through all of that.

I sleep in fits and starts. The only decent bit of sleep seems to be right before the alarm goes off. I dream of Debi riding on top of me, her Buddha belly rising and falling to a rhythm, while Leonora stands by the bed, wearing only her blouse and suit jacket. She produces her Lochgelly tawse from behind her back, as well as a pair of handcuffs.

'So, Simon, you must be tchained to the bed to enchoy experience todally...' she says, in an East European accent.

I wake up with a dry mouth and a huge stonk on. The line of coke before bedtime probably wasn't the best idea. First thing I do before I get dressed, even, is flush the rest of the bag of cocaine down the toilet. I'm going to need a totally clear head for this negotiation.

I shit, shower and shave, and feel ready to rock. One of my new shirts underneath one of the Ted Bakers and I'm looking pretty fucking solid, imho. Time for breakfast. I don't negotiate on an empty stomach.

***

I walk up from Picardy Place and then along Princes Street towards the office around eight. I've got my holdall with me, the one I've been living out of for the past few days. My mouth is still dry, despite the three cups of coffee I've washed breakfast down with. It's a pretty standard Scottish spring day, which is to say a bit of wind, a bit of rain and a bit of sun all thrown into the mix. Cold, but not enough to freeze your gonads off.

Then up Lothian Road, and across, into the jungle. That's what I think of it as: a jungle of modern office buildings that have been thrown up since the Nineties, all sleek and corporate, with fancy detailing or something fancy about the windows that the architects threw in as added value just to show how flash the firms working there were. Edinburgh's financial district: lawyers, accountants, financiers: all scrabbling around trying to keep enough plates in the air to afford the fancy rents now that the arse has fallen out of the market. A pretty steamy jungle, with a lot of big beasts going quite hungry.

I get into the office about half past eight, flipping my ID at Bobby (he tries to smile but, being a Jock, it looks more like he's got indigestion) and head on up to my floor. I want to dump my stuff at my desk, before I face the music.

The gang's all here. Al, Bradley, Leonora, Danielle, are all tip-tapping away at their keyboards with the support staff. As I walk across the open plan, every man jack of them is watching me. I no longer have to think I'm paranoid to know that. I put the bag down and straighten up and there's Al, watching me over the partition.

'Tony was looking for you,' he says.

'Good.' My voice sounds more confident than I am. 'Because I was looking for Tony.' Back out through the double doors and across into part of the office where the partners have their offices. The secretaries don't appear to be paying me any attention. Presumably, they're not in on the whole thing. Just as I reach Tony's door, though, his secretary looks up, and says, 'Tony's in meeting room 5. He said to send you right up.'

Back across the open plan, I wink for one of the fruitier secretaries who catches my eye. Then up in the lift.

Gemma stops doing her nails when I walk in. 'Tony's in – '

'I know,' I say. The coffee is playing havoc with my stomach by now and I can feel a familiar build up in the plumbing. I hope to keep gassing the bastard as a last resort in this negotiation.

Meeting room 5 is one of the smaller rooms on the top floor. It's tucked away at the end of the corridor near the gable wall of the building. One side is a glass wall that looks out onto the corridor; the other end has a window, looking out over the New Town.

Both Tony Hand and the Rottweiler are there, of course. Standard operating procedure: confuse and disorientate your opponent before the negotiation even starts. I'm ready for them though. At least, I think I am.

The Rottweiler is standing at the window as I walk in; Tony Hand is half way down the table at the far wall, sipping a coffee.

'Kenny Futret said you wanted to see me,' I say, just to throw them off guard.

'Who?' Tony Hand's face is expressionless.

'You know, the bent cop you sent to try and blackmail me with a bag of cocaine last night, after putting the frighteners on me by following me around half of south Edinburgh. That Kenny Futret.'

The Rottweiler turns his head from looking out the window. 'No idea what you're talking about. As far as I'm concerned, we're here to sack you this morning. You've persistently refused to follow specific instructions – '

I've just sat down, but I stand up again. 'Fine. In that case, consider this a resignation. I'll just take everything I know so far to the cops who aren't bent. I do believe there are some of them.

I think they'd be particularly interested in what you're planning for the 30th April.'

Again, a standard tactic, although I don't like overplaying it. Threaten to walk away. This time, though, it works. I get two steps towards the door before Tony Hand says, 'I wouldn't do that if I were you. Nobody listens to DS Martin down at Fettes.'

From the window, the Rottweiler offers, 'He's all washed up. He's about to be thrown off the Force, you know. For insubordination. At least the two of you have something in common.'

The fact that the two of them are talking suggests they're actually pretty keen for me not to go. I stop and turn round.

'Is that the best you can do? Of course your boy Futret has managed to get something cooked up against Martin. So he's been put on suspension. So what? And what about Derek Boyes?'

That makes the Rottweiler turn right round from the window and glare at me. 'Who?'

I sigh, dramatically. 'Oh, come on, Wallace. You can do better than that, can't you? He's your co-director in at least ten companies. Although I did note that he's not on the board of Wrong Box.'

Big Doggie starts to undergo a strange transformation. It's a bit like these old Jekyll and Hyde films, where the guy takes a potion and then turns into this really unconvincing looking monster. I suppose they didn't have prosthetics and all that in the black and white days, but you know what I mean. Bulging eyes, cord standing out on his neck. I swear he grows two collar sizes.

'What the fuck do you think you've been up to when you've been supposedly working, eh?' He's almost incoherent with rage. He starts towards me and I actually think I may have to take the cunt on physically. Not exactly a pleasant thought: the Rottweiler may have run to paunch a bit these days, but he's still a big lad. Fortunately, Tony Hand steps in.

'Calm down, Wallace. In fact, sit the fuck down, both of you. Let's talk about this like adults. Okay, Simon. So you've done a bit of digging at Companies House. Wallace and I are co-directors of some of the property companies we act for, along with Derek. So what?'

We've now moved to the second phase of the negotiation. We've had the initial manoeuvres: the foot over the top of the ball gambit, the threatened walk out and the Rottweiler's tantrum. Now it's a case of each side finding out what the other knows and wants.

I have to play my cards carefully though. I can't let them know anything directly that's come from Karen Clamp, obviously.

'So, Derek Boyes just happens to be the head of a gang from Auchendrossan that's into drugs, prostitution, trafficking, the whole bit. Plus, of course, money laundering, which is where you guys come in.' I sit down, eventually, and stick my hands behind my head. 'What really interests me, Tony, is how a respectable couple of types like you got in with someone like Deek.'

I nearly call him Pimpy Boy by mistake. 'I mean, as you may know, I paid a trip down to Auchendrossan myself a few days ago.' It feels like months ago that it happened, that night with Debi and Elena. 'I don't suppose he was an old school pal?'

Tony smiles and Big Doggy, who's done what he's told and sat down at the head of the table, actually chuckles.

'Actually, he was. He was a scholarship boy.'

I smile back. The three of us are like old pals now, shooting the shit. 'He won a scholarship to Heriots? How did he fit in?'

The Rottweiler chuckles again. It's a low, grumbling sort of sound, that I've never heard the like of before. I think I preferred his Mr. Hyde transformation. 'That was the point. He didn't fit in. Oh, he was bright, of course: but he could only afford the one uniform from Aitken and Niven so that's what he had to wear every day, no matter how much we dirtied it for him. Still, at least his hair got a good wash when we used to stick his head down the toilet.'

'Then one day he had had enough. He turned up at the school gates with a team from Auchendrossan and gave us all a good stiff kicking.' This is Tony Hand. He jerks his head at the Rottweiler. 'Wallace here squealed like a stuck pig. We all gave Deek a bit more respect after that, I can tell you.'

'I'll bet.' This is all very interesting, but it's what's called the "getting to know you" phase of the negotiation. It's not actually getting us anywhere. It's just giving them time to think.

'He left after fourth year, of course. Only got a couple of O grades. He was already dealing at the school gates. You can take the boy out of Auchendrossan…'

'Why 30th April? You're pushing all the assistants – or at least all of those that are trusted with the files – to close the deals by 30th April. What happens then?'

Tony shrugs, trying to look disinterested. However, he can't help a glance at the Rottweiler, who meets his eyes and then looks away, fiddling with a packet of shortbread. 'It's the end of the financial year. We need to get all the deals completed, for tax reasons.'

'Really?' I try to keep my body language as neutral as possible. 'So you, Deek and Wallace have had a cosy little Board meeting down at Auchendrossan to sort all that out, have you? Perhaps while the three of you were playing Winchester biscuit over Debi and Elena?'

The Rottweiler surprises me. His look of disgust is actually convincing, when he looks up.

'We don't touch those girls. We don't know where they've been. We're not like you, Simon, obsessed with sex.'

I'm so busy trying to press home my advantage I forget. 'Oh, I think you should ask Tony about that, Wallace. He's not above sampling the goods.'

Then I remember. Shit. I know that from Karen. Tony's eyes narrow. 'How would you know that?'

I glance over at the Rottweiler. He's cast his eyes up in disgust at Tony, but now he's looking straight at me as well. Top negotiators can read body language like a book, and they know I've given away something here. 'What, do you think Martin hasn't been carrying out some surveillance of his own?' I say. Never lie during a negotiation. It will catch up with you. Time to get this one back on track. 'Anyway, I'm not here to talk about shagging rights. That may be a side benefit, of course, but it's the main deal I'd like to sketch out with you.'

Tony Hand smiles. 'And what main deal would that be, Simon? What is it that you want?'

At last, down to business. 'To be made partner. Whatever it is you guys are building up a huge war chest for, on 30th April, I'm pretty sure the old school tie doesn't extend to you telling Derek Boyes all about it. My best guess? You're planning to launder every last penny of the crims' money through these transactions and then disappear somewhere with it. Let's hope the ash cloud disappears by then, eh?'

There's a silence and the two of them exchange glances. There's a long silence. Eventually, the Rottweiler sticks his last card on the table.

'Here's a counter offer. It wouldn't be too difficult to make you disappear beneath some of these fancy new tramworks that the Council are putting in. By the time they dig you up, we won't be somewhere where we have to worry about it.'

I have to admit, there's a cold chill goes down my spine. The cunt actually wouldn't turn a single hair at the thought of having me done away with. If it wasn't clear to me before I came in the room, it's clear to me now: they're going to take the money and run, presumably to somewhere that doesn't have an extradition treaty.

I try to look as relaxed as possible. 'That's true. But best case is that the cops will be in the office right in the build up to you guys disappearing, asking all sorts of nosy questions. And, of course, there are other people now who know what you guys are up to. Futret has been turned over so, unless you've got the Chief Constable himself in your pocket, Martin should have no trouble getting his job back.

'Besides, much as you'd like to, Wallace, I don't think you're going to kill me yourself. You'd have to get Derek or one of his lads to do it for you. Which gives me an opportunity to spill the beans to them. And I just don't think they'd take the trouble to carry out a full investigation once I told them you were planning to do a bunk.'

The Rottweiler looks like he's about to explode again. Tony, on the other hand, looks ashen faced. He makes a delicate little movement with his hand in the Rottweiler's direction, cutting him off before he says anything else. Then he turns to me. 'Okay. Let's talk turkey, Simon. You say you want to be made partner. We can't do that for you but we could give you the same as the others. You see, organising something like this isn't easy, so we've had to let the others in on where the money's coming from. Those of them that we think we can trust, obviously. As you've noticed, only some of the assistants and associates handle the Walter Scott deals. Each of them has been promised ten million as a bonus on 30th April.'

'But they don't know – '

'We're not complete bastards, Simon.' Tony Hand actually looks like he means this. 'We plan to tell the inner circle about skipping the country. Wallace here has been making the arrangements. I dare say he could get a couple of extra tickets: the Brazil flight isn't exactly oversubscribed at the moment.'

So there it is. They're offering me ten million to shut up and fuck off with the rest of them to Brazil.

'So the crims think – '

'As far as Derek and his lads know, we're about to arrange for a huge wad of cash to go their way and we take our usual 10% cut. They're right about the huge wad of cash but none of it is going to Auchendrossan. It's what you might call a 100% fee situation.'

I smile. Time for my counter offer. 'I like that idea of adding an extra zero. How about we make my share one hundred, instead of ten? After all, I will have the extra inconvenience of having to throw D.S. Martin off the scent at the last minute.'

'True,' says Tony. He glances at the Rottweiler, who is now looking bored with the whole thing. 'Okay, Simon. You've done your homework. A hundred million it is.'

And that's it. It's as simple as that. Actually, it's too simple. The bastards caved too easily, which has me worried.

I walk down to the second floor, using the stairs for once. The whole thing is like some sort of a dream. As I'm walking up to my desk, Al stands up and comes round to my side. He sticks out his hand: Tony must have phoned down ahead of me.

'Nice work, Si. Tony says you've got balls like church bells. Welcome aboard.'

I look round. As it so happens, it's only the ones in the inner circle who are in at the moment. Leonora looks up from her computer and purses her lips at me in a way that means, *More of the same for you, big boy*. Brad gives me the thumbs up. Danielle says, 'Always knew you'd work it out, Si.'

Just then my moby bleeps and it's Karen Clamp, texting me to ask what's happening.

What indeed, Karen? What indeed? Then, just as I'm settling

down to do some work, the iPhone chimes a second time. It's not Karen again, as I'm expecting: it's Yvonne.

Si, I'm pregnant. We need to talk. LOL.

Suffice to say I'm not laughing out loud as I sit staring at the screen, trying to make sense of the writing on it.

CHAPTER 23
NEW ARRIVALS

They start arrivin about two in the morning, the next night.

It's one of those nights you often get around Easter, where the wind picks up, like it's blowin the last of the winter out the door. Of course, with a rubbish Cooncil flat like mine, the windows and doors all rattle like crazy, so I'm lyin awake anyway, listenin to the wind whistlin round the empty Ivanhoe block.

It's no as if it's a comfortable feelin, knowin that the block's standin there in darkness apart from any of the deck access lightin that's still workin: the whole big maisonette block, like some sort of gap tooth in the dark. It might all be under Oddjob's protection, but even Oddjob has to sleep sometime. And the jackals and hyenas round here never sleep.

It's like one of these mini vans some of the taxis use: you can hear the door slidin back and then low voices as people get out. Then feet on the external stairs, goin past the flat. That van goes away, but almost as soon as it has, another one arrives: the door slides open and more folk get out. Low voices. All men, from the sound of it. Doors bangin up and down the block as they get moved in. And so it goes on: it sounds like they're fillin the block from the top down. Next, I hear the diesel engine of a bigger bus, bringin the last consignment of them. More feet on the stairs, and then feet trampin about the flat above me.

Suddenly, my front door rattles: someone's tryin to get in. I spring out of bed but then I hear a voice shoutin somethin in some Eastern European language and the guy who tried my door goes away. Then the flat below me comes alive with foreign voices and folk movin about.

Don't get me wrong. I'm no a racist. These folk are comin into our country because they can't get a job in their own one, and our lot are too lazy to get off their backsides and do all the rubbish work that these folk do. All the same, it is a bit strange lyin there in the dark, listenin to all these voices, knowin that no one of them will be speakin English.

They keep their voices low: the only raised voice I've heard in the whole thing was the shout that warned off whoever was thinkin my flat was next to be filled. That must have been their gangmaster.

I lie there in the dark, listenin to them movin about above and below me, bags bein thrown down, doors bein opened and shut. Then, from below me, the clink of a bottle and some glasses. Low voices. Then, quite quietly, the ones below me start singin.

Just then, Candice comes through.

'The men below me are singin a song, Mammy,' she says, climbin into the bed.

'I ken, hen,' I say. She snuggles in. 'They'll probably be workin shifts, so they might come and go at odd hours.'

She raises her head off the pillow. 'It wasn't them that woke me up, Mammy. I had my dream again. The one where the men have taken me in a van to a garage. You're no there, but then you turn up. I think one of the men might be Kevin, but he won't smile at me.'

'It's just a dream, Candice,' I tell her.

***

When the door goes, mid-morning, I'm thinkin maybe it's one of the new neighbours come to borrow a cup of sugar. Or maybe their gangmaster. Worse than that, it could be Oddjob, or Pimpy Boy, come to see how I'm gettin on with their proposal.

In fact, it's none of the above.

The guy and the lassie have Cooncil written all over their faces: that superior, we wouldn't normally be seen dead in a cowp like this, but it's just a job to us kind of look. There's a shifty kind of look to Cooncil people too, like they're always thinkin of what the politically correct thing is to say instead of just tellin the truth like somebody normal.

'Mrs. Clamp?' The lassie's maybe about thirty, with short, blonde, bobbed hair and wee specs. 'I'm Judith Barnes, and this is my colleague, Tom Jack.'

Jack the lad is an older gadgie. He's leanin on a stick like he's got a gammy leg and he has a drinker's nose. His specs are perched on top of his mottled bald head. He's got a tweed jacket on and a tie that's like the archaeological record of every hot meal he ever had.

'Do you mind if we come in, likes, Mrs. Clamp?' he says. 'We're from the Cooncil.'

'City of Edinburgh Council Housing Division,' Judith Barnes says, flipping me some sort of ID.

Let the games begin, I think to myself. 'Whyever no?' I say to them.

In the living room, Jacky boy plants himself in my armchair, while the lassie perches on the edge of the sofa as if she's no sure what she'll catch off it. 'We've been reviewing your file, Mrs. Clamp,' she says. 'We see that you've made several complaints of anti-social behaviour in relation to your neighbours downstairs. They're not Council tenants, of course.'

'Oh aye?' says I, thinkin, *Oh ho, what's comin here?*

'We've been speaking to the cops...' Jack the lad starts up from his armchair but the lassie interrupts him.

'We've recently started a new data sharing agreement with various partners across the community safety sector,' she says.

'So you've been speakin to the cops,' I say.

'The police are one of the partners in the data sharing agreement, yes,' the lassie says. She's determined to keep up the jargon. Part of her tactics. Confuse the enemy with meaningless rubbish.

She goes on. 'Yes, and we have information that suggests that this may not be an appropriate environment to bring up a small child.' She stops, and then she actually blushes. She lowers her voice and says, 'We understand that there may be unlicensed sexual activity taking place in the flat below you, Mrs. Clamp. We don't know if you were aware of this, although the nature of some of your complaints suggests that you had a bit of an inkling.'

'It's no place to bring up a young lassie, on top of a brothel,' Jacky boy says, translatin for me.

Judith Barnes shoots him another look. 'Yes, well, it's all just alleged, but as you are the parent or guardian of a young girl, Candice Clamp I believe...'

Data sharing. Oh aye. They've been data sharing with somebody all about me. Somebody that goes about Auchendrossan with a manky shell suit and thinks he runs the place.

'We're here to offer you a flat in another part of town, likes,' Tom Jack says to me. 'There's a couple of nice ones on offer, and we could get you moved pronto.'

There's kind of a lull in the conversation. I can't quite believe what I'm hearin. Five years. Five years I've been in this crummy flat and there's no a week gone past that I haven't contacted the Housin Department about gettin out. And now, the minute Pimpy Boy moves all his immigrant workers into the rest of the block, the Housin Department turns up to offer me somewhere else.

It's all just too neat.

I stand up. 'I'm afraid your information is out of date. The two lassies who were runnin the brothel have moved out. There's some nice East European lads moved in downstairs and they're perfect neighbours. This flat may no be a palace so far as youse are concerned, but it's absolutely fine for me.'

They leave soon after, lookin confused as anythin. Jack the lad gives me a right funny look as he stumps out the door. 'You'll no get time to reconsider, Mrs. Clamp,' he says.

'Fine,' I say to him. All the while thinkin, *Have I burned my boats here?*

***

Mid-mornin, I phone Heid-the-Baw. I ken he's probably in work, but I have to speak to him about what's goin on down here.

'Simon English?' He sounds distant, like I'm some client or somethin.

'It's me,' I say.

'Yes, hi.' Still distant. Then it sounds as if he's walkin as he talks. 'How can I help you?'

'Are you with someone at the moment?' I sound like some sort of jealous girlfriend, but I need to know whether the line is secure.

'Yes, that's right, er, I was. Okay. I can speak now. What's happening Karen?'

I explained to him about Oddjob and Pimpy Boy's visit and how they plan to turn me into some sort of wage slave, washin and ironin for the Romanians.

'That doesn't sound so good.' He's bein distant again. 'Still, it might be best to play along for now.' Then, more quietly, 'Did you get away okay the other night?'

'I think so. It was Kenny Futret that was followin you, wasn't it? I don't think he saw me.' I'm fairly sure he didn't see me. Mind you, in fairness, I'm no easy to miss. Distinctive, as ma mother once said in one of her more sober moments.

There's a pause at the other end of the line. Then Simon says, 'Might be best, actually, if you just play along for now. I think the way things are going, it'll all be over in a week or so.'

'What do you mean, it will all be over – ' I say, but he cuts me off.

'Got to go now. Call you later, okay?' The line goes dead. I sit there, starin at the moby for a minute, and then it bleeps with a message. It's him, givin me the name and address of an old University pal who "does domestic". I have no idea what that means, but I take it that he means me to go and see him.

I phone them and make an appointment for late afternoon, after I've picked up the bairn and taken her to Jessie's. Then I phone Jessie.

'I've got some news,' says Jessie. 'I'll tell you when you come round with Candice, but let's just say I'm movin, but not very far. Kevin was round to see me. He's always talkin about you, you know, Karen. I think he might have a wee crush.'

I think of Oddjob and shudder. The only crush I can think of he might have is puttin some poor gadgie's head in a vice.

***

Things start to go downhill when I pick up Candice from school that afternoon.

'I don't want to go to Aunty Jessie's again,' she says. 'All she does is go on and on about Princess Diana. It's borin.'

'Now, now, Candice. That's no way to talk about your Aunty Jessie,' I say, although it is true that Jessie has been gettin more and more obsessed with the Diana conspiracy. I wish she could see that it's stoppin her seein what's goin on right under her nose, with Pimpy Boy and the Cooncil. I'm still seethin about those two clowns from the Cooncil tryin to get me moved today, so I'm no really payin attention when Candice says somethin else.

'What was that?'

'She's no even my real Aunty. My only real Aunty is Aunty Elaine, and we hardly ever go to see her.'

'Well, she is in Pilton,' I say. I can tell I'm no goin to win this argument. We're at the front door of Jessie's block. 'Where are you goin anyway?' Candice says. 'Is it that business partner of yours again, Simon English?'

I shush her. 'No so loud, Candice.' We're in the stairwell by now. 'Simon English, Simon English, Simon English,' Candice starts singin at the top of her voice. 'There's only one Simon English.'

'Will you be quiet, Candice? Anyway, I'm no goin to see him. I'm goin to see a lawyer about the flat.'

Candice sits down on the bottom step of the stairs. 'I want to come too,' she says. 'It's my flat, as well, Mammy.'

I look at her and despite panickin that somebody's heard her shoutin out that name, I can't help but wantin to laugh. She's eight years old, but sometimes she's goin on twenty-eight.

'Candice, it's no' – '

'Simon English,' she says, quietly.

On the way up into town, I phone Jessie and explain that Candice wants to come shoppin with me after all. I turn to Candice.

'Need to know basis for Aunty Jessie, from now on,' I say. 'She may have been turned.'

***

The office is in one of the side streets off Broughton Street. There's a big brown sign with white letterin on it. Daniel Brannigan, WS.

It's fair to say things could have gone better.

The receptionist looks me up and down and gives me a wee half smile. 'I'm afraid Mr. Brannigan has been called away, Mrs. Clamp,' she says, 'But I've managed to fit you in with an appointment with Ms. Child.'

The lassie's name is quite appropriate, because she looks about fourteen. And "appropriate" turns out to be her favourite word. As in not appropriate.

'Ms. Clamp?' She's got jet black hair, scraped back and tied into a ponytail which makes her forehead look even bigger. She's a skinny wee thing, with bright blue eyes that seem to stick out somehow. When she sees Candice behind me, her eyes stick out even more.

'Oh, I didn't realise you would have one of your children with you,' she says, cold as ice. Then she mutters somethin I can hardly catch, somethin about it not bein "appropriate" to have children in an office environment. I sit down and Candice sits down in the other seat, as quiet as a mouse. I realise I haven't really thought about how to explain this.

'It's about buyin my Council flat.'

'I see,' she says, lookin disappointed. I gather there's no much money in legal work to do with Cooncil flats.

'And what's the address?'

'3/2 Ivanhoe Court, Auchendrossan.' I can almost see her flesh crawl when I mention the name of the estate.

'I see,' she says again. 'And have you filled in the application form?'

'No yet.'

She sniffs. 'Have you thought about how you're going to pay for it? Have you seen anyone about a mortgage?'

I think for a minute. 'Aye, well, there's the thing. It's what you might call a private mortgage. A man from the estate is givin me one.'

'Pardon?' She looks disgusted. Dirty minded wee hussie.

'A mortgage. The man that owns all the other flats that all the Romanians have just moved into.' This throws her completely.

'Romanians? I'm sorry, I'm not following you Mrs. Clamp. And, by the way, I don't think it's appropriate to refer to people just by their nationality…'

I feel my temper startin.

'I called them Romanians because I know nothin else about them, except that they come from Romania. Is that okay with you, Miss Child?'

I can see the colour risin in her cheeks now, like some laddie from the class above has asked her out on a date.

'Perhaps we got off on the wrong foot, Mrs. Clamp. I simply meant...'

I've had enough by now though. 'I'm no goin to stand here and be accused of bein a racist,' I say, then realise that I'm sittin down. I stand up.

'I really don't think it's appropriate...'

'Come on Candice,' I say. 'We're leavin.'

On the way out, I say to the receptionist, 'I've walked out of better law firms than this one in my time.'

Which I realise, on the bus back to Auchendrossan, is actually true.

***

Pimpy Boy is lurkin around near the front door of Ivanhoe when we come up. He mogers over.

'Alright Karen? You got an answer for me yet?'

'I've just been to see my lawyer, to set wheels in motion,' I tell him.

'But Mammy...' Candice says and I grip her hand, just a wee bit tighter, and she stops what she was goin to say.

Pimpy Boy looks from me to her and back again, gives a strange kind of wee smirk and then slopes off in his shell-suit.

I hope Heid-the-Baw kens what he's doin.

CHAPTER 24
CRAIGENDARROCH

They leave it until the Thursday before to ask me.

By then, of course, things have changed. Only just over a week before they close all the Walter Scott deals, so the rest of the client base can go to hell in a hand cart, so far as those of us in the inner circle are concerned. Wherever we're going, a week on Friday, it doesn't look like we're coming back: calls go unanswered, other deals are ignored or put on the back burner, while we all try to tie everything to do with the Walter Scott companies up with a big red bow.

The only exception is this licence to occupy that Rhona, who's not in the inner circle, of course, is trying to sort out for New St. Andrew's House. She keeps getting earache about it from the Rottweiler, and she keeps coming to me to ask for advice about it. Not that I mind that in the least: it's just difficult to talk to her face instead of her chest, it's so magnificent. Male hormones. Terrible curse.

'The client's desperate to get in on this particular date, but the current owners just aren't interested,' she says.

'So who are your clients?'

She shrugs, setting off an earthquake in the mountain range beneath her blouse. *Look up, look up.* 'Dunno,' she says. 'I just get my instructions direct from Wallace, who speaks to them.'

'Aha.' *Interesting.* Still, I can't be seen to be taking too much of an interest. The only time I raised it with Tony he gave me a strange look and said, 'You don't need to worry about Wrong Box.'

Anyway, I'm sitting at my desk on the Thursday when Al + Bradley slide over. It's first thing, which tends to be the time inner circle conversations take place, before Rhona, who's not in the inner circle, of course, makes it in from whichever awful Fife town it is she commutes from.

'Got a big weekend coming up this weekend,' Al says. The big ginger one looks pleased with himself. 'Wondered if you'd be interested.'

'Thought we'd all be chained to our desks, with Rottweiler hitting us with a big stick till we close all these deals,' I say. The mention of a thrashing reminds me of Leonora's little experiment with the tawse. My arse tingles at the memory. The python tingles, too.

Bradley looks amused. 'Nah. We're getting there with all of them, even the Edinburgh Council one, now you're on board.'

That is true, although there are still some nips and tucks to be ironed out. Not that I'm in any way voting for working the weekend. 'So?'

'Craigendarroch,' Al says. 'The timeshare, you know? The firm has a week – this week, in fact. It's often used for entertaining clients and such, but we've bagged it for this weekend. Go up on Friday night, back Sunday. Pile of scran to stick in the microwave, beers, sauna, swim, game of snooker maybe, more beers. What do you think?'

'And who would we be?' This all sounds better than a poke in the eye with a sharp stick, of course, but not if it's just Laurel and Hardy here.

Al grins. 'Thee, me, Brad the Impaler. Leonora and Danielle. It's a three bedroom. That leaves space for you to bunk down with your little criminal lawyer, if you like.'

This gets me thinking, and the python's doing some thinking of its own, stirring down below. Something doesn't add up though. 'So it's a three bedroom…?'

Al is still grinning all over his big ginger face. 'Yeah. Brad and Leonora have bagged the master, of course. You maybe didn't know about me and Danielle.'

Danielle, who's sitting nearby, looks up and smiles. 'It's mainly in Al's head, of course, him and me. But I've said that if he's a very good boy, I'll share the second bedroom with him and then we'll see if he can be a very bad boy. That leaves the fold down bed in the living room to you and Sylvia, if you can close the deal.'

Brad is concentrating hard, a sure sign that he's trying to come up with something funny.

'And if you don't, keep the porno well turned up to drown out any other noise you might be making.'

'No problem,' I say. This could be an interesting negotiation.

To be honest, when I text Sylvia, I'm not expecting anything better than a straight knock back. When she texts me back straight away, that's what I'm expecting, but instead she says:

Not sure. How about a quick bite at lunchtime to chat thru?

It's good as I could have hoped for.

I stare at the text for a full minute before deleting it and then email Sylvia to make the arrangement. My moby is still drawing my eye, though: I should really be texting Yvonne, except I've absolutely no fucking idea what to say to her. After I got the text from her that she was pregnant, I did try to phone her, but she was all, 'Hi Tracey, yes, everything's fine.' According to the read out on her mobile, I'm Tracey, so Gary doesn't get suspicious when he sees it going off. The fact that she was calling me Tracey on the phone means the big monkey must be at home. Fuck.

The morning goes past in a blur. There's some serious work still to be done on the Edinburgh Council deal: it's predicated upon us getting most of our goodies up front by way of a cash payment from the Auchendrossan gang. The price of the land is fairly nominal, but the City Council wants to get its hooks in the share of the developer's profit once the bricks and mortar go up, so they're looking for assurances of where the funding is coming from.

That's a bit tricky on two fronts. Firstly, the funding is coming from drugs, whores and human trafficking and, secondly, the firm is planning to grab it up, do the bank transfer equivalent of stuff it in a poly bag, and run off to Brazil with it. I can see now why Tony Hand and the Rottweiler wanted me to have nothing to do with the deal: anyone who wasn't on the inside would wonder why what the Council was asking for was unreasonable.

Before I know it, it's one o'clock, and I go down to Pret-a-Manger to meet Sylvia. She's wearing the same suit she had on when I first laid eyes on her, all those years ago it feels like, when poor Jimmy Ahmed was lying tits up in my bath. Underneath the suit, there's a powder blue blouse which has a couple of buttons open at the top and the button at the navel undone too.

There's a flash of a fold of tummy as we sit down with our chorizo and cheese wraps, and the python starts to slither from its nest.

'So,' Sylvia says, between mouthfuls, 'This is some sort of corporate bonding exercise, then?'

'It is actually. Tony Hand apparently certifies it as an internal training course so we even get CPD points for time spent in the sauna.'

Sylvia actually giggles. 'And who's going?'

I tell her. She chews on her wrap for a bit, thinking. I'm thinking, too. Mainly, of course, it's the python that's doing the thinking for me. The python is capable of excellent forward thinking on operational matters, but really I'm trying to concentrate here.

Then Sylvia says, 'All the bad boys and girls then?' She looks at me, and I can't make out what the expression on her face means.

'And you and me,' I say, with a wink.

'You mean you're not a bad boy? How disappointing,' she says. She puts her wrap down and wipes her mouth with a napkin. 'Do you want the rest of this? Go on then. Well, I suppose I could tell my boyfriend I was away on a corporate weekend, integrating with my new colleagues.'

The python takes this as a signal that Thunder Birds Are Go and I actually look down to check that he's not visible to the naked eye, down my trouser leg. Just then, my moby goes. It's Karen Clamp.

'Sorry, I've got to take this,' I say to Sylvia. 'That's great, though.'

To be able to hear myself think amongst all the Jock lawyers and surveyors cluttering up Pret-a-Manger, I have to go outside.

'It's me,' she says. Thank fuck mobys tell you who 'me' is, these days.

'Yes, hi. How can I help you?' I'm trying to get somewhere far enough away from the door to be heard, while keeping an eye on Sylvia.

'Are you with someone at the moment?' She sounds like some sort of jealous girlfriend, for fuck's sake.

'Yes, that's right, er, I was. Okay. I can speak now. What's

222

happening, Karen?'

She's got quite a story to tell. The crims want her to buy her flat from the Council, with them financing it. There seems to be some sort of bizarre thing with her doing washing and ironing for immigrants built into the deal. To be honest, it sounds like she's gone a bit tonto, but I hear her out.

'That doesn't sound so good. Still, it might be best to play along for now.' Then, more quietly, I say, 'Did you get away okay the other night?' Now I'm sounding like the sensitive boyfriend.

'I think so. It was Kenny Futret that was followin you, wasn't it? I don't think he saw me.'

Thank fuck. It's slowly dawning on me how precarious her position is, right now. 'Might be best, actually, if you just play along for now,' I tell her. 'I think the way things are going, it'll all be over in a week or so.' Just at that moment, the guy on the other end of one of my transactions heaves into view: yet another overfed public schoolboy called Brodie.

'What do you mean, it will all be over – ' she says, but I cut her off.

'Got to go now. Call you later, okay?' When I get rid of Brodie, I text her the name and address of an old University pal who does domestic.

By the time I get back, Sylvia has gone and our place has been taken by two goons who have shoved our wraps to one side on the table. I snatch mine and the rest of Sylvia's up, give them a look and then stroll back to the office, thinking all the time that Sylvia may have changed her mind.

Back at my desk, though, there's an email from her:

> I may regret saying this but …. what are
> the sleeping arrangements?

I email her back:

> Dunno yet. Will confirm. Pick you up at
> 5.30 Friday night. Bring toothbrush.

It's best to present these things as a fait accompli.

***

We go straight from the office on Friday night. For once, I've brought the Lexus in from Stockbridge and squeezed it into one of the tiny parking places the firm rents along with the office. By the time Sylvia comes round, the rest of them have headed off already: they've loaded up Al's car with the booze, mostly, and the boot of mine is stuffed with Waitrose ready meals that the girls have got organised.

I'm still in my suit, but Sylvia's obviously got changed at her office, into tight jeans, a camisole top and some sort of long lambswool cardigan type thing. She looks fantastic, but she also looks nervous. When we get in the car, she suddenly leans over and gives me a peck on the cheek.

I catch her, just as she pulls away, kiss her on the lips, and it turns into our first full on snog. It's one of those moments when there's like a bolt of electricity going through your whole body: it feels like I've been waiting to do this for so long, I can't quite believe it's happening. The python, meantime, is purring down my trouser leg like a Panzer Division going into Poland. My hand slips under the cardy, brushes aside the flimsy camisole and at last I'm in contact with the Buddha belly.

Just as I start a bit of stroking action, though, Sylvia pulls away.

'That's enough for now,' she says. 'Just remember, I've got a steady boyfriend.'

'I won't tell him if you don't,' I say, starting the Lexus.

The journey up to Ballater is a good two and a half hours, even giving the Lexus its head. Sylvia prattles on the whole way. I get a blow by blow account of her working week: it sounds absolutely gruesome dealing with these lowlifes.

'So, where do most of your clients come from, then?' I say.

'Oh, all over. The outskirts mainly, of course: all the sink estates like Craigmillar, Pilton, Auchendrossan.'

Auchendrossan. That's why the firm has taken over the one she works for, of course. They want the firm's business all dealt with in-house. No doubt they're going to buy Gordon Drummond, her partner, out. Or at least that would be the plan if they weren't planning to scarper with all the money next Friday. If *we* weren't.

'Have you ever heard of a character called Derek Boyes?' I ask her innocently.

'Gordon handles him himself,' she says. 'He's something of a major player. Where did you hear of him?'

'Read about him in the paper, I think,' I say.

She's quiet for a bit and then she says, 'You know, when I told my boyfriend I was going on some sort of corporate bonding thing, he said I should be careful I didn't get too bonded in.'

I'm thinking about Leonora and imagining her tying Sylvia up with silken ropes. 'Really?'

'Yes.' She says. 'There was something Jim said one time about your firm. Said there was something funny going on but when I asked him to explain, he went all quiet. What do you think about them?'

Something is only now starting to dawn on me. 'You mean Jim Martin?'

'Yes, Jim.' I glance over at her. We're on the A93 by now, twisting our way through fantastic countryside in the dusk. One thing I have to say about Scotland. It's a shame it's full of Jocks, because the scenery is amazing.

'You mean Jim Martin, DS Jim Martin, is your boyfriend?'

I can feel her staring at me. 'Well, duhh.'

Fuck. In fact, fuck, wank, fanny, bastard. How could I have been so stupid?

***

It's eight o'clock by the time we make it up the A93 and along to Craigendarroch. It's pitch black, of course, and it takes a bit of figuring out to find the right lodge, especially with Sylvia yapping away twenty to the dozen. As soon as we pull in beside Al's great big fuck off four by four, though, we're met by the two of them, who descend on the Lexus like a two man rolling maul.

'Beer! Scran! Beer! Scran!' is about all we can get out of them, as they raid the boot for the ton of Waitrose ready meals. Then they're off up the steps into the lodge, barging into each other like only Jock rugger buggers do, dodging and feinting.

'Misread my quadruple bluff, there,' I hear Bradley say, as Al goes crashing into the side wall at the top of the steps. Such larks. Such tools.

I turn to Sylvia, who's gone all quiet. 'Okay?'

'Yeah,' she says. She turns and looks at me and pats my hand. 'Let's take it slowly, okay?'

'Sure,' I say, Mister Sensitive personified, at least until I can get those shreddies off her and the python can work its magic. Right up until then, I'm working from a Nora Ephron script. Sylvia goes to say something else, and then there's a hammering on the car window.

'Are you guys coming in or what?' Bradley shouts. 'There's beer and scran.'

I open the car door, unfortunately not quickly enough to knock the thick cunt off the driveway into the rockery below. 'You bet,' I say and go to unload my bag from the back. Sylvia gets out too and we head into the lodge together, Bradley leading the way like he owns the fucking joint.

Inside, the lodge is one of those ones with the bedrooms on the ground floor and a set of stairs up to a big living cum dining area. The bed that Sylvia and I are down for is folded up into the wall behind some wood panelling. It's plush, in the way these time shares always are; a whole herd of cows have gone into the leather sofas and there's a reasonably up-to-date flat screen telly that the boys are watching.

In fact, things are pretty much split along traditional lines: Danielle and Leonora are busy unpacking the food into the fridge, while the rutting stags are at rest on the couches, a bottle of Deuchars each in front of them. There's a half-finished bottle of white on one of the kitchen tops and two empty glasses beside it: wine for the ladies, indeed.

'Hey, guys!' I say, with as much enthusiasm as I can get up. 'You all know Sylvia?'

'Come through, come through, Sylvia,' Leonora says, 'and leave these useless men to their silly games.' Soon the three girls are all air kissing and giggling over the wine glasses like they're old pals, although Leonora does give me a look at one point that says, *Yes, but will she whack your arse with a leather belt like I could?*

'Be back in a minute boys.' The two goons have started to wrestle themselves out of the couches again – it looks like they've brought a Wii with them, so there's lots of alpha male grunting going on over whatever it is they've been playing – but I suddenly feel an urgent need to visit the bathroom. It's been a long journey but, apart from the obvious, a little toot of nose candy from the supply in my sponge bag seems in order right now.

When I come out of the bathroom, the two of them are waiting for me, Al in his denim shirt and chinos, while Brad has gone for the plaid shirt and jeans look.

'Breath of fresh air needed, Si,' Al says to me, with a wink.

Over his shoulder I hear Leonora shout, 'Be back by nine, boys, or the food will all be gone.' Then we're off out the lodge door, down the steps and on the road to the hotel bar, and I'm stuck between the two cunts with their arms over my shoulders like we're the fucking front row in a scrum.

Bradley starts this low kind of growling sound and I'm expecting some cheesy rugby song, maybe the one about the hairs on her dicky-di-do, but then the two of them start chanting again: 'Beer, Eckies, scran! Beer, Eckies, scran!'

I'm expected to join in, of course, so I do, although I manage to convince them to shut up when we actually get to the main hotel building.

The bar by the swimming pool is pretty full. It's Friday night, after all, so a lot of people have just arrived and come for a drink. I tell them I'll stand the first round, so they find a table while I order up. By the time I've come over with the pints, they've already got their Ecstasy tabs ready, although at least they've had the sense to hide them in their great paws rather than set them out on the table.

Al holds out his hand as if to shake mine. 'Welcome to Craigendarroch, Si, and welcome to the team proper.' I shake his hand and, of course, come away with the little pill nestled in my own palm. I neck it as discreetly as I can, although I do notice the barman glancing over at us as I do so. Other heads are turning, too: the bar's one of these family friendly type places, so there are lots of kids running about and folk who've brought their grannies.

Just for a microsecond, I see us as the rest of the bar probably sees us: three big noisy bastards who have come clattering in and are up to something dodgy by the looks of it.

'Thanks, guys. Listen, let's keep the volume dial down in here, okay? Don't want to draw too much attention to ourselves.' I take a big gulp of lager to wash down the E.

'Sure, Skip,' Bradley says, frowning as he downs half his pint in one go. 'There's some serious drinking to be done.' He wrinkles his brow more deeply, clearly trying to push one more thought down the pipe than his brain is up to. 'I take it you've had that particular kind of medication before? Your reputation kind of precedes you.'

'Sure, many times,' I tell him, patting him on the shoulder. The truth is, I've never combined Es with cocaine before and I generally have the sense not to set the two of them afloat on a sea of lager but, hey, let's see how it goes. As long as it doesn't reduce me to a gibbering wreck telling the cunts everything I know, I'm prepared to give it a shot.

Too bad that the most immediate effect does seem to be that I run off at the mouth. 'Tell me,' I say, 'since we're all in the same scrum together now. What did happen to Jimmy Ahmed?'

Al gets a far away look in his eyes, like he's trying to remember that name from way back and before I can stop myself, I'm saying, 'You know, the guy in my bath?'

It's Al's turn to frown. Brad is too busy hoovering up most of the rest of his pint. He puts his finger to his lips and I realise that I'm the one that's been speaking too loudly this time. 'We don't know,' he says. 'Tony and Wallace handle that side. All we knew was that something was going to happen that would keep you out of mischief. And here you are.' He grins.

'Definitely didn't go according to plan, that one,' Brad says. 'Anyway, ready for another pint?'

And there it is. Jimmy Ahmed doesn't merit more than a mention when there's a drinking competition to be had. Brad has finished his pint; Al is not far behind. I've had about a third of mine so far. 'Same again,' I say. I try to keep my voice down this time.

CHAPTER 25
SHE SEWS SHELL SUITS

Friday mornin. I open the door and there he is, manky white shell suit man himself, Deek Boyes, a.k.a. Pimpy Boy. He's got a pen behind his ear, and some sort of form in his hand.

'Oh hello, Karen,' says he. 'I was just passin and thought we could have a look at the Cooncil form to buy your flat together. Any chance of a cup of tea?'

I stand aside and he struts past. Someone must have told him that story about Sean Connery walkin on the balls of his feet, and he's tryin to imitate it.

'Milk and two sugars, Karen,' he calls out, once he's ben the livin room.

'Just make yourself at home,' I say and make the tea. The kettle's just boiled anyway.

'Any biscuits?' he shouts through.

'I've none in, Deek,' I say. *None that you're gettin anyway,* I think to myself, as I bring the teas through.

He's made himself comfy on the couch so I head for the armchair, but he pats the leatherette beside him. 'Come and sit beside me, Karen, and we can have a look at this thing together.' He gives me this weird kind of smile. 'I promise, no funny stuff.'

I look at him. He's a couple of years younger than me, but his lifestyle seems to be agreeing with him. When he was a kid, he had really bad acne, but that seems to have cleared up. He's got one of those fancy haircuts guys younger than him go for now, all styled with gel and that and a wee pencil thin moustache. The shell suit is still manky, but when I sit down beside him I can smell he's got some sort of expensive aftershave on.

He looks at me. 'You know, Karen, you and me go back a long way, eh? Right back to when we were weans.'

I'm no at all comfortable with this. Sittin beside him, I mean, chattin like we're old pals. He was never a pal of mine.

'Oh, aye, Deek,' I say. 'I ken a lot about you that some of your cronies won't.'

His cheesy grin falters a wee bit at that, but then he says, 'I like you, Karen. You don't take any sh*te from the Cooncil, useless f*ckers that they are, excuse the French.'

Oh ho, thinks I. <u>*Aye, let's talk about the Cooncil.*</u> 'What were they doin round here yesterday, tryin to re-house me?'

I'm studyin his reaction and he makes a good job of lookin genuinely surprised. 'They were what?' There's another expression crosses his face. It's hard to describe, really, but it makes me think: *There's someone from the Cooncil no gettin their brown envelope this month.*

'So they offered you somewhere else out of here? What did you say to them?'

I shrug. 'What was I meant to say to them? I told them to get raffled. I didn't think your offer would stand if I was moved somewhere else.'

What else can I do? Here he is, the laird of all he surveys in Auchendrossan, and Pilton and Muirhouse as well, for all I ken. He can snap his fingers and clear out a whole maisonette block and put a squad of immigrant workers in. He's got the cops and the Cooncil tied up and all I've got is Simon English. And he's no even returnin his calls at the moment. I have to go along with it, at least for now. For the bairn's sake, like.

'Correct,' he says, lookin satisfied. He takes a slurp of his tea and takes the pen from behind his ear and taps the form in front of him. 'Will we have a go at fillin this in then?'

'Whyever no Deek?' I say. I'm surprisin myself here, how co-operative I'm bein, I mean.

***

I meet Candice at the school gate as usual and take her hand.

'Come on, hen. We're going up town to Morninside this afternoon.'

She looks up at me, her wee face all concerned. Teachers might say her spellin's all skew whiff but she's good at pickin up my moods. 'But, Mammy, it's Friday.'

'It doesn't matter, Candice,' I say. 'We can go to Morninside on a Friday just as well as a Saturday or Sunday. Mammy is in need of a bit of a break from this place.'

The bus arrives just then and we go up the stairs to the top deck. There's a front seat free, even though the other one's filled by an old jaikie. The flies are practically buzzin round him, but when Candice gives him a shy wee smile, he brightens up a bit. That's the effect Candice has on anyone.

'Alright, hen?' the jaikie says and then falls asleep.

On the way up town, Candice is all excited about this change of routine. 'Are we still havin fish suppers tonight, Mammy? Will we be back in time? Can I go to the ice cream place and still get fish and chips later?' She's distractin me, but in a good way.

The lettin agency is a block or so down from the bus stop. 'Now, Candice,' I say, interruptin her just as she was about to point somethin out in a shop window, a monkey or somethin. 'We're goin to this shop that lets out flats. It's kind of a pretend game, so don't say anythin about what Mammy tells the woman, okay?'

Candice looks up at me and her mouth falls open. 'A pretend game! With the wifey in the flat shop! Can I pretend too, Mammy?'

I can't help smilin. 'No, Candice. Just you pretend that you don't ever say much, for now.' I can see her face fall, so I say, 'It's like bein a secret agent. You have to keep a poker face. Do you know what a poker face is?'

She shakes her head and then I poke her. 'It's no' laughin when someone pokes you,' I tell her, and she's still gigglin when we go into the lettin agency.

I don't know why I expected a lassie, but it's a guy. He's a young gadgie and he's been hittin the spray tan gun pretty hard. Jet black, gelled hair, and eyebrows that look like they've been drawn on. One of them arches as I walk in the door with Candice and come up to the counter.

'Can I help youse?' he says, lookin as if it's the most unlikely thing in the world that he could.

'We're lookin to rent a flat in the area,' I tell him. I feel Candice grippin my hand, ready to burst into floods of giggles again. She doesn't know, of course, that I'm dead serious. I've never been in a private let, but it couldn't be worse than livin in Auchendrossan as a one woman steamie.

The lettin agent's eyebrow cranks up another notch. 'I see,' he says. 'Most of our clients don't let to DSS, by the way.' His nostrils are flarin as if he can smell the fact that we're DSS.

'Do I look like I'm on the social, is that what you're tryin to say?' I say, tryin to keep my anger down.

'Just a standard question,' he says, lookin disinterested. I notice his nails for the first time: the boy has had a manicure. 'Are you?'

I take a deep breath. 'Aye, it so happens that we are temporarily in receipt of housing benefit till I can get my business started.'

He looks triumphant. 'Well, you might want to try this place. They're students and they're looking for a flat share.' He pulls out a single printed sheet of A4 with an address, but no photograph. Then he gives me a slightly less snotty look. 'They're worth a try, anyway.'

***

The flat is up three flights of stairs, so I'm sweatin like a race horse at Aintree by the time I knock on the door. Candice has stayed quiet for now, but I can hear her thinkin, no idea what the old girl's up to, but we'll let it play for now. She's wise way beyond her years in some ways, that one.

The door opens and it's a lassie with rings through her nose, ears and lower lip. She smiles.

'Aye?'

'I've come about the spare room,' I say, expectin her to shut the door in my face.

Instead, she opens it wide. 'Oh, right. You'd better come in then,' she says. 'Hiya,' she says to the bairn, as we go in, then she shouts through and this gadgie appears.

The two are like chalk and cheese. The lassie with the piercins, when the door's fully open, is biggish made and dressed all in black: black leather trousers, black Metallica t-shirt and a black leather jacket. The gadgie, on the other hand, looks like he's just stepped out of an Agatha Christie whodunit: tweed waistcoat, trousers, brogues. He's even got a cravat on. He's tall and skinny with his hair slicked back. All he's missin is a monocle.

'Well, hi,' he says. He's no quite as friendly as the lassie. She's got the bairn all giggles already, makin faces at her and that.

'Erm, aye,' I say. 'I was wonderin if I could see the room.'

'Sure,' the lassie says. 'I'm Norleen, by the way, and this is Scott. Scott's Dad owns the flat.'

The bairn speaks up as we go into the room. 'I'm Candice, and this is my mum, Karen,' she says and then dissolves into another fit of giggles. Even Scott can't help smilin at her.

It's no like there's a lot to see in the room itself. Bare floorboards, a double bed and a wardrobe that looks like it came out of a skip. Then I look out the bay window.

This side of the flat looks out onto the main road in Morninside. Shops, cafes, posh folk strollin up and down and no a junkie or a jaikie in sight. Just posh folk.

'I'm, erm, DSS. Is that a problem?' I say, lookin at Scott.

He frowns. 'So you get your rent paid by the Council? Is that right? Housing benefit? That can't be rocket science, can it?' Then he leans his head towards the doorway. 'We haven't shown you the kitchen and living room yet. Would you like a coffee by the way?'

And there it is. There's the moment where I think, *I could get away from Auchendrossan. No to some other Cooncil hell hole. To this place. Candice could go to the local school and I could see if I could get a job in one of the wee shops, maybe. Get away from Pimpy Boy and Oddjob, and all the low life Auchendrossan scum.*

The kitchen looks like a bomb's hit it, but then I'm no exactly Nigella Lawson. We sit in the livin room, with the sun pourin in through the two bay windows, drinkin coffee.

Then Scott has to go and spoil it all.

He exchanges glances with Norleen and she nods, slightly.

'Well, if you're still interested, Karen, we'd be very happy to give it a try. Obviously you'd need to get a spare bed for Candice, so it would be a bit of a squeeze. There's a deposit, obviously, of the first month's rent. When would you like to move in?'

All I hear, really, from all of that, is the word deposit.

'How much is the deposit?'

He blinks. 'It's the first month's rent, £550.'

I take a deep breath. 'I see. Well, I'll need to get back to you about our movin in date, in that case. You see, I'm in the process of settin up a business and I've a slight cash flow problem at the moment. It's just a temporary thing obviously, while I'm gettin my business plan together, likes. I could give you a ring in a couple of days to confirm.'

Scott's noddin, but you can see he's no buyin it. 'Oh, okay. Well, here's the number. Of course, we do have other viewers.'

'But you're my favourite one,' Norleen says in a stage whisper to Candice. Candice doesn't even giggle, she just smiles and squirms a wee bit.

Out in the street, on the way back to the bus stop, Candice says, 'We're no goin to get to stay there, are we Mammy? I mean, you've no really thought it through, have you, the deposit and that?'

'Just shut it, Candice,' I say, immediately wishin I hadn't, but she doesn't say another word to me, all the way to the bus stop, all the time waitin for the bus and all the way on the bus back to Auchendrossan.

I can't say I blame her.

***

The next mornin is Saturday mornin, but there's no let up in the charm offensive by Pimpy Boy. He chaps the door just as I'm makin a coffee to go with the Farmfoods croissants I splashed out on (there's another mistake I'll never make again).

When I open the door, there he is in all his manky glory. There's someone behind him that I take at first to be Oddjob. Then, when I stand back to let them in, I see who it really is. He's got a huge melon head and I've seen him twice before. Once goin into the flat below, when I passed him on the stairs, and once, briefly, the first time I tracked down Simon English at his office.

Tony Hand.

'I got your form into the Cooncil yesterday, Karen,' Pimpy Boy says. 'I didn't know how you were placed with a lawyer yet, so I thought I could get my own one down to have a bit chat with you about the process.'

'Oh aye, right?' I point them towards the living-room. Melon Head's givin me a funny look as he goes past. And then I turn to Candice, who's standin beside me.

'Out you go and play the now, hen,' I say to her quietly. 'This'll be borin grown up stuff.'

234

'But I might be able to – ' she starts, but then thinks better of it, and heads out to play down at the green. No that there's any other kids to play with now, of course, with Pimpy Boy havin moved all the families out to make way for his East European slave labour.

Pimpy Boy's sittin back on the couch, arms across the back, as if he owns the place already. He jerks his head at Melon Head.

'This is Tony Hand, one of the top lawyers in Edinburgh, likes. I use him for all my business interests.' Tony Hand is still lookin at me, obviously tryin to work out where he's seen me. Pimpy Boy goes on, 'He's no generally available on a Saturday mornin, of course, but I told him this was important. I'm as keen as you are to get this whole deal signed up as soon as we can, Karen, just so as we know where we all stand.'

I decide to beat Melon Head to the punch. 'Have we no met before?' He looks grumpy already, no doubt about bein dragged out of his bed on a Saturday mornin by scum like Pimpy Boy, but now he frowns even harder.

'I don't think so,' he says. You can see, though, that he's still thinkin it over.

Pimpy Boy looks amused. 'Maybe on one of your visits down here, Tony, to view the property portfolio?'

I jump right in. 'Aye, that's where I've seen you. I've passed you on the stairs. You were goin up to one of the other flats.'

Hand looks confused for a minute and then nods, briefly. 'That must have been it.'

'Anyway,' Pimpy Boy says, gettin things back on track, 'My good friend Karen here is buyin her Cooncil hoose and I've agreed to help her fund it. It's a small type of transaction in the grander scheme of things, likes, but it means a lot to her. So would you be able to draw up the contract for us, Tony?'

Tony Hand's eyes widen. He sits back on the couch a bit, and I realise I've no even gone through the rigmarole of offerin them coffee or anythin. 'No, I couldn't act for both of you. The Law Society…'

Pimpy boy's lookin at me and winkin. 'Well, Tony, me and Karen aren't goin to tell the Law Society, if you aren't. Can you no just do this on the side, likes?'

Tony Hand shoots him a look. 'No, I couldn't. Not unless you want me struck off. And where would you be then, with all your other transactions?'

That shuts Pimpy Boy up. There's a bit of a pause. In the meantime, Tony Hand is lookin at me funny again.

'Unless,' he says slowly, 'You're actually both clients of the firm's already.'

I get a feelin like there's a block of ice runnin down my back.

CHAPTER 26
LIKE THE BUSES

There are certain rules in the land of Jock. One of them is that everyone has to get their round in, no matter what the consequences. Even if it decreases your chances of a shag by about ninety-five percent.

So, three pints later, we're heading back to the timeshare lodge late. My head is totally spinning. Just so you don't need to do the research yourself, a toot of coke, a tab of ecstasy and three pints of Stella don't mix terribly well on an empty stomach. Plus, of course, I'm totally paranoid about giving something away to these two goons.

Not that they're paying much attention: they're back to their barging each other game, knocking each other into the rhododendrons and giggling like a couple of Heriot's boys on helium. When we get back to the timeshare, though, the mood changes.

'You're dinner's in the dog,' Danielle says, when we come in. The girls have been hitting the Chardonnay pretty hard, but they're still not pleased.

'Boys will be boys, eh?' Leonora says, slapping the plates of what might have once been Thai green curry down on the table.

Sylvia, meantime, is smiling sweetly at me. 'Good news, Simon,' she says. 'I've had a chat with Danielle and we've re-arranged the sleeping arrangements. We've got the twin-bedded room downstairs. Al and Danielle can have the double up here.'

Oh, great. Everyone's laughing, looking at the expression on my face.

'You can still push two singles together, big guy,' Brad says chortling away as if this is the funniest thing anyone ever said since Bob Monkhouse lost his joke book.

'Not if Sylvia has anything to do with it,' Danielle says, slyly, and they all burst out whinnying and laughing, like this one, if possible, is even funnier.

Things get worse when we sit down to eat.

'Splash out some of that cab.sauv.,' Bradley says to Danielle. He's grinning from ear to ear, but then he would be, the bastard, since he's got Leonora in the big double room with the en-suite and, if he cleans up his act from now on, a chance of exploring the A to Z of perversions with Miss Lochgelly later on. Meanwhile, I'm going to be in the twin room with Miss Frosty Pants, probably lying awake listening to him grunting. I'm thinking about all this, as I neck half a glass of the red at one go.

'Steady on there, tiger,' Al says to me, looking amused. 'We've only got a case of this stuff to last us all weekend.'

'They've got wine shops up here, even in sheep shagger central' I try to say, although it comes out a bit more like 'Shum shopsh wine in shipshagginshentrl.' Everybody laughs but they're looking at me now, wondering why I'm so pissed on a couple of pints.

'If you don't slow down and behave yourself, you're not even getting in the same room,' Sylvia says and they're all laughing like hyenas again, when the Perrier award wining hyena has just cracked the line that clinches the prize for him.

I feel strangely disconnected from the whole thing. It's like I'm watching a movie, but the sound and the camera work don't quite match up. There's also a kind of jerky thing going on, like my eyes are some sort of CCTV camera jumping from one scene to another: Leonora, looking at me in a slightly concerned way now; Sylvia, still laughing at her own joke; Brad, already shovelling food into that great rubber lipped maw of his.

I look down at the plate. Food. Must get some food in to try to counteract all the booze and pharmaceuticals. I shovel some of it onto my fork, although it seems bloody slippery stuff, that won't stay on. Eventually, I stab a big bit of chicken and ram it in. It doesn't taste of anything. I try to tell them this but they just fall about laughing again.

I decide to just keep quiet and maybe they'll pick on someone else. Maybe they won't notice that the room is starting to spin. I'm aware of Danielle saying something, something that is probably directed at me, but I decide to ignore it.

Then everything goes black.

When I wake up, I have this excruciating pain all over my face, particularly my left eye. Then I realise I've ended up face down in the Thai green curry. It feels like a piece of chilli has embedded itself under my eyelid.

'Fuck!' I rear up suddenly, which makes the whole lot of them laugh even louder – push my chair back – and stumble for the bathroom. I'm aware I'm stumbling a bit, but I make it to the bathroom okay. My eyeball now feels like it's been dipped in acid, but then half my face is on fire: a tip for you, if you're wanting to moisturise, don't use Waitrose Thai green curry. I manage to wash it off and look at my face in the mirror: a bit blotchy and there's still a few grains of rice in my hair, but, otherwise, not too bad.

'Are you all right, Simon?' It's Sylvia's voice, on the other side of the door.

'Never better,' I say and get the last of the curry off. My eyeball pain is now reduced to a dull throb.

When I come out, the cunts have got the decency to look mildly concerned. I give them the line about moisturising with ready meals and they seem to understand enough of it to at least laugh a little. Then I say, 'Just nipping downstairs for a minute,' and clamber downstairs to the room.

Of course, I never make it back upstairs. The minute I sit down on the bed, I realise what a great idea it would be to just pull the covers over me and have a little sleep. I'm vaguely aware of people looking in on me at various points and then everything goes black again.

***

When I wake up, I've got vague memories of dreams about lions prowling round the timeshare. Lions and hyenas. Eating Thai green curry.

In fact, just before I wake up, an image flashes into my head of two hyenas shagging, looking over their shoulders at me and laughing.

'Misread my quadruple bluff,' the hyena on top says.

I wake up again, properly this time. My bladder and my head are competing to see who can be sorer than the other. Must go for a piss. If I can get my head off the pillow.

Sylvia. Fuck. I get my head off the pillow and she's awake, on one elbow, watching me. Even in the half dark of the bedroom, and in my feeble state, I still notice that she's wearing extremely sensible pyjamas.

'How are you feeling, now?' she says.

'Actually, better than I thought I would,' I say. This is a lie, but I know that it's important not to show weakness.

Sylvia's bed is the one nearest the window. She turns over and opens the curtain a crack, just enough to put some light into the room. 'So. Are you going to behave like a total prat all weekend? Because if that's the case, Simon, I'm going to get Danielle to give me a run to the nearest railway station this morning. If you can't hold your drink, you shouldn't try to keep up with the others.'

Oh, fucking great. So now, in her Jock vision of the world, I've made a prat of myself not just by passing out into the main course, but failing to keep up with Al + Bradley. Now would probably not be the time to tell her about the drugs. Lots of humble pie to eat before I get to eat anything more interesting. Or even dream of getting my paws on that Buddha belly of hers.

'You're absolutely right, of course, Sylvia, to be so annoyed. Look, let's start again can we? It looks like it's a lovely day out there – ' Certainly, it feels like the sunlight is melting my retinas through the gap in the curtain. 'So, maybe we could go for a walk this morning, have a chat. How would that be?'

She harrumphs a bit, but by the time we've chewed the fat a bit more, she's agreed at least not to go back to Edinburgh right away. I haul myself out of bed – still with my clothes on of course. Standing up feels not too bad.

I'm looking for a clean shirt and boxers when Sylvia says, 'You can get dressed in the toilet upstairs. I'll be up in a minute.'

Fine, then. I tiptoe up the stairs and pass the half-open door where Al and Danielle have been no doubt doing the nasty all night. I can hear them awake, talking in low voices.

In the bathroom, I grab a quick shower and start to feel human again. Then it's time for breakfast with the Addams family.

At breakfast, I'm still the comic turn, although I do start to play up to it a bit. You can see them storing up the story about me blacking out into the curry for future dinner parties with their awful Jock friends: 'Then there was that guy, you remember, what was he called, oh yeah, Simon English. And the funny thing is, he was English, hahahaha. Well, we had him up at

240

Craigendarroch...'

Except, I suddenly remember, we're all off to Brazil at the end of next week. So, they'll have to learn fucking Portuguese to regale their pals with that one.

Remembering that makes me realise the situation I'm in. Why on earth did I agree to come up here with them? To keep them from being suspicious I suppose. But why did I bring Sylvia? I realise that I've probably put her in some sort of danger by doing so, at least possibly. Not that she knows anything, of course. Unless Martin's told her more than she's letting on.

And then I think of Yvonne, and her text message, and that brings me down even further. A quick dip into the sponge bag and a quick post-breakfast toot helps to kick start the day a bit better, though. Somehow, we all end up going for a 'little walk' which turns out to be a full on route march over several mountain ranges. Danielle and Leonora are well up for it, yomping away uphill, but Sylvia hasn't brought the right kind of boots.

'How much further is it?' she keeps saying, like some kid. Eventually, when we're on the down slope and heading towards a pub for lunch, I say to her, 'Do you want a piggy back?'

She eyes me suspiciously. 'Is that just an excuse so that you get to touch me?' The rest of them are further on and have stopped to wait for us to catch up.

'Of course,' I say and she actually laughs. 'But it will stop your feet hurting.' She shrugs and then hops aboard my back, while the rest of them give a sort of cheer. I must admit, it is good to feel her clasping her arms around me, even if it's the incorrect mounting position, as it were. She starts to warm up, and is yapping away ten to the dozen again by the time we reach the pub.

The Gruesome Twosome are up at the bar getting the beers, so, while Danielle and Sylvia go off to the toilets, I sit down next to Leonora.

'Just lemonade for you, skip?' Brad shouts across to me.

'Yeah, right,' I shout back and everybody laughs.

I laugh all the louder because, while Brad is otherwise occupied and everyone else is looking the other way, Leonora has just stroked my cock.

241

Yes. That's right. You heard it right. She just does a quick look around, to check nobody else is looking, nods and smiles at me and runs her hand down the python, which immediately tries to escape from my jeans to get some more petting.

Leonora winks at me. 'Someone's feeling better,' she says.

***

After lunch, and the long march back to Craigendarroch, it's time for the leisure facilities. Al + Bradley decide to go to the gym first, which suits me fine: the less I see of those two tools over the weekend, or, indeed, ever, the better.

I'm disappointed to see that Danielle and Sylvia have both gone for boring one piece swim suits: it turns out that both of them are serious swimmers, so they get into a competitive kind of splash up and down, all a bit alpha female.

Only Leonora has made an effort, with a black bikini. She's skinny, but athletic. After a couple of swims up and down, she looks at Danielle and Sylvia doing their Rebecca Adlington impressions and then sideways at me.

'Fancy a shot in the steam room? See you in there in a couple of minutes. You first.'

Thank fuck the water is quite cold: it's keeping the python down a bit.

The steam room has some fat Aberdonian in it when I go in, who wants to talk to me about football. I tell him I'm more of a rugby man and that shuts him up. Then Leonora comes in, and he takes the hint and fucks off.

She is one cool customer. She comes in and sits down beside me. Not so close that anyone would be suspicious, but within reaching distance. I've been careful to sit in the corner where your shape can't be seen through the door of the steam room.

'What now?' I say.

'Brad had brewer's droop last night, so I'm needing some quick relief,' she says. 'Give me your hand.'

I have to lean over a bit to reach where she's leading my hand but as soon as I realise where it's going, I forget about any of the discomfort.

'Down there,' she says and gasps as my fingers make contact.

242

That is one very bad, and very wet, pussy.

'Oh yes,' Leonora says, 'Yes. Yes. Come on. Do it faster. Yes.'

So there we are. Let me tell you, as a hangover cure, sitting in a steam room, bringing a thoroughly perverted woman to the peak of orgasm while your girlfriend and her boyfriend are somewhere about outside, would probably now be in my top ten tips. I'd never realised before that I enjoyed the element of danger, but then as Leonora bucks and gasps beneath my attentive hand, I realise that she's got quite a lot to teach me.

We're both getting so involved in it we only just notice the dark shapes of people appearing at the door of the steam room in time. I whip my hand out from her bikini and, on instinct, assume a kind of crash position, as if the heat is just too much for me.

'Ah, so that's where you got to,' Sylvia says as she and Danielle come in with Al + Bradley. 'Simon, are you all right?'

'I think he's getting there,' Leonora says, cool as a cucumber.

***

You know, pussy really is like the buses. You wait around for weeks sometimes for one and then two come along at once. The only problem is, you can't hop aboard both at once. Or only very rarely. Besides, my near death experience with the two tarts in Auchendrossan had put me off that particular fantasy for a while.

The rest of the afternoon and evening runs along fairly predictable lines. A couple of drinks – all together this time, so no eckies for the gruesome twosome – followed by a meal in the hotel. Back at the lodge, Sylvia had still thrown me out when she wanted to get changed, but there was a look in her eye that suggested things might be different.

When it gets to bedtime, however, she's still playing a bit hard to get.

'I'm just not sure if I'm ready, Simon,' she whines.

'I know, I know,' I say, Mr. Sensitive Man of the Year again. 'But I've been quite a good boy today, after all.' *At least so far as you know, sweet cheeks.* 'How about a good night kiss?'

She sits down on my bed beside me. 'Maybe.' She puts her

head to one side and I'm not so drunk tonight that I can't read there's something else going on in her head.

'Tell me, Simon. What's going on in this firm? How do they earn all these fees, especially when they can afford to send the lot of us away for the weekend to Craigendarroch?'

'You don't want to know.' It's out there before I can take it back.

'What do you mean?' There are only the lamps on in the room, casting a soft light over Sylvia's face. She looks absolutely gorgeous tonight: she's got her hair up, but a little bit of it has escaped, and she's got more make-up on her than I've ever seen before. A demure little blouse that still shows off her petite figure and tight black trousers with boots. She reaches down now and pulls one of the boots off.

'What do you mean by that, Simon?'

I take a deep breath. 'How much has Martin told you?'

Her eyes widen. 'Jim? You mean there's something criminal involved?'

I try to choose my words carefully. 'There might be. But, really, Sylvia, you don't want to be involved. Now how about that good night kiss?'

She touches my face with her hand, 'And are you involved?'

'No,' I tell her.

'That's good, then.' Her hand brushes down from the side of my face to the front of my shirt and starts unbuttoning it. 'I mean, I know you're a bad boy – ' she smiles, making good progress on the shirt buttons – 'I just wasn't sure how bad.'

If only she knew. 'You have no idea,' I say, finally getting my hands on that Buddha belly of hers, ruffling the silk blouse up and stroking my thumb past the jewel in the navel.

I hadn't had sex in a single bed since I was at university, in halls of residence, where the place was done up like a monk's cell to stop you getting too frisky with the undergrads. But, let me tell you, that wasn't going to hold the python back now.

***

Afterwards, as we lie snuggled together in the dark, she says, 'Criminal, eh?'

CHAPTER 27
DOING DOMESTIC

Tony Hand is starin at me. 'I might have seen you down here, but have I not also seen you in our offices one time? I hope you'll forgive me for saying this, Mrs. Clamp, but you're fairly distinctive.'

Sometimes my brain is no capable of thinkin quickly. This time, though, it manages to come through with somethin.

'Oh, I see. Are you in that firm I went to see the other day, Brannigan's? That lassie Miss Child has got a bit of an attitude problem, I have to say.'

Big Melon Head looks confused. 'No, no. I'm – '

I beat him to it. 'Oh, you're that other lot, Benzini, Lambe and Lockhart, are you? Aye, I did go in there for a bit of advice a few weeks ago. I got to see some prat called Simon English.' I pause, tryin to make this all as convincin as possible. 'You're no goin to get him to do my conveyancin, are you?'

I sneak a look over at Pimpy Boy, to see how he's takin all this. As soon as I do, he starts creasin himself laughin. Tony Hand is smilin, too.

'Karen, hen, they couldn't make you up,' Pimpy Boy says after a bit. 'How many firms of lawyers have you fallen out with, exactly?'

I shrug, playin along with it. 'One or two.' Which, technically, is absolutely correct. So now they have me pegged as some sort of nut that goes around botherin random firms of lawyers.

Tony Hand's still smilin. 'Well, don't worry, Mrs. Clamp. Simon doesn't do domestic in any case. I think I'll get Rhona Gallagher onto your case. She's a very nice girl – I'm sure you'll like her much better than Simon, who can be a bit abrasive at times. Now, if I can just take some details…'

And there it is. I'm off the hook – I think – for now, although Tony Hand only has to ask the snotty receptionist lassie and he'll find out I asked for Simon English specifically. Then I'm sunk.

When he's gettin ready to leave, Tony Hand says somethin that makes me completely paranoid. 'Yes,' he says, turnin to me and chucklin at the door. 'Simon took quite a lot of getting used to for all of us. I'm sure you'll like Rhona, Karen. She's a very nice girl. And Simon's going to be a very busy boy over the next week for us.' And then it's him and Pimpy Boy off down the stairs like a couple of old pals.

I stand at the window, watchin Candice out on the green. She's taken the old tennis racquet and ball out with her: that seems to be her favourite game at the moment, just knockin the tennis ball into the air and then tryin to keep it up in the air. She dodges about the green, eyes fixed on the tennis ball: up it goes, quite high into the air sometimes, then she scurries about tryin to get the racquet underneath it to punt it back up again. One, two, three, four times she manages it, before she gets the edge of the racquet instead of the strings the next time and the ball shoots off across the green. She doesn't give up easily though.

We're safe for now, I keep tellin myself. But why is Simon English goin to be kept so busy? It might just be that they're loadin stuff onto him to keep him out of mischief, like he said they did before. But, all the same, I want to talk to him and find out what's goin on.

When I phone, it goes straight to message. 'It's me,' I say. 'Can you give me a ring as soon as. Things are happenin down here and I need to find out where I stand.'

Simon has told me he is workin with the cops, with the straight cops, a guy called Martin, he thinks he can bring the whole thing crashin down: Pimpy Boy and his gang, Melon Head and the firm, the whole lot. He's no actually told me how he intends to do that. And, anyway, what if they've turned him? All they'd need to do with a prat like that would be to offer him a load of money to go along with whatever they're plannin.

I need to keep goin with plan B, which is no more cunnin than gettin out of Auchendrossan altogether. If only I had five hundred and fify pounds.

Then I think of my sister, Elaine. Her man used to work at Marconi, got made redundant, and then, straight after, got a job workin through in Glasgow. Elaine told me last year they were keepin the redundancy money, for a rainy day.

I open the window of the flat, but wait until Candice has missed the ball again before I shout down to her. 'Come on, hen,' I tell her. 'We're goin to visit your Aunty Elaine.'

***

I phone ahead, like I always have to with Elaine. She doesn't like surprises.

'That would be fine to see you, Karen,' she says, but there's a tightness in her voice that suggests there's somethin that wouldn't be fine at all about it. I'm thinkin it's just that she doesn't have any time for me, when she says, 'Mum's here at the moment.'

'Is she stayin long?' I say. We're at the bus stop and the Pilton bus is just pullin up. *Last chance to abort the mission.*

'It's a bit hard to say,' Elaine says, 'but why don't you come anyway?' There's that tightness in her voice, but she's tryin to sound right about the whole idea of a family gatherin. 'I'm sure James will be delighted to see his wee cousin.'

Candice is tuggin my arm. 'We need to get on the bus, Mammy,' she says and, right enough, the bus driver is glowerin at us for wastin a microsecond of his time. I step on and that's us committed, especially given how much Lothian buses charge for cartin you twenty yards.

'I'll see you soon, Elaine,' I say into the phone and then ring off. Candice has already got the money ready, and then it's off upstairs as the driver puts the foot to the floor.

Up the stairs and onto the top deck, me scannin the place for likely suspects. Nobody obviously psychotic, but a woman and her kids have taken over the two front seats, so we sit a wee bit back.

I'm thinkin all the time about Tony Hand. If he goes back to the office and checks with that wee jumped up receptionist, he'll find out that I actually asked for Simon when I came in. Not a great prospect. I try phonin Simon English again on the bus. His phone is still switched off. Have they got to him already?

Candice, meantime, is pointin out things of interest on the way to Pilton.

'Look, Mammy, there's a man with three Rottweilers. I wonder what he feeds them?'

'Probably his kids,' I say, without thinkin.

Candice gives me a look. 'Sky McClatchey says hers is just a big soft lump, Mammy,' she says, quite the expert all of a sudden on all things related to dogs. She suddenly thinks of somethin. 'Oh, I was forgettin! Fifi and Bonbon will be there as well! I haven't seen them in ages!'

It says somethin for my family that Candice is more excited about seein the poodles than any of the humans. I mean, Elaine's no a bad sort at all, or I wouldn't be goin and askin her for money. But then there's my Mum, who has surfaced from somewhere and, from the coded messages Elaine was givin me over the phone, is already drinkin at half past eleven.

And then there's my nephew, James. He's twenty now, James, but from an early age he's been collectin every kind of condition known to the medical profession.

He was five when he was diagnosed as dyslexic, right off the bat. He got an ADHD diagnosis for his sixth birthday, but he had to wait a couple of years to add dyspraxia to his trophy cabinet. At fourteen, he started drinkin (he can thank his granny for that) and throwin it back up all over my sister's posh Cooncil house. They decided that was alcohol intolerance, although he's still doin his level best to tolerate it. I'm surprised he hasn't collected the Tourette's prize yet, given the amount he swears.

That probably sounds a bit intolerant, but, for me, James only has a special need if bein the laziest guiser that ever sloped across this earth has suddenly become a medical condition. Of course, you can't tell Elaine and Rab that.

As we get off the bus, I'm still tryin to clear my head of all the old family disputes, to try to plan how I persuade Elaine to lend me £550 for the deposit for the flat. To be honest, it's no as if I could blame her for turnin me down. I mean, we get on all right, me and Elaine, but it's no as if Standard and Poor would give me a triple A ratin.

Just as we reach Elaine's gate, Candice suddenly turns to me.

'Mammy, I've just had an idea. We need to get money for that deposit for that flat in Morninside, don't we? Why don't we ask Aunty Elaine for it? Her and Uncle Rab have got loads of money, likes.'

I pause at the garden gate.

'That's a brilliant idea Candice. How did I no think of that?'

248

She fairly skips up the path to the front door, no even noticin the pack of Art Deco garden gnomes that have suddenly appeared round about Elaine's bird bath. It's her hobby, I suppose. She's got to have somethin, what with a son like James, and her husband, Rab. He never says anythin about anythin.

Mum is ben the livin room when we go in. It's no even midday, and I can see an empty bottle beside her already. She seems to have started drinkin Bacardi Breezers like she's some sort of teenager. Maybe she's headin for her second childhood or somethin.

'Daughter number two!' she shouts as I come in. Then, 'And my wee lassie – come and give granny a hug, hen!' Candice goes over and gives her a wee cuddle, poor soul. Then Mum looks up at me.

'Sun's over the yard arm,' she says, watching me for a reaction. 'Would you no care for a wee sherry, Karen?'

'I don't drink, Mum,' I tell her, for the umpteenth time.

Cousin James shambles in. 'Alright, Granny? We're no all seasoned alkies like you, eh no Aunty Karen?' And he turns and winks at me, despite the fact he's got a can of super lager in his hand.

Just at that moment, Elaine comes through with a tray of tea and biscuits. She looks hassled, but then no wonder with a house full like that.

'Ah, that's more like the thing, isn't it Aunty Karen?' says James. 'You're fond of your biscuits, are you no?'

I ignore him and say, 'Hiya,' to Elaine.

She looks at me as if she's just realised that me and the bairn have appeared. 'Good to see you, Karen,' she says. 'Could you give me a hand in the kitchen a minute?' And then she's off again, rufflin the bairn's hair on the way. 'Did you see the gnomes on your way in?' she says to her.

A hand in the kitchen, in Elaine speak, usually means she wants a word. Which is fine by me because that's what I want, too.

But then, there's no show without Punch so, the minute we start talkin in the kitchen, James has to come and see what's goin on.

***

'I could tell you're wantin to talk to me, Karen,' Elaine says. How can she ken that? My perfect sister Elaine. She even seems to have psychic powers now. She gives a wee smile which is no really a smile. 'It's just I've got this house full, as you see...'

James, meantime, is propping up the doorway of the kitchen. 'Aye, I kent Aunty Karen was wantin somethin too, Mum.'

Must be psychic genes. I take a deep breath. 'There's this flat in Morninside.'

I'm no sure anyway how to go on, but before I get any chance to, before I've barely finished saying the word Morninside, James has picked up on it like he's a parrot or somethin.

'Morninside? Morninside?' He laughs. 'What would the likes of us want in Morninside?' Then, before Elaine or I can say anythin, he's away to the living room door.

'Haw, Granny, Aunty Karen's wantin to move to Morninside.'

I can hear the old witch cacklin away ben the living room. He's set her off now. 'Morninside? Morninside?'

James comes back to the kitchen doorway, pushin his nose up with his finger. 'I say, we're all terribly Miss Jean Brodie here. I've just popped over from Auchendrossan myself. Would you care for a scone?'

Elaine's tryin no to laugh. 'So there's this flat in Morninside...'

'Aye. And there's a deposit for the rent...'

I still don't get any further. 'Haw, James. Get us another Bacardi Breezer. I need to celebrate my lassie movin to Morninside.'

'Certainly, Grandmamma. Would one like a Victoria sponge with that?'

The two of them are laughin like drains, and Elaine's shakin her head with a wee smile, lookin at me like, what can you do with them?

'...and it's £550. The deposit.'

Elaine stops lookin like she's going to laugh.

'Karen. I don't have £550 to give you.'

I feel a sinkin feelin in the pit of my stomach. 'I just thought, with Rab's redundancy.'

Elaine shrugs. 'Long gone.' She looks at James, who's now

marchin up and down the hall makin up a wee song about Morninside. *Aw, aye,* thinks I. *The flatscreen TVs and playstations and trips to London to see his favourite bands don't cost nothin.* I feel somethin buildin in me.

'Morninside, Morninside, we're all off with Aunty Karen to a flat in Morninside. Morninside, Morninside…'

'Will you fuckin shut up about Morninside!'

The words are out – that word. The word I said I'd never use – before I can think.

Elaine's starin at me. 'There's no need to swear, Karen. James has got – '

'Aye, I know. Special needs. That doesn't mean he gets to be a wee shite.' Another word I've not used since I was a kid. I feel the colour risin in my cheeks.

Elaine shakes her head. 'I think you'd better go, Karen.'

James is standin there with a big grin on his face, as if this is the best entertainment he's had all year. Candice has come out of the living room to see what all the fuss is about.

'Aye, I'm goin. Come on, Candice, we're leavin.'

At the door, I turn and say to Elaine, 'I'm sorry.'

'So am I,' she says, but her eyes are blazin.

When we reach the bus-stop, Candice says, 'Well, that went well.'

'Candice,' I say and manage to stop myself.

'I ken, Mammy,' she says, and takes my hand.

When we get back to Auchendrossan, there's a dark blue car parked in one of the spaces outside the flats. That wouldn't be unusual, except there aren't any cars parked outside the flats now: the Eastern Europeans all get moved about in vans. As I turn to go up the stairs, I hear a voice behind me from the car.

'Oh hello, Mrs. Clamp. I wondered if I could have a word?'

I recognise him right away when he gets out of the car, of course. There's nobody seems to wear a suit worse than Kenny Futret.

CHAPTER 28
EMISSION IMPOSSIBLE

Cystitis is a funny thing. I've only ever had it a couple of times before, and both times after a brisk bit of python gymnastics.

If you've ever had it, you'll know I don't mean it's funny in the Fry and Laurie sense: it's actually pretty unpleasant, having this burning sensation in your waterworks and feeling like you're desperate for a piss, even right after you've been. Generally involves sitting on the toilet, trying to get rid of the feeling, and knowing that there's not very much you can do about it.

Fortunately, an old girlfriend taught me the trick of drinking lots of water and that generally flushes it out.

Anyway, I've plenty of time to think about this, lying awake with Sylvia sprawled on top of me. Sharing a single bed sounds a lot more romantic than it actually is, of course, particularly when you have to keep sliding out apologetically to go to the bog.

'You okay, babe?' she says, when I contort myself back into position for the umpteenth time.

'Never better,' I say and she smiles sleepily and snuggles up again.

'Me too,' she says.

Both times, the sex part was pretty fantastic, I have to say. Apart from the end bit, but we'll come to that in a minute, if you'll forgive the pun. Not quite every position in the Karma Sutra, but given the restrictions of the single bed and having to stay quiet so the others won't hear too much, it was a command performance.

The only thing was, both times, it was Leonora's face I saw at the end.

Now, if you're a bloke, you're probably thinking, so what? Don't over analyse it, Simon. It's all good. And I'd agree with you, but lying awake at four in the morning with the python telling me it's potty time again, and Sylvia's arm thrown across me while she breathes gently into my ear, it all somehow seems more significant.

Plus, of course, there's the paranoid thing about Sylvia asking me questions about the firm. Plus the fact that her regular boyfriend is probably the only cop in the whole of Edinburgh who can help me take these bastards down. Plus the prospect, at the end of the week, of having £100 million and a new life in Brazil dangling in front of me.

So, when Sylvia wakes up around six, gazes into my eyes and says, 'What are you thinking?' All I can think of to say is, 'How much I wanted this, right from the start.'

Which is, at least, true.

She smiles, kisses my neck. 'It was the jewel in the navel that did it, wasn't it?'

'It was everything,' I say, as she moves from my neck down to nibbling at my chest.

One other cure for cystitis, even though it's temporary: give your python something else to think about. This time, with Sylvia up above me framed in the light from the window, Leonora doesn't make an appearance.

***

Things are quiet at breakfast. The others are either too hung over, or too distracted with trying to get the lodge back into some sort of shape, to quiz me or Sylvia about what we got up to last night.

Just before we go though, Sylvia's upstairs helping with the kitchen and I'm in our room packing my stuff when Leonora slides in.

'I hope you haven't told her anything, Simon,' she says. 'We don't need any complications.'

'Don't worry, Leonora,' I say. 'I've been tight as a camel's arse in a sand storm.'

She smiles. 'Good. I might still have to discipline you later on, of course.'

'I look forward to it,' I say, as she slips out the door again.

Drive down is quieter too, than the one on the way up. Sylvia snuggles into me as we head out of Braemar. It's fine, really, although there's a part of me finds it slightly annoying, especially as the A93 has one or two tricky corners.

After a bit, she says, 'So what happens next?'

Without thinking, I say, 'Well, there's the Edinburgh deal to close. Still a couple of sticky bits in that, but we should have it done by Friday.'

She nudges me in the ribs. Not terribly helpful when I'm taking a tight left at the high end of a good speed for it.

'I meant you and me. I mean, maybe I should tell Jim about us.'

'No!' I say. Then, 'No, not yet, Sylvia. There are still some loose ends to tidy up about my case. We don't want any personal stuff to come in the way of getting all the unpleasantness about Jimmy Ahmed laid away, do we?'

I can feel her looking at the side of my face. 'What? I thought Jim had been taken off the case? In fact, he told me he was on gardening leave. He wanted me to look into his employment position, legally I mean.'

Shit. I hadn't thought of that.

'Well...he is off the case, officially. But I think Futret is still going to Jim Martin for help. The two of them are pretty close, you know.'

'Oh,' she snuggles in closer. 'So. What are we doing this afternoon?'

Actually, my plans for the rest of the day hadn't involved Sylvia. After last night, my afternoon was going to consist of a half decent sleep, particularly as, apart from the cystitis, I seem to be developing some sort of sore throat and runny nose combo which is making me feel pretty fucking shitey.

Still, it's the python that answers for me. 'Why don't we go back to mine? We can pick up some stuff from the deli and have a late lunch. What do you say?'

***

It's early evening by the time I get rid of her. I know that probably makes me sound like a bastard but, sometimes, when you've just made it with the numero uno on your list, it's good to just have a bit of space and look back on it. Maybe it's a bloke thing. Maybe it's a bastard thing. Whatever.

Anyway, by the time she leaves, Martin, Yvonne and Tom have all left messages and my throat's starting to bite.

I start with Tom. 'How's it going, Cunty One?' I say to him.

'Been better. See these bastard doctors. And that useless fucker of a plumber, Ballingall, has been back again.'

He launches into some long rant about Ballingall and, in the end, I have to cut him off, by telling him there's another call coming in.

I'm lying, of course, but the next call is going to be trickier.

'Are you sure, Yvonne?'

'Yes, Simon, I'm sure. The doctor's confirmed it. What are we going to do?'

I don't like the sound of that *we*.

'Well, won't Gary be over the moon? I mean, you two have been trying for a baby for ages and everything...'

'You're missing the point, Simon.' There's a pause, then something that sounds suspiciously like a sob at the other end. 'We were trying for a baby together, not with you.'

'Yeah, fair point, I suppose.' Actually, there's a paranoid part of my brain running away with the idea that she knew it was her hubby shooting blanks, and not the other way around, but now is probably not the time to have that conversation.

She is definitely sobbing now. Never good when they turn the water works on you. Through big raggedy intakes of breath, she says, 'I'm going to have to tell him.'

'Wait. Don't do that just yet. Look, I'll try and get over soon, okay? We can talk this through and work out how to tell Gary together.'

'Can you get over this week? Gary's back from the rigs again on Friday.'

Friday. Fucking everything happens on Friday. 'Sure.'

When I get off the phone from Yvonne, Martin has sent me a text. *Get here as soon as you can. We need to talk.*

You know, I feel this talking thing is over-rated. I blame the psychiatrists for making people think that if they get everything out in the open, it's going to improve things.

You tell someone something they don't like. They tell you something back that you don't like. Isn't it better just to shut the fuck up sometimes? Maybe these old Jock guys that you meet that never say fuck all about anything have got it right. Maybe, when I'm older, I'll be exactly the same. Just one of these guys you see out in bars that says next to nothing most of the time then the whole crowd of them turn to him and he'll say one or two words, just the right one or two, and everyone nods or laughs or does whatever because they know he's the man.

Or like the big Indian in *One Flew Over The Cuckoo's Nest*, who says next to fuck all to Jack Nicholson for the whole film and then says "juicy fruit" and throws the whole fucking sink unit out the window to help them escape, or something like that. It's a while since I've seen that film, but he was my favourite character.

I think of texting "juicy fruit" back to Martin, but instead I tell him I'll be right over.

***

'You fucking cunt!'

This time, it's not the parrot, it's Jim Martin himself that's doing the swearing. Cameron the parrot is hopping up and down and screeching, just to lend some kind of non-verbal support, I suppose, as Martin puts me over the back of his sofa.

'If you'd just let me explain – ' I say, but it's difficult to talk when he's got me by the throat backwards over the furniture.

'What the fuck did you think you were doing, bringing Sylvia into all of this? It's bad enough having to work out a way to save your worthless arse without having to think about her as well.'

I try to shove him off but he's got the positional advantage. I always thought he looked like a tough little bastard, and it turns out looks weren't deceiving. You forget these guys are used to having a rumble on a regular basis.

'Point one,' I try to say, although with his hand round my throat and the fact that I was starting to lose my voice anyway, it sounds more like "pint in". I try again. 'Point one, I didn't know she was your girlfriend.' That at least is true, although I guess the signals were fairly obvious. I just didn't think Sylvia would go for a guy twenty years older than her, with a face the colour of a Cox's Pippin.

He relaxes his grip slightly. 'And point two?'

'I haven't told her anything,' I say. This isn't completely true, but good enough for now.

Just as suddenly as he went for me, he lets me up.

'I suppose it doesn't matter that much at this stage,' he says.

'Cunt,' says Cameron, looking disappointed that all the soapy bubble has stopped. He starts bouncing his head up and down, that way that parrots do, presumably to see if that will get us all excited again. 'Fucking useless waste of space,' he says, giving me the eye.

I ignore him. 'Look, Jim. Whatever happens between you, me and Sylvia, we have to just put to the side for now. I'll certainly be trying to avoid her being involved in anything this week, okay? And when it's all over, we can sit down and talk about things like grown ups.'

You can see he's still trying to work out a way to get to a place where he can legitimately punch my lights out, but there are more pressing needs now. 'Okay, okay. So, how do we nail these bastards?'

Good question. I sit myself back down warily, with a glance at Cameron. He's obviously got bored with the whole thing, though, and has started gnawing at his bars again. 'Well, Tom will still have that recording of Futret menacing me on his laptop. So that's something.'

Martin is nodding. 'Yes, that is something. It can get me back in the door of Fettes at least, by showing that Futret is bent. Maybe I should take that straight to the Chief Con., just to be sure your cover isn't blown.'

'Okay. I'm very keen on my cover not being blown.'

Martin scratches at his stubble. It's coming out grey, making him look even older and uglier. How the fuck could Sylvia? But then, I say that about why most women would with most men, myself included.

'And you say it's all going to go down this week? All the Walter Scott companies close their deals, the money goes into the firm's client account and they all fuck off to Brazil?'

Myself included, I nearly say, but decide not to. Not that I am, of course. Probably. I'm so busy thinking about this that I miss his next question and have to get him to repeat it.

He looks annoyed. 'I said, can you talk me through the deals again?'

'Sure. Most of them are things like shopping centres or other retail bits and bobs which the crims are buying under the front of the Walter Scott companies. There are huge wads of cash sitting in the holding company's account for transfer over to the firm's client account on Friday for the purchases.

'The crims are buying at the bottom of the market. Then they'll either transfer these retail parks on after they've developed them a bit or got permission for development, or just keep them as a steady income stream. Either way, they're getting nice clean money washing through their account.'

Martin is nodding. 'Okay. I think I understand that. But why don't your two bosses just cream the money off from the holding company's account and disappear into the sunset?'

'Because your man, Derek Boyes, is smarter than that. He alone can authorise transfers into the firm's account. And, obviously, he's not going to do that if he smells a rat. Plus, there's the Edinburgh City Council deal.'

Martin looks puzzled. 'Why is that so special?'

I shrug. 'It seems to be Derek Boyes' pet project. He wants to develop the best club in Edinburgh ever on the site and run it himself, as some sort of retirement plan. He's had enough running prostitutes and extortion rackets. But he's got a man at the bank who only shits when Derek tells him to, and he's been told not to authorise the transfer for the other deals until the Edinburgh deal is done on Friday.'

Martin is scratching his stubble again. 'And you've managed to get yourself onto the Edinburgh deal?'

'I have, but they're watching me like hawks.'

'So what do we do?'

I shrug? 'I don't know yet. But I'm working on it.'

***

I'm still working on it, two days later, and still thinking about what to do. I mean, I wouldn't be human, right, if I didn't even consider the option of taking £100 million and fucking off to Brazil with it? That kind of money could seriously insulate you from any extradition. Plus, in a way, it's a victimless crime. I mean, ripping off gangsters, although obviously that's not where the money comes from originally. I'm thinking about all of this as I sit through yet another frustrating meeting with the guys representing Edinburgh City Council. I'm there, Bradley's there,

Mr. Smooth and the guy with the beard from the Council itself. It's like banging your head against a brick wall.

I mean, this should be a straightforward deal. We buy some crappy old properties from the Council in the Cowgate, knock them down and build a brand new shiny club for Derek Boyes, lately of the Parish of Auchendrossan, to run as his own personal retirement plan. The thing is, in any deals like this, there are often gremlins and all the gremlins seems to have all come at once for this one.

First of all, there's the title, which is as dodgy as they come. Some old dog of a deed from about 1617, which talks about back courts and vennels and all sorts. I'd be surprised if Mary Queen of Scots' washing line wasn't in there as one of the boundaries as well. We put Rhona onto it and she came back with about a ten page report explaining how duff it was.

Then there's the small matter of the profit sharing agreement. The Council can't just sell us the bloody thing and be done with it. Oh no. As I may have said before, Councils are always paranoid about selling something, and then finding out that someone else makes a buck out of it. Everybody always thinks Councils are stupid and incompetent and, generally, I'd agree. But these guys are certainly trying to screw us to the wall to make sure that any money made out of the development is creamed off in both directions. So I've had Bradley trotting back and forth all afternoon to Tony Hand getting detailed instructions.

That's only a couple of the problems with the deal. I could go on but I would imagine you're losing the will to live already. Legal stuff is boring. Commercial property legal stuff is especially boring. Just trust me when I say the deal is just one of those slippery bastards that won't lie down and take it.

By seven o'clock, everyone's pretty much had enough and we let the poor bastards go. I come back to find Bradley shuffling the papers together, brow furrowed, chanting 'beer, scran, laps. Beer, scran, laps.'

'Okay, okay, I can take a hint,' I say. 'Get the Big Ginger and we can go some of that. I want you early in bed, mind. We'll need to pick this deal up off the floor in the morning.'

He nods, big rubbery lips pursed in deep concentration, and goes off to find Al. I'd said I'd meet Sylvia later on but I'd warned her the meeting would probably go on. That should give me a couple of hours to keep these two happy and then off to see her in Marchmont.

***

Beer and scran is seen to easily enough. There's any number of places round the West End and, on a Tuesday night, we've got our pick.

By then, though, I've pretty much had enough. The cold which had started up on Sunday morning after my session with Sylvia is getting worse and worse. My nose is dripping like an icicle in the Sahara and my throat is killing me.

'I think I'm going to head off now, guys,' I say as we split the bill for the food and beer.

'I don't think we can let you do that, Si,' Al says and I feel a moment of panic. What have they found out?

Then Brad says, 'You've got to try out this new place the crims have opened, Skip. Honestly. You'll love it. It's called the Diamond Cellar.'

So, before I know it, we're in this place in the New Town, not far off York Place, in one of these incredibly respectable Georgian crescents. Down the steps and into the basement flat, though, and you're in a different world.

The theme – obviously – is diamonds, as in a girl's best friend. Most of the girls are wearing some form of jewellery, although I suspect it's as fake as the rest of them. I spot one girl who's slightly more curvy than the rest of them, with what might be a ruby in her belly button. I stroll over and she looks up, flicking her hair back.

'Hi, I'm Carly,' she says. 'Would you like to buy me a drink?'

Of course I would. The sight of all this naked female flesh is getting the python vaguely interested, although he is strangely subdued at the moment. I suppose it must be the cold affecting him as well. I wipe my nose with my hanky just as unobtrusively as I can and get the girl a drink.

Meantime, I notice Al + Bradley have gone over to the barman and are exchanging a few muttered words with him. He glances across and nods to a couple of girls who teeter up to the boys on their high heels.

Well, I've made my choice. Whatever's special about these two, I'm not about to find out.

Carly takes a sip of her drink. 'Would you like a dance?' she says.

'Sure.' We go into the back room where the lap dances happen. It is pretty dingy and I'm sure some of the velvet upholstery has seen better days, but then Carly backs me into one of the booths and gets me sat down the way she wants and it feels like it's going to be all right. The music's some dreadful rubbish on a loop but she doesn't seem to notice, really, and she's soon into her routine, taking off what little she had on in the first place, bouncing up and down on my knees, stretching herself out over me, all the usual stuff.

In the meantime, I'm sitting there with my nose running, trying to hold it all in. The python, meantime, is acting strangely: all kind of shy but, at the same time, he has a tear in his eye, if you know what I mean. Not just my nose running.

Then Al + Bradley stroll in with their girls, stroll right through the back room and through a door at the back to a hidden stair. Al, just before he shuts the door behind him, mimes something to me, pointing towards the door that leads to the bar, and making the sign of a mouth flapping with his hand. He wants me to speak to the barman.

And that's the point I realise there is a difference between me and these cunts.

The minute Carly is finished rubbing me up the right way, I pay her, go back through to the bar and walk straight out. The barman shouts something after me, and when I look back, I see that he's got someone else lined up for me, a tall, skinny, blonde girl who presumably is one of the ones that goes upstairs. I just shake my head at him and keep walking.

It's a knocking shop, masquerading as a lap-dancing bar. They have rooms in the upper level for the special punters who get unlimited access, as it were. I think of Leonora and Danielle, that these two wankers were snuggling up to just two days before. I mean, a lap dance is one thing but the full English breakfast is quite something else.

And that's when I decide what I have to do.

CHAPTER 29
ODDJOBS AND ENDS

I've sent Candice to her room to play. Futret is ben the livin-room waitin for me when I come in, sittin in one of the armchairs, his wee beady eyes followin me as I go to sit down.

'I would say long time no see, Mrs. Clamp, but that's no quite right, is it?'

'What do you mean?' I try to look confused.

His wee eyes are pure borin straight into me. 'A week past Monday,' he says. 'You were up in Causewayside when I was there on a job.'

'Causewayside?' I have to think quickly. 'Well, maybe, I do have a client up in Causewayside. I take in sewin, ken? I think I maybe was droppin somethin in one night recently.'

A wee smile slips across his features. 'A client? What's the name and address?'

'I can't tell you that. Client confidentiality. Data protection.'

The smile has long gone. 'A client? And do you usually meet your clients in the pub? You see, Mrs. Clamp, I saw you coming out of the Old Bell looking like a fish out of water. And I wondered to myself, Mrs. Clamp surely couldn't have anything to do with the guy I'm following, can she? A guy called Simon English?'

This is no goin well. I shift in my seat. 'Simon English? That prat of a lawyer? Why is it everybody thinks I've got somethin goin on with Simon English?'

Futret raises his eyebrows, trying to look surprised. He's no a great actor either. 'Really? Who else has been asking you about Simon English?'

The words are out before I can think them through properly. 'Your boss, of course.'

The greasy wee eyebrows go a notch further. 'My boss? You mean DS Jim Martin has been here?'

I'm so far in now, I can't stop myself.

'Everybody kens who your real boss is, Kenny. Deek Boyes. That pimp you used to run about with when we were growin up, even though you were just a wean at the time.'

He looks like a rat that's managed to chew through a bin bag. 'You're no a very good liar, Karen. Just for the record. Was it Simon English you were meetin that night?'

I make a big sigh. 'No, it wasn't. I've only met that prat once, and once was enough. If you want the truth, I'm havin an affair with a married man. That was who I met at the Old Bell. We arrived separately and we left separately. Now are you satisfied?'

I must be a better liar than he thought. You can hear the cogs grindin round in his head. After a while, he shrugs and stands up. 'Well, it doesn't really matter whether I believe you or not. It will be up to Deek what he thinks.' And with that, he scampers off, leavin me with my heart rate doin the pasa doble and a volcanic eruption brewin in my insides. I go through to see Candice, to check that she's okay.

'Everythin alright, Mammy?' she says. 'What did that man want?'

'Nothin much,' I tell her.

The look she gives me says that even she kens when I'm lyin.

***

I finally get through to Heid-the-Baw on the Tuesday and he's still bein evasive. At least he has the decency to sound shocked at what's goin on.

'You're kiddin me?' he says, as if I sound like I'm in any mood for jokes right now. 'So they're basically running a slave labour camp and you're being shoved into it?'

'That's about it, aye.'

There's a pause at the other end. 'Karen, things are moving fast here. There is someone else on our side – a police officer.'

'No Futret?'

He laughs. 'No. Not Kenny Futret.'

'Thank fuck for that.' Now I've started sayin swear words again, I just can't seem to stop. Maybe I'm gettin that Tourette's.

'You know, I've never heard you swear before,' Simon says.

'Don't you fuckin start.'

Another pause, and then somethin that almost sounds like a sigh if I didn't ken better. 'Look, Karen. I know it's not a bundle

263

of laughs down there at the moment. Just sit tight, okay? They don't really have anything on you so just play along. Hopefully by the end of this week we'll have nailed them for good. So you can go back to your normal life.'

What an excitin prospect that will be, I'm thinkin, as he rings off. Too late. I realise that I could have asked him for the money for the flat in Morninside. Simon English has probably got £550 in his back pocket as spare change but somethin, somethin that in a less scummy place than Auchendrossan might be called pride, makes me stop myself from ringin him back.

Besides. There's one more last resort.

Candice's father.

***

There's a new routine in the maisonettes now. Wednesday dawns like any other day, with the East European workers up and gettin washed and dressed at about five in the mornin. Then the tramp, tramp, tramp of feet down the stairs, past the flat and down to the waitin Transit vans. Then the revvin of the diesel engines and they're away, away to whatever rubbish job they have to do to get to stay in Auchendrossan.

The sad thing is, they're probably glad to be here, poor bastards. There I go again.

Anyway, I'm lyin awake by that time in any case, thinkin about phonin Candice's dad. I get Candice up for breakfast and walk her to the school, still thinkin about it.

'Are you away with the fairies, Mammy?' she says, at the school gates.

'Me? No – why, are you?'

She giggles. 'Sky McClatchey says I am, sometimes,' she says.

'Then I'll need to have a wee word with her Mum,' I say, thinkin of Maggie McClatchey, the livin embodiment of mutton dressed as lamb. If she were chocolate she'd eat herself, yet here she is with her wee lassie darin to give my daughter cheek.

Candice is standin absolutely still, lookin straight at me. 'No, Mammy, you won't.'

I open my mouth to reply, but she turns and walks away, as if that's it, that's final.

Anyway, all that's fine and well, but it interrupts me from worryin properly about phonin Candice's Dad for all of thirty seconds. By mid mornin, all my anxiety issues are back and I've had to down two coffees and three yoyos to screw my courage to the stickin place. Just as well I haven't started drinkin. Maybe keep the swearin as my new hobby for now.

I've got the number of his fancy London office where he works now. I check my voicemail first, then that I've got enough credit on my mobile: anythin to put off the evil moment. Eventually, I dial the number and stab the green button.

'Bruce Reid?'

Now, I suppose at this point I should tell you, dear reader, I've no been exactly totally and utterly and completely honest with you. There's a reason why I took an interest in the strange case of Simon English and his dead client in the bath when I saw it in the paper. A reason why I decided it was worthy of a Clamp Investigation. And the reason was the name of the firm. Benzini, Lambe and Lockhart.

That, and the fact that I knew Brucie boy had been transferred to London for some reason he never told me properly, and Simon English had swapped jobs with him.

'It's me. Karen, I mean. Candice's Mum.'

There's a sigh, then, 'What can I do for you?'

I can hear other phones ringin in the background, some loud English bloke shoutin somethin, the hustle and bustle of an office. What can I tell him?

'Well, you know where I live?'

'Yes. Auchendrossan Estate. A shining example of post-war neo-Stalinist brutalism architecturally speaking. I remember it well.' He always was a sarky bastard.

'Well, you would, of course. You were here often enough.'

Wrong move. Bruce can do shirty at the drop of a hat. 'What do you mean by that? Before I met you, Karen, the only reason I came into Auchendrossan was because the conveyancing of these flats was an absolute nightmare. The Council had sold them off in loads of different ways, shares of laundrettes and so on. I was there on official business.' He's hissin at me now, obviously tryin to keep his voice down so the rest of the office can't hear.

'Oh aye. That beautiful laundrette.'

You see, when I met Bruce first, ten years ago, things were different. He was a wee munchkin of a man who came knockin round the doors tryin to sort out his title deeds, and I felt sorry for him.

That was another of my Big Mistakes.

'I repeat, what is it you want, Karen? I'm kind of busy just now.'

'Right ho, then. I need £550 to relocate me and Candice out of this hell hole.'

There's a stunned silence as he digests this and then he says, 'Any particular reason why you want to do that now?'

And that's a question I don't know how to answer. What if he's still in with the rest of the crims in the firm and is just waitin things out in London until he gets his share? Somehow, though, I just don't think so. Bruce was always so gormless, he wasn't really aware of what was else was goin on around him.

Like the first time we were intimate. I woke up and he was gone: but he was through ben the livin room scrabblin about in his briefcase for a piece of paper.

'That's it,' he said when I came through in my nightie. 'It just came to me just now. I get the Council to draft a new deed of conditions which supersedes the other one.' I thought of askin him if that had been all he had been thinkin of all the time, but I didn't really want to hear the answer, I suppose.

So, after a pause, I say down the line to him, 'Let's just say these clients of yours are makin my life very difficult. There's a flat in Morninside – '

'Morningside?'

'Aye, Morninside. Is there any reason why I shouldn't live there with your daughter?'

'Er, no, no, of course. That sounds…great. When do you need the money?'

'How soon can you get it to me?'

He tells me it will be in my account tomorrow, that he can't get to the bank today, but he'll do it by telegraphic transfer. He actually sounds quite pleased. He was always on at me to get Candice into Mary Erskine's until I pointed out it took three buses to get from Auchendrossan to Mary Erskine's in the mornin and you'd need to start the night before.

Next I ring Scott, the landlord's son of the flat in Morninside and ask him if it's still available. He even sounds half pleased to hear from me. He says that, yes, it's still free and as soon as I can get a cheque in his hands, we can talk about a movin in date. The poor wee lamb doesn't realise that as soon as I get the cheque, Candice and me will be arrivin on his doorstep and no leavin.

I spend the rest of the day makin plans for what we'd take with us. No that much we'd need, to be honest. Things have gone downhill in the flat since I had that spread in Hello magazine. Before I know it, it's three o'clock and time to get the bairn from school.

'You're still away with the fairies, Mammy,' Candice says, but she's smilin now, catchin my mood, listenin to me hummin some song off the radio – Cheryl Cole I think it maybe is – under my breath.

'Maybe I am, hen, maybe I am,' I tell her.

Then we round the corner to our block and I see Deek Boyes, and the expression on his face, and I stop singin.

'Karen, hen,' he says, jerkin his head up the stairs. 'We need to talk.'

In the flat, Candice doesn't even ask, but dumps her school bag and goes and gets the tennis racket and ball. She's goin out to the green to get away from whatever it is Deek is wantin to talk to me about. There's more than half of me wants to go down to the green and hit the tennis ball up in the air myself.

Instead, I decide to get on the front foot. 'What the hell do you think gives you the right, Deek Boyes, to come and go in my flat like it's yours already? I don't owe you anythin, at least no yet, and if you keep takin this attitude…'

He's gone over to the window, starin down at Candice runnin out to the green below.

'There she goes,' he says quietly. Then he turns to me. 'Karen, you were always somethin of a square peg in a round hole, even before you put on that weight. I genuinely, genuinely thought I was doin you a favour. I could see you as a great wee concierge for this block, just keepin the guys on the straight and narrow, doin their washin, sewin, all that stuff. They're good enough lads, ken, but we work them pretty hard so I thought someone like you could just keep an eye on them for us. It seemed like a win win negotiation.'

'Oh aye. You're just Dale Carnegie all over,' I say.

I find I'm standin at the window as well: the two of us lookin down onto the green, where the bairn has now started her tennis racket game, puntin the ball up in the air and runnin to get underneath it. She starts with one or two wee bounces and then bigger and bigger punts, goin higher and higher, and her chasin about, lookin up, this way and that, tryin to get in position before the ball comes down. Just one wee lassie in the whole of the green.

'You know, Karen,' he says, 'for a long time I didn't know what I was doin, with the property stuff, I mean. I was sittin on top of this mound of money, from all our operations, like, and it took me a while to realise what I was doin, buyin up property with it. The first things I bought were flats in Auchendrossan. All these private lets. Of course, they're the worst property investment I could possibly have made: Sixties maisonettes in a sink estate.'

He looks at me. I decide to keep my mouth shut, and he goes on.

'When I hooked up with Tony Hand and his partner, he steered me in the right direction: shoppin centres, office blocks in the centre of Edinburgh, all that sort of stuff. But still, whenever the opporchancity arose, I bought up some more of Auchendrossan. Bit by bit. It took me a while to realise what I could do with them all: house my workers. That's what they were built for in the first place, after all. But the reality is, Auchendrossan is just a tiny part of what I do now.' He gives me a strange kind of smile. 'Did you know I'm the director of twenty companies? No bad for a boy from the worst estate in Edinburgh, eh?'

I look down at the bairn, still puntin the ball up in the air with her tennis racket. I can't even remember how she got the tennis racket. It might even have been her father gave it to her, on one of his very occasional visits. 'So why are you here?' I say to Pimpy Boy. 'Why can't you just leave me and Candice in peace?'

Deek's smile fades. 'Because there's one thing I've learned in this business, Karen. You have to do the detail. If some wee scally is creamin money off the top of the drugs sales he's doin for me, I have to send Kevin round to convince him of the error of his ways. If some old biddy's a week late with her loan repayments, the same. Or if one of my girls gets a bit uppity and starts takin work in on the side, if you ken what I mean. And that's what you were, Karen. A detail. The last flat in the block. The same way that Simon English was just a detail to Tony and Wallace. Unfortunately, Debi and Elena fucked up the sortin out of that detail.'

He's pullin out his mobile phone, as if he's gettin bored with his own conversation. Needless to say, it's a top of the range iPhone. Just like Simon English, I think to myself.

He looks at me. 'And then there's you and Simon.' He's fiddlin with his iPhone now, lookin out at the bairn on the green. The ball goes up, up, reaches the top, and then starts down. The bairn scampers to get under it and this time she really middles it, back up, up …

'I've told you. I don't know anythin about Simon English. I met him the once. He's a prat. What more do I have to say?'

Pimpy Boy glances back up at me from his iPhone. 'This can still all go away, Karen,' he says. 'You can tell me now what's goin on. There's too many coincidences where you and Simon English are concerned. But you're drinkin in Last Chance Saloon.'

Down, down, down the ball comes out of the sky. Candice is racin to get there, but she won't. She's no got the time. I try to think of some explanation, somethin that will make some sort of sense.

'He's my boyfriend,' I say.

Pimpy Boy actually laughs out loud. Down the ball comes and Candice misses it. It bounces once in the long grass of the green that the Cooncil never cut often enough.

'Karen, even if that's the right answer, it's the wrong answer.' He thumbs the screen of the iPhone. Almost instantaneously, a Transit van sets out from under the block opposite where Jessie used to stay. Where Oddjob still stays. It's an ancient old Transit thing: its diesel engine rattles and growls as it heads along the link road past the green.

It stops next to the lassie. Oddjob gets out and goes to speak to Candice. He hunkers down, pickin up the tennis ball and chuckin it from hand to hand.

Then he stands up, takes Candice by the hand and starts to lead her towards the Transit.

I'm already half way across the livin-room. 'Don't you dare!' I'm shoutin. I'm no even sure at who.

Out in the hall, I hear Pimpy Boy shout after me: 'Don't worry, Karen, you're goin as well.'

CHAPTER 30
DEAL BREAKER

I knew, as soon as I said it to Martin, of course. The thing I had to do – the only thing I could do, in fact – was to bust the Edinburgh deal, in the hope it would bring the whole deck of cards crashing down.

Now, this may not sound like a big thing to you. It's just a property deal, right? But when you've spent literally weeks piecing together all the elements of a transaction with a bunch of guys in a room, tying in all the loose ends and frayed edges that keep appearing, about titles and profit share and guarantees and insolvency provisions and all the shit that it takes just to make a property deal fly, it kind of goes against the grain to then start hacking it to pieces again.

But that's all I can do to keep the whole pot boiling. Friday is the absolute deadline, but, in the meantime, I've got to keep the Edinburgh deal from getting over the line. That way, these cunts can't jet off to Brazil before Martin can convince his bosses to come in and pull the whole deck of cards down.

'I need more,' he keeps saying to me. 'Surely there must be more. The Chief Con is listening to me but he needs something to make it stick.'

'I've given you all I have,' I say.

And it's true. All I've got is that dodgy sound file taken via my iPhone of Futret menacing me a bit. I put it on my Vaio laptop, and a memory stick which I've given to Martin.

'Still nothing more?' Martin asks me. He knows I've got something else, but he doesn't know what it is. And I still don't know for definite that I can trust him. I mean, he genuinely does seem to be at home almost all the time when I phone him, as if he really has been suspended, but he could just be operating under deep cover for Tony Hand and the Rottweiler, like half of the rest of Edinburgh, it seems.

Apart from Tom, the only person I pretty much definitely know I can trust – mainly because she's so mental nobody in their right minds would have her in on a conspiracy, unless they were desperate, like me – is Karen Clamp. And she's still not talking.

By Thursday night, I'm really starting to get a bit concerned about her. I mean, why isn't she talking to me, even just to give me grief about something?

'You have to go down there,' Tom says, when I speak to him about it. So I do.

As I nose the Lexus into Auchendrossan, it takes a while to work out what the difference is. Then I twig it: no cars. The parking spaces round the flats are usually full of rusting white vans, battered looking Nissans and the occasionally shiny four by four if the main drug dealer in the block is at home.

But now, there's nothing. I could have my pick of the car parking spaces but, instead, I circle in the central roadway bit, cutting the lights and then opening the windows. Silence. I look up at where Karen's block stands: like the other blocks, it looks fully occupied, lights blazing away, apart from her flat.

And then I notice something else. On each balcony, instead of the cast and crew of *Trainspotting* chasing each other with machetes, there's a dark haired bloke, or maybe two, smoking, leaning over the balcony, chatting to each other. As one of them sparks up, I get a flash of high cheekbones and dark eyes. Karen had said they were moving Eastern Europeans into all the other flats, but I thought she was exaggerating.

One of the guys spits, looks down at me in the car, engine idling. He says something to one of the other guys. That's enough for me, and I hit the lights, gun the engine and get the hell out of Auchendrossan. By then, it's time to go up to Sylvia's flat.

***

'Hope you like pasta, Simon,' she shouts from the kitchen. Her flat, funnily enough, is the next street down from Martin's. I could probably wave at him and Cameron from the bathroom.

'I was brought up on the stuff,' I tell her, trying to get the cork out of the bottle. Of course, I'm driving, so I can only have one.

'Here it is,' she says, coming through with two steaming bowls of penne al'arrabbiata.

And so it is. *This is nice*, I find myself thinking, looking at her bookshelves and CD collection and laminate flooring and Ikea furniture. She's got something acoustic and warbly on music-wise and, after we've eaten, she snuggles into me and it really is ok. One of those hours in your life when it's just you and a girlfriend and the rest of the world can go and fuck itself.

Even when she pulls away from me and says in that whiny voice of hers, 'Do you mind if we don't, tonight, Si?' it doesn't matter that much. I think I know it's not going to be the last time ever.

That night, Thursday night, I lie awake in the dark, about a million things going through my head. Sylvia. The way she's got under my skin totally. When this is all over, I think. Martin. Cameron, the parrot. Tom with his medical problems.

And the firm, and the criminal mob they're the money laundering organisation for. Living high in the hog on the back of drug dealing, prostitution, human trafficking, you name it. So my brother, for example, can't get the medication he wants, because all the money's going on Methadone to get the schemies off smack. Brad, and the smorgasbord of sexual diseases he might be plugging himself into. Leonora too, for that matter. I hadn't thought of that until now.

***

Anyway, Friday morning dawns, and I guess I must have slept because I was dreaming about being strapped to the front of an HGV that was heading down one of these steep streets that go from George Street into the New Town, Hanover or Frederick, with no brakes and me lashed to the front like some gigantic fucking trophy teddy bear.

Martin is still trying to get his bosses to act; still no word from La Clamp; so there's nothing to be done except go into the office.

The first thing to give me a minor uplift when I go in is that there's no Bobby on the desk. I really wasn't in the mood for one of his arsey little games, although the guy who's in his place tells me he'll be in later on.

'He's working a split shift, likes,' he says to me, as if Bobby's working patterns are something I would give a flying fuck about.

The second, even more uplifting thing, is the sight of Rhona's chest greeting me as I reach my desk.

'Simon, could you have a look at this for me? It's the final draft of the licence for investigative works for New St. Andrew's House. Do you think it's okay?'

Bless her. She actually thinks I'm a nice guy. I wonder briefly what will happen to her after today? I mean, either I manage to bring the firm to its knees by having all the cunts in it arrested, or I don't, and all the cunts in it fly off to Brazil. Either way, Rhona's left minding the baby. Who's going to employ her after this?

I take a brief squint at the licence.

'It looks fine, Rhona.' I pause and then remember to be a nice guy. 'You've done some good work there.'

Rhona hooks some of that long dark hair of hers behind her ear, and smiles. 'Thanks. You know, I've heard all these stories about you, Simon, but you've always treated me really well. Thanks for your help with this.'

'My pleasure.' And it is my pleasure, watching her arse wiggle away back to her desk.

The client in that licence, Wrong Box Limited, is still nagging away at me. Karen said something about it being a film and then, before that, a Robert Louis Stevenson story. I'm not big on authors but I do know, of course, he's the guy that wrote Jekyll and Hyde. Not Walter Scott. Does that mean something?

I fire up the computer and do a quick bit of research on Wrong Box on the company's website.

Like the Walter Scott companies, it's a shell company; no returns made yet. Its directors are Wallace, Tony and a guy called Joseph Aloysius Kinnaird, with an address in what sounds like a posh bit of Liverpool.

Liverpool. Interesting.

There's a site, creditgate.com, where you can search director's names and see what other companies they're on. Kinnaird's name is so unusual, he's much easier to track down than I thought. There's a security firm, Kinnaird Security Limited, which has been going for ten years or so. And then, more recently, Kinnaird Construction Limited.

Both are registered in the Isle of Man. That's not unusual. In fact, there are so many company registered offices in the Isle of Man, I'm surprised it's not an aviation hazard, what with the sun glinting off all the brass plates when planes fly over.

'Simon.' I look up and there's Wallace Brodie's secretary. 'Have you got a minute for Wallace?'

***

Big Doggy's in his kennel, glowering at me. 'Just wanted to make sure you were getting with the programme, Simon,' he says. 'Remember, that little bastard at the bank isn't going to release the funding until you drag the Edinburgh City Council transaction over the line. So, no mistakes.'

'It's there,' I say. 'Just a final run through the documents this morning, then we sign off.'

He grunts. 'Fine. You've taken far too long over it. Now get out, I'm busy.'

You'll be busy in Saughton soon, bending down to pick up the soap in the shower, I'm thinking to myself as I head up to the fifth floor. The reality is though, that I've stalled the thing as long as I dare. We really are at the final gallop through the final version stage.

Mr. Smooth is all pally when I come in. 'Well, Simon, what do you think? That we might even have a deal to close this morning, eh?'

'Should bloody well hope so,' mutters the City Council guy, who's clearly taken a deep dislike to me over our last few weeks together. Can't say it's not mutual. Never trust a guy with tinted glasses.

Brad is making the coffee. At least he's found his level. 'Just black, Si?'

'Yes, that's fine, Brad.' I ignore the pile of crisp white paper in the middle of the table, which Mr. Smooth is already opening out, anxious to get the deal done and signed off so he can collect his massive fee from the Council.

'Alex, do you have the titles plan there? Just for a quick look.'

The City Council beard looks at me suspiciously but, sure enough, amongst the pile of crap that we've left sitting there from yesterday, he produces the scrappy plan which shows the site like some sort of multi-coloured patchwork quilt.

This is the titles plan, which Rhona drew up for us. It shows how the Council got a title to the different bits of the site. I lay my finger on a tiny snot green-coloured sliver of ground, between the pavement on the Cowgate and the entrance to Rum-ti-tum-tum's.

'See this bit here? It was acquired by the City in 1943, right? The title report says no statutory purpose and it's not held on trust, right?'

Mr. Smooth looks baffled. The City Council guy looks suspicious.

'What's your point, Simon?'

'Well, doesn't that make it common good?' When I got back from Sylvia's last night, I was doing a bit of reading. This is the last card I have to play.

The City Council guy is looking daggers at me. 'What if it is?'

One of the basic rules of negotiation: do the detail. I have here. 'Well, if it is a common good asset, you might need to go to court to get consent to sell it to us. And you haven't, have you?'

Mr. Smooth finally loses his cool. 'Simon, I can't believe that you're raising some title query at the final stage of the deal. We're ready to sign here. Do you really want to blow this deal wide open? I thought it was time critical to your clients?'

I glance over at Brad, who's pursing his rubber lips and frowning. 'No, of course not, but the title needs to be…'

'We're already giving you warrandice on the title,' Mr. Smooth says. 'What else do you want?'

I want to blow this deal wide open, like you say, Smoothy Boy. 'I was reading up on it. There's a book on the topic – '

This time, it's City Council guy that interrupts. 'Fuck that book,' he says. 'The guy doesn't know what he's talking about. You either take the title as it stands, Simon, or the deal's off.'

I turn round to look for Brad, but he's already slipped out the door. Fuck.

'Well, maybe we should look through the rest of the document just to see there aren't any other snags,' I say to them. 'More coffee anyone?'

'Fine,' says Mr. Smooth, and we start on the missives, going through them clause by clause, just to check we're all on the same page. Sure enough, we're only a couple of pages in when

Brad re-appears.

'Erm, Simon. Tony would like a word with you if that's okay.'

He holds the door of the conference room open for me, his face expressionless. As I go through, I hear him say to the others, 'I've taken instructions about the title thing, guys. Our clients will take the risk.'

Shit. They've rumbled me, finally. As I go down the stairs to the second floor, I consider just legging it out of the building. But something in me says, *Don't give the cunts the satisfaction.*

***

The first shock I get when I walk into Tony Hand's office is that Leonora's there. She smiles when I come in, and gives me a big wink: she's wearing her grey pencil skirt and jacket combo today with a creamy, retro style blouse with horn buttons. She crosses her legs and the skirt rides up enough for me to see it's stockings rather than tights.

Just at that moment, I realise that the python's ability to respond is completely and utterly unrelated to the level of danger I'm in at the time. The buttons are not the only thing with a horn on, let me tell you. Eventually, I manage to drag my eyes away from that glimpse of stocking and look Tony Hand squarely in the eyes.

Big Melon Head also has a smile on his face. 'Simon, you dog, you,' he says. 'You were going to keep us hanging on right to the last minute while you screwed around with those bastards from the Council, weren't you?'

I manage a shrug and a sort of, well, it's what I do, smile.

Tony's shaking that big melon head of his. 'Well, it just won't do, boy. Let's leave Brad to tie up the loose ends. I've pretty much given him carte blanche to get things signed up. Tick tock, you know?'

Fuck. They haven't realised what I was up to after all. I look at the clock on Tony's wall: it's half past ten in the morning. If I can –

'You deserve a break,' Leonora says. 'Every dog has his day, you know?'

Focus, Simon. The laptop with the stuff from the iPhone loaded on. Got to get it down to Fettes, to Police HQ. Just got to convince whichever cop

277

down there is straight that they need to bust these guys now. If Martin can't do it, I'll have to do it myself. No time for hideously kinky action.

Tony's got his hands clasped behind his head, leaning back in the big leather chair. 'So, you've got the rest of the day off, Si. Get yourself together. Check your passport, check you've got enough suntan oil, whatever. Remember, the flight goes at seven. You want to be on it, you've got to be here at five.'

Fuck. Must get a hold of Martin, the little sour faced bastard. What is he doing? When do we get the seventh cavalry in? What the fuck has happened to Karen? Focus, Simon, focus.

'Don't worry,' I say, trying to make my grin as broad as possible. 'I wouldn't miss it for the world. Can you just remind me how it all goes again?'

Tony nods, indulgently. 'No problem, Si. Here's how it goes: the Edinburgh deal closes. All the other, bigger deals, the ones we've been working on all week, all line up behind it, all in a row, like a set of dominoes.

'At three o'clock, I ring that snivelling little weasel of a banker that works for the crims and tell him the deals are ready to go. He authorises all the transfers through our client account: money in and on to the Walter Scott companies and money out to the City Council for that pissy little ten million deal in the Cowgate that Derek is so excited about.'

Leonora wrinkles her nose and stretches, displaying a flash of midriff underneath the creamy blouse. Disappointingly flat. Still. 'This is my favourite bit,' she says.

Tony chuckles. 'At three thirty, it's Friday afternoon and it's normal close of banking business. The little weasel goes home to whatever stone he crawls under, happy with the day's work.

'Then, at three thirty-five, a few specially authorised transactions take place after normal close of banking business, authorised by *our* guy in the bank.' Tony shakes his head. 'You'd be surprised how cheap these guys come, between you and me.

'At three fifty-five, all of the Walter Scott companies collapse into each other, leaving only Ivanhoe Enterprises. We chose that one in your honour, Si, since you were so fond of that block.'

A paranoid jolt of electricity goes through me. *What does he mean by that?*

'At four o-five, all the money that's landed in the one big pot in *Ivanhoe's* account fires off in a number of different directions – to the accounts set up for you, Leonora here, Brad, Al and Danielle, of course, and the rest split between Wallace and me. You can check, of course, to be sure that the money's there. Then at five, we all foregather here, have a quick glass of champagne, and it's off to the airport in a stretch limo. Or, of course, you can make your own arrangements, but I really do recommend Brazil at this time of year. Great weather, friendly people, and a non-existent extradition treaty. Perfect.'

He's grinning from ear to ear now, and so is Leonora. So am I, come to think of it.

'Sweet as.' All the while, I'm thinking, *Martin. Must get to Martin. Get the cops on board. Karen. Where is she? Wrong Box. What the fuck is Wrong Box?*

Tony and Leonora are still grinning away. I decide it's time to make my excuses.

'Well, I do still have a bit of packing to do, so if you'll excuse me, I'll see you guys later.'

Out at the lifts, I find I'm actually shaking. I press the down button and watch the lift come down from the top floor towards me. Five, four, three…

A set of heels behind me in the corridor. A whiff of perfume I know too well.

'Simon.'

It's Leonora. She's standing there, hand on her hip, that glint in her eye that I've come to know. The same glint in her eye she had in the sauna at Craigendarroch.

The lift pings. The python stirs.

'You don't really need to pack, do you? How about a counter offer?'

I feel my mouth go dry.

'Such as?' The lift doors start to close on me, and she reaches past me, jabbing at the button. I smell her perfume again, and the python starts to push me into automatic pilot. 'Well,' she says, brushing past me into the lift and beckoning me in. 'The day is young and young Bradley's busy tying up that Edinburgh deal, isn't he? I thought we could start with a glass of shampoo somewhere, since the sun's over the yard arm, and then maybe a little light lunch, followed by some shopping. We've plenty of time. What do you say?'

What the fuck can I say? 'Sylvia...' I manage to croak out and Leonora raises one eyebrow. She stabs the ground floor button on the lift and we start to move off.

'Really? So are you taking her with you?'

And in that moment, that crazy moment in the lift with Leonora pressing up close to me and the python going crazy down below, I realise something.

The Buddha Belly isn't everything. If I were really going to Brazil with these bastards and I had the option of taking Sylvia, I really would. But it's all academic, since I'm not going.

Which makes my next lie all the more convincing. 'No, of course not,' I say to her.

'Good,' she says, almost purring at me, like the cat that's got the cream. The doors ping open and she grabs my tie, leading me out of the lift like her pet. She waves airily at Bobby, whose eyes are just about popping out of his head at the sight of us, and out through the revolving doors. As soon as we're out of sight of the main window, she pulls me close and kisses me, hard, her athletic body pressed up against mine.

And it's that moment that somewhere, in the part of my brain that is not completely taken over by the python, that another connection slots into place.

Jimmy Ahmed.

Jimmy Ahmed was from Liverpool. Just like the guy Kinnaird, that the Melon Headed one and Big Doggy are in cahoots with in the Wrong Box company.

Liverpool. Calm down, python. Calm down.

CHAPTER 31
THE FINE ART OF NEGOTIATION

'I've got my eye on you, Simon English.'

Leonora looks at me, that glint in her eye a bit steely just at that moment. 'Tony thinks we've turned you, that you're totally on side with all of this now. I'm just not so sure, so I've decided I'm going to have to keep you tied up all day so that you don't get away from me this time.'

Champagne. I call it the truth serum. Doesn't do it so much for me, but I've known tougher characters than Leonora who've blabbed after a single glass of it. Something to do with the bubbles making the booze hit the bloodstream right on the way to the brain. There's probably a more scientific explanation for it than that, but that's pretty much it.

'What if I refuse?' I say to her.

'You won't refuse,' she says, and just the way she says it nearly has the python performing a psychic table tipping moment all by itself. What is it this woman has? She's got short hair, which I don't normally go for. No Buddha belly.

You know, if you're a woman, and you ask a man what he finds attractive in women, you'll get some old chat about personality being just as important as looks. That's partly true, actually, but it's not the first thing a guy thinks of when he meets a woman.

If you're a bloke, and you ask another bloke what he finds attractive in women, you'll get a list of vital statistics: tits, ass, legs, whether he prefers blondes to brunettes, like he's listing a set of requirements and someone's going to build one for him. And it's true that we all have our personal preferences, although as someone else once said, if you could have fillet steak every day, you wouldn't have fillet steak every day.

The truth is, the most attractive thing in a woman for most men is whether she looks as if she's up for it. And when I say up for it, I mean up for anything.

Anyway, we're in this restaurant called Wedgwood, down the Royal Mile, which is the latest place that foodie middle class

Jocks go to show how clever they are with their knives and forks.

'Are you ready to order?' The waitress looks a bit dubious, and I'm suddenly aware of the same feeling I had in the bar of the hotel at Craigendarroch: we're the loudest people there.

'Yes, yes we are,' Leonora says, laughing up at her. 'Sorry, we're kind of celebrating.'

'Sure.' The waitress looks down at her with a blank expression and I feel a twinge of annoyance. Okay, so we probably are the loudest people in the restaurant, but then the ones that look like they're sucking on lemons probably haven't had a bottle of champagne at the Ghillie Dhu for elevenses, followed by coffee, cocaine in the toilets of Starbucks and a pint at the Beehive just to bring us back down.

'I can come back if you like,' says the waitress, but Leonora waves a hand at her.

'No, no. We're fine. Two of the chilli and coriander roulades, two of the black sesame crusted mullet and a bottle of your best Sancerre. That'll do us.'

The waitress struts off without another word, and it's just me and Leonora, with the rest of the restaurant desperately earwigging to hear what this drunken, horny pair are going to say next.

'Just going to powder my nose, darling,' says Leonora. You can feel the sigh of disappointment round the room but every male eye is on Leonora's arse as she sashays off towards the toilets.

The minute she's out of sight, of course, I'm texting everyone I can think of.

To Karen: *Where are you? Let me know you're okay.*

To Martin: *Can't get away right now and can't hold up the deal any longer. Will get to Fettes as soon as. In the meantime, tee up cops to intercept them at office or airport.*

To Tom: *Can you find out anything you can about Joseph Aloysius Kinnaird? Google him, see what you can dig up on him.*

There's a reason I'm getting Tom to do this. He's got so much time to sit at home at the computer, he's developed quite a capacity to hack into stuff he shouldn't be into. Like the Criminal Records Office.

The starters arrive, and the bottle of wine. Still no sign of

Leonora.

I Google Kinnaird Construction and find a site for them. It's a really shit site, as basic as they come, with pictures of JCBs and dumper lorries. A gallery shows some of the incredibly dull buildings they've helped to build. One thing catches my eye, though: at the bottom, in big green letters, they've put on their homepage: DEMOLITION OUR SPECIALITY.

Then my iPhone pings with a message. It's from Leonora.

Do you want to know what I'm doing right now?

I laugh and text back. *The starters are getting cold.*

A second later, the message comes back. *I'm getting hot.* I'll let you fill in the blanks for what else she says in her text, but suffice it to say, she's definitely just using one hand to operate the mobile. What a bad, bad girl. The python tries to tip the table over again.

Eventually, she reappears, a big grin on her face. 'Nice appetiser,' she says and I think most of the restaurant has worked out that she's not talking about the starter.

The rest of that meal is a blur. I think we ordered a bottle of red as well: I think the food was pretty good but, to be honest, it wouldn't have mattered if it wasn't. Then, before I know it, it's coffees, liqueurs and out onto the Royal Mile, where everything seems to be moving very quickly. I check my watch: it's just after two. Tick tock.

'Now for the shopping,' Leonora says. 'Come on.' She grabs my hand and drags me across the street, just about putting us both under a taxi. She laughs, pulls up her blouse to show her midriff to the taxi driver and is instantly forgiven. Obviously a flat tummy man, then. Then it's off down Cockburn Street, to a little place I'd passed before but had never had any reason to go into.

I had a girlfriend once who liked to be spanked, although it was really just a gentle bit of botty-patting before the main feature. We never took it any further than that.

So, to be honest, this shop is something of an eye opener to me. Whips, thongs, strap-ons, lube and more leather and PVC than you could shake a stick at. Leonora seems to be in her element. In fact, she seems to know the shop assistant.

'I'll have this, and this, and this,' she says, as excited as a kid at

Christmas. By the time she's finished, we've both got two bags to carry.

Outside the shop, she kisses me again, hard. The short walk down Cockburn Street and retail therapy seems to have sobered her up a bit.

'Your place,' she says.

Almost before I know it, we've got a taxi at the station to rattle us down to Stockbridge, we're in the flat, she's all over me and then she has the whole contents of the shop spread out on the bed in front of us. That's when she starts to get all bossy.

'Wear this, and this, and this. I'll be back in a sec.'

I've got the gear on as instructed when she reappears: she's opted for a PVC catsuit that's more skin than suit, and thigh length boots.

'Down on your knees, doggy,' she says. I've cleared the bed of all the other stuff in readiness, but she's got the lead attached to the dog collar before I can say anything and is hauling me through to the living-room. Let me tell you, laminate flooring can be a bit fucking painful on bare knees. Even in a state of extreme pythonism.

'This is all happening so fast, Leonora,' I say, but my voice is muffled by the gimp mask. I don't know if you've ever tried one of these things, but it's pretty difficult to breathe, despite the air hole.

Leonora just ignores me anyway. 'No time for talking now, doggy. Save your tongue for more important things.'

Sure enough, she hoists herself up in the armchair so that her box is at the right level for me on my hands and knees.

The wrong box, I'm thinking to myself. As I start to tease and please her, I think about the word "box" as it applies to a woman's business end. I mean, I've never quite understood how it came to be a euphemism, if you see what I mean. There's nothing in that area box shaped. Unless the girl were to trim her lady garden into a box shape, in which case, presumably it would be a box hedge, haha, but, in general, you've got a triangle or a rectangle in the case of a Brazilian and everything down below that is pretty much not following the laws of geometry.

And it's while I'm thinking about all this, and how Leonora is the wrong box but the right box, that something clicks into place, somewhere in a bit of my brain that is still functioning, despite the python, and I know exactly what I have to do.

Easy for now, though. Got to play the game. Leonora is basically your classic sub/dom, in that she likes to dominate, and then be dominated. After a bit of to-ing and fro-ing in the living-room, she looks up at me and purrs, 'Now you have to tell me what to do.'

'Okay,' I say. I lift her up, carry her through to the bedroom and throw her roughly, but not too roughly, onto the bed.

'Stay there,' I tell her. 'You've been a very, very bad girl.'

The rest of the stuff we bought is now down at the side of the bed, so I have to stretch across whilst keeping Leonora occupied with my hand to get the item I want.

'I'm afraid I'm going to have to take you into custody,' I tell her, slipping the handcuffs on. Thank fuck tight Jock bastard Reid splashed out on a decent bed frame, one that I can cuff the other end to. The silken ropes are probably less secure, but I use them anyway, tying up both hands and feet. Leonora really is so into it all that she doesn't realise what I've done until she's tied to the bed hand and foot.

'Oh Simon. Now you have me at your mercy.' She really does look fantastic, lying there tied up, I have to say.

'This has been a revelation to me, Leonora, really it has.' I can't resist going down on my hands and knees over her: the python still has control of most of my brain. I take off the gimp mask.

'So what now?' Leonora is still smiling, gazing into my eyes, but I can see she is searching for a clue.

'What happens now is that I put the duvet over to cover you and keep you comfortable and go out for a little while. Then I help the cops bust the others.'

Her expression is changing. 'You're lying.'

'Nope,' I say. 'Deadly serious. D.S. Martin's just getting the manpower together to pull the whole lot of them down to Saughton. We've got all the evidence we need.'

'Don't make me laugh. D.S. Martin couldn't find his arse with both hands. Is he all you've got?'

'Not exactly,' I say, thinking, *Pretty much.*

Leonora's face changes from a sneer into a smile. Ever so gently, she edges her pelvis up, so that she's rubbing it against the python. 'Come on, Si. If you were so certain you had the proof, you would've brought it all crashing down before now. The only reason you can be waiting until the last minute is because you don't have all the ducks lined up in a row. How about a counter-offer?'

With hands and feet tied, she can't move a lot, but what she's moving is certainly moving mountains. 'It's not too late,' she murmurs. 'We can still get away with the money. We're stuck with Brad and the rest of them on the plane, but, after that, it's a whole new ball game.'

Bump, bump, she thrusts herself against me, gently, insistently.

'Tell me something,' I say. I'm not surprised to find my voice hoarse. 'Minus the money, would you still be doing this?'

Bump, bump. 'Of course, but you with the money is an even better package.'

I'm not quite sure how I manage to do it, but I lever myself up and away from her, so that she can't reach me with her pelvic thrusts. I clamber off the bed, pull the duvet out from under her and settle it back down on top of her.

'You stay nice and snug here,' I tell her. 'I will be back.'

Leonora laughs uncertainly, as she watches me pull my clothes back on. 'You bastard. Aren't you even going to finish what you started here?'

'No time,' I tell her. Just about dressed. *Must find Martin. Still no word from La Clamp. What the fuck is Tom doing?*

'I could scream the place down, you know,' she says.

'I know. But then the neighbours will call the cops and what are the chances of you getting one of the bent cops? And, even if you do, the bent cops report to the Auchendrossan crew, don't they?'

She doesn't say anything to that. I go into the living-room, pick up my laptop, put my shoes on and go back through to check on her.

'Hold tight, honey,' I tell her. 'Back soon.'

It's getting on for half past three and the light's fading a bit, so I can't quite read the expression in her eyes. I don't suppose it's a situation she finds herself in every day, after all.

'Be careful,' she says.

Then I'm off, out of the flat, down the stairs, checking for messages. The one from Tom makes me pull up short.

Kinnaird is into heavy stuff. Convictions for GBH, attempted murder, conspiracy, armed robbery. Only started security firm after he got out of last long stretch. Severe health warning.

I suppose I'd been expecting this but, all the same, it makes me pause on the landing. It sounds as if Tony Hand and the Rottweiler are branching out into a similar partnership with a bunch of gangsters down in Liverpool now. But why? Why would they need to do that, when they're about to do a runner to Brazil? And what possible interest would they have in getting poor Rhona to get the Wrong Box company access to the rotting hulk that is New St. Andrew's House?

Construction. Specialists in demolition. Fuck.

I'm still thinking about all of this, still thumbing the iPhone for messages, with the laptop tucked under my arm, when I go out of the flat door and turn into the street. I've sobered up a lot now so I'm surprised at how quickly two guys walking towards me are walking towards me.

Then I look up from my iPhone and the big one, the big square one built like a brick shit house, the one that looks like a Bond villain, hits me in the solar plexus and I go down like a wardrobe full of donkey jackets.

'Simon fucking English. Excuse the French. Won't you step this way?'

Big, meaty hands, hauling me up, the door of a van sliding open and me hurtling inside. Inside, the smoked glass makes the place even darker. Oddjob and Derek Boyes clamber in after me, Boyes sticking the laptop to one side on one of the leather seats. The driver guns the engine, the door slides shut, and we're off.

Derek Boyes is shaking his head at me, and smiling sadly. 'Simon,' he says. 'Simon, Simon, Simon. You've led us a merry dance today. We gave you a call at the office, but we were told you were away for the day. Checked down here, but there was no sign. So, Kevin and me have been in some pretty fucking lush places round the West End looking for you, let me tell you.'

He smiles at me, like we're old pals. I'm still struggling to breathe after Oddjob's punching me in the guts. It was like getting an iron girder slammed into your ribs. 'Sorry to

287

disappoint,' I manage to croak.

This seems to amuse Derek Boyes hugely. 'Simon, you're a constant big bag of surprises,' he says. 'Now, down to business. Here's a pop quiz for you. Give the correct answer and you don't get another punch in the guts from Kevin.'

I straighten up. 'Good incentive.'

He puts his fingers to his lips. 'Shush now, you're starting to annoy me. Question one of one. What, exactly, is the nature of your relationship with Karen Clamp?'

I suddenly realise, with a horrible sinking feeling, that they've got Karen. Of course they've got Karen. That's why she wasn't returning her calls. I try to think clearly. What would she have said?

Derek Boyes is still smiling at me, whistling slightly through his teeth. Then he makes the noise that they do on Countdown, that quiz show Mum watches obsessively. 'Duh dut duh dut derrrly dut boom! Going to have to rush you there, Simon, old chap.'

'She's my girlfriend,' I say, and Oddjob punches me right in the stomach again. It's lower down, this time, so it's actually the stomach rather than the solar plexus and the remains of the fancy lunch at Wedgwood make their way up to my gullet. I only just manage to hold it down.

'That is the correct answer,' Derek Boyes says. 'Well done there, Simon.'

As soon as I can speak I say, 'So why did he still punch me?' I look up: I find that my vision's gone a bit hazy, probably because my eyes are watering. Derek strokes his chin, just a regular comedian now.

'Good question,' he says, turning to Oddjob. 'Why did you, Kevin?' The Oddjob guy shrugs his mountain-like shoulders. 'Just cause,' he says, in a way that makes it sound like "just cause" rather than "just 'cause", if you see what I mean.

The van lurches to a halt. I realise we're at the lights at Blackhall. They seem to be heading out of the city. I look over at the sliding van door beside Derek. There's just no prospect of me being able to grab up the laptop, flatten Derek, open the door and make a run for it before the Oddjob guy flattens me again.

Derek seems to know the way I'm thinking. 'Thinking of leaving us so soon, Simon? I really wouldn't, you know.' He sits back, relaxing against the metal wall of the van as it moves off again. 'You know, Simon, you and I are very similar. In many ways, like.'

'Really?' I try to keep my voice as even as possible.

Derek Boyes starts laughing. It's a high pitched, hyena type of laugh. With his mouth that far open, it's really not a pretty sight: all these years of deep fried Mars Bars have taken their toll on his tooth enamel.

'Really?' he says, mimicking me. Then he stops laughing. 'Aye, really. Here's the thing. People underestimate me. They think I'm just some clueless druggy bastard from the schemes whose head's full of mince. But if there's one thing I've learned, Simon, it's that you have to know how to negotiate.'

'Oh aye. I know all about negotiation. Read up on it when I was in Saughton for a wee stretch. Competitive, co-operative, the Harvard method. You'd be surprised how co-operative a negotiator I can be. It's just when I get competitive, that's usually when Kevin here has to break some heads open for me.' He winks at Oddjob. 'He's no much of a negotiator, our Kevin. Very much on the operational side.'

'I can see that,' I say. I feel I have to say something. I'm trying to keep an eye on where we're going, just in case I ever get back from it, but it's hard to see out and I'm trying not to be too obvious about it.

'Aye, you would see that, Simon. Like I say, we've a lot in common, you and me. People think you're an arsehole as well, so they underestimate you. But you understand that this is all a negotiation too, don't you?'

I sit back, trying to make my body language as positive and open as possible. That's what you do, when you want your opposite number to trust what you're going to say. 'So let's negotiate,' I say. I glance out the front window. We've turned left at the Barnton roundabout, heading for Gogar.

Derek has his fingers to his lips again. 'No yet, Simon, no yet. Let's get you to our little hideaway first. Then you can catch up with Karen and Candice.'

Fuck. They've taken the kid as well. I feel a sinking feeling in the pit of my stomach, but that could just be the after effects of Oddjob's fist. I check my watch. Quarter to four. To think that, only fifteen minutes ago, I was still aboard Leonora. Maybe I should have stayed there after all.

'I think you should know, time is kind of of the essence here,' I say to him. 'If you want to stop Tony and Wallace getting away with all your money.'

That makes Oddjob sit up straight. There's a flash of doubt in Derek's eyes. Just a flash, before he folds his arms and says, 'Nice try. But these cunts know which side their bread is buttered on.'

Time for me to do the silence thing. That lasts for a full minute, before Derek gets Oddjob to hit me again so hard I'm not even able to speak for another five minutes.

By then, we've pulled up outside a totally nondescript industrial unit. From the sound of the planes, I can tell it's somewhere pretty close to the airport. That and the acres of cars beyond the chain link fence. Not that there's anyone in any of them to see what's happening.

Oddjob has to help me stand when I get out of the van. I'm still struggling for breath.

'Come away in,' says Derek. 'We've tried to make it as homely as possible. For the lassie, like.' He swaggers on ahead of us: the driver, who I haven't even been paying attention to, comes and supports my other side.

'Nice to see you, to see you nice,' he says, as Derek Boyes pulls the battered metal door open and we go inside.

Futret.

CHAPTER 32
THE HARVARD METHOD

Karen gives a pretty fucking convincing impression of being my girlfriend when I stagger in the door. She grabs me off Oddjob and puts me in a cross between a bear hug and a head lock, all the while saying loudly: 'Darling, darling, what have they done to you?' She shoots a look at Oddjob. 'If you've hurt him, I'll swing for you, Kevin.'

The big heavy looks genuinely upset. 'No permanently I've no. He'll be okay, Karen. I didn't ken...'

'Aye, well.' She pulls me close again and whispers in my ear, 'What the fuck is going on, Simon?'

'Just follow my lead, okay?' I murmur in her shell like. She smells none too savoury, but then, in fairness, I suppose they don't really do showers in industrial units. 'How long have you been here?'

'Two days,' she growls. 'Where have you been?'

'Looking for you, some of it,' I say. That is, at least, true: of course, I've also been at Sylvia's flat (weirdly I feel slightly guilty about that, with the bear-woman crushing my already bruised ribs). The office, obviously, my flat with Leonora, and so on. The crims must have been incredibly unlucky not to get a hold of me.

The vast majority of the time, of course, I've been at the office, and that would have been the obvious place for them to take me. Interesting that they didn't.

Derek Boyes, meantime, is watching our performance closely. He claps his hands slowly. 'Very fucking touching, I must say. Come on then, you two. We have some questions.'

Karen looks round and I get a chance to see the front part of the unit for the first time: they've partitioned a bit off and there's camp beds, couches, even a flat screen TV at the end wall. Sitting in front of it is a little girl: I take it this must be the kid that Karen keeps going on about. As we head towards the opposite corner, where there's a small office type place walled off, the kid looks round.

'Just stay there the now, Candice,' Karen says. She shoots a look at a hunched figure on one of the couches. 'And you. Look after her or you'll have me to answer to.' The hooded figure on the couch is coughing and sniffling but pauses long enough to raise a middle finger at Karen.

The office itself is typical of a scabby industrial unit like this. Various nondescript papers, calendars of women with their tits out, a desk littered with various invoices and files, and a chair behind it with part of the cover torn off, so that the foam is slowly oozing its way out. Oddjob busies himself unfolding some stacking chairs for the rest of us to sit on, while Derek installs himself in the chair behind the desk.

'Any chance of a coffee?' I say. The fancy lunch at Wedgwood with all that wine is far behind me, but I could still do with some caffeine to help me think more clearly. I check my watch: four ten. Tick tock.

'Aye, why not?' Derek says. He seems highly amused. 'Kevin, could you get a coffee for Mr. English and I'll have one too. Milk and two sugars. Karen?'

Karen shakes her head. Oddjob goes over to the wall which has a window looking out on the yard beyond: there's one of these cheapo coffee machines there that pump out raw diesel. In my current state, though, I'll take anything. And anything will do to break the ice. Like I've said, the Getting To Know You stage is important in any negotiation. And this is going to be one hell of a negotiation.

'Nice place you have here,' I say. 'I mean, quite a handy front operation.' Derek laughs, that high pitched, hyena type laugh.

'You really think so? It's just one of my business interests, Simon. It ticks over nicely. This new kiss and fly tax the airport's going to bring in will do it no harm either.'

Oddjob plants down one of these shit brown plastic cups that you get from these coffee machines. The stuff in it might once have been in the same warehouse as a coffee bean, but that's about as close as it gets.

Then Karen kicks off. 'Youse have got no right to hold us here. The police are on to you big time, Deek. It's only a matter of time before they track you down. Same goes for you, Kevin.'

Derek has stopped smiling now. 'Don't waste my time, Karen.

The only cops I don't have in my pocket are the ones that couldn't find their way out of Fettes with a map and a fully fucking functioning GPS system. So they're not a major worry, believe me. What does worry me, is what you and your so called boyfriend have been up to and whether, contrary to all appearances, your man here isn't a total fanny, and is in some sort of scheme to do me and Kevin and the rest of the boys out of our hard earned cash.'

'Hard earned?' Karen is about to say more but I lay a hand on her knee.

'We're wasting time here.' I pause, long enough to lean back in the chair and glance out the window. Just on cue, a jet slides into view, on its way down. 'It's ironic, actually, that you've brought us here to the airport. I wonder if Tony and Wallace are going to leave their cars here with you later on this afternoon.'

Derek looks confused, then interested. 'Why? Where are these two cunts going?'

I smile. 'Brazil, or so they say. With all your money.'

Derek laughs again, but it's an uneasy sort of hyena sound, like a hyena that's looking over its shoulder waiting for a lion to come out of the bushes and bite its arse. 'What do you mean?'

I take a sip of the diesel oil formerly known as coffee. It actually manages to taste worse than it smells. Then I meet his gaze. 'As you rightly say, Derek, this is a negotiation and here's how it's going to go. You're going to put Karen and Candice in a car and take them to a place of safety. Then they're going to phone me and tell me that they're safe. In the meantime, you and I and Oddjob here are going to be in a car on the way up to the office where you can ask Tony Hand and Wallace Brodie whether I'm telling the truth or not.'

Derek is laughing again. A full on, I've run off with the best bit of the antelope kind of laugh. 'What did you call Kevin? Oddjob?' He laughs again. 'You know, I never thought of that, but now you mention it, you're right.'

Oddjob – Kevin – doesn't look so impressed. 'Who's Oddjob?'

Kevin, still laughing, shakes his head. Oddjob has made a move towards me but Derek waves him to sit down again. 'All in good time, Kevin. All in good time. Actually, Simon here is paying you something of a compliment, if you only knew your

James Bond films.'

Oddjob looks none the wiser so Kevin goes on. 'Okay, okay. That's an interesting proposition you have there, Simon, so here's my counter-offer. Karen and Candice stay exactly where they are until you tell me everything. And if I think you're lying, I get Oddjob here – ', he chuckles, obviously quite taken with the name – 'to start on one or the other of you. I think, just in the interests of equality, I'll get him to start on Karen.'

Time for another card.

'No deal. In case you haven't noticed, your man Kevin there has a crush on Karen as big as the car park outside. He wouldn't touch a hair of her head, or Candice either.

'So, take them way out of the way, and I'll tell you everything you need to know about how these guys are about to rip you off big style. But we do need to hurry a bit. Otherwise, all that money that went into these Walter Scott companies today is about to disappear under your nose. And most of the rest of Benzini, Lambe and Lockhart with it.'

I don't want to tell him about Wrong Box unless I have to. Karen is watching me, but keeping quiet for now.

Derek, meantime, is stroking his chin. He's got a couple of days stubble on it, as if he's been away from his usual routine as well. 'Karen and the kid stay where they are. There's an easy way to check if you're telling the truth, Simon.' He jerks his head at Oddjob. 'Kevin. Can you get the laptop from through by and switch the Wi-Fi on?'

As Oddjob disappears, Derek says, 'You won't know this, but we've got a man at the bank looking after everything. He phoned me at half past three to say all the deals had gone through and the money was in place.'

I'm explaining to him about the after banking business deals when Oddjob reappears with the laptop. Derek boots it up, snaps a couple of keys, stares at it intently and then swivels it round so that I can see it. 'No coconut or cigar, Simon. The money's all where it should be.'

Fuck. He's tabbed open all the Walter Scott company accounts. According to the screen in front of me, each one is sitting with a healthy balance in millions, just as they were meant to be at half past three today.

Then Karen pipes up, 'That doesn't mean anything, Deek. It wouldn't take a genius to put a divert on the system so that when you view the accounts, it looks like everything's hunky dory.' She turns to me. 'I read about it online. The government do it all the time, to try to hide things like budget deficits.'

Thank fuck for paranoid conspiracy theorists. Derek grabs the laptop back from me, tabbing between the various accounts. He looks up, 'That could be true. But it still means you don't have any proof that Wallace and Tony are trying to rip me off. Or why to fucking Brazil.'

I play my last card. 'Have you heard of a guy called Joseph Aloysius Kinnaird?'

Derek frowns. 'The name rings a bell. Joe Kinnaird, from Liverpool?'

'That's right. Did you know that Wallace and Tony are also in cahoots with him, in a company called Wrong Box?'

'Ron Box? Who the fuck is he?'

I ease the laptop out of his hands and call up the Companies House website. I get the company details I'm looking for on two tabs and then swivel it back round.

Derek stares at the screen. 'Wrong Box Limited. Directors: Anthony Hand, Wallace Brodie, Joseph Aloysius Kinnaird. Okay. So, they're in another company with another guy. So what?'

I flick on my iPhone and show him Tom's message. 'You can double check this if you want but, basically, Joe Kinnaird is in the same line of business as you are. Now, look at Kinnaird Construction, his main front company. I think you'll see a name you recognise.'

Derek goes back to the laptop and clicks on the other tab I've opened up at Companies House. 'Kinnaird Construction Limited. Directors: Joseph Aloysius Kinnaird, James Ahmed.' He looks up. 'Jimmy Ahmed?'

'The same Jimmy Ahmed Debi and Elena dosed up with Rohypnol on a night out with me. The guy that ended up tits up in my bath. Remember him? The thing is, if Tony and Wallace haven't told you he was the M.D. of a Liverpool firm in the same line of business as you, what else haven't they told you?'

Derek looks like he's about to say something but Karen gets there first. 'The Wrong Box is a novel by Robert Louis

Stevenson, Deek, if they didn't teach you that at Heriots. The main characters are the last survivin folk who are entitled to a bunch of money. Does it no strike you as strange that they've set up a company with that name? Whatever your bank says, they're plannin to move the money across to this new lot and leave youse with nothin.'

Derek just stares at her. His mouth is working, but no sound is coming out.

'Come on, Deek. Did you really think the old school tie counted for that much?'

'I think she has a point, boss,' Oddjob says.

That seems to make Derek's mind up. He shoots a look at Oddjob, 'Thanks for that, Kevin, but I don't pay you to think.' He turns to me. 'You're coming with us. It's all a bit thin, but there's definitely something no right about all of this.'

'Fine. But we can drop Karen and Candice off on the way.'

He shakes his head. 'No way.'

'In that case,' I say, folding my arms, 'I'm not going anywhere. At least, not without a fight. And fights take up time you don't have, Derek, if I'm telling the truth.'

If this all sounds terribly tough and macho to you, the truth is I'm absolutely fucking shaking inside. The last two punches Oddjob dished out were just him warming up.

There's a long pause and then Derek says, 'Okay. Let's get on with it, then.'

Tick tock. It's quarter to five, on a holiday weekend, and since the Jocks decided on no congestion charge, the roads will be absolutely clogged. I stand outside the office while Karen gets herself and Candice organised. In the office, I see Derek open a drawer and hand something to Oddjob. It takes a moment to register what it is: some sort of a hand gun. Then Derek takes another one out of the drawer for himself and stuffs it into the waistband of his shell suit.

I turn around and Karen and Candice are there. Candice is looking up at me, shyly.

'Simon, this is my lassie,' Karen says.

She's a pretty little thing: about eight, probably, but bright as a button. 'Hiya,' she says.

'Hi,' I say. I never know what to say to kids.

The hooded figure on the couch looks across and I see for the first time who it is. It's Debi, but even with her hood down, it would be hard to recognise her: big rings under her eyes, hair all greasy and plastered down, and a nasty rash of spots round her mouth. She stares at me, but doesn't seem to recognise who I am. I dare say she's had a few paying clients since then.

Futret appears from somewhere, again, with a big bulge under his jacket that I take to be another shooter. 'Let's go,' he says. Then Oddjob and Derek appear out of the office and we're off.

We emerge up the sliproad into a traffic jam, heading for the Gogar. I check my watch again: five o'clock. Fuck, wank, fanny bastard.

Derek looks round at me, apparently less worried. 'What time did you say they were leaving the office?'

'We were meant to get together at five for a glass of champagne and then a limo was collecting us to take us all to the airport.'

Derek nods. 'I suppose it just depends how much champagne the winos want to drink.' He turns to Futret, who's driving, 'Better put the blues and twos on, Kenny,' he says.

***

I don't know why it hadn't occurred to me that the cunts would be cheeky enough to use a police siren and pretend we're all undercover cops. It does give me a bit of a chill, sitting there, realising just how much influence the guy in the front seat has: cops, Council, if Karen is to be believed, even the taxi drivers all dance to his tune. What he said was true. People underestimate him because he looks and sounds like a schemie Jock loser.

He was right about that bit. We've got fuck all else in common, of course.

Derek looks round. 'One thing I don't understand about your story. If Wallace and Tony are about to rip me off and fuck off to Brazil with the rest of the firm, why do they need Joe Kinnaird on board? What's he got to do with it?'

Just at that moment, my moby rings, which is handy, because I don't have an answer. That's the bit I haven't worked out yet.

Just what is the Wrong Box company all about? And why do they have this side deal going on about New St. Andrew's House?

Meantime, it's Tom on the phone. 'What the fuck is happening?'

'I'll get back to you soon,' I tell him. 'Everything's cool, okay?' I say and ring off.

Derek nods his approval from the front seat. 'That's the idea, Simon. We don't need any complications.' He looks sharply at me as the moby goes again. 'Answer it, then switch the fucker off.'

It's Martin. 'Where the fuck are you?' I can tell where he is: in his living room. The parrot is squawking in Anglo Saxon in the background.

'I'm a bit tied up right now,' I tell him.

'I can't get the Chief Con to act without them interviewing you, Simon,' Martin says. 'You need to get to my place pronto.'

'I'll get back to you,' I tell him, and ring off, only for the moby to go straight after.

Derek turns and shoots me a warning look.

'Sorry, I have to get this,' I say. 'It's totally unconnected.'

So it is: the display shows it's Yvonne ringing.

'Hi.' I try to keep my voice as relaxed as possible, in the circumstances.

'Hi Tracey,' a sarcastic male voice says, 'or should I say, Simon. This is Yvonne's husband. Gary. We've not had the pleasure yet, although it sounds like you've had the pleasure of my wife quite a bit, you cunt.'

I actually start laughing. Of all the people to phone me at that moment, this was the one I was least expecting. 'This isn't exactly a good time…'

I can imagine the little bulldog's neck bursting through his shirt collar at the other end of the line. 'Not a good time? Not a good time? Then tell me, you English cunt, when would be a good time to discuss the fact that you've got my wife pregnant? Where are you right now? Stay right there. I'm coming over.'

'Kind of in transit at the moment,' I say, smiling at Derek and rolling my eyes as if to say, 'wouldn't you just know it?'

Gary stops shouting and brings his voice down to an even tone. I can hear Yvonne in the background, saying something to him. 'Shut up, Yvonne. Listen, English cunt. I'm heading into Edinburgh now. Yvonne says she doesn't know where you live, so I'll meet you at your office. You'd better be there when I get there.' Then he hangs up.

Oh great. I shrug and smile again at Derek and make a show of switching the iPhone off. He turns back round, looking disgusted.

By now we're racing along Corstorphine Road, having screamed round the Gogar roundabout in the midst of all the mayhem. Futret is tanning the arse out of the van, overtaking, running red lights, the full lot.

Meantime, my mind is racing, too. The Wrong Box. The last men standing take the money.

I look across at Karen, who's cuddling Candice. 'That thing you said about setting up diverts on accounts so that things look the same if you rang in from a particular IP address?'

'Aye?'

'I guess that means you could do a similar thing by setting up diverts in the computers in the firm's office? So, for example, all the associates and assistants could think they were checking their bank accounts and seeing their share of the money diverted in and, in fact, it was all fake?'

Karen shrugs. 'Do I look like Bill Gates? Aye, I suppose so.'

Derek is looking back at me, quizzically. 'What's that supposed to mean?'

'It means that Wallace and Tony were planning to rip the whole lot of us off.' I think of saying more but then stop myself. If we were all being ripped off, then Tony and the Rottweiler were hardly going to jump on the same plane with us. Not just the Wrong Box, the wrong plane.

Fortunately, Derek is thinking of something else. We've now clattered through the Haymarket junction and we're heading for the West End. 'Where do you want to drop them off?' he says, jerking his head at Karen and Candice.

'West End will do fine,' I say.

We pull into the side and I get out with Karen and Candice: I'm relieved to see that Oddjob stays in the van, watching me closely though. He's just out of earshot.

I make a great play of kissing Karen and patting Candice on

the head. She giggles. I take out my wallet and hand them all the cash I've got in it.

'There should be about a hundred here,' I say. 'Take a taxi down to my flat. There's a woman chained to the bed who's probably desperate to pee by now. Keep her handcuffed but you can untie her other hand and her feet. There's a pail under the sink in the kitchen if she needs to go.'

Karen blinks, twice. 'What on earth…?'

'Don't ask. But don't trust her either. Just make sure she's comfortable and then get yourselves to a place of safety. Is there somewhere you can go?'

She nods. 'Aye, I think so.'

Candice pipes up, 'We're going to stay in Morningside, Simon.'

'Morningside?' I say.

'Don't you start,' Karen says and leads Candice towards the taxi rank.

'Come on, English, get back in here,' Oddjob says from the van. I get in and the van screams off, cutting across two lanes of traffic and heading up Lothian Road towards the office.

Let the games begin, you cunts, I'm thinking, as we pull up on double yellows right outside.

CHAPTER 33
THE OLD QUADRUPLE BLUFF

To all external appearances, it looks like business as usual at the office. Bobby's still sitting there, wearing a high vis jacket today, I notice: must have had to do something outside and it would be against health and safety not to wear it, no doubt. He looks up when I come clattering in, laptop under my arm, with Derek, Oddjob and Futret in tow. I pass him by without a glance, but as we reach the lifts, I hear the familiar, annoying voice: 'Mr. English? If you'd just like to sign your guests in, please.'

I'm going to ignore him but Derek, who obviously hasn't dealt with him before, decides to go back.

'We don't need to sign in,' he says, leaning over Bobby's desk. 'We own this entire fucking building, including you.'

Bobby stays perfectly still. 'There's no need to swear,' he says, very slowly, as if speaking to someone whose first language isn't English. Come to think of it, that pretty much covers Derek and most of the outer Edinburgh population. That's not the way Derek sees it, though. He leans over and grabs Bobby's tie, pulling him close so that they're nose to nose.

'Fucking take a telling, you jumped up wee shite,' he says. 'Any more of your attitude and I'll have Kevin here deal with it. And you won't like Kevin when he's angry.'

To be fair to Bobby, he stays perfectly calm. 'If you don't let go of my tie,' he says, 'I'll call the police.'

Of course, that weasel Futret has been waiting for this moment. He produces his warrant card and shines it in Bobby's face. 'I am the fucking police,' he says.

Beside me, the lift pings. 'Come on, guys,' I say. 'We're wasting time.'

Derek lets go of Bobby and we all pile into the lift. Derek jabs the buttons for floors two and five, which are both labelled with the firm's name, of course. He looks at Oddjob. 'Kenny and I will take the second floor. You go up with Simon to the fifth, but don't let him out of your sight.'

As the lift doors open on the second floor, there's a strange

301

kind of silence. It's amazing how, even at the lifts, you can hear that low frequency buzz of people working, muttering to each other, walking across the carpeted floor. It's only when you hear the silence of an empty office that you realise your ears normally pick these things up.

'Looks like we might be too late,' I say.

'We'll see,' says Derek and draws his gun, as he and Futret head out.

Then the lift doors shut and it's only me and Oddjob. He stares at me as the lift picks up again. I feel the urge to say something, anything, to break the silence.

'Look, Odd – er, I mean Kevin,' I say. 'I don't think the thing with Karen and me is going to work out. So, you know, you have my blessing, if you get my meaning.'

'You were going to call me Oddjob again, weren't you?'

I shrug. 'Well, yes. Sorry, but – '

He smiles and his eyes almost disappear into his cheeks. 'Don't worry, likes. I quite like it, actually. I ken who Oddjob is, by the way: sometimes you just have to play dumb in front of the boss.'

I smile and nod.

'We didn't mean to do Jimmy Ahmed in, ken?' he says. 'He was getting a bit lairy with Elena, and that's why she called me up. I put a sleeper on him just to calm him down a bit, but I wasn't to ken he'd taken that bad reaction to the drugs, eh? No my fault.'

'Sure,' I say, thinking, *so Jimmy didn't just die of the Rohypnol poisoning. And if a jury's in a hanging mood, it might turn out to be murder after all.*

There's a bit of a lull in the conversation. Suddenly, a final bit of the puzzle slots into place in my head. Just as the lift doors ping open, I say to Oddjob, 'It was you stuck Jimmy's toe up the tap, wasn't it? Why?'

He looks at me a bit sheepishly, and grins. 'Aye. My OCD, likes. The thought of that tap, going drip, drip, drip…'

We walk out onto the fifth floor. It's empty too, of course: I half expect to see Gemma painting her nails at the reception desk, but there's nobody.

There's something else, though, other than people.

Modern demolition ordnance doesn't look like cartoon

versions of dynamite. There's no big box with TNT stamped on it. All the same, it's fairly obvious that the stuff attached to the external walls of the building, and all round the internal ones too, are some form of explosive materials.

Oddjob gets on his mobile to Derek. 'Boss, we have a problem.' Then he explains.

In the lift on the way down, Oddjob is smiling strangely at me.

'Do you think I should get one of those bowler hats? You know, the ones with the razor blade in them?'

'I think that was the other guy,' I tell him.

Derek and Futret get in at the second floor. Derek is wide eyed. 'Looks like you were right. The cunts must have given the rest of the staff the afternoon off, gathered here at five and then got spooked when you didn't turn up. They can't have been long away when we arrived.'

The doors open and we're on the ground floor.

'We'll get them at the airport, although I would have preferred to have done it here,' Derek says. 'Too many folk in the way at the airport. Plus there's the security.' As if remembering, he tucks his gun away beneath his shell suit again. 'You're welcome to come along for the ride, Simon, but things could get messy.'

'No, I've got things to do here,' I tell him.

The three of them turn to go, then Derek stops and turns round again. 'That's why they needed Joe Kinnaird, isn't it? Demolition expert. Blow the whole fucking building and you've covered your tracks pretty well. Everybody's looking the other way for a terrorist attack, while you fuck off to Brazil. I have to give the guys credit. It's ingenious.'

Then he turns and the three of them head off towards the airport.

I walk slowly back up to the reception desk. Bobby is staring at me, as if he wishes his eyes could shoot some form of laser beam technology and fry me on the spot. His face is purple. He seems to be struggling to get some words out.

I pull a chair over and sit across from him. 'Bobby,' I say, quietly. 'I know that you hate me. I know that people I came into this building with threatened to assault you. None of that is important right now.'

He's staring at me, still trying to get some coherent words out.

His eyes look like they're about to pop out of his head. 'You...he...'

'Shush now, Bobby. Listen very carefully. The top floor of this building is wired with explosives. I don't know when it's due to go off but it will probably be in the next hour. This is your chance to be a hero. Phone 999 and get the bomb squad on the way. By the time they get here through the traffic, you'll have single handedly cleared out all the guys on the first, third and fourth floors.'

He's still looking at me, but his expression has changed to one of disbelief. 'Have you – ?'

'I wish I had lost my mind, Bobby. If you don't believe me, go up to the fifth floor first, but hurry. And when you're speaking to the bomb squad, you can tell them that New St. Andrew's House is also wired to blow.'

'New St. Andrew's House?' he says and writes it down, as if he's taking directions for ordering a taxi. I stand up and turn to go.

'And where are you going?' he says.

I look back at him. 'I think I've just read a quadruple bluff properly,' I tell him. 'But even if I have, I've still to put the winner away.'

Outside the building, I phone Martin.

'Where are you?' he says. 'What's happening?' In the background, I can hear the parrot add, 'You ignorant cunt.'

'Do you have a car that works?' I ask.

'Yes, of course, but – '

'Then get in it and pick me up outside the Filmhouse, okay? Quick as you can.' He rings off and I walk slowly back up out of the business district and on to Lothian Road. All around me, Jock professionals are scurrying past, on their way to this and that, even if it's only to All Bar One, or some other such place. In the distance, I can hear the sound of sirens. *Good boy, Bobby,* I think to myself. *But every solution brings a new problem.*

I've just reached the Filmhouse when a familiar figure appears. 'Simon English?'

It's Gary. All five feet eight, all the way round of Gary, the Scottish pit bull with a grievance.

'Gary, listen, I know you're upset about Yvonne but now is

not the time. Let's get together – '

And then he kicks me hard, in the bollocks, and I go down.

As he follows up with a volley of kicks with what feels suspiciously like steel toe capped boots, it occurs to me that I've had quite a day of it, physically I mean: from being dragged around my flat in a dog collar by Leonora, to having my ribs broken by Oddjob, and now this.

Still, it's hard to find your motivation for fighting back when you've been having an affair with the chap's wife and made her pregnant: besides which, being kicked hard in the nuts is the worst pain known to man. Women say childbirth is worse, but then no man ever volunteers for being kicked in the nuts a second time, so I rest my case.

Anyway, I'm crouched there on my knees, taking the kicking as best I can, when I'm aware that the rain of kicks has stopped. I look up and see Gary being put in a half Nelson by a face I recognise. Short, sandy hair and a whisky sour complexion. A face I could kiss right now just for sheer joy that he's stopped Gary killing me.

'Who the fuck are you?' Gary says. 'This is between me and him.'

'I'm sure it is,' Martin says to him, calming him down. 'What did he do?' he says, releasing Gary long enough just to show him his warrant card.

'He's made my wife pregnant,' Gary says.

You can see Martin suppressing a smirk. 'That doesn't surprise me, sir. He's always doing that sort of thing. However, I need him right now, so I'm going to arrest him for assaulting your foot with his head, if that's okay?' To me, he says, 'Get in.'

Martin's unmarked car, complete with flashing light, is parked up on the pavement. I get in, Martin lets go of a confused looking Gary, jumps in the driver's seat and we're away.

'Where to?'

I've been thinking about this. 'Well, they've wired one building at the West End and one at the East End to explode, so I reckon we can deduce something from that,' I say. 'Let's go up Lothian Road and I'll explain on the way.'

'Okay,' Martin says, wheeling us around in the midst of the tea time traffic and heading uphill.

I give him a brief résumé of what's happened to me so far today, leaving out detail in the bit with Leonora, obviously. I think again of the quadruple bluff analogy, but decide to opt for something simpler. 'You know how, in rugby, they talk about blind siding the opposition?'

'More of a football man myself,' Martin admits. 'If you can count Heart of Midlothian FC as a football team.'

'Anyway,' I say, slightly impatient now that we're clear of Tollcross and heading along Melville Drive by the Meadows, 'As I understand it, it's when you set up a scrum, or a ruck or whatever, and it looks like the ball is coming out one side and then the big guys at the front, the forwards, they slip it to the little guy that stands just behind them – is that the scrum half? And he goes up the other side while the opposition are looking for some big cunt to break loose with it on the other side. Well, that's what Wallace and Tony have been up to. All the time, they've had us looking at one side of the ruck, while they've been slipping up the other side past us. Go right here, by the way.'

Martin glances over at me as he turns right towards Causewayside, heading out of town. 'Are you sure you've not taken too many kicks to the head from that guy? You're not making much sense.'

'Okay. Okay. Here's the thing. Wallace and Tony set up a series of deals and they set up a double cross of the crims whereby the money comes in today and then disappears off from the companies which they've set up with Derek Boyes. To do that, they need the help of some tried and trusted associates and assistants in the firm – they can't do all the work themselves.'

Martin grunts. 'Okay. I've got that so far.'

'Yeah, so far so good. Let's leave aside the fact that they're also double crossing those same associates and assistants by carrying out illusory transfers of millions of pounds into their own accounts, preparatory to everybody flying off to Brazil tonight. Let's concentrate instead on the Wrong Box Company.'

'The Wrong what? Where are we going by the way?'

'Just keep heading for the ring road,' I tell him.

He puts his foot down and runs yet another red light. Looking over, I see King's Buildings flash past: it seems like months ago since my little caper with Kenny Futret down here.

'To double cross the crims properly, they needed to set up a diversion. They had no idea whether the crims might be on to them. So they got in tow with Joe Kinnaird and his demolition company, just to be on the safe side.'

Martin glances across at me again. 'The safe side of what?'

'Think about it. As we speak, there's bomb squads, fire brigades, ambulances, all fully engaged at two major incidents in the city. That ties up the whole of the police force and also, incidentally, completely clogs up the middle of the city. At both ends. The Wrong Box Company was a means to an end but it was also symbolic. They were going to be the last two guys standing. The tie up with the Liverpool criminal, the bomb threats, all a huge paga on one side of the ruck while they steal up the other side. The Wrong Box Company broke the pattern, using a Stevenson novel instead of one by Walter Scott. That was the piece of the puzzle I couldn't get.'

'Which way on the bypass?' Martin asks. We're at a cross-roads, literally. 'I mean, you've got the final piece now, right?'

'Er, not as such.'

'What the fuck do you mean, not as such?' Martin's looking at me like I'm some sort of simpleton. 'You mean, you don't know where we're going?'

Behind us, the traffic's starting to build. Some impatient bastard toots his horn.

'Go left,' I say, thinking. Actually, there is some sort of gut instinct going on there.

Just as Martin does so, heading into the eastbound bypass, my iPhone goes off. It's the Schemie Savant.

'Karen, am I glad to hear from you,' I say and I mean it. I explain everything as Martin hurtles us towards the end of the bypass.

'So, they made it look like they were goin for the airport, which would mean goin by the West End, but they've also created a diversion at the East End?'

'Correct.' There's a pause and she sighs.

'Do I have to spell it out? They're goin east. I think you're going to tell me either Wallace Brodie or Tony Hand happened to have a pilot's licence.'

'They both have,' I say.

There's another pause, then she says, 'Well, the only airfield I ken out there's East Fortune.'

I relay this to Martin and he nods, crossing both lanes to get to a turn off. 'The old World War Two airfield? That makes sense.'

I thank Karen. 'That girlfriend of yours isn't too happy with you, by the way,' she says.

I smile as I ring off, picturing Leonora and the pail. Then I remember something, and turn to Martin. 'By the way, you might want to radio in to your boss that there's some guys with guns heading for Edinburgh airport.'

'I'm glad you mentioned it,' Martin says, giving me a funny look. 'I had actually worked that bit out for myself.'

***

It's twenty miles from the centre of Edinburgh to East Fortune airfield, but it feels like we do it in about ten minutes. The gates for the main bit are all locked up, of course, so Martin has to take the long way round, battering along a track up the side of the perimeter fence.

'Always meaning to change this car,' he mutters. It's an old Vauxhall, although, in fairness, the engine's got a good bit of grunt in it and he's fairly caning it along this track. The runway slowly comes into view, and, sure enough, there's a Cessna sitting on it, its engines already idling.

'There it is.' I point, and Martin grunts again.

'Fine,' he says. 'But how do we get through the fucking fence?'

'It does come to an end, eventually,' I say, pointing ahead of us this time.

Martin guns the engine even harder and we're flying along this dirt track, almost literally. We're going past the section of World War Two planes, parked at the side of the runway: in between them, I can see us now going way past the Cessna. I can see heads in the windows of the modern plane, faces peering out at us.

We reach the end of the fence at last, bump over the rough grass at the side and then we're on the runway. Bump, bump, onto the tarmac, and then Martin turns the car so that he's facing the Cessna in the distance.

'Okay,' I say. 'What's the plan?'

Just at that moment, the Cessna starts to move forward, slowly, taxiing for take off.

Martin floors the accelerator. 'Drive straight at the cunt. If you have a better plan, I could do with hearing it right now.'

Fuck me sideways and call me Sally on the weekends. He actually means to ram an aeroplane. He really is that mental. Unfortunately, as the plane starts to pick up speed, I can't think of a better plan than playing chicken with the Cessna.

'Short of you knowing how to hotwire a Spitfire and flying it, I guess not,' I say.

Martin doesn't reply. He's concentrating on keeping in line with the Cessna, which is now veering off slightly to one side. We're picking up speed. Seventy. Eighty. Eighty-five. Ninety. The Vauxhall's engine is roaring, but underneath it you can still hear the guttural clatter of the Cessna's engines.

Closer. Closer. Closer. Fuck. The Cessna starts to pick up more speed. We're about two hundred yards away from it now, tanking along.

Closer. Closer. One hundred yards. Fuck, wank, fanny bastard.

Suddenly, the Cessna wobbles in a semi-circle, ever so slowly, moving out of our way.

'He's going to try to take off in the other direction,' I tell Martin.

He nods and, as we draw up alongside the Cessna, he throws the car into a left turn, like he's Jeremy fucking Clarkson on Top Gear testing out a Maserati. The tyres make an unholy sound like a banshee being castrated, and suddenly we're sliding sideways right in front of the Cessna's wheels. The pilot has no choice but to pull up, so close I can barely get the passenger door open.

Martin's out of the car first, but I'm not far behind him.

Martin backpedals, until everyone in the cockpit can see him down below. He raises his warrant card, like it's some kind of psychic protection.

'Lothian and Borders police! You're all under arrest.'

By the time the shot rings out, I've already run round to the side with the door on it. It's too high up for me to reach, but then it opens.

Of course I was expecting to see Tony Hand's big melon head, or the Rottweiler's snapping jaws. Instead, the figure that appears is female. Chestnut curls. Cute, pixieish nose. The Buddha belly, of course, is hidden under the flight overalls she's wearing.

Sylvia.

She has to shout to be heard above the sound of the engine. 'Simon. Get out of the way. There's no need for you to be hurt.'

I'm almost at a loss for words. 'What are you doing there? Have they kidnapped you?'

It's then that the big melon headed one makes his appearance in the doorway. 'Not exactly, Simon. You see, we never quite trusted you – or the rest of them – to be quite honest. After the unfortunate accident with Jimmy Ahmed, we decided that Sylvia would operate under deep cover, just to keep an eye on you. I don't know what you've done with Leonora but, frankly, I don't care either. All that bunch had to do was do their jobs in closing those deals. It was Sylvia here who had the really hard work, keeping Martin occupied, and then you.'

Sylvia has the good grace to look slightly embarrassed. 'It was fun, Simon, you and me. Really.'

There's a shout from the front of the plane. They can't have killed Martin yet. 'Simon – run for cover, for fuck's sake! Behind the car!'

That, of course, would be the sensible thing to do. Instead, I stay exactly where I am and shout up to the two of them, 'You utter cunts. You fucking greedy bastards. You know, I don't know if it's something to do with the Jock character, but you're the most greedy, grasping bastards I've ever come across, and dealing with greedy, grasping bastards is part of the job in commercial property. You could have had a perfectly good life just by staying legit, but, no, you had to go one better, didn't you? And it didn't matter who got in your way.'

Tony Hand is cupping his hand behind his ear, trying to get all of this. When I run out of breath, he shouts back down: 'Very interesting, Simon. The important issue for me though is that you're in the way right now. I'm afraid I'm going to have to cut this negotiation short.'

And then he shoots me in the leg.

It feels like somebody has punched me really hard, just about the knee, and I go down. The door in the plane shuts, and then the Rottweiler starts reversing the Cessna back from Martin's car. When the pain hits, it's pretty bad but, by then, I've realised that one of the Cessna's wheels is about to run right over me unless I move. Somewhere in the distance, I can hear police sirens going.

You know when you see in the movies somebody rolling out of the way of a train or a car or whatever. It looks easy, right? Well, let me tell you, it takes everything you've got to move when one leg is utterly useless beneath you. I can see the big tyre heading for me, picking up speed, and it's all I can do to flap myself out of the way. I just manage to do it: the tyre grazes past me, seeming to go more slowly now. I go to put my hands over my head, to protect myself against any more bullets that come raining down.

Then the button of my coat catches in the frame supporting the wheel, and it starts to drag me backwards.

Still sirens, getting closer. Unless that's some sort of aural hallucination. I've no option but to get up, rather than be dragged along the airfield. Once I'm up, of course, the pain in my leg kicks in big style. I'm hopping along, one arm snagged on the aeroplane, trying to get my fucking jacket off: I'm not sure what inspires me to jump onto the hubcap and cling onto the spars, so that I can get my jacket off more easily – but whatever it was that gave me that stupid idea, that's what eventually wins me the gallantry medal because, just at that point, the Chief Constable's special crack unit appears, surrounds the Cessna with police marksmen and it's all over, with me hanging onto the plane like some sort of fucking mad action hero. Pretty ironic, really, when all I was trying to do was to get detached from the fucking thing.

I'm not really aware of much of what happened after that, but the three of them must have given themselves up pretty quickly. Next thing I know, I'm on a stretcher, and I'm looking up at the Chief Constable. I know he's the Chief Constable because he's got loads and loads of braid on his cap and he hasn't even bothered to wear a flak jacket.

'You're a very brave man,' he says. 'Thank goodness we got that tip off from your boss down in London, to back up what Jim Martin has been saying to me for days. I think I owe Jim an apology.'

The Velociraptor. So he was the one that pulled a few strings. I look up at the Chief Con. 'Martin?' I'm surprised how croaky my voice sounds.

'He took one in the shoulder, but he's going to be okay,' he says. Just then, there's a ringing noise from his breast pocket, and he pulls out his mobile.

'Yes, we've just caught up with them. Do you want a word with Simon?'

And then he hands the phone down to me, lying on the fucking stretcher. It's the Velociraptor.

'Simon?' he rasps. Forty a day man, the old Scaly One. 'Had a few doubts about whether you were losing your marbles when we spoke the other week, but then Bruce Reid came to see me about some woman there called Car Clamp...'

Then he starts to say something else, but he's wasting his breath because everything goes black.

***

It'll take a while for the Crown to sort through all the files and get enough to prove a case. That's why Leonora turning Queen's Evidence is such a good negotiation. She's got enough to put the rest of them behind bars for a good stretch.

Both bombs went off, but with nobody hurt. I don't think anybody mourned the loss of either the firm's office or St. Andrew's House. Maybe the insurance companies.

The Velociraptor's promised me my old job back, but there's some shit to sort out here first. The firm's in a hell of a mess, obviously, but my clinging onto the wheel of the Cessna has gone the rounds, so the clients and the Law Society think I'm some sort of a hero. The firm's made me up to partner and Rhona to associate and the pair of us are working long days and nights. Brains as well as breasts, that girl.

Sylvia's up in Cornton Vale, awaiting trial, her Buddha belly a distant memory. Amazing how quickly the python can get over things when distracted. At least there's Leonora to keep me company if, by keeping me company, you mean getting tied to the bed and thrashed with birch twigs. The python's rapidly acquiring a taste for it, though.

Tom and Mum are fine. The Health Board saw sense about his medication after I threatened to sue their arses. I think the prospect of the headlines about the hero's disabled brother was what clinched the deal. He's still a cunt, but he's still my brother. Keeps badgering me to get a ground floor flat so he can come out on benders with me more often.

Edinburgh does seem a slightly more bearable place with Tony, Doggy, Danielle, Al + Bradley, Oddjob and Derek Boyes behind bars. Joe Kinnaird, apparently, was down in his gaff in Liverpool, waiting for his share of the loot to roll in, when the Merseyside fuzz felt his collar.

Still, it'll be good to get back to God's Own Country.

Things have settled down with Gary and Yvonne. He seems to feel some Jock point of honour has been satisfied by the kicking he gave me, so they're keeping the baby and playing happy families. Turned out he was playing an away fixture of his own, after all.

And la Clamp? Currently scaring the fuck out of the Morningside posh, working in some coffee shop or other. I'm seeing her on Tuesday, to go through her business plan for her sewing and alterations empire. We've even found a vacant shop that fits the bill and I'm getting a surveyor pal of Jerry's to screw the landlord to the wall on the rent for her. *Pro bono*, as these Edinburgh cunts say.

She's even applied for a business development grant, from the Council.

About the Author
Andrew C Ferguson

Andrew C Ferguson is a local government solicitor who lives in Fife. He is author of *Common Good Law* and co-author of *Legacy of the Sacred Chalice* and *Local Planning Reviews in Scotland.*

His short fiction has been published widely in magazines and anthologies, including *The Hope that Kills Us; Sporty Spec: Games of the Fantastic; A Mosque Among the Stars;* and *Nova Scotia: New Scottish Speculative Fiction.* His poetry has appeared in the magazines *Chapman, Brand, Iota, Word Salad Magazine, Gutter* and *Farrago's Wainscot.* He is also a spoken word performer and musician, writing a regular blog at www.andrewcferguson.com.

More Books From ThunderPoint Publishing Ltd.

The Oystercatcher Girl
Gabrielle Barnby
ISBN: 978-1-910946-17-6 (eBook)
ISBN: 978-1-910946-15-2 (Paperback)

In the medieval splendour of St Magnus Cathedral in Kirkwall, three women gather to mourn the untimely passing of Robbie: Robbie's widow, Tessa; Tessa's old childhood friend, Christine, and Christine's unstable and unreliable sister, Lindsay.

But all is not as it seems, and gradually secrets are revealed until past and present collide with unexpected and devastating results.

A story of betrayal and redemption, The Oystercatcher Girl is as beautiful and secretive as the Orkney of its setting.

The Bogeyman Chronicles

Craig Watson

ISBN: 978-1-910946-11-4 (eBook)
ISBN: 978-1-910946-10-7 (Paperback)

In 14th Century Scotland, amidst the wars of independence, hatred, murder and betrayal are commonplace. People are driven to extraordinary lengths to survive, whilst those with power exercise it with cruel pleasure.

Royal Prince Alexander Stewart, son of King Robert II and plagued by rumours of his illegitimacy, becomes infamous as the Wolf of Badenoch, while young Andrew Christie commits an unforgivable sin and lay Brother Brodie Affleck in the Restenneth Priory pieces together the mystery that links them all together.

From the horror of the times and the changing fortunes of the characters, the legend of the Bogeyman is born and Craig Watson cleverly weaves together the disparate lives of the characters into a compelling historical mystery that will keep you gripped throughout.

Over 80 years the lives of three men are inextricably entwined, and through their hatreds, murders and betrayals the legend of Christie Cleek, the bogeyman, is born.

The House with the Lilac Shutters: and other stories
by Gabrielle Barnby
ISBN: 978-1-910946-02-2 (eBook)
ISBN: 978-0-9929768-8-0 (Paperback)

Irma Lagrasse has taught piano to three generations of villagers, whilst slowly twisting the knife of vengeance; Nico knows a secret; and M. Lenoir has discovered a suppressed and dangerous passion.

Revolving around the Café Rose, opposite The House with the Lilac Shutters, this collection of contemporary short stories links a small town in France with a small town in England, traces the unexpected connections between the people of both places and explores the unpredictable influences that the past can have on the present.

Characters weave in and out of each other's stories, secrets are concealed and new connections are made.

With a keenly observant eye, Barnby illustrates the everyday tragedies, sorrows, hopes and joys of ordinary people in this vividly understated and unsentimental collection.

'The more I read, and the more descriptions I encountered, the more I was put in mind of one of my all time favourite texts – Dylan Thomas' Under Milk Wood' – lindasbookbag.com

Mule Train
by Huw Francis
ISBN: 978-0-9575689-0-7 (eBook)
ISBN: 978-0-9575689-1-4 (Paperback)

Four lives come together in the remote and spectacular mountains bordering Afghanistan and explode in a deadly cocktail of treachery, betrayal and violence.

Written with a deep love of Pakistan and the Pakistani people, Mule Train will sweep you from Karachi in the south to the Shandur Pass in the north, through the dangerous borderland alongside Afghanistan, in an adventure that will keep you gripped throughout.

'Stunningly captures the feel of Pakistan, from Karachi to the hills' – tripfiction.com

QueerBashing

By Tim Morriosn

ISBN: 978-1-910946-06-0 (eBook)
ISBN: 978-0-9929768-9-7 (Paperback)

The first queerbasher McGillivray ever met was in the mirror.

From the revivalist churches of Orkney in the 1970s, to the gay bars of London and Northern England in the 90s, via the divinity school at Aberdeen, this is the story of McGillivray, a self-centred, promiscuous hypocrite, failed Church of Scotland minister, and his own worst enemy.

Determined to live life on his own terms, McGillivray's grasp on reality slides into psychosis and a sense of his own invulnerability, resulting in a brutal attack ending life as he knows it.

Raw and uncompromising, this is a viciously funny but ultimately moving account of one man's desire to come to terms with himself and live his life as he sees fit.

'...an arresting novel of pain and self-discovery' – Alastair Mabbott (The Herald)

Changed Times
By Ethyl Smith

ISBN: 978-1-910946-09-1 (eBook)
ISBN: 978-1-910946-08-4 (Paperback)

1679 – The Killing Times: Charles II is on the throne, the Episcopacy has been restored, and southern Scotland is in ferment.

The King is demanding superiority over all things spiritual and temporal and rebellious Ministers are being ousted from their parishes for refusing to bend the knee.

When John Steel steps in to help one such Minister in his home village of Lesmahagow he finds himself caught up in events that reverberate not just through the parish, but throughout the whole of southern Scotland.

From the Battle of Drumclog to the Battle of Bothwell Bridge, John's platoon of farmers and villagers find themselves in the heart of the action over that fateful summer where the people fight the King for their religion, their freedom, and their lives.

Set amid the tumult and intrigue of Scotland's Killing Times, John Steele's story powerfully reflects the changes that took place across 17th century Scotland, and stunningly brings this period of history to life.

'Smith writes with a fine ear for Scots speech, and with a sensitive awareness to the different ways in which history intrudes upon the lives of men and women, soldiers and civilians, adults and children'
- James Robertson

A Good Death
by Helen Davis
ISBN: 978-0-9575689-7-6 (eBook)
ISBN: 978-0-9575689-6-9 (Paperback)

'A good death is better than a bad conscience,' said Sophie.

1983 – Georgie, Theo, Sophie and Helena, four disparate young Cambridge undergraduates, set out to scale Ausangate, one of the highest and most sacred peaks in the Andes.

Seduced into employing the handsome and enigmatic Wamani as a guide, the four women are initiated into the mystically dangerous side of Peru, Wamani and themselves as they travel from Cuzco to the mountain, a journey that will shape their lives forever.

2013 – though the women are still close, the secrets and betrayals of Ausangate chafe at the friendship.

A girls' weekend at a lonely Fenland farmhouse descends into conflict with the insensitive inclusion of an overbearing young academic toyboy brought along by Theo. Sparked by his unexpected presence, pent up petty jealousies, recriminations and bitterness finally explode the truth of Ausangate, setting the women on a new and dangerous path.

Sharply observant and darkly comic, Helen Davis's début novel is an elegant tale of murder, seduction, vengeance, and the value of a good friendship.

'The prose is crisp, adept, and emotionally evocative' – Lesbrary.com

The Birds That Never Flew

by Margot McCuaig

Shortlisted for the Dundee International Book Prize 2012

Longlisted for the Polari First Book Prize 2014

ISBN: 978-0-9929768-5-9 (eBook)

ISBN: 978-0-9929768-4-2 (Paperback)

'Have you got a light hen? I'm totally gaspin.'

Battered and bruised, Elizabeth has taken her daughter and left her abusive husband Patrick. Again. In the bleak and impersonal Glasgow housing office Elizabeth meets the provocatively intriguing drug addict Sadie, who is desperate to get her own life back on track.

The two women forge a fierce and interdependent relationship as they try to rebuild their shattered lives, but despite their bold, and sometimes illegal attempts it seems impossible to escape from the abuse they have always known, and tragedy strikes.

More than a decade later Elizabeth has started to implement her perfect revenge – until a surreal Glaswegian Virgin Mary steps in with imperfect timing and a less than divine attitude to stick a spoke in the wheel of retribution.

Tragic, darkly funny and irreverent, *The Birds That Never Flew* ushers in a new and vibrant voice in Scottish literature.

'...dark, beautiful and moving, I wholeheartedly recommend' – scanoir.co.uk

Toxic
by Jackie McLean
Shortlisted for the Yeovil Book Prize 2011
ISBN: 978-0-9575689-8-3 (eBook)
ISBN: 978-0-9575689-9-0 (Paperback)

The recklessly brilliant DI Donna Davenport, struggling to hide a secret from police colleagues and get over the break-up with her partner, has been suspended from duty for a fiery and inappropriate outburst to the press.

DI Evanton, an old-fashioned, hard-living misogynistic copper has been newly demoted for thumping a suspect, and transferred to Dundee with a final warning ringing in his ears and a reputation that precedes him.

And in the peaceful, rolling Tayside farmland a deadly store of MIC, the toxin that devastated Bhopal, is being illegally stored by a criminal gang smuggling the valuable substance necessary for making cheap pesticides.

An anonymous tip-off starts a desperate search for the MIC that is complicated by the uneasy partnership between Davenport and Evanton and their growing mistrust of each others actions.

Compelling and authentic, Toxic is a tense and fast paced crime thriller.

'...a humdinger of a plot that is as realistic as it is frightening' – crimefictionlover.com

In The Shadow Of The Hill
by Helen Forbes
ISBN: 978-0-9929768-1-1 (eBook)
ISBN: 978-0-9929768-0-4 (Paperback)

An elderly woman is found battered to death in the common stairwell of an Inverness block of flats.

Detective Sergeant Joe Galbraith starts what seems like one more depressing investigation of the untimely death of a poor unfortunate who was in the wrong place, at the wrong time.

As the investigation spreads across Scotland it reaches into a past that Joe has tried to forget, and takes him back to the Hebridean island of Harris, where he spent his childhood.

Among the mountains and the stunning landscape of religiously conservative Harris, in the shadow of Ceapabhal, long buried events and a tragic story are slowly uncovered, and the investigation takes on an altogether more sinister aspect.

In The Shadow Of The Hill skilfully captures the intricacies and malevolence of the underbelly of Highland and Island life, bringing tragedy and vengeance to the magical beauty of the Outer Hebrides.

'...our first real home-grown sample of modern Highland noir' – Roger Hutchison; West Highland Free Press

Over Here
by Jane Taylor
ISBN: 978-0-9929768-3-5 (eBook)
ISBN: 978-0-9929768-2-8 (Paperback)

It's coming up to twenty-four hours since the boy stepped down from the big passenger liner – it must be, he reckons foggily – because morning has come around once more with the awful irrevocability of time destined to lead nowhere in this worrying new situation. His temporary minder on board – last spotted heading for the bar some while before the lumbering process of docking got underway – seems to have vanished for good. Where does that leave him now? All on his own in a new country: that's where it leaves him. He is just nine years old.

An eloquently written novel tracing the social transformations of a century where possibilities were opened up by two world wars that saw millions of men move around the world to fight, and mass migration to the new worlds of Canada and Australia by tens of thousands of people looking for a better life.

Through the eyes of three generations of women, the tragic story of the nine year old boy on Liverpool docks is brought to life in saddeningly evocative prose.

'...a sweeping haunting first novel that spans four generations and two continents...' – Cristina Odone/Catholic Herald

The Bonnie Road
by Suzanne d'Corsey
ISBN: 978-1-910946-01-5 (eBook)
ISBN: 978-0-9929768-6-6 (Paperback)

My grandmother passed me in transit. She was leaving, I was coming into this world, our spirits meeting at the door to my mother's womb, as she bent over the bed to close the thin crinkled lids of her own mother's eyes.

The women of Morag's family have been the keepers of tradition for generations, their skills and knowledge passed down from woman to woman, kept close and hidden from public view, official condemnation and religious suppression.

In late 1970s St. Andrews, demand for Morag's services are still there, but requested as stealthily as ever, for even in 20th century Scotland witchcraft is a dangerous Art to practise.

When newly widowed Rosalind arrives from California to tend her ailing uncle, she is drawn unsuspecting into a new world she never knew existed, one in which everyone seems to have a secret, but that offers greater opportunities than she dreamt of – if she only has the courage to open her heart to it.

Richly detailed, dark and compelling, d'Corsey magically transposes the old ways of Scotland into the 20th Century and brings to life the ancient traditions and beliefs that still dance just below the surface of the modern world.

'…successfully portrays rich characters in compelling plots, interwoven with atmospheric Scottish settings & history and coloured with witchcraft & romance' – poppypeacockpens.com

Talk of the Toun
by Helen MacKinven
ISBN: 978-1-910946-00-8 (eBook)
ISBN: 978-0-9929768-7-3 (Paperback)

She was greetin' again. But there's no need for Lorraine to be feart, since the first day of primary school, Angela has always been there to mop up her tears and snotters.

An uplifting black comedy of love, family life and friendship, Talk of the Toun is a bittersweet coming-of-age tale set in the summer of 1985, in working class, central belt Scotland.

Lifelong friends Angela and Lorraine are two very different girls, with a growing divide in their aspirations and ambitions putting their friendship under increasing strain.

Artistically gifted Angela has her sights set on art school, but lassies like Angela, from a small town council scheme, are expected to settle for a nice wee secretarial job at the local factory. Her only ally is her gallus gran, Senga, the pet psychic, who firmly believes that her granddaughter can be whatever she wants.

Though Lorraine's ambitions are focused closer to home Angela has plans for her too, and a caravan holiday to Filey with Angela's family tests the dynamics of their relationship and has lifelong consequences for them both.

Effortlessly capturing the religious and social intricacies of 1980s Scotland, Talk of the Toun is the perfect mix of pathos and humour as the two girls wrestle with the complications of growing up and exploring who they really are.

'Fresh, fierce and funny…a sharp and poignant study of growing up in 1980s Scotland. You'll laugh, you'll cry…you'll cringe' – KAREN CAMPBELL

Lightning Source UK Ltd.
Milton Keynes UK
UKHW02f1957280518
323364UK00004B/43/P

9 781910 946145